MAYS LANDING

a novel by J.C. Mercer

This is a work of fiction. Names, characters, organizations, places, events, and incident are either products of the author's imagination or used fictitiously.

Text copyright © 2016 by J.C. Mercer

ISBN-13: 978-0-9974530-2-7

ISBN-10: 0-9974530-2-8

J.C. Mercer

for Dana

Contents

Chapter 1. THE COSMIC CHAMPAGNE

The nurse told me I had been dead for over four minutes. As a third-year medical school dropout, I feel fairly qualified to state categorically what a crock of shit that is. Even after "clinical death," typically defined by the cessation of vital functions such as heartbeat and respiration, brain death doesn't usually occur for a good five or six minutes later, when the brain runs out of oxygen and becomes irreversibly damaged. In truth, the exact moment of death is somewhat arbitrary and basically occurs when in the opinion of the attending physician there is nothing left that can be done to revive the patient and the pronouncement of death is made, along with the current local time, which then goes on the official death certificate. Doctors love to perpetuate tales about bringing patients "back from the dead" to elevate their self-perceived godlike status, as if those present in the Bellevue Hospital emergency room on Manhattan's East Side that rainy autumn evening were witnesses to some divine miracle.

Likewise for all those so-called out-of-body and near death experiences you may have heard about, such as feelings of euphoria, walking through a tunnel toward a bright light, or visions of your grandparents or favorite uncle beckoning you to join them in the afterlife. Spiritually reassuring no doubt, but all with very earthly scientific explanations. As your brain becomes oxygen deprived, a condition known as cerebral anoxia — even a third-year dropout can show off by flaunting medical terms — and begins to die, it releases a wide range of sensory altering chemicals. These include endorphins, euphoria-inducing hormones known to suppress pain and cause the "runner's high" that many experience after exercise, as well as powerful anesthetics like ketamine, which combine to create a cacophony of "neural noise," an overload of often faulty information to your brain. The common experience of being in a long tunnel with a bright light at the end, for example, is generally attributed to the retina at the back of the eye becoming starved of oxygen and its nerve cells firing at random. The majority of these nerve cells live in the most sensitive part of the retina, the fovea, which is the bright spot that looks like the end of a tunnel.

The only true recollection I have of my brief excursion to "the other side" is a strange, effervescing feeling, as if I was some kind of giant Alka-Seltzer tablet. No glimpses of God's face, no revelations or answers to life's deepest questions. In fact it was just the opposite; if anything I was struck by the randomness, the meaninglessness of it all. If spending eternity drifting in an endless sea of ginger ale is not exactly what you had in mind as a reward for a life well-lived, I apologize. However, we've all heard stories of near-death survivors who claimed to have visited the "other side" and then lead inspired lives in this world, secure that there is a better life waiting for us in the next. I suppose what follows is a chronicle of someone who came back from the experience pretty sure that there isn't.

To understand my thoughts in those first moments when I regained consciousness, it is important to consider the amount of preparation that had gone into my suicide attempt. This was no pathetic "cry for help," but the culmination of weeks of careful planning. When I finally closed my eyes I knew with 100% certainty that I would not open them again in this world. Thus, I naturally assumed the darkness, interspersed with what appeared to be flashes of broken light to be part the experience of being dead, the afterlife, or whatever came next. Not altogether unpleasant, I thought, except for a growing soreness in my throat.

As my surroundings came into focus, I realized I was in a dark and unfamiliar room. The glints of light were in fact reflections off metallic structures, furniture or equipment of some sort, from city lights trickling in through giant windows to my right. Perhaps I had been reincarnated, as some person now with a searing headache to go with the sore throat and what felt like rocks in my stomach. As I began to make out the familiar shapes of a hospital bed, drip bag, night table, and the drawn curtain to my left a sickening sense of dread crept over me. My sore throat must be an aftereffect of gastric lavage: a long tube crammed down my esophagus to pump my stomach. My headache was undoubtedly the product of dehydration, hence the drip bag. I was probably also getting, or had already received, glucose and thiamine (depleted from the body by the alcohol), as well as Narcan or some other opiate.

I wasn't dead, or even reincarnated. I was just another failed suicide attempt.

Footsteps echoed faintly in the distance.

Anger, frustration, and shame swirled inside me. My worst-case scenario, one that I had taken great pains to avoid, had in fact come to pass. I was a medical school dropout who could neither cope with the real world nor successfully orchestrate his own suicide to escape it. I would now be forced to live in ignominy, laid bare to the world as the weak, self-absorbed nutcase that I was. To quote my father, I was now firmly entrenched "on the tail end of the bell curve" of humanity.

The slightly ajar door across the room suddenly swung all the way open, spilling in light from the hallway. A short, roundish silhouette paused briefly in the doorway before stepping inside. As she approached, the light from the window illuminated a nurse wearing an unbuttoned sweater over her uniform, upon which hung a nametag bearing the Bellevue Hospital name and logo. I was apparently in the presence of Nurse Chavez.

"You're awake," she stated, reaching down by the foot of my bed and taking the clipboard that hung there. "You gave us quite a scare ..."

And then she went into the part about how I had been dead for over four minutes. I suppose she expected a big thank you. My voice was weak and scratchy, however, and I didn't feel like educating her on the distinction between clinical and brain death.

"Do you know where you are?"

"Bellevue?" I cleared my throat.

"That's correct. I need to get some additional information from you. This will only take a moment."

She was obviously uncomfortable. Attempted suicides do that to even the most hardened hospital staff; there's always the fear you'll say something that sets them off on a manic episode. She started with the easy questions, confirming my name, social security number, and other basic information while recording my blood pressure, temperature, and pulse rate. I'm twenty-five years old, yes that's my address, no I don't have any insurance. She avoided eye contact, scribbling on the clipboard with a pen.

"Is this the first time you've tried to hurt yourself?" she asked, finally looking up at me for the first time.

I knew the question was coming but still wasn't prepared with an answer.

"Well ..." I stumbled, "I wasn't, exactly, necessarily, trying to ..."

Nurse Chavez flipped through the paperwork on the clipboard.

"You had a trash bag filled with helium tied over your head? Is that correct?"

"I was trying out a new look."

Nurse Chavez ignored this.

"May I ask what medication you've taken in the last twenty-four hours?"

I shifted uncomfortably on the bed.

"Some sleeping pills."

"Prescription?"

"Yes. Seconal. About a dozen. One hundred milligrams each."

"Anything else?"

"Demerol. Four fifty milligram tablets. Also Percodan, six, five milligrams each."

"Anything else?"

"Yeah, Thorazine—"

"Hold on."

She put her pen in her mouth, pulled out the sheet she was writing on, flipped it over and started writing on the back.

"Go ahead."

"Thorazine, I forget how many, fifty milligrams each. Also propoxyphene."

She hesitated.

"P-R-O ... here, let me."

I took the clipboard from her and wrote out the name, along with the total dosage of 300 milligrams.

"That's all," I said, handing her back the clipboard. I didn't bother telling her about the bourbon.

She finished writing, and then stuck the pen in the metal clip at the top of the clipboard.

"There's a fresh hospital gown in the bathroom if you'd like to change and wash up." She motioned past the curtain to my left. "Would you like some help?" she added, only because she was supposed to.

I realized I was still in my street clothes. My wallet, which I specifically remembered leaving in the front pocket of my jeans, was missing.

"Can I have my wallet back?"

Nurse Chavez hesitated before answering. "You'll get your personal effects when they discharge you. Try to make yourself comfortable and get some rest." She placed the clipboard back at the foot of my bed. "There will be someone along to speak with you shortly."

She spun around in a practiced move designed to discourage conversation, and walked briskly out of the room, closing the door to the same three-inch crack it was open when she entered.

I shuddered. I knew what was coming next: a full psychiatric evaluation to determine if I represented a risk to myself or others. I could potentially be put on psychiatric hold and transferred to the psych ward for more tests and further evaluation. Pain seared through my head as I attempted to sit upright. My only alternative was to flee, despite the fact that they were most likely holding my wallet to prevent exactly that.

With great effort I was able to swing one leg off the side of my bed, and then the other. I rested a moment, noticing the bits of dry vomit encrusted on my dark t-shirt and jeans. I cursed my weak stomach as one of the factors that most likely betrayed my suicide attempt, although the plastic bag and helium were supposed to have made it fail-proof. An audible groan escaped me as I slid off and grabbed the side of the bed. I was hunched over, struggling to remain upright. The floor spun beneath me.

"You'll never make it."

I froze. The voice came out of nowhere.

Chapter 2. T-BONE

"Probable suicide? They'll at least have you on line of sight observation."

I looked up. The voice, male, was coming from behind the partially drawn curtain to the left of my bed.

"They're supposed to be able to see you at all times."

Two stumpy bare feet, covered with an unnatural amount of hair, extended from behind the curtain. Grotesquely long toenails, almost an inch in length, curled from the tips of the toes that remained.

"That's why they leave the door cracked open."

There was a metallic rattling of chains from the other side of the curtain. I slowly pulled it back, fully expecting to find some mythological half-man, half-beast shackled to the wall on the other side.

"Sneaking out of Bellevue's no joke ... unless you have me to help, that is."

The man was chained to the bed, a fancy Posey four-point setup: adjustable padded cuffs secured to both wrists and ankles. It was much more elaborate than anything I had seen on my rotations at Columbia. In the dim light I could make out his features: stocky and very short, almost dwarf-like, no more than five feet. I also noticed he was missing toes on each foot. He was older than I had expected, late fifties, maybe sixties. Wiry gray hair protruded from all sides of his head, and virtually all of the exposed flesh not covered by his hospital gown was layered with thick body hair, like some diminutive, geriatric bear.

"Soon as you help me out of this we can go." He smiled at me through a set of crooked teeth.

I looked over the straps that secured him.

"What, these?" He rattled his restraints. "Don't worry about these, not like I'm some criminal or anything. I do this for a living. I'm a test jockey. Professional lab rat."

I just stared at him blankly. He had a lazy left eye that hung half-shut most of the time, then twitched sporadically.

"What you might call a human guinea pig, although personally I don't think that's really accurate ... was doing a phase one on some new cold medicine and had an AR — adverse reaction — took me a while to calm down is all. Sent me here for observation."

"Sorry ..." I muttered apologetically, backing away.

"Hey, I'm fine now. Really."

I went over to the door and peeked into the hallway while my new hairy dwarf friend kept yammering behind me.

"When they catch you they're going to lock you up in the psych ward."

Down the hallway to the right was a large, circular desk and work area where four corridors intersected. Nurse Chavez and two other nurses were stationed there.

"You ever been in the psych ward at Bellevue? It's the Superbowl for wackos. Doesn't get any bigger than that. Never been myself, but I heard stories ..."

I peered the other way down the hall where a custodian wearing a baseball cap and oversized headphones was mopping the floor.

"The residents there like to shit into trash bags and swing them around at each other." He chuckled from his bed behind me. "Last of the gladiator sports. Probably be at least a week before a real doctor sees you."

I spun around and walked quickly back to his bed. Fuck it. The worst he could do is kill me, which had been my original intent anyway.

"Atta boy." He smiled as I grabbed his wrist and began fumbling to unstrap him. "Ya gotta unbuckle it first, then pull off the strip ... yeah, like that."

Within minutes he was free, bending over with his arms outstretched and doing calisthenics, which produced a wide array of cracks and pops in his back and joints.

"Ah Christ that feels good. Hey, I don't think we been formally introduced."

He thrust his pudgy hand out.

"Thomas Bonicelli. Everyone calls me T-Bone."

I was casting my fortunes with someone named after a cut of beef.

"Mays," I muttered, extending a weak handshake.

"Mays? That your first or last name?" He clenched my hand with a firm grip and then roughly yanked off the plastic identification band around my wrist with his left hand.

"Just Mays," I winced, as he released my hand and ripped off his own wristband. He made his way to the door and motioned for me to follow him.

"Keep your eyes open and your mouth shut," he whispered as he nudged the door open a few more inches. A shiny plastic plate on the door read: Room E-5072. He stood just inside the doorway peering at it, for what purpose I had no idea, until I realized he was looking at the reflection of the nurses station.

He glanced back at me and gave a wink.

"Don't worry. I was green once too."

T-Bone yanked me by the arm, pulling me into the hall and carefully closed the door to its original three-inch gap. His gait was like a duck, perhaps because of the missing digits on his feet. He led me to the opposite wall and out of view of the nurses station, then turned the other way, giving me a shove as we continued in the opposite direction.

The custodian with the headphones mopping the floor loomed ahead of us. He looked up slowly as T-Bone motioned for him to take his headphones off.

"You know which way to dialysis?" he asked.

The custodian adjusted the left side of his headphones, exposing one ear.

"¿En qué dirección a la diálisis?" T-Bone repeated.

The custodian shook his head no, then fixed his headphones and went back to work. T-Bone shrugged, then took a sharp right, yanking me behind him.

14

"You gotta be an expert in hospital security in my line of work," he told me in a low voice as we continued down the tiled hospital corridor. "ID cards, fingerprint scanners, I seen it all. Used to consult for some of the biggest hospitals in the world."

Somehow it didn't seem likely to me, but I didn't argue.

"The key is confidence," he continued. "They got cameras everywhere, but nobody knows what to look for. Unless you're running around with an axe. It's all, what's the word …"

Something caught his eye in the darkness inside one of the passing rooms. He put up his hand, motioning for me to stop, then one finger indicating for me to wait. He disappeared through the door, then re-emerged almost immediately chewing on a half-eaten chicken breast.

"… reactive. That's it. Except maternity. You definitely wanna steer clear of there. Always tight security. And the psych ward …"

I followed him as he turned around and backed through a pair of swinging double doors and continued down another hallway.

"You know I couldn't help overhearing your conversation with Nurse Ratched back there."

T-Bone tossed the remains of the chicken breast into a canvas laundry trolley at the side of the hall and began to push it. "She was right about one thing, you know. Don't make sense to off yourself like that."

The squeaky wheels of the laundry bin echoed through the hallway.

"Take it from me. I make a good living through my body. Like a professional athlete. Or a supermodel."

He appeared quite different from a supermodel or a professional athlete, but I was in no mood to quibble. I just wanted to get out. We came to a service elevator in a small alcove. T-Bone stopped and pushed the button.

"I mean, look at you. You got good hair. Nice teeth. Two healthy kidneys, I betcha. Plenty of bone marrow."

A bell rang as the elevator doors opened.

"How's your sperm?"

Fortunately T-Bone didn't wait for a response and pushed the laundry bin into the elevator. I followed as he pressed one of the buttons and the doors closed behind me.

Inside he caught me glancing at the nails emerging from his toes like talons, and he grinned.

"Cosmetic companies pay a hundred fifty for every nail over an inch long. Couple more weeks and that's almost a grand you're looking at."

I cleared my throat. "Nice."

He shrugged. "I could grow my fingernails too, but them I can't cover up so easy. Bad for business."

The elevator doors opened revealing cinder-block hallways and concrete floors in what was obviously the basement level.

"Gotta maintain a professional demeanor," T-Bone explained as he pushed the laundry bin into the hall.

As I followed him I could hear a commotion from up the hallway. Tall carts containing stacks of trays were being dollied in and out through swinging doors by what looked to be kitchen staff in white uniforms wearing paper caps.

"Hey, you know I'm outta here after my blood work this morning. I usually hang out at Saint Chris's when I'm washing out between experiments. It's on 48th and 10th, the big church, just go down in the basement."

T-Bone effortlessly pushed the laundry bin off to the side of the hallway and replaced it with a wheeled cart filled with trays that towered over him. The staff seemed to pay him no mind, as through the swinging doors I caught a glimpse of the polished metal of industrial sized refrigerators, freezers and other kitchen appliances inside.

"Good group up there. Maybe you wanna stop by while you, you know, sort things out and everything."

We turned another corner and he stopped in front of an enormous metal door.

"We're here."

The words "FIRE EXIT Do Not Open Alarm Will Sound" were emblazoned upon it.

"Any door that says fire exit has to be left unlocked. Building codes and everything."

I hesitated. "What about the alarm?"

T-Bone scoffed. "If those things really worked you'd have alarms going off all the time. Just for show. Here, watch this." He leaned forward and gave the door a push, getting the entire weight of his body behind it.

There was the immediate thunderous clanging of a bell, not the electronic kind but a real ringing like in an old-fashioned firehouse.

"Sonofabitch ..." T-Bone muttered, genuinely surprised. He looked at me and smiled weakly, shouting over the clatter. "You better take off, kid."

I stepped outside into a dimly lit underground parking lot, spinning around to get my bearings.

"Over that way. It'll lead you up to 27th and First." T-Bone pointed, still shouting to be heard over the alarm. I started to run toward a tunnel leading to the street.

"Remember, Saint Christopher's All Souls Kitchen on 48th and 10th," he shouted after me. As I entered the tunnel, I could see the streetlights and city traffic opening up out of the darkness thirty yards or so ahead of me.

"Good luck kid!" was the last thing I heard from him as I stumbled forward. I fixated on the lights far ahead, fighting nausea, with my mouth tasting like tin foil. The irony of the situation, even in my desperate state, was not lost on me. I was finally getting my near-death experience, even if it was happening while fully conscious. Perhaps I had been too quick to dismiss all those "crossing over" stories after all, I thought to myself as I blindly followed the light at the end of the tunnel ahead of me where, unknown to me at the time, another life waited on the other side.

Chapter 3. THE GHOST OF 125TH STREET

I walked past three hospitals on the way back to my apartment that morning. Three. Lenox Hill, St. Luke's Roosevelt, and Mount Sinai. I had heard stories of "negative wallet biopsies": emergency medical service personnel routing patients to public or private hospitals based on their ability to pay. However, passing three hospitals through rush hour traffic from West Harlem all the way down to Bellevue, a public hospital on the Lower East Side of Manhattan some eighty blocks away, with a flatlining suicide attempt in the back of the ambulance seemed extreme. Still, I couldn't think of any other explanation. Had I been a distinguished graying-at-the-temples executive who had wrapped his luxury car around a streetlamp, I was pretty certain I would have ended up at Lenox Hill.

By the time I passed through midtown on the long walk back to my studio it was past dawn and the worst of my nausea had subsided, with my splitting headache receding to a dull throb. As my immediate physical discomfort began to fade a curious, almost MDMA-like (methylenedioxyamphetamine, better known as ecstasy) euphoria began to overtake me. Colors and sounds seemed more vivid: the deep morning blue that enveloped the streets, the metallic rattle of shopkeepers lifting the grating that covered their storefronts, and the flashing lights of Times Square.

I had died in my mind. And then come back. Most people spend their entire lives preparing themselves mentally for death. I was way ahead of them, somehow above all of that now, no longer one of the death-fearing mortals scurrying about with petty material concerns. I even felt a strange relief that my wallet was back at Bellevue. I had no identity anymore. I was a spirit, a wraith, playing with house money with each moment of life that passed from this point forward.

Other than a shower and change of clothing, I really had no pressing reason to return to the studio apartment I had been living in for the last four months. After dropping out I left my medical school roommates in an on-campus apartment and moved a few blocks uptown, which might as well have been in another country. If anything I was returning to the scene of my crime to work out what could have possibly gone wrong, and what detail I missed which resulted in my unwanted rescue.

I decided that a northern approach to my apartment would be the best plan of action; however diminished my earthly presence had become I still wasn't about to chance a confrontation with my landlord. I walked up Amsterdam Avenue and across 125th Street toward Broadway. There I ducked into a laundromat a few doors from my building, where I could cut through the alleyway in the back. This had become my preferred method of entrance when trying to return home undetected, usually because of unpaid rent.

As soon as I entered the laundromat, I could feel a palpable change in the mood. The morning chatter beneath the whirring of the washers and dryers came to an abrupt stop, and I felt the eyes of a dozen Hispanic *madres de familia* following me as I walked quickly to the back doorway. No doubt I had been the subject of much gossip in the last day. A new pair of expensive sneakers was enough to cause a stir on my block; I could only imagine the commotion being carried out comatose on a stretcher would have caused. Even the laundromat manager, a foul, ill-tempered obese woman who would curse at me in Spanish every time I cut through to the back exit only scowled this time as I passed the small table where she sat stacking quarters into neat rows.

I skipped out the back door and down steps of crumbling concrete to the alleyway. Above me garments flapped from clotheslines strung between the buildings as I made my way through piles of boxes and garbage to the dumpster behind my apartment building, which rested beneath the shadow of a rickety metal fire escape. I reached to the top of the dumpster and hoisted myself up, my stomach churning again not from the physical activity but the stench from the garbage within it. I paused for a moment, steadying myself in a crouched position on the corner of the dumpster, deciding if I needed to vomit again. The wave of nausea passed, and I carefully rose to my feet. I had performed these acrobatics enough times over the past few months in conditions ranging from near sleepwalking to falling-down drunk that it didn't present much of a problem, although the stench from the dumpster seemed particularly rank this morning, either from my heightened sensitivity or a dead animal inside.

I reached up and grabbed the bottom rung of the rusty metal fire escape ladder. One, two, three, I pulled myself up arm over arm until I was high enough to catch the bottom rung with my left foot, then swung my right leg over a metal guardrail and climbed onto the fire escape landing. Another rest, catching my breath and wiping the dirt and rust off my filthy hands, and then I made my way up the narrow metal steps. Despite my condition, I bounded up two steps at a time, anxious to appear as only a blur to the occupants behind the passing windows.

Fully out of breath by the time I reached the sixth floor, I bent over the railing and steadied myself a moment, then turned to face the opaque window of my apartment, which was covered with a film of grime. I dug my nails into the decaying wood on the top pane until I had enough of a grip to push it down a couple of inches. Reaching through the opening, I groped inside for the screwdriver stuck into the sash as a makeshift lock and pulled it out. Completely drenched in sweat at this point, I pushed the top pane back up, then lifted the lower pane all the way, which provided an opening wide enough for me to crawl through, and stumbled inside.

It was quite a sight to behold.

My emotional descent had happened gradually enough that I didn't really notice the sight, smell, and sounds that now overwhelmed me in the 12' x 16' oversized closet I had spent the last four months of my life in. Trash, including plastic cups and bottles with mold growing in them welcomed me. Chinese food, pizza boxes, paper plates, junk mail, as well as a large unopened pile of letters bearing the logo of Columbia Medical School lay strewn about. They formed a kind of decaying topsoil above the lower layers of old medical textbooks, my dirty scrubs and other assorted clothing. Breaking the silence was an unsteady buzzing from flies and the faint crinkling of paper, either from the light breeze flowing through the open window or roaches and other assorted vermin tunneling under the garbage. It was the smell that surprised me most however. It wasn't overpowering, at least immediately, nor was there any one particular scent that stood out above the old food, body odor, urine, and other stenches. It was the way they combined to form such a very distinct and pungent essence of ... what? Despair? Hopelessness? This is what I imagined they would smell like.

The colored balloons reading "West End Novelties" that still floated around the ceiling added an eerie, birthday-party-gone-wrong feel to everything. They had come with the commercial sized helium tank I had rented, which rested beneath a layer of clothing next to my mattress. I had inflated them in a kind of morbid going-away celebration I had thrown for myself the day before, washing down my assortment of pilfered barbiturates with alcohol before pulling a two-ply garbage bag filled with helium over my head and affixing it with elastic bands around my neck.

I had spent months in this room alternating between debilitating depression and the uncontrollable anger so deeply entrenched not only in my life but my family history that I had given it its own name. I called it The Rage, and it was typified by a complete loss of any physical or verbal self-control. While most visible during the daily conflicts between my parents, it could appear in full force out of nowhere, from the most seemingly innocent of triggers, such as a Christmas toy or new piece of furniture that stubbornly refused to be assembled and would end up getting thrown through one of the windows of our three floor colonial in Lexington, Massachusetts. Despite, or more likely because of, my father's outward and explosive manifestation of The Rage, I did my best to implode inwardly, as privately as possibly, thrashing beneath blankets, pulling hair, and muffling screams with my pillow. That was my condition in the months here following my premature departure from medical school. Suicide is perhaps the ultimate act of implosion, so it's no surprise that the end result was my Exit Plan: a fail-proof scheme to end my life.

Except that my Exit Plan had failed.

I cast a glance back out the fire escape window at the tenement buildings staring back at me. Hundreds of windows. Was it possible someone had seen something? Obviously somebody must have called emergency services. As I looked around I began to discern subtle changes and things out of place that must have been a result of my rescue. What appeared to be yellow police tape came in through the crack of the closed front door, and a path through the debris had been cleared to the futon mattress at my feet. I grabbed a t-shirt to change into which, while not strictly speaking clean, at least didn't have chunks of vomit on it.

"Parkhill."

A man stepped out of the bathroom.

He was big, broad, with a wide handlebar mustache twisted on each side. Fiftyish, with salt-and-pepper hair in a knit blazer and open shirt, he had a beefy, cop-like physique although there was no badge that I could see, nor did his demeanor or body language make me think law enforcement. He seemed too hesitant, even slightly nervous. Like the nurse at Bellevue, the tentative tone of his voice indicated he knew he was addressing someone who had just attempted suicide.

"Who ...?"

I was so surprised it was all I could get out. My t-shirt fell to the floor, and I stumbled backward toward the window.
This man I had never seen before was trying to respond, as if he couldn't tell me who he was, or our relationship was so complicated that it defied words.

"It's okay, Parkhill. I'm here to help," was all he could offer, then flashed a weak smile and took a tentative step toward me. "Like a guardian angel—"

He took another step forward, and I instinctively spun toward the open fire escape window, banging my shin on the sill as I leapt through. My ears were pounding so hard I couldn't hear if he was behind me as I bounded down stairs one flight at a time, then hopped the railing at the bottom to land back on the dumpster. Another jump down to the concrete of the alleyway, falling forward onto my hands. My shin throbbed as I straightened again, and ran as best I could, hoping to make it back out through the laundromat before my churning stomach failed me for the second time that day.

Which direction to run? Not much choice. North or uptown meant Harlem and eventually the slums of the South Bronx. East or west and I'd hit the East or Hudson River pretty quickly. So I headed downtown, limping slightly on my aching shin. I would have given anything for a Percocet, or even a Xanax or Klonopin to calm my nerves. I was shaken by the mystery guest in my apartment, my self-described guardian angel, to the point where I began to wonder if I had hallucinated the whole thing. And why did he call me Parkhill? I despised my first name, and never voluntarily offered it to anyone; those who did know it were usually good enough to respect my wishes and call me by my last name. Only my father still called me Parkhill.

I considered my next move. I naturally assumed this would be another suicide attempt.

If I learned one thing during my two monthly rotations in the emergency room at Columbia University Medical Center, it was how difficult it is to end one's life painlessly and effectively. Even physician-assisted suicide is an imperfect science, and amateurs attempting to end their suffering by washing down a handful of Tylenol with a bottle of scotch are bound to be disappointed. The cruel irony is that many victims of these ill-prepared suicide attempts wake up brain damaged from a lack of oxygen, permanently disfigured because of an errant gunshot wound, with a damaged liver or kidneys from an overdose, or severe burns to their gastrointestinal tract from swallowing battery acid. Many of these I had the opportunity to witness first-hand. A successful suicide attempt wasn't something that was entered into lightly and required careful preparation. What I needed was time, a place to sit and think.

It would be a lie to say I came upon Saint Christopher's All Souls Kitchen at 48th Street and 10th Avenue, which I discovered was located in the basement of one Saint Christopher's Church, purely by accident. I suppose subconsciously I must have known where I was going. I didn't have a cent to my name, nor any identification, as if I had been dropped onto the planet with nothing more than the clothes on my back. I passed a group of derelicts sitting in lawn chairs in front of the drab church. I realized I now had more in common with them than a medical student at a prestigious university. Most wore heavy coats despite the warm weather. One person in a garbage bag vest with his head and arms poked through the sides was pushing a shopping cart full of junk. A small crowd had gathered around it and were having a spirited argument over a kitchen appliance. I did my best to look tough and bored as I finally found the large wooden entry door, separate from the church entrance, passed through the darkened vestibule and down a set of stairs.

The sheer dimensions of the interior surprised me; it was similar in size and décor to a large high school cafeteria, albeit one with a significantly older and more ragged population. The majority of the space was taken up by wooden tables attached to the floor, most of them full. Roughly a third of the patrons would be immediately recognizable as homeless, although I was surprised at the percentage of people who would not be out of place pushing a shopping cart down the aisle of the nearest supermarket or picking their kids up from soccer practice. There was also a significant number of children, drinking milk or juice from tiny cartons, running between the tables and being scolded by their mothers, even though I presumed school was still in session.

I became aware of how hungry I was. Far across the room, a long cafeteria-type counter with trays of food separated the masses from a kitchen area. Apparently I had missed the lunchtime rush, and most of the staff were now sitting at a long table on the other side of the counter, eating and laughing among themselves, some wearing disposable food service hats. I hadn't intended on eating anything, a ghost like myself being above such earthly needs, not to mention the fact that the fare would probably be disgusting. Still, I found myself drawn toward the food counter, working through the crowds, past a wall plastered with anti-drug and inspirational posters, a worn cork bulletin board with job postings that looked like it hadn't been updated in decades, and a dark office with the words "Social Services" emblazoned on the window.

As I approached the back, I took a plastic tray from a trolley cart and moved down the food counter to inspect the various options. I paused before a long metal platter containing the remnants of some swirly pasta in a meat sauce sitting unmanned under a heating lamp. I peered closely into the tray, which seemed to me a giant Petri dish for bacteria, wondering how many children had sneezed in it. Instead I grabbed one of the remaining unidentifiable sandwiches (with one side wheat bread, one white) from a neighboring tray, and swiped a miniature carton of milk from a plastic tub filled with mostly melted ice.

I took a seat at the end of one of the tables and attempted to block out the din that surrounded me to get down to the matter at hand of reviewing available suicide options. The degree of difficulty would be much greater now that I did not have a cent to my name. I couldn't afford to construct another helium-filled "suicide bag" to put over my head. In my research I found this to be the most preferred method as the inert gas prevents the panic, sense of suffocation and struggling during unconsciousness known as the hypercapnic alarm response, caused by the elevated levels of carbon dioxide. Making use of the helium tank sitting back at my apartment didn't seem to be an option anymore. Buying a gun was also out of the question. I might be able to find enough rope to hang myself from a tree, although that required some engineering and was likely to attract attention. There was the whole jumping off a bridge or tall building thing (self-defenestration is the official term). That sounded like a rather terrifying last few seconds, like one of those scary carnival rides I hated, except that this one ended with the splattering of my brain. More importantly, I didn't want an ending that would draw attention to myself. I was not making a protest or statement to the world, and had no self-absorbed desire to stage some grandiose departure. This also ruled out other attention-grabbing methods such as self-immolation (setting oneself on fire), hopping down on a subway track and electrocuting myself on the third rail or pulling an Anna Karenina and leaping in front of an oncoming train. Not my style, nor was anything that would cause prolonged or even short-term discomfort such as starvation or dehydration. I was contemplating whether I could create an incision on my wrists with a plastic serrated knife deep enough to induce sufficient hemorrhaging when I became aware of someone calling my name.

"Mays!"

I looked up to see T-Bone skipping down an aisle toward me. He was dressed completely differently from when I last saw him twelve or so hours ago, sporting a bow-tie and a plaid sports jacket circa 1974 and an almost-presentable pair of dress slacks, although as he got closer I was able to discern the pattern of assorted stains and tears. His wild hair was now parted, and he carried a small, thickish notebook, one of those Filofax personal organizers that buttoned shut with a strap. It was apparent he was wearing what for him must have been formal attire, almost like he was going on a date.

"Eww ... whaddya wanna eat that for?" he asked, looking at the remains of my half-eaten cheese sandwich.

"Worse than prison food. You wouldn't believe the stuff they find in there. You hungry? Let's get you some real food."

He reached gently under my armpit and lifted me out of my seat.

"How you doing for cash, you got money? Yeah? No? That's what I figured. C'mon."

He pulled on my arm; I instinctively hesitated.

"We can't have you walking around with no money like you're some kinda bum on the street, can we?"

He gave another tug on my arm, and this time I followed. I didn't have much to lose at this point. I actually was a bum on the street, and if he was going to murder me it would at least solve my current dilemma.

T-Bone led me through the tables toward the front entrance, waving and acknowledging his colleagues as he passed: "Hey, Pac Man. What's with the hair? Looking good there, Baby Doll.

Kendrick, you wanna check on Peehole when you get back? I'll pick up a sandwich for him. Thanks, babe …"

Despite his bravado no one seemed to pay him much attention or provide a reaction except an occasional nod. He arrived at the large entry door and pulled it open, holding it for me.

"Here we go. First we gotta get you some walking around cash."

He gave me a wink as I stepped through the doorway, or maybe it was just the tic he had in his lazy left eye.

"Trust me. Make you feel like a new man."

Chapter 4. THE ORIGIN OF SPECIES

We walked for the better part of an hour, all the way down to the financial district near Battery Park on the southern tip of Manhattan. I said little, listening to T-Bone speak in broad terms about the important role we were about to play in the propagation of the human species, natural selection, and evolution. It sounded at first as if we were on our way to start a new civilization in a distant galaxy, or board a giant ark that would repopulate the planet. It wasn't until we passed Washington Square Park in Greenwich Village that it began to dawn on me where we were going.

I was going to sell my sperm.

As we got closer to our destination, he filled me in on the basic procedure. Most laboratories would pay between $50 to $200 cash for each ejaculation, provided the sperm met basic criteria (they check the number of sperms, how many are alive, and how active they are). You could only do it once every 48 hours (you generally needed that long to build up enough of the little guys anyway), although the number of fertility clinics in the greater New York City area made it easy to bypass this rule by spreading your seed in round-robin fashion among multiple sperm banks.

We entered a nondescript office building across from Battery Park and took the elevator down while T-Bone attempted to pat down my tousled hair and issue last minute guidance.

"Just act natural. Remember, you could be fathering hundreds of children here. You don't wanna look like a moron. Don't drool or anything, and remember to spoo directly into the cup, they need more than a dribble."

The elevator doors opened into a basement office suite that had a sterile, hospital feel to it. T-Bone led me across the lobby to a sliding window along the far wall beneath a large sign that read "ReproChoice Laboratories."

I was given a clipboard with some forms to fill out by a cheerful lab assistant sitting at a counter behind the window, a young Asian girl in a white lab coat who looked like she was in third grade. We retreated to the waiting area where T-Bone jotted down the address and phone number for St. Christopher's soup kitchen, then paced around me as I filled in the rest. Most of the information was for my anonymous profile, which would be read by prospective clients of the sperm bank. There was no bonus or monetary incentive for having my particular profile and corresponding syrup chosen from the hundreds of other donors, although you wouldn't know it from T-Bone's incessant tips on how to market my gene pool.

"Add a couple of inches to your height. They like 'em tall. That's all the interests you have? Put a few more down there. Everyone wants a well-rounded kid. Add some sports or something. Like a track star. And a musical instrument. It don't matter what, harpsichord, banjo, whatever. There, say yes to yoga, yes to tai-kwon-do ..."

He spent a good twenty minutes helping to make my seed more attractive to a potential host, another quality product the sperm bank could add to their catalog of self-described captains of industry, scholars, world-class athletes and other templates of human perfection. Finally we returned the paperwork to the cherubic Asian woman sitting behind the glass, who smiled as she took my clipboard. On the other side of the window beyond her I could see industrial-size stainless steel freezers, along with file cabinets and other assorted laboratory equipment.

"Here ya go. I think you're gonna be real happy with Mays here, Sonja. Regular stud horse." T-Bone slapped me on the back proudly.

I cringed as the lab assistant, apparently called Sonja, looked over the contents of the forms. She finally placed the clipboard underneath the counter, where she pulled two clear plastic cups with screw tops from a drawer.

"How about some reading material?" T-Bone asked, and Sonja reached back under the counter, this time straining to lift an eight-inch high stack of magazines. She pushed the pile across the counter to T-Bone.

"It's for the kid mostly," T-Bone shrugged. "Helps the first time." He was flipping through the impressive collection of pornographic magazines, then stopped at a copy of *Black and Stacked*, opening up the centerfold to consider it.

"They have a nice collection of Asian stuff, if you're into that kinda thing," T-Bone said vaguely in my direction. "Personally not my cup of tea. No offense there, Sonja."

Sonja just smiled pleasantly as T-Bone tucked the magazine inside the Filofax notebook he carried and slid the pile over to me.

"Uh, I'm good ..." I stammered.

T-Bone shrugged and slid the magazines back across the counter. "We'll be in the collection rooms if you need us."

He said it like he was running off to make copies as he took my arm and whisked me through a pair of double doors, then down a long corridor with noticeably different décor. The floors were carpeted, and oil paintings of pastoral landscapes lined the walls on one side, with the other being taken up by a series of evenly spaced doors. Muzak wafted softly from somewhere.

"You have any problems just knock on the wall. I'll be right next door," he continued, as if the thought of him jerking off in the room next to me would be reassuring.

He stopped outside one of the doors and reached in, feeling along the wall until the lights came on in what I presumed to be one of the aforementioned collection rooms.

"I'll be waiting right here when you're done," T-Bone said as nudged me inside and closed the door behind me.

"Remember to lock it!" I heard from the other side of the door. I pushed the lock button on the doorknob, then turned back around to get my first full look at the room.

It was a perfectly square room, which couldn't have been more than twelve feet on each side. Most of the space was taken up by an enormous worn reclining chair with a stand-alone reading lamp arching over the back. My immediate reaction was that I would be jacking off in my father's study. There was a small night table next to the chair, upon which rested a box of tissues and some kind of lotion or hand soap in a square plastic push-button dispenser.

I gingerly touched the seat of the chair, shuddering to think of the acts that had been performed over the years on its cracked leather, then reached down and pressed the handle of the soap dispenser. A pearly white lotion oozed out of the nozzle and onto the table.

It was all suddenly too much. I had to get out of there. This instant. I rushed to the door and swung it open.

T-Bone was standing in the doorway.

"All set?"

He was holding his plastic cup, a half inch of opaque white liquid now covering the bottom. I stared in amazement.

"Conditioned response." T-Bone shrugged, reading my incredulous expression. "I get within a block of these places my dick plumps up like a frank on the grill."

He turned me around and gently pushed me back into the room.

"C'mon, it's not like you've never done this before," he said as he shoved his copy of *Black and Stacked* under my arm. "You just never got paid for it."

The door closed behind me again.

I supposed he had a point. I locked the door and walked back to the leather chair and sat down, leaning back and taking a deep breath.

I'm thirteen again. Back in my bedroom in Lexington.

I opened the magazine to a picture of a bald black woman sitting naked on a horse while she cupped her breasts. I could hear T-Bone humming from outside in the hallway, which wasn't helping matters.

I turned the page. Two naked and well-endowed black women sticking their tongues in each other's mouth. Okay, that was a little more appealing.

I unzipped my fly. Another deep breath. I reached inside the flap of my boxers and gently retrieved my member. Another deep breath as I closed my eyes, resting my head against the back of the chair and began to massage gently with my fingers. The bizarre events of the day began to wash out of my brain as I became fully erect, moving my fist up and down the shaft of my penis. At least this might relieve some stress, I thought to myself as a warm feeling began to build inside.

THUMP! THUMP!

I jumped six inches off my chair as a loud banging rattled the door. I could feel my gonads shrivel like raisins and go scurrying for cover inside my stomach.

"HOW'S IT COMING MAYS?"

We were waiting outside the window in the front reception area twenty minutes later, watching Sonja examine a sample of my semen under a microscope.

"Is it soup yet?" T-Bone asked.

She smiled, then reached into the drawer below her and counted out small bills, which she then handed over to T-Bone and me. I couldn't help but stare at them in amazement. Cash. I had to admit it may have been the easiest fifty bucks I had ever earned.

"Can I take a look?" T-Bone asked her. Sonja shrugged and pushed the microscope across the counter to T-Bone. I watched, appalled, as he leaned over and peered into it, slowly turning a knob to adjust the focus.

"Check it out, Mays," he said in fascination as I stuffed the money in my pocket and spun around to leave. "It's like a million little tadpoles all with your face."

An hour later we were spending our newfound income inside a nearby fifty-cent hot dog joint T-Bone knew about. We stood at a counter and looked out onto the street as we ate. A half-finished six pack of beer we had brought rested between crumpled ketchup-stained napkins. It was the evening rush hour in the financial district; hordes of businessmen and women dressed in power suits, secretaries wearing running shoes with their heels tucked safely in their purse, all moved past us in a sea of gray and blue. Steps leading down to the subway swallowed most of them, while others stood in the street jockeying for position as they hailed cabs.

"Look at them all," T-Bone said, shaking his head. "Another day of kissing ass. Sucking up. Selling out."

He took a bite of his hot dog.

"You know about the Grecians, Mays?"

I shook my head no to indicate that I didn't.

"An ancient warrior civilization," he continued with his mouth full. "Every male had only one purpose in the world. To become the best warrior he could be. The only thing that mattered was how you could fight. The soldiers had all the respect. All the glory. To die in battle was the ultimate honor."

He took another bite of his hot dog.

"It was known as the Grecian Formula."

I could see how the ancient Spartans might be easily confused with the popular men's hair product.

"Look at them, Mays. It's the Grecian Formula all over again. Except instead of chasing glory on the battlefield, they're chasing money. Dollars."

He looked up at me for affirmation or at least a response. A shrug was the best I could muster.

"Right now they're sitting in bars and on the subway, telling war stories. How much toothpaste or stool softener they sold today. The more money they make, the more people will kiss their ass. The more women will want to fuck them. A bigger palace. A better neighborhood. Better schools. Better doctors. Move up the food chain. The legendary warriors get worshipped. Get to make all the rules. Parading through the streets in fancy cars."

He lowered his voice.

"But what they're doing, see, is selling themselves. Piece by piece. Every day. Until you're not yourself anymore. You're not even a human being really. You have no thoughts of your own. You think you do, but you don't. You're just a part of the machine."

I watched him and took a swig of my beer. He seemed sincere, even if it all amounted to an elaborate rationalization of someone who, like myself, had proven themselves unable to hack it in the real world.

"That's how we're different from them, see? Me and you. We have free will. We have a choice. We choose not to be a part of that world. We choose a different path."

"By jerking off in a plastic cup?" I scoffed. It was an almost involuntary reaction, but I immediately froze, not knowing whether I had crossed some kind of boundary that might set him off. T-Bone looked at me, the only noticeable response being an almost imperceptible twitch of his lazy left eye.

"Yeah, I've sold my sperm," he shrugged, turning back to the passing commuters. "Also my hair, toenails, teeth. Some bone marrow every now and then. Even a kidney." He shook his head thoughtfully as he polished off the last of his hot dog.

"But at least I still have my soul."

"Sperm, that's just the beginning," T-Bone continued as we walked up Ninth Avenue a couple of hours later. "I mean, it's important, don't get me wrong, quick cash and all, but the real action is the experiments."

It was well past sunset, the last remnants of the autumn sun filtering through the skyscrapers to cast long shadows about us. We were now drinking malt liquor out of forty-ounce bottles, concealed in brown paper bags.

"Phase one, two, three ... drugs, medical devices, health products, being out there on the edge of the envelope, changing the world. Weren't for guys like us there wouldn't even be a such thing as aspirin."

He stuffed his Filofax into his armpit and grabbed my arm as he turned onto one of the cross streets, taking a swig from the beer in his other hand.

"You don't, uh, worry about things like side effects?" I asked him as delicately as I could. T-Bone belched and gave a couple of shudders, like an old car whose engine still sputtered even after it was turned off.

"Meh. Not so much."

Another yank of the arm, and we were walking into a narrow cobblestoned alleyway, me following blindly behind him.

"What do you think the first guy ever put a contact lens on was thinking?" T-Bone continued. "You think they knew what was gonna happen? How about disposable razors with three, four, five blades? You know how many faces got tore up in the trenches before they finally got that right?"

Dumpsters and stacks of trash bags lined the walls of graffiti-covered brick amidst the vague smell of urine.

"We're a dying breed, Mays. Test pilots. Pushing the boundaries of modern medicine. It takes a special kind of person. Cut from a different cloth—"

He stopped short, and I almost ran him over, knocking him forward onto a metal grating on the ground below us at the end of the alleyway. We couldn't walk any further. T-Bone turned to me and grinned.

"So whaddya wanna do?"

We were at the end of a deserted alley somewhere below midtown. I had lost track of exactly where. I suddenly wondered whether everything that had happened today was designed to lead me here. Perhaps there was some dark agenda behind his charity, and I was about to find out what it was.

"What do you mean?" I asked, fighting the tide of panic rising inside me.

"What do I mean? I mean you're a young stud with cash in your pocket. You're the prince of the city. Whaddya wanna do? Eat? Get drunk? Birddog pussy? You name it." He took the last swig from his beer and let out a belch, tossing the brown paper covered bottle against the wall where it shattered. "The night belongs to you."

I just looked at him, feeling confused and overwhelmed by the almost liberating effect that my suicide attempt, my new identity, or rather lack of any identity at all, was having on me. I was a ghost, transformed into only a faint shadow of the person who used to be Parkhill Mays. Suddenly I felt like I might collapse.

"I need to sleep," I answered finally.

It was the truth. I was exhausted, my mild alcohol buzz and the events of the past day having finally caught up with me. I felt like I could lay down on the ground beneath me right there and fall asleep, which given my predicament was unfortunately a very real possibility.

"That's what I figured."

T-Bone took the Filofax and reached behind to secure it between his belt and the small of his back. He took a breath, then bent over and grabbed the large, rusty metal grate embedded in the cobbled stones below. Letting out a grunt he pulled it back on its hinges as it creaked mightily, revealing an opening with almost vertical steps that descended into the darkness.

"To the Bat Cave then," he let out, gently steadying the grate until it rested on its hinges at an upright angle. "Trust me, it's safer than a shelter. You don't wanna know what goes on in those places."

I was motionless, staring down into the foreboding darkness while T-Bone caught his breath.

"You got some other place to stay?" he asked, obviously reading my hesitation.

Finally he shrugged, brushing the pieces of rust off his hands, then lowered himself to the ground and carefully made his way backward down the steps, using it more as a ladder than a staircase.

"Good luck to ya then, kid."

I watched as his body disappeared below street level, then finally out of sight altogether. The traffic echoed in the distance as I stood still in the dim alleyway. Seconds passed, then minutes, until finally the panic of being alone overtook any fear I had of T-Bone and whatever waited for me in the darkness below. I turned and knelt on the ground, then took a first few tentative steps down the staircase, just as T-Bone had done. Perhaps I was already too late, I thought to myself, and he's disappeared forever.

"Close the top behind you!" T-Bone's voice echoed from somewhere below.

I pulled the dirty grate with one arm until my head was below street level and let it slam shut, closing my eyes beneath the shower of tiny rust particles. I continued to work my way down the steps as the broken light that filtered through the grating above me faded, the last remnants of a topside world that I no longer belonged to. It was the same world I had tried to escape from just the day before and failed, although as I descended deeper into the darkness, it occurred to me that in fact I may have actually succeeded. I had only found a different way out.

Chapter 5. THE MOLE PEOPLE

Eyes. It was as if I could feel them upon me in the darkness, watching from all angles.

"Just keep holding on to my shoulder … that's it …" T-Bone whispered as we made our way forward. I had bumped right into him when I reached the bottom of the steps. He had obviously been waiting for me.

"It takes a while for your eyes to adjust to the dark—"

There was a sharp CLANG nearby, like metal hitting metal.

"It's all right, he's with me," T-Bone said loudly, although the tentative tone of his voice didn't inspire confidence.

"They're just letting everyone know we're here," he explained in a hushed tone, although I had no idea who was being warned or who was doing the warning. I continued walking directly behind T-Bone with my hand on his shoulder as the metallic clanging continued for a few minutes, seeming to travel along pipes to the side of whatever tunnel we were in. The only traces of light were thin streams that filtered through an occasional grating above us, and the darkness seemed to exaggerate the faint sound of dripping water beneath the din of the city traffic.

"We just gotta go down one more level. Follow me, grab on to the handles here." T-Bone gently lowered me to the ground until we were both on our knees, then seemed to turn himself around. "Sit down on the floor now and scoot forward … there you go."

To my horror the ground seemed to disappear all at once, my legs dropping over the side of a cement wall of indeterminate height; all I could see was pitch blackness below. T-Bone took my hand and placed it on what appeared to be a metal bar on the side near the top.

"Now you're just gonna turn around and go down the ladder, just like last time, easy does it, follow me."

From the sound of his voice he was already descending. I slid forward, feeling for the top rung with my foot, then turned around and began to climb tentatively down behind him.

Ten ... twelve ... fourteen steps ... how high up was I? It was probably good that I couldn't see anything. Then my foot touched the bottom, more of a gravelly surface this time instead of rock or cement. I felt T-Bone's hand touch my shoulder.

"There ya go. Now just follow along behind me here."

I gripped his arm, taking small steps forward. Shades of blackness alternated on either side of me, like I was walking between giant pillars or other large structures.

"You okay? You want to stop?"

"No," I managed. I was hyperventilating. Never before had I imagined there could be so many variations of black, which appeared to dissipate ahead of us into a giant vertical slit of brown.

"There it is ... right there. Say hello to the Vajayjay."

I had never heard the term Vajayjay before, but as we approached I realized he was referring to a giant crack in a wall of concrete that almost filled my entire field of vision. At its widest point it was about three feet across. I could see through to the other side that, though still dark, was distinctly lighter in color, flickering as though flames burned beyond. Even in the darkness I had to admit it did bear a striking resemblance to an oversized labium minorum.

"Eeeeeeuuuuuuoooooohhhh yeah that feels good." T-Bone squeezed through the gap in the wall with disturbing pleasure. Through the dim light I could make out a satisfied grin on his face from the other side as he beckoned me to follow.

I carefully stuck my foot out and slid through the hole in the concrete. On the other side distant lights now revealed more detail; I looked around.

We were standing before an underground subway track, although it was immediately obvious from the decay and debris it hadn't been used in many years. All around us were large cement pylons interspersed with ancient beams, cobwebs and antiquated garbage that had disintegrated into unrecognizable heaps. About twenty feet to our right, the track disappeared into a much narrower tunnel; to our left, light and shadow seemed to dance from somewhere in the distance. From the echoes of our movements the space we were in felt cavernous, at least a couple of stories high, although the details faded into black in most directions and it was difficult to precisely judge the size.

"This way." T-Bone took my arm and we headed left, following the track toward the distant lights. "You'll find your way around here soon enough. There's a couple of entrances actually. The Vajayjay is the safest, but there's one on 31st and 7th behind Papaya Mike's you can use in a pinch—"

Another loud CLANG echoed nearby; I nearly jumped out of my sneakers. T-Bone didn't flinch. There was enough dim light now that I could make out an antiquated sign on one of the cement pylons that read:

Spitting On the Platforms or other Parts of this Station is
UNLAWFUL
Offenders are Liable to Arrest
By Order of the Board of Health

"The people down here, the mole people, most of them are okay, but you gotta watch 'em. You hear crazy stuff, you know, the webbed feet, the cannibalism, but most of it's bullshit."

I had never heard the term mole person before, and certainly never heard anything about them having webbed feet or eating each another, although I would have believed pretty much anything at that point.

"Trust me, you're actually a lot safer down here than topside," he nodded upward. "The big corporations, they don't run things down here. You don't have to sell yourself. Nobody owns anybody else here. Everybody's equal."

Ahead of us the flickering light seemed to be emanating from behind a pile of rubble. There was a faint rumbling sound, and I felt the ground vibrate beneath me; a train was passing somewhere above or below us, I couldn't tell.

"I know guys ain't been topside in years. Trust me, they got everything down here. Food, running water, art ..."

He motioned proudly to the faintly visible concrete wall twenty feet or so to my left. I could vaguely make out what looked like a huge mural in spray paint, some kind of blue face, but little of the detail.

"I probably wouldn't hardly ever go topside myself if I wasn't still trying to fix things up there. You know, with the experiments and everything. I'm sentimental that way. Plus, these mole people, at least most of them, they're not so sophisticated like you and me, and, well, to be honest ..."

He gave a shrug as we passed the large pile of debris to our right, where the space before us opened to reveal the source of light we had been following.

"... they kinda look at me as their leader."

It was a subway platform, obviously long abandoned. A fire burning in a metal trashcan in the center revealed dirty mosaic tiles on the back wall bearing a now indistinguishable pattern. A dozen or more figures were silhouetted against the backdrop, leaning against each other, sitting in chairs, lying on mattresses, almost all eerily still. Only their distorted shadows moved, dancing on the wall behind them in the flickering firelight.

It was like a painting, this surreal scene beneath the surface of New York City, some kind of dysfunctional extended family portrait. You had to stare for a moment before you noticed the almost imperceptible movements. What looked to be a woman, dark, sitting by the fire, was rocking back and forth, arms clutching a bundle. At the far edge of the platform sat a large black man in white coveralls beneath an army jacket. I recognized him as one of the people that T-Bone had spoken to at the soup kitchen. He was different now though, holding his head in his hands and staring down at the platform, humming or muttering to himself.

"Hold on a sec, I'll introduce you to the gang here." T-Bone took a few steps in the direction of the muttering black man and called out enthusiastically. "Special K! What's going on Kendrick—"

A low, guttural scream echoed through the chamber as the man reared back his head, letting out an anguished cry that faded into a kind of helpless, whimpering yelp.

"PRINCESS!"

No one on the platform flinched, although T-Bone stopped dead in his tracks.

"I'll tell you what," T-Bone said, clearly having second thoughts. "I'll tell you what, let's get you some sleep and we can come back some other time. C'mon."

He took my arm and we continued down the track into a smaller enclosed tunnel. The light from the subway platform behind us cast long shadows, and I couldn't help looking back until we disappeared around a corner. My eyes were adjusting to the darkness now as I could make out a series of low arches in the wall to the side of the track. T-Bone approached one of them, and I followed.

"This here is about as far down as you want to go by yourself." He motioned further down the track. "Just 'til you get the lay of the land. Safety first and everything. Watch your head ..."

We ducked under one of the narrow arches, and on the other side was a small alcove. It was filled for the most part by a large piece of machinery that appeared to be built into the ground, a transformer or something obviously dormant, which sat enclosed in a filthy chain link fence. The ground around it was covered with a layer of garbage: bags, paper cups, broken furniture, and other debris. I also became aware of the overwhelming smell of feces.

"This is it," T-Bone announced proudly. "Welcome to the Bat Cave."

We slogged through the garbage toward the far corner of the alcove.

"Most of the time I'm on the road travelling for experiments. I been pretty much everywhere. Cleveland. Detroit. Houston. Lauderdale. But when I'm in town, this is where I stay. I call it the Bat Cave. Not much, but it's comfortable."

Both the garbage covering the ground and the stench of human waste became thicker, making it difficult to walk. I covered my nose and mouth.

"That's it, just breath through your mouth. Sorry about the smell. I do it on purpose. Keeps the riff-raff away, if you know what I mean."

Of course, I had no idea what he meant but followed anyway, breathing through my mouth as instructed.

"Right up here ... there you go ..."

T-Bone stepped up on a catwalk, a concrete shelf that extended from the far wall about three feet above the ground.

"You'll probably want to sleep here. Above the trash and stuff."

I climbed up next to him, following his voice, a vague dark shape in a sea of shadows.

"Wait here a sec, don't move ..."

I could hear him stepping away from me. As his footsteps and breathing faded I became aware of rustling sounds from the trash below me.

"Here you go kid. Up here."

T-Bone's voice was somehow coming from above me now. Looking up, I could make out the outline of his head sticking out from a narrow crawlway above me.

"Catch."

Something soft bounced off the top of my head and landed on the catwalk at my feet. I got to my knees and felt around. It was a torn throw-cushion, like something you'd find on your grandmother's sofa, now soiled and, from the feel of it, covered in stains.

"I'll keep a look out from up here," I heard T-Bone yawn from above. "Try to get some sleep, Mays."

Feeling much more like a first line of defense against intruders than protected by a watchful guardian from above, I nonetheless took the pillow and tried to get comfortable on the concrete step. I thought about asking for a blanket or something to lie on but decided against it.

"Takes some getting used to down here. It's different ya know," T-Bone murmured. "You see all kinds of shit. Stuff most people never see."

There was a short snort, and then steady breathing that quickly escalated into a full-blown snore. T-Bone was asleep.

I placed my head on the soiled pillow, then lay still wondering if it would be possible for me to sleep like this. I tried closing my eyes. Then I opened them. Then I closed them again, and the last thing I remember thinking was how strange it was that in the total darkness it really didn't make much of difference whether they were open or shut.

Chapter 6. JOSEPHSON CANTU-NAFE

I have no idea how long I slept or what time it was when I awoke. In fact, I had just learned my first lesson in subterranean living. Not only did the absence of light play tricks on the brain to distort the sense of time, but the complete lack of topside yardsticks gauging time measurement, such as daylight, timepieces, social expectations or decorum, meant people generally lived by basic biological needs. They ate, slept, fornicated, and got high when their body instructed and as external conditions made it possible. Yet even beyond the obvious observation that few of us had to show up for work the next morning or lunch dates to be kept, the past or future in a larger sense were constructs we had little use for. The past usually consisted of memories ranging from negative to horrific, from which most of us were trying to escape, nor did contemplating future prospects that were likely equally as grim provide much comfort.

When I finally struggled to rise from my concrete mattress, pain seared through my aching neck, back, and joints. I called T-Bone's name twice with no response, and it became clear I was alone. Staggering through the debris of the Bat Cave in the darkness, I forced myself to fight another rising tide of panic. I made my way out of the alcove and onto the subway track where my fears of abandonment were once again quickly allayed.

"Over here, Mays!" T-Bone's voice echoed in the distance.

I turned to see a small fire flickering thirty or so yards back up the track. There were figures gathered around it, including the unmistakable diminutive outline of T-Bone.

As I made my way toward them I could see Kendrick, the angry man from the subway platform now sitting placidly by the fire. He was holding a long stick with the carcass of a rat impaled upon it. Sparks popped and crackled on its burnt exterior as Kendrick rotated it above the flames as if toasting a marshmallow. Next to him was a contraption I concluded was a primitive rat trap. It consisted of a large plastic bucket with a piece of rope pulled taut across the opening, through which an empty soda can with holes punched in the top and bottom was strung. Foul-smelling black water filled up the bottom two-thirds of the bucket. The idea was to put some kind of bait on the top of the can and as the rat crossed the rope to retrieve it, it would inevitably fall off the can as it rotated under its weight. After swimming and scratching on the side of the bucket, it would eventually become exhausted and drown.

Across from Kendrick sat a woman who I also vaguely recognized from the subway platform. It wasn't any familiar physical characteristic as much as her silhouette, specifically the way she rocked subtly back and forth. She was dark-skinned, black or Hispanic, although it was almost impossible to gauge her exact ethnicity or age beneath the matted, wild hair, and the huge lesions and open sores that covered her face. I couldn't help but stare at them. At the very least they represented some advanced cutaneous fungal infection, or more likely hepatitis. I almost didn't notice the object she had clutched in the arms of the filthy raincoat she wore: a small plastic doll.

T-Bone was already in midday form, gesticulating wildly and waving his Filofax.

"It's called imminent domain. Trust me, this area here is just like SoHo was before the boom in the 70s. All the way down to the exit on 31st Street. Wide open spaces, street access, you got privacy. Just a matter of time until they run outta room topside. Everything down here's gonna be worth a fortune. But you know what we need first?"

"Imminent domain," Kendrick replied dutifully, as he calmly took the simmering rat from the flames and examined it.

"Damn fucking right." T-Bone slapped my shoulder as I came to a stop by the fireside. "This here is a business associate of mine, Mays. Mays, this is Kendrick, otherwise known as Special K, and this here's Baby Doll."

Neither of them made any acknowledgement. Kendrick was cutting the rat off his stick with a knife he'd pulled from his boot, but most of my attention was focused on Baby Doll. I knew it wasn't the time or venue, but I had to say something.

"Um, ma'am, no offense but … you really should see someone about that." I was touching my face almost unconsciously. "I could maybe take you to an ER if you want—"

Baby Doll let out a hysterical, toothless laugh that seemed to unnerve even T-Bone, or perhaps it was just me he was embarrassed by.

"Yeah, come on Mays, we got a busy day ahead of us," he said as he tugged my arm and headed further up the track. As I backed away from the fire, the glint of Kendrick's knife caught my eye. He was slicing up the abdomen of the charred rat with a precision and dexterity any surgeon would have been proud of.

"This way, Mays!" I heard T-Bone shout, and I finally turned and stumbled after him.

We had to climb back out through the Vajayjay, up to the street again, and walk a couple of blocks to get to the uptown local. I, like many people, had the misconception that the New York City subway was a matrix of interconnected tunnels. As T-Bone explained to me, abandoned sections like the one I had spent the night in were very rare and usually cut off from the main arteries due to the incredible expense and human capital that go into building, powering, and maintaining these massive underground marvels. There was the narrow stretch of track on the lower level A/C/E going from Port Authority down to 28th street, and the lower levels for the BMT and IRT lines at City Hall and Bergen Street, and the unused platform at Chambers Street. Some were used by the Transit Authority as storage facilities, but others served as underground time capsules and homes to a volatile ecosystem of mole people or anyone seeking refuge from the topside world.

As we clambered down the steps to the subway entrance on 34th Street and 8th Avenue, T-Bone further enlightened me on the finer points of clinical trials in the pharmaceutical industry.

"Phase one trials are the first kind of tests they do with humans. They just want to make sure you don't drop dead. Doesn't matter if the drug does what it's supposed to do. As long as you don't start coughing up blood, they're happy."

He gave a quick look around the station as we walked past a glass booth in which a bored transit worker counted money.

"Phase two they wanna check to make sure it actually does what it's supposed to do."

T-Bone deftly pulled one of the turnstiles halfway backward and swung his hips through, then waited expectantly for me to follow. I hesitated.

"No big deal ... gotta keep down the travel expenses, eat into your margins. Go ahead."

I followed his instruction as he cast a glance toward the token booth.

"Once it passes phase two it moves to phase three, which is kinda the same thing but with more people," T-Bone continued. "Plus they compare it to other stuff, like competing products and whatever else to see if it works any better."

There was a growing rumble from an approaching train down the track.

"Some go on for months. Free room, meals, entertainment. And at the end of it all, a big fat check. I already got one lined up this summer in North Carolina. Some new anti-depressant wonder drug."

T-Bone looked at me and brightened. "Hey, you know it might do you some good."

He chuckled until he saw I wasn't laughing. I suppose it wasn't a joke to me, given my long history of mood stabilizing, anti-psychotic, anti-anxiety, and anti-depressant medications.

"Anyway it goes for three whole months," T-Bone went on, raising his voice as the train roared into the station. "Very hush-hush. Very exclusive. Don't worry though. I can get you in."

He bragged with the air of someone scoring reservations at a chic Manhattan hotspot. The subway car screeched to a stop, and we entered through the sliding doors. T-Bone gave me a wink, although again it just may have been his twitching lazy left eye.

"The research director there is a very close personal friend of mine."

"You have got to be kidding me!"

T-Bone slammed his fist down on the table in anger as I flipped through a thick loose-leaf notebook containing hundreds of clinical trials, including the purpose of the study, dates and duration, eligibility, and compensation. It was the third clinical trial recruitment agency we had visited that day, not to mention the stops at four area universities and the public library, where we pored through online classifieds and the no fewer than nine periodicals dedicated to the pharmaceutical industry.

"I'm sorry, T-Bone. They need women," explained Roz, a kindly, almost grandmotherly woman, with spectacles and her hair in a bun. "I put him on the waitlist. I'm sure he'll get in eventually, a trial this size. You know how these things work."

Roz's official title was Placement Coordinator, and she looked comically out of place in the white lab coat she wore, which, as is the case for 90% of people working in anything remotely related to science or health care, was strictly for show. There was a handful of other Placement Coordinators sitting at desks in the shabby, windowless office space around us, all looking equally out of place in their lab coats, talking on phones or assisting other prospective human guinea pigs.

The entire exhausting but strangely exhilarating day had been a crash course in the different types of opportunities available to professional lab rats. Most large-scale trials by the big pharma corporations were filled by specialty recruitment agencies, like the one we were in, who were paid a fee that was usually proportional to the degree of difficulty in finding suitable participants. Criteria could include pre-existing conditions, age ranges, gender, or other specific characteristics. For example, a fair percentage required smokers, which T-Bone explained I couldn't fake since they would test a hair sample, or specific mental or behavioral disorders, which I usually could fake or didn't need to. This business arrangement was further complicated by the fact that many of these agencies would subcontract or split commissions with other agencies, particularly for very hard to fill trials, so in fact you often had multiple agencies recruiting for the same study.

Beneath the level of giant pharmaceutical clinical trials were companies testing or performing focus groups on individual products. These could include trials to determine if a new whitening toothpaste actually outperformed its competitors (and didn't destroy tooth enamel in the process), choosing the catchiest name for a new fruit drink, or law firms looking to prove that the chemical preservative being used in their client's canned yams was not in fact toxic. There were also paid community gigs like training recruits for the Jersey Shore Lifeguard Association, the 92nd Street YMCA, or the New York City Police Academy, feigning drowning or getting blanks shot at us while running through a "funhouse".

Then there were the academic institutions, which while less lucrative than their corporate counterparts, were shorter in length and usually paid in cash. These could include everything from psychology undergraduate students performing basic Rorschach tests to Ph.D. candidates fulfilling requirements for their thesis on *Skip Rope or Dinner: Factors Contributing to Caloric Restriction and Exercise*. Business considerations aside, these were also usually far more interesting than the commercial trials. The highlight of my day had been talking our way into a study at the Fordham Theological Seminary targeted at people who believed they were Jesus Christ, presumably to observe all of these would-be Messiahs interacting together. This opportunity to attend an exclusive cocktail party for the sons of God was far more incentive to me than the meager stipend.

Finally there were those classifieds placed by individuals that fell into the general category of "anything goes." While some may have been legitimate, there were others, like the one that sought subjects for a study "exploring human limits in mummified asphyxiation" that delved into much darker territory with, to put it mildly, very questionable scientific value.

I had already lost track of everything we had signed up for, although T-Bone was taking copious notes in his antiquated Filofax. The scheduling was actually the most difficult part. Some trials required you to stay onsite at a facility for multiple days, weeks, or even months, known as "lockdown." This was generally undesirable as it precluded participation in other experiments in parallel, although it could be worthwhile for particularly lucrative trials such as the one T-Bone was currently arguing to get me included in.

"Do you have any idea the sacrifices I've made for this agency?" T-Bone continued to berate Roz indignantly.

"I'm looking for a trial with something benzo-ish, maybe even a sedative," I interjected politely to Roz, trying to diffuse the tension. I used the same tactic whenever my parents would argue. "Like a Luminal, with just a touch of Demerol to take the edge off ..."

"Celoxis? Ring a bell?" T-Bone pressed. "The phase twos? Eleven days without a bowel movement. *Eleven days.*"

"Maybe a new generic version of Nembutal?" I asked. "Something that starts slow and builds gradually ..."

"Do you have any idea what that feels like, Roz?"

"With an amphetamine kick, but a pure, speedy kind of rush, not the teeth-chattering, muscle clenching kind ..."

"I went six days without a movement on a cruise to Alaska," Roz replied to T-Bone after giving it some consideration. "For some reason, travelling always fills me up with bricks."

"Fine. I didn't want to have to do this," T-Bone announced with finality. "But you leave me no choice. I'm going to have to go over your head."

Roz, however, was nothing but helpful.

"You can write a letter to the clinical trial fulfillment department at Josephson Cantu-Nafe."

Hearing the full name of the giant pharmaceutical conglomerate caused me to let out an almost involuntary scoff in disdain.

"My dad's on the board of directors. I could ask him."

I blurted it out so quickly that I didn't even realize what I was saying, and my face flushed immediately.

"Your dad's on the board of JCN?" T-Bone asked me, suddenly interested.

I tried to shrug it off.

"Yeah. I think so ..." I remembered some giant trophy or plaque of achievement thing with the JCN logo he got well before I was born sitting on a shelf in his study, along with all the other JCN pens, paperweights and assorted tchotchkes that littered his office.

I turned back to Roz to escape T-Bone's stare, then pointed to a random line in the binder of trial listings in a feeble attempt to change the topic.

"How about this one?"

Roz ran her finger under the listing and read through her spectacles. "Estrogen replacement therapy?"

"Um. Below that."

"Do you have Mongoloidism?"

An hour later I was coughing up my lungs as I chased T-Bone down First Avenue. I did my best to conceal the long skinny cigarette I clutched in my hand. I appreciated the fact that T-Bone had wanted me to start with something mild, but it was embarrassing being seen with what was clearly a woman's cigarette.

"So I need to start smoking so I can stop smoking?" I asked him as I wiped the tears from my eyes.

"Exactly. Kicking nicotine addiction is a billion-dollar industry. You wanna make it in this racket, you need a piece of that."

I did indeed want to make it in this racket. By this point I was in fact quite excited at the prospect of my new career.

"I see myself more as a specialist. Just the high-end stuff. Opioids, benzos, maybe dabble in dissociatives on the side ..."

"Doesn't work that way," T-Bone said dismissively as he ducked into the entryway of a shiny midtown skyscraper. "I gotta pee."

I expected him to go inside through the revolving doors. Instead he just stepped to the side and unzipped his fly.

"I always piss on Fortune 500 companies," he explained, nodding toward the logo of an immediately recognizable global manufacturing company visible though plate glass windows. "Higher up the better. Extra points for anything in pharmaceutical, finance, or energy. My way of sticking it to The Man."

I watched in horror as a stream of urine sprung forth from his midsection.

"So. What, your dad a scientist or something?"

He spoke casually, paying no mind to the crowds that rushed past and, for the most part, paid no mind to him.

"A surgeon ... cardiac ..." I didn't want to talk about my father at all, and I certainly didn't want to talk about it with someone urinating in public. "Had a procedure named after him."

I figured the details of a pulmonary autograft, also known as the Friedkin-Mays procedure (although no one ever really called it that) would not be of particular interest to him. It involves replacing a diseased aortic valve with the person's own pulmonary valve, with a pulmonary homograft (with a valve taken from a cadaver) which is then used to replace the patient's pulmonary valve. My father was one of the pioneers who proposed it, then first performed it in the early 1970s amidst much fanfare in the medical community.

"Some kind of big shot, huh? So that's how come you wanted to be a doctor too? Like your old man?"

Pools and rivulets of urine from what seemed like an unusually voluminous pee were forming all around T-Bone as he looked at me expectantly. In truth, I actually didn't think I wanted to be a doctor solely because of my father. I had always done well in the sciences, an attribute I had obviously inherited from him (along with a number of his other darker inclinations). Unlocking the truths that lay in the core elements of our natural universe, especially the human body, had always provided a refuge from the much less manageable world of human interaction, emotion, and family dysfunction which to me defied any logical explanation.

To be fair, however, it was almost certainly because of my father that I always assumed I would be a surgeon. He came of age during the glory days of cardiac surgery, after the advent of the heart-lung machine that maintains the circulation of blood and oxygen content required during open heart surgery. This technological innovation transformed the field from a highly experimental curiosity to nothing less than an alternative to death for millions of sufferers of heart disease, and was responsible for the one of the largest spikes in life expectancy in the history of our species. In the process it also triggered the meteoric rise of surgeons, particularly cardiac surgeons, into the rock stars of the medical community, with all those practicing cognitive medicine (and actually interacting with patients), nurses, and the rest of the medical ecosystem merely supporting cast members. Another by-product was a phenomenon that to this day is still omnipresent among the surgical community, including my father: the God Complex. The experience of stopping someone's heart and starting it again will do that to a person. In short, becoming a run-of-the-mill anesthesiologist or pediatrician never seemed like an option to me.

"We don't talk much," was all I said to T-Bone, who finally tapped his penis and zipped his fly. I tried to look casual as I took another cough-inducing puff from my feminine cigarette.

I hadn't had any interaction at all with my father since I heard rumors that he had called the attending on my surgical rotation. I don't know what my father said to him, nor am I even 100% certain that they spoke, although it seemed clear that something had caused a disturbance in the natural pecking order. As a third-year medical student, I was of course at the bottom of the hospital food chain. My role there was basically a glorified office assistant with additional tedious or unpleasant patient-facing tasks, such as taking vital signs and cleaning up messes. Just above me were nurses, still treated like scum, although they at least got paid (and weren't paying to be there like I was). Then there were the interns, to whom I reported. Above the interns were residents, who were just interns in their second to fifth year. Next came the fellows, sub-specialists who required even more training, and at the top of the ladder was the attending. So the morning the attending surgeon asked me to tag along with him to the operating room and get scrubbed up, I was immediately suspicious. A short thirtysomething bodybuilder type with a shaved head and spectacles, he proceeded to make a big show in front of the whole OR of asking me to remove the auto-retractor that was holding open the neck of the patient, who was suffering from stage IV follicular thyroid cancer. He then proceeded to force me to hold the patient's neck open for the entire duration of the seven-hour surgery with these two manual retractors each the size of a spatula. Seven hours of holding the same position with no other movement or breaks for the bathroom. The only time I flinched was when he hit the jugular and a geyser of blood spurted forth, and I instinctively leaned backward lest I get shot in the eye with a stream of hepatitis. The attending, to his credit, didn't flinch at all, but made some comment I was too flustered to understand about the Friedkin-Mays procedure, or the Friedkin-Mays flinch. I didn't really understand him, and did my best to smile at the sniggering and laughter around the room.

Just the memory of it caused my stomach to churn like a washing machine, so loudly I was afraid people passing on the street might hear it. I suddenly felt a panic attack coming on, accompanied by an intense craving for the calming effect of a benzodiazepine.

"So what, you got a trust fund or something?" T-Bone asked as we continued through the crowds down the sidewalk. He was talking in a low voice, obviously aware that this might be a sensitive subject.

"Nah, no, nothing like that," I lied.

"Good for you," T-Bone nodded approvingly, if not altogether convincingly. "Take it from me, you did yourself a favor. Doctors? The worst of the worst. Whores to big pharma. Puppets for the insurance companies. Bunch of hypocrites ..."

His voice trailed behind me as I became distracted by a pile of garbage bags and other discarded items that sat on the curb. Something in one of the large open cardboard boxes had caught my eye. With the last stub of the skinny cigarette dangling from my lips, I reached in and carefully pulled out a pile of old quilted blankets, like the kind movers use to wrap furniture.

T-Bone whistled in appreciation behind me.

Chapter 7. BIG THUNDER

Back in the Bat Cave that evening, I was carefully arranging the quilted blankets I had salvaged on the floor of the catwalk. Folded over, they made a passable mattress. I felt immensely satisfied, more so than I had in months.

"You know, you remind me a lot of myself when I was your age. Bold. Ambitious." I heard T-Bone yawn from above.

"I think I need a street name," I responded enthusiastically from my upgraded boudoir below. "Something cool sounding. Like Blade. Or Nails."

"Whoa. Better slow down there, kid."

"What about Big Thunder?" I asked hopefully. It had been the brand name of my first bicycle, and one of my few happy childhood memories.

"You don't just give yourself a street name. Doesn't work that way."

"So what do I have to do?" I asked, sprawling out luxuriously and closing my eyes.

"Well. Big Thunder. It's like this," T-Bone yawned again, and I could tell he was about to fall asleep. "First thing you gotta do is understand everything you learned up to now is bullshit."

He was absolutely correct.

Freedom. That's what it felt like, at least at first. I suddenly had something that had been missing for quite some time: a future. A bizarre, twisted, uncertain future I never could have imagined just a few days before, but a future nonetheless. I had a new life, a new identity, and a second chance. I had put so much effort into the careful planning of how I would end my life with inert gasses, pills, razor blades, rope or firearms, not knowing that I had an alternative. The old Parkhill Mays was dead, gone from the world without having to go through the emotional or physical trauma of actually ending it.

I became fearless, throwing myself into my new lifestyle with a maniacal intensity, fueled by a never-ending quest for the latest industrial-grade mood altering chemical compounds, and a complete disregard for my own physical well-being. Most of all, I was driven by an innate desire to prove myself to T-Bone, no doubt tapping into my lifetime of accumulated deep-seeded father issues. T-Bone, my new surrogate quasi-father figure, whose chosen profession I pursued with the same fervor I had with my biological father. I wanted so desperately to please him that I almost drowned myself a few days later at a lifeguard training class at the 92nd Street YMCA. After swimming to the bottom of the pool and swallowing almost a liter of chlorinated water, I lost consciousness until a team of lifeguards was able to resuscitate me. Two other volunteers and one lifeguard trainee were so traumatized they quit on the spot, while T-Bone gently informed me that my showboating was making him and the rest of the volunteers look bad.

A simple trip through the department store with T-Bone was an adventure. He could identify which bath salts containing cathinone, the amphetamine-like stimulant, were edible, and which brands of cough medicine contained the hallucinogenic dextromethorphan (DXM or DM) without any of the nausea-inducing side ingredients like chlorpheniramine, phenylephrine, or other sugars or thickeners. We soon fell into a comfortable pattern together, selling our sperm three to four times a week, which gave us a nice base income. These would be interspersed with the formal clinical trials, for which we would have to wait for a check to be mailed to St. Christopher's. Sprinkled throughout these were the academic institutions: medical schools, science and psychology departments running one-time or short-term studies.

"When do we get to try the pharmaceutical-grade cocaine?"

I posed the question to T-Bone at PEAK Laboratories, a clinical exercise testing facility in Bergen County, New Jersey. We were among twenty-plus other study participants. All of us wore white terrycloth bathrobes with the corporate logo of a mountaintop emblazoned on it, and were peddling exercise bikes aligned in neat rows. To the casual observer it looked like a high-end spa or exercise class.

"Doesn't work that way," T-Bone replied next to me, engrossed in a copy of *Cat Fancy* magazine as he peddled. "It's not always glamorous like that."

Behind each exercise bicycle was an electronic box mounted on a wheeled stand sporting a number of blinking lights and a small digital display. Long plastic tubes, approximately half an inch in diameter, stretched from the front of the device, under the bathrobe of each bike rider and up into their rectum. The machines, it was explained to us, contained sensors designed to measure the three pillars or Holy Trinity of flatulence: sound, temperature, and gas concentration. Every time it detected any flatulent activity, our associated fart-o-meter would emit a high-pitched beep, like the kind you hear on someone's voicemail after they tell you to leave a message. It was loud enough so that you'd hear them consistently going off around the room, which had the general effect of making us sound like an alien race communicating through our sphincters. My monitor emitted an almost constant ringtone. T-Bone of course seemed to be able to break wind on demand, like a metronome, with one perfect fart per minute.

"You gonna wear that on your head everywhere we go now?"

T-Bone asked the question without looking up from his magazine. He was referring to the authentic vintage leather aviator's cap and goggles on my head. It was unstrapped, the goggles resting comfortably on my forehead. Along with my bathrobe, it was the only garment of clothing I wore. As part of my new identity I accumulated a collection of used clothing that was not only weather-appropriate but odd looking enough to discourage any human interaction, especially when covered with what I considered to be my very manly film of urban grime and stench. I had found the aviator's cap and goggles, my *pièce de résistance*, in an old thrift store.

"It keeps away the riff-raff," I answered mid-fart, above the electronic tone of my monitor.

The color display on our monitors would output, among other things, trace levels of hydrogen sulfide, which is the major compound contributing to smell. A typical fart contains anywhere from .001 to 1 parts-per-million (PPM) of hydrogen sulfide. Our threshold for smell begins somewhere around .005, and exposure for more than an hour to anything above 1 PPM actually represents a health risk. 25 PPMs of hydrogen sulfide (the level reached by some industrial livestock operations like cattle farms) can cause shortness of breath and dizziness, while a single breath of 1000 PPMs is enough to put most of us in a coma or induce pulmonary edema. Temperature also plays a factor. Hotter farts not only provide a more fertile breeding ground for hydrogen sulfide producing bacteria, but also amplify the range of the fart as gasses move faster at higher temperatures.

"There's a time to look crazy, and there's a time to blend," T-Bone responded, still not looking up from his magazine. "And a time to wash. Christ, I can smell you even in here."

While not logistically impossible to bathe using a single faucet from an antiquated sink in the pitch-black decrepit subterranean bathroom within walking distance of the Bat Cave (T-Bone did it, usually for a sperm donation, which he always prepared for like a blind date), the amount of time and effort involved was such that I made little attempt at personal hygiene. My face was mangy and unshaven, and I kept my hair tied up in a ponytail when it wasn't matted beneath my aviator's cap, until it reached the requisite length to be sold online or in local salons T-Bone knew about.

"What do I have to clean up for?" I protested.

"It's one of those things. You gotta take care of yourself. Otherwise you'll end up like the other bozos sleeping out on the street."

"At least they have a street name," I responded, suddenly feeling defensive.

T-Bone gave a weary of sigh.

"Mays. That's your street name."

"But that's my real name."

"Should be easy to remember then."

I lowered my head, going into a full-blown sulk as more tones were emitted from my monitor. The foul gray legume-based paste they served when we first arrived was wreaking havoc on my gastrointestinal system. A nurse wearing a disposable white respirator mask (they didn't offer them to the participants) came by every thirty minutes or so to check our blood pressure, heart rate, and monitor readings. If we didn't show enough activity they'd serve us another helping of the bean mush to further jumpstart our system. The little pill they administered to us halfway through the trial supposedly contained enzymes that would prevent gas by breaking down complex carbohydrates, although it was clear I had either been given a placebo as part of the control group or they needed to go back to the drawing board.

My show of disappointment had the desired effect, and T-Bone finally lowered his magazine and looked at me.

"Fine. I was gonna surprise you, but I got us a gig testing a new digital epinephrine auto-injector. Two milligrams every ten minutes for two hours. Pure adrenaline. *And* we get 50 milligrams Librium at the end to bring us down."

"Really?" I immediately brightened.

"Done deal. Just gotta pass a physical to show your heart won't give out."

"Thanks, T-Bone!" As if in appreciation the monitor behind me emitted a series of rapid machine-gun fire tones.

"No thanks necessary." He beamed like an indulgent father, going back to his magazine as his own monitor let out a single beep. "Seeing you light up like a Christmas tree is thanks enough."

We would, of course, have to lie routinely to get into so many trials and experiments. Somehow T-Bone's warrior code for improving the human condition as a pharmaceutical test pilot didn't take this fact into account. Almost all required you to list whatever medications you were taking, which we would always fabricate or leave blank, although to be fair it would have been difficult to give an accurate listing even if we wanted to. Lest anyone pass judgment on my lack of scientific integrity, I am confident that none of our misdeeds cheated the world out of a cure for cancer. Most were harmless, such as the focus group coordinator who believed her client's new flavored milk shrunk our retinas to the size of a pinhead, when in fact we had just spent the night before having strobe lights flashed at us in a meat locker in a study having to do with the effects of body temperature on retinal dilation and visual field perimetry. We were nothing more than statistically irrelevant rounding errors, mere droppings of bad data in an already confused Petri dish of market research, double blind studies, and clinical trials.

In short, anyone who didn't get too caught up in larger ethical concerns and had a fairly good tolerance for getting poked, prodded, and with an abundance of bodily fluids wouldn't have too difficult a time selling their body to science as a full-time endeavor, albeit one that didn't pay particularly well. In a good week we could expect to clear what was roughly on par with a minimum-wage worker at a fast food restaurant. Sometimes better, often worse, and of course it was all much more sporadic than your typical 9 to 5 job. In fact, the never-ending search for a steady supply of lucrative, perfectly interlocking trials, experiments and focus groups was itself almost a full-time job. T-Bone had a rotation of sources, including clinical research laboratories, local recruitment agencies, colleges, newspaper ads, and searching online using the computers in the New York City Public Library.

There had been many "new starts" in my life before, occasions when my parents decided (by choice or necessity) that a new school, new soccer team, or new summer camp would be the cure for my "adjustment issues." Usually it was only a matter of time before my moodiness, emotional highs and lows, missed social cues, or general awkwardness would set me apart from my peers. In this world where addiction, mental and physical handicaps were the norm, "fitting in" had little meaning. For many it was an undiagnosed or untreated mental illness that left them unable to cope with the topside world in the first place. In a sense this was the cohesive glue that held us all together in a kind of psychiatric ghetto, with a seemingly endless influx from nearby psychiatric hospitals like Bellevue, St. Luke's, and New York Presbyterian. They were flushed out into the streets, many given only cab fare and directions to nearby shelters or soup kitchens like St. Christophers's, where they would sometimes appear still in their hospital gown. Despite whatever walk of life we had come from, for most of us every conscious moment was a never-ending battle against not only external physical elements but hopelessness and despair.

And, of course, The Rage.

I had always assumed that my own family's specific form of mental illness was genetic defect passed down through generations like an heirloom. The many different colors, shapes, and sizes of The Rage I witnessed living on the street made me question to what extent environment plays a factor. The unforgiving conditions made the Hunger Rage and the Overwhelmed Rage fairly common, which fueled a need to escape that invariably introduced the Delusional Rage, often accompanied by the Substance Abuse Driven Rage (and just as dangerous Detox/Withdrawal Rage). The Paranoid Rage was typically a long-term side effect, while competition for scarce resources could nurture a kind of Predatory Rage that could escalate into a Homicidal Rage. These more outward-facing forms of derangement directed toward others weren't my style, preferring a more Self-Destructive Rage, even Passive Rage. I was the imploder, no doubt the result of my father's terrifying explosions. I did however discover a new kind Self-Preservation Rage that was helpful in keeping others at bay.

This particular variety I discovered on one of the first sub-freezing nights of the fall. Unable to sleep I took the initiative to gather enough garbage to build a small fire on the tracks outside the Bat Cave. T-Bone emerged shortly thereafter and admonished me not to start fires unless Kendrick was around, as they tended to attract attention and potential unwanted visitors from great distances. That didn't stop him from sitting next to me and warming himself, however. I was still exuberant enough to engage in one of my favorite topics of conversation, lethal doses for different prescription and over-the-counter medications.

"Don't get me wrong. Pentobarbital. Secobarbital. Always the safest bet. *If* you can get your hands on some. Big if."

I leaned over to the fire and lit the last of my thin feminine cigarettes, tossing the empty pack into the flames and taking a luxurious toke.

"Over-the-counter it gets risky. Ninety aspirin should do the job. Depends on your weight. You could take about 30 50 milligram Benadryls. 45 Excedrin, 78 Dristan will have the same effect. Hell, even 120 NoDoz and there's a decent chance—"

I stopped mid-sentence and looked up.

There were three high-powered flashlight beams pointed directly at me. I couldn't make out the figures behind them in the darkness, some fifteen feet away, nor had I heard anyone approaching. I immediately turned to T-Bone for guidance.

He had disappeared, completely gone from the very spot he sat in just seconds ago.

I turned back to the flashlights. They were still, and I could almost feel the figures behind them sizing me up.

That was when the Self Preservation Rage began to swell inside of me, a kind of shaky, fuck-everything madness. It seemed to power me to my feet, slowly, and without rushing, my cigarette clenched tightly in my lips.

Reaching beneath my chin, I snapped the strap to my leather aviator helmet tightly around my head. Then I pulled the goggles down over my eyes and stared straight ahead into the lights.

I stood there, trembling. I don't know how long I waited, or what I was waiting for. I thought about screaming. I thought about charging them. What I did was take the last puff from my cigarette and toss the butt into the fire.

Finally, the three figures turned and started walking in the other direction. I watched them through my dirty goggles until they disappeared around a corner of the tunnel.

"You're learning, kid."

T-Bone emerged from the darkness behind me.

"Getting yourself some defense mechanisms. That's a good thing."

The Rage as a defense mechanism. I had to think about this. I felt myself collapse to the ground next to the fire.

"Where did you go?" I asked him. "It was like you just disappeared."

"That's my defense mechanism," he said with a shrug as he settled down next to me. "Takes practice. But you'll get there."

I stretched out on the ground, still shaken but feeling pleased, waves of relief still pulsing through me.

"We might have to come up with a street name for you after all," T-Bone added.

"You know, I think I'll just stick with Mays," I decided, pulling the goggles off my eyes and positioning them on my forehead.

"It's my name, after all."

There was a *KERPLUNK* of a rat rolling off the tin can suspended by rope and into a dirty bucket of water from the rat trap nearby. It must have been a large one, as it struggled mightily, enough that I feared it might actually knock over the bucket of water and escape. T-Bone and I just sat and listened, until finally its scratches became more infrequent. I wondered if the rat was floating in the sea of effervescing bubbles just as I had been, perhaps scurrying down a tunnel toward a bright light, or if its spirit was really somewhere else now, or had just been extinguished forever.

Chapter 8. RAT CITY

I suppose it was inevitable that the honeymoon I experienced with my new off-the-grid lifestyle would come to an end. Perhaps it was the fact that, while I was constantly under the influence of any number of untested substances, it was one of the rare stretches of my life when I was not taking any prescribed anti-psychotic/depressant or mood stabilizer. I started to question whether the initial freedom and euphoria I felt may have all just been part of the manic bipolar-driven high I typically experienced before another unbearable low. The changing of the seasons from autumn to winter and corresponding drop in temperature certainly contributed to my growing disaffection. During particularly cold spells I'd go into a kind of quasi-hibernation for hours, sometimes days on end, shivering beneath layers of blankets and negative thoughts.

I suspect the main culprit however was simply witnessing first-hand the brutal conditions of this underground world that I had, until recently, found so liberating. There's a cliché in books and movies about indigent people being merry and happy-go-lucky, free from the everyday bonds and concerns of the rest of us. Living outside the confines of civilization, with all of its inefficiencies and injustice, would make people somehow more civilized, in the same way we think of it as a good thing when an injured animal is returned to nature, "the wild," and away from man-made dangers. As I quickly discovered "nature" is an unforgiving place, a day-to-day struggle for basic resources and survival, where every life form fell into the category of predator or prey.

As in the wild, the threat of violence was a constant stressor. Almost daily, T-Bone would have stories of whose gear had been stolen, who froze to death, who was missing, and who was in the ER after being beaten with a busted table leg. He made his informal rounds, wandering the city and checking on lost souls like myself, each with a past as dark and twisted as the tunnels that run beneath the streets. I wasn't sure how wide T-Bone's loosely held flock extended or how many it numbered, or even his underlying motivation for casting such a broad social net. It was part philanthropy, part social interaction, part intellectual curiosity, part ego, and part something else entirely, an endless reservoir of energy I could never fully understand. Sometimes he'd tell me about what he saw, sometimes he'd make me go with him, particularly if he knew I wouldn't believe him and chalk it up to one of his crazy stories (as I often did).

I witnessed first-hand the body of the sleeping homeless man under the plaza of the Metro North station in East Harlem who was set on fire apparently by a passing gang. Despite the half-hour subway ride uptown we still made it there before any law enforcement. A crowd had assembled. T-Bone didn't recognize the body, although it would have been difficult with third-degree burns covering the face and torso. As we were watching a pair of obviously sky-high homeless teenagers started undressing each other and fornicating on a bench across the plaza, which gradually began to siphon the onlookers around us who went over to watch.

There were others, like Peehole, thus named because of his small size. He couldn't have been more than fifteen years old. The story I heard from T-Bone was that he was from rural Pennsylvania and had run away from home when his boyfriend broke up with him. The only sign he was awake, or even alive, was the faint sobbing and muffled cries of anguish that would emanate from within the abandoned dumpster he lived in. Watching him, for whom simply making it through a single day was a momentous task, was a constant reminder of just how cruel nature could be to produce something so broken, so fundamentally ill-equipped to survive. Death seemed preferable to an existence consisting of daily mental torture laying in his own filth and waste. Eventually T-Bone was able to talk him out, relocating him into a community of LGBT runaways occupying a building in East New York that operated as a loosely-run brothel.

Then there was Baby Doll. I was awoken in the Bat Cave one night by a sound that I thought, given my surroundings, must have been a dream.

> *Sleep my child and peace attend thee,*
> *All through the night*

It was a lullaby, clear if not entirely melodic, and still more exquisite than anything down here could have produced. I lay listening for a moment, and then slowly rose, as if drawn to the sound.

> *Guardian angels God will send thee,*
> *All throuqh the night*

Outside the Bat Cave, I looked up the track to see Kendrick and T-Bone asleep by a fire. Sitting upright next to them, identifiable only from her back and forth rocking, was Baby Doll, singing to no one in particular.

> *Soft the drowsy hours are creeping,*
> *Hill and dale in slumber sleeping*

This was the same Baby Doll who was barely able to communicate with the outside world, speaking in different voices and prone to bursts of manic laughter. She would wander in and out of the Bat Cave on occasion to seek refuge, and took whatever assistance or abuse people provided her in the way of food, drugs, and beatings.

> *I my loved ones' watch am keeping,*
> *All through the night*

And yet there she was. As T-Bone observed, I was still in the process of developing rudimentary self-defense mechanisms. Since I didn't feel like being sad just then, I went back into the Bat Cave and wrapped myself up in blankets trying to block out the sound. Yet it was as if the music kept playing inside my head anyway.

She disappeared shortly after that and we never heard from her again. I did however catch T-Bone staring at something months later during lunchtime at St. Christopher's. He often did that; staring at something a little too long, shuddering at odd moments, like his body was slightly out-of-tune after the years of abuse. This however went on long enough that I finally followed his eyes to the shopping cart pushed around by one of the regulars at the soup kitchen, who had been wearing layers of trash bags when I first met him. The shopping cart contained the usual hodge-podge of scrap metal, old take-out food and other sundries, and I was about to chalk it up to T-Bone's long-term cognitive damage when I finally saw it too, the small plastic doll, crammed in the bottom.

"Mays! You listening?"

We were sitting on the concrete in the darkness beneath an unfamiliar enclosed overpass in Hunts Point, located in the bowels of the South Bronx, watching a virtuoso graffiti artist named Little Andre create one of his masterpieces on a warehouse across the avenue from us. T-Bone had heard he was working and insisted we come all the way up to see it. It was a few hours before dawn and cold, although a small crowd of onlookers were still scattered throughout the darkness around us, spilling out onto the avenue. Most of the streetlamps were broken, but scattered flashlight beams crossed as they followed Little Andre's careful motions, creating a bizarre opening night atmosphere.

"So anyway, they're supposed to be studying this medication for blood pressure," T-Bone continued.

From what I could make out Little Andre was a gangly, skinny black kid with a baby face. T-Bone had explained to me that there had been a Big Andre as well, an older brother (Andre was some variation of their last name), but he had been missing for months. Incarceration and accidental death were occupational hazards for graffiti artists, who routinely scaled tall bridges, billboards, live subway tracks, and other treacherous locales in search of high-traffic canvasses to display their art.

"Helps angina or something so more blood can get to the heart. Only pretty soon I notice that my dick's been hard for like a day and a half. Not regular jerk-off hard, but tree trunk, diamond cutting hard, like this heat-seeking missile ..."

Little Andre was painting some kind of Hell creature, a winged bat-like monster with a furry tail and skull head with bright yellow eyes that pierced the darkness. Giant 3D letters below read UNIVERSAL DESTRUCTION in fiery letters. It was at once hideous, breathtaking, and brilliant. It made me think of The Rage. And my father.

"So it's a couple of years later," T-Bone narrated obliviously, "at the same lab but for a different study. I don't know it at the time but they're giving me the exact same medication, only this time I'm hooked up to this thing called, I kid you not, a RigiScan."

Further down the avenue a group of freegans were engaged in a "dumpster dive," foraging for food in an old dumpster behind a closed take-out Chinese restaurant. Freegans were plentiful in this neighborhood, many of them living illegally (squatting) in abandoned warehouses like the one Little Andre was adorning. Reusing unwanted food and clothing was part of their creed, so as not to perpetuate what they saw as our fundamentally corrupt economic system run by giant corporations that destroyed the planet. The freegans had set up an assembly line leading out of the dumpster, with some mining for potential viands that they would then toss out to the others, who would perform a basic level of quality control and either throw back into the dumpster as refuse or pack into small crates.

"Like this electric boa-constrictor they wrap around your cock," T-Bone continued, fully engrossed in his tale. "It squeezes every 30 seconds to see how hard it is, how wide it is at the shaft, then they hook it up to this little computer strapped to your leg. And I'm supposed to wear this for two weeks, sleep with it even."

Ironically enough, despite their mutual anti-business, anti-government, anti-everything leanings, T-Bone had little patience for the freegans, whom he derisively called the freakings. He loved to tell stories like the freegans' failed attempt to liberate scores of cattle from a beef farm in upstate New York, who only stared back at them motionlessly instead of fleeing to freedom when the fences impounding them were cut open.

"So naturally it's not the most comfortable thing in the world, and there's not much going on down there until a couple of days later when I'm at the library of all places, using the computer there looking for trials, but it's against the rules because they close in five minutes and you're supposed to be off the computers at least fifteen minutes before."

I had a theory explaining T-Bone's disdain for the freegans, despite the almost nihilistic, believe-in-nothing philosophy they both shared. For the freegans, their steadfast belief in nothing, or rather the complete rejection of all the pillars our modern society, still represented what might be described as, for lack of a better word, something. T-Bone, despite his lip service to a utopian underground society, truly believed in nothing, a complete absence of anything that ran much deeper than the freegans; an ingrained distrust of any governing body, organization, ideal, or anything that could even possibly be construed as something.

"So all of a sudden, she's standing above me, this librarian, big woman, and she's wearing this jacket with these big Joan Crawford shoulder pad things, and she says to me '*You must leave now.*' And it's the way she said it, in this low, kind of dominating tone of voice, just ordering me what to do, like she's so physically disgusted with me that sets me off like a rocket, and all the sudden BEEP BEEP BEEP my RigiScan starts lighting up—"

"*FIVE-OH!*"

The shout came from somewhere in the darkness, setting off a flurry of activity like a starter's gun at a track meet. I saw Little Andre jump off his stepladder and grab a light he had set up. I looked next to me and T-Bone was gone, as if he had evaporated, just as he always did at the first sign of any trouble, before the other assorted beams of light from flashlights in the area disappeared.

Five-O, as in Hawaii Five-O, was slang for law enforcement, although the term had been generalized to mean any unidentified visitor. I stood still, upright in the darkness, not knowing which direction to run in, while a single flashlight beam turned the corner of the avenue and made its way into the darkness of the enclosed underpass.

"Hello?" came a shaky male voice from behind the approaching flashlight beam. "Hello? My name is Paul Aviland and I'm with Operation HOPE, the New York City Homeless Outreach Project."

In addition to St. Christopher's All Souls Kitchen, there were a number of other non-profits catering to the homeless. Operation HOPE was among the more visible, as they tended to go down into areas most others wouldn't. I had even seen them in some of the tunnels and abandoned stations near City Hall. It was certainly something I would never do. Most were unpaid, descending into the depths and darkness of the tunnels to seek out the diseased and mentally unstable, where they would typically get fleeced and paid little mind.

"If anyone here is in need of medical attention please come forward. I also have sandwiches if anyone is hungry."

Their efforts always struck me as more pathetic than heroic, overmatched and overwhelmed as they were, much like the solitary part-time social worker who supposedly worked at St. Christopher's but I had never seen. Operation HOPE-less seemed like a more appropriate name.

"Give me the food," the voice behind the flashlight whispered to someone else, apparently his partner, ridiculous in that it was so quiet the sound of his hushed voice echoing off the walls around us might have been on a loudspeaker.

"I just gave it to you," a different voice whispered back, beneath a sudden fast patter of receding footsteps. There was a pause while the footsteps disappeared, presumably along with the supply of sandwiches.

"Let me see the flashlight then."

No sooner had the words left his lips than the point of light began to move quickly away from them, as more footsteps bounced through the darkness in the opposite direction of their voices.

"Come back ..."

I suddenly became aware that the stolen flashlight was heading in my direction, as if whoever had taken it was making a B-line toward me. I attempted to backpedal but was disoriented in the darkness, and it seemed no matter which direction I moved I was unable to get out of its path.

"Can whoever took our flashlight please give it back?"

Bump!

A force not much more than waist high collided with me, thumping down to the pavement before me as I stumbled backward. For an instant the beam from the flashlight was pointing directly upward at me. I squinted and shielded my eyes. The beam moved away again, and I heard the small figure that had crashed into me scramble up from the ground. The light from the flashlight then continued past me at its previous velocity, but not before I was able to catch a fleeting glimpse of its new owner.

It was a child.

Nine years old? Ten? I couldn't even tell if it was a boy or a girl, just a young dark face with big eyes beneath a hooded sweatshirt disappearing into the darkness, leaving behind only the voice of one of the hapless social workers from Operation HOPE.

"Could someone please show us the way out of here?"

A child. I was unable to get the thought out of my head hours later back at the Bat Cave, nor did I understand why I was troubled by it when I had worked so hard conditioning myself not to be troubled by anything. T-Bone had told me there were families living down here, although as with much of what he said I took it with a grain of salt. Suddenly however, his notions of an underground civilization sounded less far-fetched. I wondered if a thousand years from now the differences between the rich and the poor might not be just economic and social but physical as well, a Darwinian adaptation where underground and topside meant not just different worlds but different species.

The final straw that forever shattered any lingering romantic notions of my alternate lifestyle, ironically enough, began as a humanitarian mission. T-Bone roused me from a hibernated state in the Bat Cave one evening after we completed a trial procedure where a tiny patch of pubic hair was grafted onto the scalp as part of an experimental replacement technique. We had been provided a small supply of Percocet to manage the pain, and T-Bone had given me his share. He kept shaking me until I was coherent, then told me to follow him. I did, not only because I usually did whatever T-Bone told me to do in circumstances like this, but there was an unusual sense of urgency in his tone and mannerisms. He sounded almost stressed, which was never a word I would associate with him. I was gingerly touching the few strands (I wouldn't even call it a patch) of unnaturally wiry hair now affixed to the lower back of my head as I followed him out of the Bat Cave and further down the track, well past what I knew to be safe. T-Bone was waddling ahead of me at a fast clip, either out of urgency or the general unease of leaving our unofficial comfort zone.

"Fucking Kendrick ... never around when you need him," was all T-Bone muttered.

It became so dark that I finally had to take my accustomed position walking behind him with my hand on his shoulder. Vibrations from passing trains increased in frequency and intensity to the point I was beginning to worry about getting run over or electrocuting ourselves. Somehow T-Bone could tell when the track forked to the left, and turned sharply after some distance, and then again, and then it seemed we were off the track entirely and walking on gravel. It was during this time he explained to me the destination and nature of our trip.

We were going to a place called Rat City.

Perhaps it was the lingering effects of the Percocet, but my first thought was of the famous experiment done in the 1970s known by a similar name. The experiment consisted of hordes of rats locked into a tiny, overcrowded cage and given the choice to drink out of two drop dispensers, one containing water and the other morphine. Almost all of the rats drank the morphine. Then instead of packing them all in a tiny cage they set up an elaborate rat city, like a giant playground for rats. There was plenty of food, balls and wheels to play with, and private places for mating and giving birth. None of the rats would take the morphine. Even after they tried sweetening it, there was nothing they could do to entice the residents of Rat City to become junkies.

I made the mistake of mentioning this to T-Bone.

"Oh yeah?" T-Bone asked as a light appeared at the end of the tunnel we were walking in. "You know I mightta been in that one come to think of it. Did they run it at Rosedale Clinical?"

We emerged from the tunnel into a much larger open underground space. A subway car, slow moving, made its way along tracks above us. From our angle below I could see it wasn't a regular passenger car but one of those long flat-bed maintenance cars loaded with dumpsters of trash.

I assured T-Bone that this was a different experiment, and tried to get him to tell me why we needed to visit this particular Rat City.

"Favor for a friend of mine with a medical condition. Should be no problem for a guy like you," he waved dismissively. "So what happened with the experiment?"

The maintenance car came screeching to a stop, disappearing from view behind an elevated platform ahead of us. There was a large cement structure supporting it that rose up from the ground at our level. Dim light filtered down through the tracks to the ground and walls that appeared to move and change color in the distance.

"I dunno, lost funding or something, maybe the professor got canned." There was some reason that escaped me why it wasn't universally accepted, I mused, becoming aware of dark shadows moving around to the side of us. "Methodology was fucked up or something ... not everybody believed it."

"That methodology was flawless!"

T-Bone's tone would indicate that he in fact was the one responsible for publishing the results of the study. I was slowing down as we approached the activity ahead of us; the odor that had been growing steadily had become almost overwhelming.

"That's what they're doing, don't you get it? Just feeding us morphine."

"Why not just take your friend to the ER at Bellevue? I'm not a real doctor," I protested, trying to change the subject back to the matter at hand. "What medical condition are you talking about?"

"She been complaining about her lower back and stomach. I got suspicious so I checked. Turns out she was pregnant and didn't even know it."

I stopped suddenly, both out of surprise and to let a pair of oversized rats, who were clearly not intimidated by me, scuttle past.

"How do you know?"

T-Bone pulled me along by the arm and gave a shrug.

"The head coming out of her vajajay was a clue, but you're the doctor."

I had "gowned up" for a half dozen or so L&Ds (labor and delivery) during my OBGYN rotation at Columbia, including a couple of caesarean sections, which were cool because the incision is huge and they let you stitch it up. I knew it wasn't going to be my field; given my depression I had grave misgivings even bringing people into a world with light and sunshine. The darkness and spectacularly unsanitary conditions into which this baby would not only be delivered but presumably live made the thought utterly appalling to me.

"T-Bone, no—"

"It's just up ahead here. This is where they transfer all the dumpsters from the garbage cars before it gets taken to Jersey to sort out," T-Bone explained.

Packets of rat poison that resembled artificial sweetener for coffee were dispersed through the litter on the ground below us.

"They store them in these locked rooms that are supposed to keep the rats out. The city replaced the doors a few years back, but it don't make no difference. They're in the walls."

And with that we came to a stop inside the perimeter of Rat City. I felt the contents of my stomach shoot upward as I beheld the sight, which was something no amount of Percocet could have braced me for. The light filtering down through track above us revealed a layer of trash and debris almost completely covered with swarms of rats. They were of varying sizes, from mouse to small dog, with a handful of truly frightening cows that seemed to be of a different species. I instinctively covered my mouth and nose in an unsuccessful attempt to lessen the impact of the overwhelming stench. It was a surreal site, the waves of dark brown and black that seemed to flow together, with a uniform high-pitched squeaking sound in the background representing the underground equivalent of crickets. There were three or four major arteries, creating visible traffic patterns around the exposed cinderblocks of the cement stanchion leading up to the platform and garbage rooms above us, the mouth of a river where a seemingly endless supply of rats would pour into and fall out of.

I felt the brush of rodents scurrying across my feet and against my legs as T-Bone led me through the sea of vermin. On the far side of the cement structure was an out-of-service freight elevator, clearly designed to bring large items to the platform above us, that obviously hadn't been used in years. The doors were open, revealing a dark elevator shaft inside. T-Bone stepped in and pulled me behind him. I could see lights flickering above us, along with a whimpering sound above the cacophony of squeals and distant clanging from dumpsters being unloaded from the subway car.

"It's me!" T-Bone shouted, and an aluminum work ladder appeared out of space above us and clattered upright on the ground next to him. Peering closely, I could see it descended from a small trap door in what appeared to be the floor of the immobile freight elevator suspended about ten feet off the ground. As I made my way up the ladder behind T-Bone, it looked like the shaft and elevator itself was quite large, maybe twelve by eighteen feet, although once I climbed through the opening in the floor I became completely disoriented. There were flashlight beams from along the sides that moved wildly in the darkness, blinding me at times, but for the most part focused on the dark-skinned woman lying on her back on a thin mattress in the center.

T-Bone introduced her to me as Egypt. She was not, as her name might suggest, a hot exotic dancer, but a morbidly obese black woman who instead looked the size and shape of the Gift of the Nile. She must have weighed over 300 pounds, and I could understand how her pregnancy might have gone unnoticed. Blankets covered her body unevenly, with rolls of exposed flesh visible between the cracks. I was about to protest to T-Bone once more, but realized it was pointless. We couldn't move her to an ER even if we wanted to; in fact, I wondered if it were physically possible for her to have left the elevator in many months.

I politely introduced myself to Egypt using the most professional, matter-of-fact tone I could muster, then got down on my knees. I asked for more light to no one in particular, and the beams around the room magically followed me as I lifted her knees and spread her legs.

She was in active labor, her cervix fully dilated and the top of the baby's head "crowning" or protruding through.

"I'm gonna shit ..." Egypt wailed.

"That's the baby moving through the birth canal, it's putting pressure on your rectum, it just means the baby is coming out—"

There was another agonizing scream, as a short burst of urine and fecal matter spurted forth. I tried to dodge it but ended up getting sprayed. The contractions were becoming closer together, seemingly only minutes apart, and the baby was clearly ready to come out. I told T-Bone I was going to need a sheet or blanket to wrap the baby in, the cleanest they had, and one was handed to me.

"Just keep pushing," I coaxed as the next contraction started. The baby was passing through her pelvis face down, which was good, and I gently supported its head.

"That's perfect, Egypt, just like that."

Its umbilical cord was loosely wrapped around the neck, a not uncommon occurrence. I fumbled to create a loop wide enough for the baby to slide through, then gently turned its head to the side to help the first shoulder emerge. Through another set of screams, I then lifted the baby toward the mother's stomach to help get the other shoulder through.

"One more push, that's all I need."

There was a final wail from Egypt and the baby, a boy, was through. The entire delivery had taken less than ten minutes. I held him at a 45-degree angle for a moment to drain the mucus and fluids. There was a gasp, and then the reassuring sound of his crying. I wrapped him in the surprisingly clean blanket that had been provided me, and placed the baby on his mother's chest and into her outstretched arms as I had been trained to do. I then leaned over on my hands and knees and tried to catch my breath, covered in fluids, still taking in what had just occurred.

There was a rumbling beneath the crying sounds of both the baby and his mother, then a long screech as the maintenance car above us began to pull out of the station. The whole elevator began to shake.

"Oh god, there's another!" Egypt cried out suddenly, but I reassured her it was only the placenta, which came out relatively easily. Knowing it was unlikely there was a pair of sterile surgical scissors laying around, I waited until I could no longer feel a pulse in the umbilical cord and did my best to break it free with my hands, cutting through the slippery surface with my dirty fingernail and then pulling it apart. Finally, I looked up behind me at the figure of T-Bone and scrambled to my feet.

"T-Bone," I whispered frantically.

Between the flickers of light from the flashlight beams I could see him grinning as if he was the lucky father.

"Not bad, kid."

"We can't leave him here."

His smile faded immediately.

"T-Bone, listen to me. This baby can't stay here. He can't live like this."

I was frantically whispering to him, but he kept talking over me.

"What are you saying? You want to take her baby?"

"If there's one thing I know, in this whole fucked up world, it's that this is no place for a baby, not if we can help it—"

"We can't steal their baby—"

"T-Bone, listen to me—"

I stopped as his eyes got wider and his gaze moved over my shoulder. I spun around. All of the lights were now pointing at us, and I was blinded. I turned back to T-Bone.

He had disappeared.

Then the lights disappeared as well. I stood motionless in the pitch darkness for a horrible instant with the sickening realization that something very bad was about to happen.

Then came the arm around my neck. Someone was choking me from behind, someone large. I gasped for air, using both hands to try to loosen the arm when suddenly it felt like there was an explosion on the side of my head, then another behind my ear. I was being choked and beaten simultaneously. There were two more blows to the side of my head from my unseen assailants, then the arm was removed from around my neck and another crushing blow came down inside my right shoulder, sending me falling onto my knees and forearms.

At this point I was pretty sure I was going to die, not quite as sure as I was when I put the helium bag over my head, although this was likely to be messier. There was a kick to my rib cage, then another, and I finally covered my head in a fetal position on the floor. I rolled over in an attempt to escape the punishment but more fists rained down, hitting my exposed sides and the arms I protected my head with. I rolled over on the floor again and could feel with one of my legs the floor disappear at the corner of the open trap door. I made a last-ditch effort to pull myself toward it, knocking my face into the top of the aluminum ladder. A final kick from behind sent me through the opening and falling into space, just as they might have disposed of a rat who had invaded their humble but meticulously maintained home.

Chapter 9. THE RAPTURE

There are actually striking similarities between giving birth and being on the receiving end of a true beat-down. Everything from the cries of pain and pleading for it to stop, lack of bladder and bowel control, to the shallow whimpering sounds, she while in labor and myself when I awoke trying to breathe through what I was pretty sure was a fracture of my seventh or eighth rib on the left side and my medial clavicle or collarbone.

The first image to appear before me when I became conscious again was of tiny green fluorescent splotches glowing in the darkness, seemingly suspended in midair. My entire head throbbed and my left eye was so swollen I could barely see out of it. The right side of my face was raw to the touch and covered with tiny pebbles and rat droppings, like I had been dragged face-down by my feet. Even the slightest attempt at movement would send pain shooting up my spine, and I wondered if this is where I had been left to die, in this refuse pile of dirt and rotted wooden beams.

As things came more into focus I could see the green shapes floating in black ink were actually mushrooms growing out of the earth around me. The glow radiated from the mushroom's gill, the papery rib under the cap. It was astonishing to me that any plant life, even a non-photosynthetic fungus that didn't depend on sunlight to grow, could survive in conditions like these. Then again, I supposed the same could be said for all of us living down here.

"They call 'em jack-o-lanterns."

T-Bone's head lowered itself into my field of vision.

"Just don't eat 'em, you'll shit your guts out."

Breathing was so painful that I dared not respond, and instead only continued letting out whimpering sounds with each shallow exhale.

T-Bone got down on his stomach in front of me and pulled something out of his coat, a dirty parka he wore in the winter.

"We gotta move you," he said, biting open what appeared to be a tiny plastic bag and spilling the powdery contents onto the back of his fist.

"You need to take this or it's gonna hurt too much."

I didn't even ask what it was, not caring at that point. However, there was no way I was going to be able to snort anything in my condition.

"Can't ... breathe ..." I managed to get out, and T-Bone seemed to understand

"We'll need to shoot it then. I'll find a needle from somewhere ..."

Panicked, I immediately consumed the powder in a series of small, exceedingly painful snorts. Prescription painkillers can be crushed and sniffed for a more intense and immediate high, but it was clear I was under the influence of something I had never tried before. The nausea came first, then leveled off at what felt like a manageable level, followed by a kind of numbing warmness.

"Give it a sec. How you feeling now?"

It was at least easier for me to talk, and the whimpering that accompanied each breath seemed to have subsided.

"I. Um. What." I explained.

T-Bone nodded to someone who had apparently been standing behind me the whole time. Suddenly I was being elevated above the sea of bioluminescent mushrooms in which I had been laying. I was aware that I must have been in pain, for the dull scream echoing out in the darkness seemed to belong to me, but in my brain it was abstract somehow. The ground began to move below me, as I could make out the army jacket of Kendrick. He had me slung over his shoulder, seemingly without much effort, and was walking with T-Bone. As they moved, I remember hoping not to throw up on Kendrick. I could hear T-Bone preaching about some experiment that sounded vaguely familiar.

"... this giant city for rats, it went on for miles, like the size of Cleveland. I was on the team that helped build it ..."

My nausea was getting worse, so bad I almost missed the physical pain to my ribs, neck, and spine. I kept feeling like I was about to fall off Kendrick's shoulder and tried to get them to slow down, but all that came out of my mouth was a moan.

"The fuck rats need a city for?" I heard Kendrick inquire, and noted he was in an unusually chipper mood. I wondered if T-Bone had bribed him with whatever substance he gave me.

"You're missing the point there. It's a metaphor see ..."

Finally I couldn't hold it in anymore, feeling the pain in my ribs even through my drugged condition as I hurled down the back of Kendrick's army jacket.

"... you know, like when they try to cure cancer in lab rats," T-Bone droned on.

Either they didn't notice the stream of vomit making its way down the back of Kendrick's jacket or they chose to ignore it.

"That's what I'm saying," I heard Kendrick posit. "Who gives a fuck rats have cancer? They need to worry 'bout the *human beings* first."

I recognized we were back in the Bat Cave, where Kendrick finally lowered me to my makeshift bed on the catwalk. The last image I remember is the two of them looking down at me in the darkness, Kendrick removing his vomit-covered army jacket and T-Bone chuckling to himself.

"Rat City, that's us, boy."

I had come full circle.

"I just need a one-pound bag of Epsom salt. Try to find the unscented kind," I instructed T-Bone from the same position on my concrete bed over a week later.

My physical wounds were the first to heal: the cuts and bruises on my face, then my collarbone, and finally my ribs. The mental part of the ordeal was a different story entirely. I had spent my days lying still for the most part, trying to manage the pain in my chest, using a plastic trash bag for my waste, not touching most of the food and water T-Bone brought me, and sinking deeper into the same spiral depression I had in my studio apartment before my suicide attempt.

"And two Claritan-Ds, thirty tablets, the kind they keep

behind the counter. You have to ask for it. Make sure it has pseudoephedrine. They'll only let you buy one at a time so you'll need to go to different places."

I had taken the first step, I realized, down my current path that would inevitably lead to permanent disability. Even T-Bone, with his rock-solid constitution and hardy disposition, betrayed the obvious toll his chosen lifestyle had taken over time, including the twitch in his eye, bad teeth, the occasional involuntary shudder, his duck-like gait and awkward movements, all the result of years of injuries gone undiagnosed and untreated. This was what I had to look forward to, a life of steadily decreasing physical and mental capacity that upon reflection didn't seem like much of a life at all.

"Then at least 500 milligrams of diphenhydramine. You can definitely find it in Sleep-Eze and NyTol, but most sleep medications should have it."

I was overcome with hopelessness, and, of course, The Rage. Here I thought I could escape it by changing my name, my clothing, my life, as if it wouldn't recognize me beneath the ridiculous aviator cap and goggles that I no longer bothered to wear. But it had found me, sometimes immobilizing me with despair, while other times I'd twist and writhe beneath my blankets, stuffing the filthy throw-cushion I used as a pillow into my mouth to stifle the shouts.

"Then just three of those big Tylenols, extra strength, plus a liter and a half of bourbon. Doesn't have to be the good stuff."

As was the case the last time, there was only one escape, one inevitable conclusion I could arrive at.

"Here's $98 dollars. It's all I have left." I held up a wad of bills from underneath my blankets.

"You can't knock yourself off here," T-Bone informed me flatly.

I just looked up at him, not having the energy to argue. Granted, it wasn't as fully fleshed out as my last Exit Plan, but I needed some tools to work with.

"House rules," he shrugged. "It'll stink. Attract attention. Bad publicity."

"I'll go somewhere else then."

T-Bone gave a weary sigh.

"Fine. Come with me." He snatched the $98 from my fingers and made his way toward the entrance of the Bat Cave, then looked back at me impatiently. "Come on," he repeated.

I struggled to rise, then followed him clumsily as he led me further down into the tunnels. We were once again headed in the same general direction of Rat City, although I was quickly and completely lost with all of the turns he made in the darkness.

"You ever stop to think this all might just be a figment of your depressed personality?" he asked me as we walked.

"I'm not depressed," I answered. "That's the thing. It's not me that's depressed. It's life. Life is depressing."

"How come you never wear your little pilot's cap anymore? It used to make you so happy."

"Any rational human being. If they had a choice ... do you really think anyone would choose to be born?"

I was struggling to keep up behind him, clutching his shoulder with my hand. We entered a particularly narrow passageway that seemed to intersect two larger tunnels.

"Think about it," I reasoned. "The things that are supposed to make this all worthwhile. Love? Probably causes more suffering than anything. One person always loves the other more. It never lasts. I don't know anyone who's been happily married. My parents have been married almost twenty-six years. They can't stand each other. My dad cheats on her. Makes fun of her body. She stays in bed all day loaded on painkillers."

There were nearby vibrations from a train passing around us, although I couldn't tell from what direction.

"Children? That's the biggest joke of all. All the dreams you have for your kids when you bring them into this world. Recipe for disaster. Fucks up the kids and disappoints the hell out of their parents. You don't believe me? Ask my folks."

Finally, we emerged out onto a stretch of subway track I didn't recognize.

"So most people go along sucking dick every day at a job they hate, too afraid to die."

"Here we are," T-Bone said finally, turning around to face me. "Have a seat. Be sure to face this way," he added, pointing down the track ahead of me. "It'll be easier."

I hadn't intended on such a violent exit, getting run over by a subway train. T-Bone obviously didn't think I'd go through with it, judging by his demeanor. That shaky, fuck-everything flavor of The Rage began tingling through my system. I got down and my hands and knees and made myself as comfortable as possible, staring straight ahead as instructed.

"Should be a train along any minute," T-Bone informed me, taking a seat on the ground about ten yards to the side of the track on my left. He was barely visible in the darkness.

"You're going to watch?" I asked incredulously.

"Yeah, never seen this before believe it or not," he mused, pulling out a pack of cigarettes. "Although you keep talking about this depressing shit I'll be on the track next to you before long."

"That's why we invent things like God and Heaven, you know," I continued as T-Bone lit his cigarette. "To sweeten the pot. Like, when I was a kid in Sunday school, we learned about the Rapture—"

I stopped. The ground beneath me began to tremble.

"The Rapture," I continued. "It's when the end of the world comes, and God takes the good people to Heaven and leaves the assholes to suffer and die."

The faint vibration began to steadily build, and there was an audible rumbling in the distance coming from behind me. My breathing started to quicken.

"Organized religion is just another way they control us," I heard T-Bone respond. Through my peripheral vision I could make out the glow of his cigarette. "Work hard at the factory, don't make waves, you get to go to Heaven."

Pieces of litter and dust were blowing about from the oncoming draft. I forced myself to stare ahead stoically

"So my Sunday school teacher, she has us each write a Rapture letter to our parents telling them how great things are in Heaven and how we can't wait to see them."

The rumbling was growing louder, as the stretch of tunnel we were in was suddenly illuminated from bright lights shining behind me. T-Bone had to raise his voice to be heard.

"It's the same like they do with the Arab kids. Promise to get their dick sucked for eternity if they strap on a bomb," he shouted. "Or in the old days when the Pope used sell salvation at fifty grand a pop to get the ceiling painted."

The rails were visibly shaking, and the clatter made conversation all but impossible. I closed my eyes.

"So we're all, hi Mom, hi Dad, Heaven's great," I yelled. "I watch TV all day, drink soda and have candy for breakfast. And our teacher, she's egging us on, encouraging us. And I remember thinking ..."

The noise was deafening now, seemingly directly behind me.

"... if this afterlife thing is so great ..."

I screamed what I thought was as good an epitaph as any:

"WHY ARE WE WASTING OUR TIME HERE?"

There was a shower of sparks and bright flashes next to me, a blinding display of pyrotechnics as the subway train roared past on an adjacent track ten yards to my right. The wind rushing past knocked me forward onto my stomach, and I was momentarily unable to catch my breath. I lay there face down, hyperventilating as the sound of the train gradually dissipated. I realized I had wet myself.

"Sonofabitch," I finally heard T-Bone chuckle. "Gotta hand it to you, kid. Once you set your mind on something ..."

There were footsteps, then dollar bills fluttering to the ground in front of my face.

"Here's your 98 bucks," he said simply. "Let's get outta here. Get drunk or something."

I looked up as T-Bone flicked away the last of his cigarette and helped me off the ground.

"We'll stop by St. Chris's. Kendrick's making his sesame chicken."

"What if you spend eternity fizzing away like a giant Alka-Seltzer tablet?"

I stared at the back of my milk carton at St. Christopher's that afternoon, as if the answer was hidden in the nutritional information listed on the back. T-Bone sat across one of the long wooden cafeteria tables from me, opening the mail that had arrived for us. The soup kitchen was only half full, lunch having ended over an hour ago. Back behind the serving counter, the kitchen staff and other volunteers were sitting at a table, laughing and eating their lunch. They always seemed to be having such a good time, whether serving up sesame chicken or mopping floors. I found it annoying.

"What if that's all there is? Then what's the reward?" I mused. "Why go through all this suffering? What's the reason?"

"Look, you got another check!" T-Bone handed me a slip of green paper, a check for $235 from RCL Laboratories, Inc. Raritan, NJ. "Whaddya say we cash it and have ourselves a little celebration?"

"I don't see any reason for it. Living, I mean ..."

I could see T-Bone's shoulders slump in disappointment. I knew he was tired of hearing about this. I didn't care.

"... no reason for it at all," I muttered.

"Audrey!"

T-Bone shouted, brightening suddenly. He was looking over at the social services office. The door was open. It was the first time I had seen the door open in the dozens of times I had been there.

"Hey, Mays, Audrey's here!" T-Bone almost giggled, scrambling to his feet. "C'mon!"

I watched him skip between the tables toward the open door as I sullenly finished my milk. I hadn't seen him this ebullient since the first time he took me to jack off. He paused outside the office door, and then I heard a female voice squeal his name from inside.

And then Audrey Flores appeared in the doorway. She gave T-Bone a hug and they began talking animatedly, like old friends who hadn't seen each other in ages catching up. It wasn't like her physical looks would stop traffic. I could tell she was short, about the same height as T-Bone, and a little pudgy. Her black hair went just past her shoulders, and had what appeared to be purple highlights. A fashionably torn, off-the-shoulder sweatshirt revealed a black tank top and elaborate flower tattoo that started at the top of her arm. She wore multiple earrings and a chain around her neck and was gesticulating wildly as she spoke, a variety of bracelets and bands rattling about her forearms above her rolled up sleeves. I guessed early to mid-twenties, my age or perhaps a little younger.

But it was her smile.

Something so refreshing, even exquisite about her smile took my breath away and seemed to light up the room around her, even one as cavernous and dreary as St. Christopher's. I watched intoxicated as she waved her arms, laughed, shrieked, and touched T-Bone's shoulder. I finally rose and stepped hesitantly toward them, moving almost unconsciously in a semi-circle and out of her line of sight. As I got closer, the door to her office swung open a little further, and something else caught my attention. It was there in the reflection of the glass on the window of her office door, superimposed over Audrey's melting, gigawatt smile.

It was me, or rather my image reflected in the glass. My matted hair protruded from under the hood of my open soiled sweatshirt and filthy quilted winter coat, face still slightly misshapen from the recent beat-down and covered in scabs. My many layers of t-shirts and jeans were filthy, threadbare and torn. Just as quickly as the vision of Audrey filled me with warmth was it now replaced with waves of humiliation. The extent of my descent, the reality of my current existence, could not have been more painfully clear. I was no longer of this world, more at home in a city of rats than civilized society.

I saw T-Bone glance toward me, and I immediately spun around in the other direction.

"Hey, Mays!" T-Bone shouted behind me. As he gave chase I broke into a run, fighting through the crowds on my way to the door, wishing I could sink back into the ground where I belonged.

"Come back, Mays ..."

Chapter 10. THE SHELF

For most people, myself included, the descent into a homeless existence doesn't happen in a linear fashion or follow a gradual downward path. To be sure there are tell-tale signs and milestones along the way, but more often the journey begins with a couple of bad breaks such as loss of a job, personal tragedy, or addiction, and ends with a very steep and precipitous drop.

I call it falling off the shelf, and it occurs when you are so completely devoid of what are considered to be the minimal entry requirements as a member of civilized society that re-entry to the topside world is no longer practical. When putting on a clean shirt for a job interview and presenting a valid form of identification or home phone number becomes a challenge, let alone a polished resume or previous job references, and when your face, teeth, or mannerisms betray months or years of sleeping on concrete, eating from garbage or abusing substances, the path back to the surface becomes implausible indeed.

I saw a perfect example of this a few days later as T-Bone and I took the subway to the NYPD Police Academy out in Flushing, Queens. We were both being paid $30 plus breakfast to be in a "funhouse," where we'd jump out from behind boxes and have blanks shot at us by prospective members of New York's Finest. I saw a man, clearly on the edge of this shelf, right there on the precipice. It was the morning rush hour and the subway car was packed, and I stood surrounded by professionally dressed men and women most of whom would clear out at or near Wall Street. I was sullen, as I had been since running away from Audrey in the soup kitchen. I found myself wistfully remembering the simple pleasures I had enjoyed before I had fallen off the shelf, such as taking a hot shower, going out to dinner, or flirting with a girl, and how I now avoided looking around when walking on the sidewalk for fear of catching my own reflection in the passing windows.

Passengers exited and entered at the 14th Street station. My eyes were shut as I tried to block out the bustle around me and, despite the fact it was the dead of winter, my painful sunburn. T-Bone and I had spent the better part of the previous day under a sunlamp testing a men's body rub that was supposed to emit a masculine scent and provide a testosterone-enhancing nourishing hydration formula to the skin while at the same time protecting against the sun's harmful ultraviolet rays. It had left my upper body a checkerboard of blotchy squares ranging in color from pink to bright red.

I heard the doors close. Then close again. And again.

"Get out the door, please!" an irritated female voice echoed out of a speaker above me. I opened my eyes.

Pressed against the window of the subway doors was a middle-aged man, unshaven, gripping a brown paper shopping bag he had managed to squeeze into the subway car while the rest of his body was out on the platform. His face was beet red as he continued to try to push through the doors.

"Get OUT THE DOOR, please!" the conductor's voice echoed again.

To the casual observer the man trapped in the doorway may have looked like your average middle management corporate lapdog in a worn brown suit, afraid of missing the morning conference call. Upon closer examination, however, one could pick up unmistakable clues that this was a man standing on the edge of the shelf. His white shirt was dirty and covered with stains. The brown suit he wore was threadbare and had rips in the pockets and seams. Even further though, his angry, creased red face and unkempt thinning gray hair belied a hardship that ran much deeper than his current predicament, sandwiched between two doors on the downtown local. It was almost as if he was making his last stand.

"I can wait here all day, people," the voice from the speakers announced smugly. There were audible groans all around as the realization that she was probably correct spread through the subway passengers.

"Take the next train," pleaded a tall, slender black man, notable for his traditional African garb and multi-colored hat, although his accent was all New Jersey.

"It's self-absorption," announced a professionally dressed young woman, probably an administrative assistant, in running shoes and glasses, her heels no doubt tucked away in the large bag she gripped tightly to her chest.

The doors shuddered again as the gray-haired man only kept pushing forward, swinging his brown paper shopping bag for momentum and ignoring the new round of protests that erupted around him.

"Oh for goodness sakes—"

"Do you understand what you're doing?"

"Get out the damn door needledick!"

The din continued to rise as the man kept trying to force his way inside until the light blue of a police uniform could be seen behind him through the glass. The giant hand of the transit cop outside yanked him unceremoniously back through the doorway and out onto the subway platform. His brown paper shopping bag ripped open and lay in a shredded heap on the floor of the subway car inside as the doors finally closed completely, dozens of old and torn paperback books spilled out. Perhaps he had been planning to sell them.

The subway car lurched forward, and nobody said a word as it rattled ahead. The administrative assistant who had diagnosed him as suffering from self-absorption apparently recognized one of the titles of the worn paperbacks lying on the floor and stuck it in her bag, then looked straight ahead as if nothing had happened.

Meanwhile, I thought about the man I had just seen and wondered if an afternoon in central booking or a night in jail would be enough to push him off the shelf completely. Perhaps, before long, he would become a regular at St. Christopher's or another passing shadow trapped between life and death in the underground world I now found myself a part of.

"You know, I used to be quite the ladies' man in my day."

T-Bone lowered his copy of *Seventeen* magazine to reveal his expanded face, stretched wide beneath an ill-fitting plastic facemask covering his eyes and nose. His hair was neatly tucked away beneath a plastic shower cap, and his hairy legs and bare feet protruded from under his hospital gown.

"I have whatcha might call a silk tongue."

We were sitting in a sterile white room with a half dozen other fellow human specimens for a rather clandestine test of some chemical by-product of a synthetic multi-nutrient fertilizer. The manufacturer was publicly stating it was completely harmless and did not in fact cause blisters or asthmatic symptoms in a disproportionately large percentage of its employees, and that the class action lawsuit being filed against it was frivolous and without merit.

"Stop." I pretended to be engrossed in my copy of *Good Housekeeping*, something about quick and easy recipes for holiday entertaining.

"That Audrey, she's a good girl you know. Might be just the thing to help you with your depressive personality disorder."

"I don't want to talk about it, T-Bone."

I hated that he had been able to diagnose everything that had happened back at the soup kitchen. I hated that all of my emotions and motives were so readily apparent to the outside world. I hated that my painstaking efforts not to care about life or anything in the topside world had been derailed by something as embarrassingly ordinary as a simple schoolboy crush.

"At least she's not still with that Manny guy. Sick dude, did time a few years back."

I looked up from the picture of an eggplant encased in green jello in my magazine. T-Bone was obviously pleased to have finally gotten a response. I looked back down in a belated attempt to discourage further conversation, then turned the page, hoping "Thirteen Steps to a Flatter Stomach" would provide some distraction.

"Truth is I kinda burnt myself out during that prophylactics experiment at Camp Lejeune a few years back. Big government thing. For the military. Lasted eight weeks—"

He was interrupted by a loud snort from above us. I startled and looked up to see an opaque gas descending from the grated ceiling in uneven spurts, beneath a frighteningly loud wheezing that sounded like a giant aerosol can from above. It was as if we were being crop-dusted. T-Bone didn't flinch.

"WHY WHERE YOU TESTING CONDOMS FOR THE U.S. MILITARY?" I shouted through the din.

The roar stopped suddenly, as quickly as it had started. T-Bone's voice echoed calmly through the gray-blue fog settling around us.

"I'm actually not at liberty to discuss it."

A day later we were at the New York Medical College in Westchester County, an hour north of New York City, letting third-year medical students, as I had been months before, stick their fingers up our ass.

"You know, you could always invite her on one of these experiments," T-Bone pressed.

There were about a dozen of us, all men in hospital gowns sporting varying degrees of dishevelment, leaning spread-eagled against the sides of portable beds. A group of medical students were gathered behind each of us taking turns, as apparently there were not enough rectums to go around. This was not surprising considering we were only being paid $100 for what amounted to a very gentle version of a prison gang rape.

A male instructor's voice echoed somewhere in the background.

"The pelvic floor, located below the rectum, is made up of many different muscles, including the puborectalis ..."

I grimaced as a finger made its way up my anal cavity. The finger felt female for some reason, but I didn't want to turn around and associate a face with it.

"You know the research director up at Lake Placid is a close personal friend of mine. Very romantic up there. You could do a little weekend getaway and make some money on the side."

T-Bone continued talking breezily on the other side of the hospital bed I was leaning against, his face no more than a foot from my own. In his typical fashion he seemed completely immune to the invasive classroom exercise taking place, chatting amiably as the crowd of students behind him in rubber gloves explored his colon.

"Hey, you know if she has her ovaries?"

I finally hissed at him through gritted teeth.

"T-Bone, can we please not talk about it right nooooowwwww—" I winced as the finger reached a new high water mark in my rectum.

"... up to the sigmoid colon at the top ..." the instructor's voice could be heard in the background.

"You gotta do something."

"I'm not going to do any*thing*—" I grimaced again as the index finger of the doctor-in-training behind me foraged further up my colon.

"Why wouldn't you?"

"Because, T-Bone, I am a filthy, homeless dropout who spends each day degrading himself selling any body part or fluid people will pay for and each night sleeping underground in a pile of trash."

I swung my head around to confront what turned out to be a very slight Indian male, who looked up at me in surprise.

"And if you put your hand any further up my ass it's going to come out of my throat."

I resumed my spread-eagled position. The finger was removed from my anus, and another one, unfortunately thicker, began to test the exterior hesitantly.

T-Bone just stared at me for a moment. I tried to avoid his gaze.

"I know that," he said finally.

His response caught me off guard.

"Really?"

94

"Of course. You look like shit. You stink to high hell. The best you could hope for is that she feels sorry for you. And not like a good kind of mercy-fuck sorry. Just the thought of holding your hand would probably make her puke."

I was speechless.

"She wants someone safe. Prince Charming. Don't worry though ..."

T-Bone broke into a broad smile that for the fleetest of moments made me consider the possibility that there were things in this world that made life worth living, and perhaps he was one of them.

"... I already got a plan worked out."

The next morning I followed T-Bone to JC Penney, where we bought fresh clothing, a pair of chinos and a collared shirt; he wanted to buy me a shiny titanium-like interview suit, but I protested that it didn't fit my cover story of a third-year medical student. He did insist on taking me to one of those old-fashioned barber shops in Manhattan, where, after getting my hair washed and cut, he made me get one of those vintage shaves with a hot towel and straight razor.

"How's it feel, huh?" I could hear T-Bone ask excitedly.

I was reclining back in my chair with a wet washcloth covering my eyes. Mentholated thick and creamy lotion had been applied all over my face and neck. It was cool and hot at the same time, very soothing; I had to admit T-Bone had stumbled upon something.

"I never volunteered for anything in my life." I protested, trying not to move my mouth so the straight razor gently mowing my face wouldn't nick me.

"Not to worry. It's like anything else. All about figuring out what they want to hear," I heard T-Bone explain. "They want to hear that you want to make a difference, save the world. Tell them you have a brother or sister whose life was saved by someone like them, a drug addict or something, that'll lend credibility."

"Isn't there some kind of training or degree I need?" My voice had a nasal tone to it as the barber pushed my nose gently upward, then to the left and right shaving the hard-to-reach corners of my face.

"You'll be scooping tuna salad. It ain't brain surgery. If Special K can do it you can." He was referring to Kendrick, who at least had been a cook in the military. I brought nothing to the table. "And remember, Audrey only works Thursdays, twice a month."

"I told you I couldn't care less about Audrey."

"Fine. Forget about Audrey. Do it for you. When was the last time you fixed yourself up like this? I can't remember the last time you didn't stink. Look at you now."

The barber wiped my face with the washcloth and spun the seat around so that I faced the mirror. I sat up and admired myself, clean-cut and shaved for the first time in months.

"You're a regular movie star."

And then I saw him, through the mirror, standing out on the sidewalk through the plate glass windows behind me. The man with the handlebar mustache, my guardian angel, the one I had seen in my apartment the morning after my suicide attempt. He was wearing an overcoat this time, holding a newspaper but looking up over it at me through the mirror. Our eyes met for only an instant but he was staring at me unmistakably, and I immediately swung around.

He was gone.

"Whatsa matter?" asked T-Bone, confused.

"Did you just see him?"

"See what?"

"That man, he was standing there, staring at me."

"Who?"

"I've seen him before."

"Seen who before? What are you talking about?"

I watched the passers-by for a moment, trying to reconcile the coincidence or understand why this man might be following me until I felt the towel dab my face again. It was T-Bone this time.

"C'mon. Let's get you to St. Christopher's before you mess up your clothes."

I was sitting in the office of Yvette Bishop-Gray, the executive director of the St. Christopher's All Souls Kitchen. As I looked around, I could see she had gone to great pains to make it as soothing an environment as possible, an oasis from the noise and chaos outside her closed door. The light was dim, emanating only from a shaded desk lamp along with several fragrant candles that were strategically placed around the room. Tapestries, interspersed with motivational and life-affirming posters, adorned the ceiling and walls. Running water from a miniature decorative fountain on a shelf trickled peacefully behind me. There were potted plants everywhere, and differently styled comfortable furniture that had obviously been brought in from the outside.

Yvette was a heavy-set woman with a light brown complexion and an attractive face, with a pile of graying braided dreadlocks that protruded in all directions atop her head that added almost a foot to her stature. She wore a giant sweater that looked like a bathrobe and comfortable looking slipper things with toes extruding the ends. She peered up at me from the application I had just filled out and took another sip from a cup of herbal tea, her eyes magnified behind wide-rimmed purple and black glasses.

"So. Why do you want to volunteer?"

I stared at her like a deer in the proverbial headlights. T-Bone had prepped me a dozen times but still the answer seemed to stick in my throat.

"Because ... I want to ..." I stammered. "... help people?"

Yvette burst into laughter.

"I don't know, do you?" she asked.

My face flushed but I managed to smile. I could feel my famously weak stomach begin to flutter.

"Um, yes, I do," I answered, trying to sound resolute.

I didn't understand why I was so nervous for this. I had been on many more difficult and important interviews. College. Medical school. Yet it seemed to me this was far more than volunteering for a soup kitchen. Although I was loathe to admit it, it felt more like an audition for the topside world of eating utensils, personal hygiene, and human interaction.

She looked back down at my application.

"You're still in medical school?"

I nodded. I had to put something on the application, and being a medical student was my last full-time commitment.

"You know you'll just be making sandwiches and cleaning up here. There's probably a lot of other things you could be doing more in line with your experience. Have you heard of the Homeless Outreach Program?"

I nodded again. They were the ones in the Operation HOPE t-shirts who went underground and to far corners of the city to be routinely abused. No, I had no interest in that whatsoever, even to get laid.

"The director is a friend of mine. I'm sure they'd love someone with your skills."

"Actually, the time commitment was more than I, I mean, I just have so much respect for the work that you people do. I know the amount of work that's involved and I ... I don't want to over-commit."

Yvette looked at me with a half-smile.

"You can only work Thursdays, Mr. Mays?"

"Yes." I didn't tell her to just call me Mays, and wondered if it was some weird soup kitchen etiquette to call each other Mr. and Mrs.

"You know what kind of doctor you want to be yet?"

"Well actually my father was a cardiologist," was always how I started my standard answer to that question, which surprised me but in a pleasant way, as it was one I actually had a ready answer for.

"But what do you want to be?" she interrupted before I had the opportunity to complete my canned response.

I hesitated, marveling somewhat at her unusual combination of external warmth and empathy atop a core foundation of no-nonsense, bottom-line directness.

"To be honest I ... I really don't know."

It was true, especially now. More than she could have known. I must have looked pathetic, because she smiled at me sympathetically.

"Well, you still have some time right?"

I nodded. She was making marks and writing things on my application, probably the reason I was being rejected.

"There's no rush. I think you're just like me."

I was flattered but clueless as to how we might be alike, or how she could possibly know anything meaningful about me based on the lies I had been telling.

"Five years ago I was a business operations specialist for the IRS. Some of us ..."

She smiled again, then grabbed a couple of pamphlets from her desk and handed them to me.

"... just take a little longer to find our place."

And I was in. While landing a non-paying volunteer opportunity at a soup kitchen may not seem like much of an accomplishment, I felt exuberant. Not because I had climbed back up on the shelf of civilization I had fallen off of months ago. I hadn't. I was still living hand-to-mouth underground. It did seem for the first time that I was no longer in a free fall; perhaps I had at least found a bottom. I had just passed myself off as a normal, above-ground human being. A few weeks ago, I would have thought such a feat impossible, even if just a year ago I wouldn't have considered it a feat at all.

Chapter 11. SAINT CHRISTOPHER'S ALL SOULS KITCHEN

I was a nervous wreck before my first day at the soup kitchen, leaving the Bat Cave early to arrive at St. Christopher's over an hour before it was open to the public, and fifteen minutes before I was supposed to be there for my lunch and dinner shifts. I had a one-hour break in between, which was typically spent by the volunteer staff having their own meal and hanging out in the kitchen. This socializing time was the most frightening to me, in the same way I would worry about having someone to sit next to in the lunchroom on my first day of school. I walked to the front of the line that already stretched around the corner and tried to open the giant wooden doors with the official air of a staff member who was authorized to enter the building early. The doors were, of course, locked. I knocked on the door, realizing how pathetically faint it must sound from the inside of the cavernous old structure. Behind me, an old Puerto Rican woman with a scarf over her head was holding the hand of a girl, no more than ten or eleven, who looked to be her granddaughter. They both stared at me blandly with varying degrees of bored curiosity and amusement.

I pounded on the door, cursing silently as I cut the skin on my knuckles and put them to my lips as blood appeared. I waited another ten minutes, knocking occasionally and trying to avoid the glances of the onlookers, when a teenager I recognized from the kitchen staff arrived. He was a skinny black kid in his mid-teens with a leather coat worn over a hooded red sweatshirt that almost covered immense headphones. His eyes and expression were masked in opaque wraparound sunglasses that he wore even inside, which gave him the appearance of a kind of cyborg. The rhythmic movement of his head back and forth to the almost entirely inaudible beat from his headphones added to the effect. I wasn't about to attempt to make contact but instead followed him as he walked past the front door and around the block to an inconspicuous walk-down stairwell and into a building I never would have imagined was even connected to, much less a part of, St. Christopher's. We came up into a coatroom, where I recognized the soup kitchen's industrial school cafeteria smell. Other volunteers were removing their coats. Having gone with a layered look of multiple shirts beneath a heavy sweatshirt, I walked past the coat hooks and benches in a business-like manner and through a swinging door. In the hallway I could hear a voice I recognized as belonging to Yvette, the director who had interviewed me, for some reason above the crash of ocean waves.

"It's all about communication. And commitment. About honoring the commitments you make to others." I followed her voice toward the door to her office, which was cracked open, and peeked inside. Yvette was sitting behind her desk talking to none other than Kendrick. He was slouched in his chair across from her, with a sullen, angry look on his face. The sound of ocean waves was emanating from a small speaker on her desk, making it sound as if she and Kendrick were talking on a beach at high tide.

"If you need to miss a shift you have to communicate that—"

They both looked up at me, then to my right hand for some reason. In my excitement I hadn't noticed the damage to my knuckles was worse than I had thought. A trail of blood marked my path down the hallway, and was dripping onto the floor outside her office.

"Sorry, maybe if you have some iodine or isopropyl ..."

Yvette grabbed a few tissues from a box on her desk, then got up and walked over to me.

"Welcome, Mr. Mays. Why don't you wash up and help Kwami at the dessert station?"

I thought she was going to hand me the tissues but she instead bent down in front of me and smeared the floor where a small pool of my blood had gathered.

I backed away and nodded as if I knew the location of the dessert station or who Kwami was, while from behind me I heard Yvette apologize to Kendrick beneath the sound of crashing waves.

"Excuse me while I try to get all this blood off the floor ..."

Continuing down the hallway toward the distinctive, stale smell of old milk I made my way into the kitchen area. I had seen the kitchen before from the other side of the long counter that separated us from the masses, but will admit to a twinge of self-importance at seeing the "back-of-house" side of things for the first time, like being able to sit at the cool kids' table. I took a short walk around to get my bearings.

The "hot stations" were in the far rear, comprised of some industrial ovens with grease-blackened burners next to a grill that looked like it dated back to the industrial revolution. Two large women who I guessed were of Irish descent, one blond and one brunette, were loading metal lasagna pans the size of tombstones into an oven. Behind me, past a couple of big white lift-up top freezers, were stacks of dishes and a steel sink, beyond which was another smaller sink clearly meant for washing hands in; taped above it were all kinds of health advisories along with dispensers for plastic hats and gloves.

I almost ran to this scrub-in station, which was like seeing a familiar friend at a party where you don't know anyone. I turned both handles and took my time to adjust the temperature, luxuriating in the water. It sent waves of stress-relieving warmth throughout my extremities as I did my typical surgical scrub, all the way down the elbows, starting with the fingertips. Make sure to get soap under the fingernails, then each individual finger, careful to spend extra time between thumb and forefinger on the left hand, then right, to make sure there aren't any little grimy deposits. Then each wrist. Then forearms, the fronts first, rinse, then the backs, rinse, then the left-right sides of each arm. Then the elbows and crooks in my arm, flexing to make sure I got everything. I did have to pick away a few pieces of torn flesh by the second knuckle on the ring finger of my right hand, or, as we in the medical profession refer to it, the middle or second phalange above the proximal interphalangeal joint of the second finger. I wasn't aware that I was taking a particularly long time or that anything was out of the ordinary until I heard chuckling behind me.

"Baby, lunch is going to be over before you finish."

I turned around to see a middle-aged Puerto Rican woman with light brown skin and a pretty face. She was giggling uncontrollably and standing next to one of the big Irish women, the blond. Unlike her friend she was not laughing, although you could tell it required all her effort.

"Stop, Rosa," the big Irish one hit the other one on the arm.

"It's all right, take your time," Rosa apologized through laughter.

I started to introduce myself but ended up just stammering something unintelligible as I dried my hands on a roll of paper towels and grabbed a pair of sanitary gloves and a hat from the cardboard dispenser. I did my best to flash a pleasant smile as I begged off to find safety in another part of the kitchen.

I put on my sanitary gloves, which were not the tight, surgical kind but more like fingered baggies with a loose elastic around the wrist. I didn't see any of the other volunteers wearing anything on their heads, so I decided to forego the plastic bouffant cap, which, in addition to making me look like a sperm, would waste the extensive preparation I had spent on my hair.

I spotted the most likely candidate for the dessert station. The young man I had followed, who I assumed to be Kwami, was scooping chocolate pudding from a long tray into small bowls. When he had accumulated a dozen or more bowls of pudding, he would give each one a quick spritz of whipped cream and place them on a tray in a tall wheeled cart. I stood there a moment, watching in silence, hoping he would notice my presence and welcome me into the brotherhood of volunteers. There was no response except for the nodding of his head in rhythm to the faint tinny sound emanating from his headphones. It became clear that I was going to have to take proactive action. I shot out my hand sudden enough that I was sure to get his attention.

He paused, looking at my outstretched hand. Slowly he pulled down his hood.

"I'm Mays." I smiled winningly, even though he clearly couldn't hear me beneath the mammoth speakers strapped to his ears. Finally he reached up and pulled them down to his neck.

"I'm Mays," I repeated. "You must be Kwami?"

It wasn't much of a conversation starter but I didn't have a lot to work with. He stared at my hand for another moment, then took it, looking at me solemnly through his impenetrable wraparound sunglasses.

"It's impervious," he said sternly.

I was confused.

"I'm sorry?"

"It's impervious."

"What's impervious?"

"I am impervious."

"Impervious to what?"

"No. My name. I-M-P-E-R-V-I-U-Z. Imperviuz."

Was his name really Imperviuz? Was I in the right place? This looked like the dessert station. Kwami, or Imperviuz, was putting on his headphones again. I was losing my opportunity.

"You know, I can do the whipped—"

His hood was up and he was scooping again, although this time I took the liberty of squirting the whipped cream on each bowl. He didn't seem to mind, and I was thrilled to finally have a job, making sure each dessert had a perfectly formed a curly-Q plume of white deliciousness on top. I was so immersed in my work that I didn't notice when Kwami, or Impervious, or whatever his name was stopped suddenly.

"AM I GOING TOO FAST?" I shouted at him, but could see he wasn't looking at me but over my shoulder. I spun around.

Kendrick was standing there. He was wearing his poofy plastic food service hat, which added half a foot to his height and made him even look even more intimidating. In fact, as I looked around the kitchen, everyone was wearing their plastic food service cap now. Feeling a little bit like the last gazelle to have heard the onrushing cheetah, I spun around to look at Kwami, who was not only wearing his plastic cap but had somehow managed to place it under his headphones and hood in the nanoseconds I was turned around.

"Oh, hey, Kendrick," I said like we were bosom buddies and immediately put on my cap. It was strange seeing Kendrick in this completely different environment, where he obviously held some kind of unspoken power over the rest of the kitchen staff, who treated him with a hushed deference. It didn't seem to be because of any title or official position he held there, but either his previous formal culinary experience as a cook, or volatile disposition and size, or perhaps a combination of both.

"I was just, putting the, on the, the chocolate pudding—"

"It's French."

"I'm sorry?"

"French eggless double chocolate mocha mousse. Topped with real cream. 'Sup Kwami."

Kwami, as I supposed he actually was called, was somehow able to hear him despite the headphones, and nodded back to Kendrick, who picked up one of the completed desserts and held it in front of me.

"French. Eggless. Double. Chocolate. Mocha. Mousse."

He looked at me expectantly, like he was waiting for me to repeat it.

"French eggless double chocolate mocha ... mousse?" I replied hesitantly.

"Topped with real cream."

"Topped with real cream," I added with slightly more confidence.

He nodded approvingly and put the dish back down. It was the most positive feedback I had received all day. I couldn't tell if he was training me or if this was part of some initiation, but Kendrick then took me to each of the different stations in the kitchen. He said nothing more than the name of each particular dish, which was always far more grandiose than it appeared to warrant. There was some kind of jello-fruit thing that he described as "winter fruit salad with yogurt-honey pine nut dressing." The lasagna was "spinach and pesto baked zucchini lasagna." Even the frozen dinner rolls were "low carb whole grain." I tried to sound appreciative as he showcased his role as the de facto executive chef, while at the same time doing my best to commit each name to memory in case I was expected to answer questions about each course, like a captain at some fancy midtown restaurant.

It was with some relief that I was returned to the familiar confines of the dessert station. I helped Kwami load the rest of the bowls of French eggless double chocolate mocha mousse topped with real cream onto the dolly and we carted it over to the servers on the front lines by the counter. At 11:30am the doors opened. I have to admit there was an excitement leading up to the moment when Yvette finally yelled for the doors to be unlocked. Mr. Chin, an elderly Asian man with an unpleasant disposition, was the building person with all the keys, and normally he would be the one to do it while Mrs. Daugherty (as I heard Yvette call the big brunette Irish woman) would assist with crowd control. She also tracked how many people came through the door with a little mechanical counter, which would then be reconciled with the number of dishes or "plates" served. A good sized kitchen like St. Christopher's could do up to 300 plates for any given meal. Then the customers would file in, making their way around the perimeter to the counter where the servers would greet them. There was plenty of conversation about the latest ailments, weather, and what was for lunch today and how it compared to lunch or dinner yesterday or last week.

Guests were allowed to come back for seconds after 12:30pm, when everyone had been served. By the time the cafeteria was full, I was already starting clean-up. Kwami was kind enough to mentor me through the "station break-down checklist," or, to be more exact, he would point to each item and watch as I completed it, his head still moving in tiny rhythmic motions to the beat of his headphones. Each station had its own set-up and break-down checklist, along with other notices like reminders to wash hands after using the toilet and nutrition-based cartoons. Once each station completed clean-up, the volunteer staff would gather by two long metallic picnic tables. I could feel my pulse quicken when Kwami pointed to the last step in the dessert station break-down list and walked off. I rolled up the thick rubber doily-patterned mats and placed them under the table as the other stations had done, soaking myself with rancid water in the process.

My clean-up duties fulfilled, I pulled off my cap and gloves and casually tossed them in a large trashcan over behind the caged pantry area. I peered through the shelves over to where the volunteer staff was congregating, having a good vantage point to observe everything without being seen.

Audrey was sitting at the table.

I hadn't even been sure it was one of the Thursdays she worked. She was seated next to Rosa. Probably not a good sign. She had brought her own salad in a clear plastic box and was opening it while Rosa cursed at a leafy sandwich wrap that fell apart as she ate it.

"What are you waiting for?"

I jumped, then spun to see T-Bone, grinning in excitement, his lazy eye fluttering like a moth.

"What are you doing here?"

"I'm your wingman, remember?

"Please go. This looks weird."

"Weird? You're the one hiding behind the pantry cage."

His unassailable logic only frustrated me.

"I got my rap down. I'll tell her this story about how you saved my life and what a big hero you are."

"T-Bone, please, please no ..."

"Or better yet, saved an animal. A hurt animal. Women eat that up. Like you saw a dog with three legs by the side of the road and had to stop."

"I'm not listening."

"Or started a shelter for blind cats or retarded pets or something—"

"You're not even supposed to be over here."

"Who else are you going to sit with during lunch?"

I just looked at him, struggling for a response. Nothing came to mind, so I rolled my eyes like it was a stupid question in the first place.

"I'm fine. Just go." I turned him around and nudged him back in the direction of the general population.

"Really. Go."

He reluctantly shuffled his way toward the demilitarized zone demarcated by the serving counter. Realizing whatever cover I had was blown, I made my way to the end of one of the two adjacent picnic tables where there were leftovers along with assorted lunchmeats and other items laid out for the staff. I took a couple of plastic utensils, the fruit jello salad thing, and a French eggless double chocolate mocha mousse. Much to my relief, I spotted Kwami sitting midway down the bench, almost between the two tables, with a space to his left. It was time to cash in those valuable relationship-building chips I had earned serving as his dutiful apprentice.

"WHAT'S UP, IMPERVIUZ?" I asked in a voice loud enough to penetrate the deepest nuclear-proof underground bunker as I took a seat next to him.

Kwami didn't even look at me, although the surrounding conversation immediately died down.

Bastard. After I did everything except kiss the hem of his soiled sweatpants, even called him by his ridiculous stage name. No matter. I occupied myself with my jello salad. The conversation around me picked up again. Audrey was sitting only two seats away from me on the other side of the table, still talking with Rosa as she stabbed pieces of her salad with a plastic fork.

One of the dishwashing staff further to my right, an older man who looked like he could be one of the guests at St. Christopher's, was carefully unwrapping saltines and sticking them between the layers of his lasagna. One of the first things you learn about working in a soup kitchen is that nothing is wasted, including condiments. Anything consumable got consumed.

With conversation out of the question I decided I needed some caffeine to power myself forward, so I excused myself to no one in particular and went to pour myself a cup of coffee. Leaving it black like the macho graduate school student I was pretending to be,

I returned to my seat only to find my chocolate mousse had disappeared.

Audrey was eating it.

She caught me looking at her as I sat back down again.

"Oh *fuck* did I just take your chocolate pudding?"

"It's French eggless double chocolate mocha mousse with real cream topping!" I blurted out enthusiastically. I was so starved to make conversation my mouth didn't wait for my brain.

Audrey and Rosa burst out laughing. I looked down the table to where Kendrick was devouring a giant plate of pasta for support, but he didn't bat an eye.

"I'm so sorry sir, was that your French double chocolate chip cookie mousse?" Audrey gushed sarcastically.

"Er ... you can have it."

"No, that's okay. I didn't know it was yours."

"Audrey, he don't want it *now*," Rosa explained to more laughter as Audrey slid the half eaten dessert to the center of the table. My chivalrous gesture rebutted, I just stammered awkwardly for something to say until a voice above me made almost jump out of my seat.

"Did you know that Mays saved my life?"

It was T-Bone. He was standing directly behind me.

"You meet Mays here? Very close personal friend of mine. Saved my life."

At this point I was hoping the cafeteria floor would open up and consume me.

"For real?" Audrey gasped in more mock incredulity. "Like pulled you out of a burning car or some shit like that?"

"No. He changed my mind." T-Bone replied, not an ounce of levity in his voice. "I mean, he *changed* my *mind*."

His tone of voice was different, more serious somehow, with a gravitas that seemed to overshadow the satellite conversations taking place around us. The kitchen got noticeably quieter.

"I couldn't move for two weeks," he went on, then reached over to my, or Audrey's, half eaten bowl of what might easily be mistaken for chocolate pudding. "I was testing one of those big traction machines. Spinal decompression. Got paid almost a grand. And I shoulda known better because it was right after Thanksgiving, which is like this fucked up anniversary for me. And I'm sad because I'm thinking back to the accident, back when I had a wife and a little girl. Driving back from the holiday dinner at her Aunt Charlotte's in Poughkeepsie."

Some of the front-of-house volunteers who had been cleaning the serving counter were looking over and listening now as well.

"Two weeks and there wasn't even hardly anyone there to talk to. All I could do was think. Just lie there and think. And my brain goes into this, this circle where I'd get one sad thought, then another. And no matter what I do, I can't get out of this circle. Like I'm going around and around, only it's getting worse."

He took a random spoon laying on the table and began to take slow, small bites of the dessert.

"So I collect my pay, get royally fucked up and fall asleep somewhere I don't remember. I think they found me half-frozen in Washington Square Park. Lost some toes. Wake up in the emergency room and I see this mug," T-Bone continued reflectively, motioning toward me. "Some kind of almost-a-doctor. And I don't give a shit, I tell him everything. Everything I've lost. My family. How I live. Now. Every fucking day. And I ask him a question: why would someone like me want to live?"

Even Kwami had his headphones removed.

"And he listens to everything, and I'm thinking he's going to tell me I need to get clean, get a job, turn my life around, some motivational bullshit, but he doesn't do any of that. It was the most beautiful thing. He said just the opposite."

T-Bone let a measured spoonful dissolve in his mouth, and then continued.

"Cry. Puke your guts out. Get high. Shit it out, whatever it takes. Fuck. Get hurt. Despair. Fight back. Let go."

There were dozens of us now, watching him thoughtfully take minute bites of his dessert.

"Just live. Every. Day. Every fucking moment. That's what it's about. That's what everything is about."

He shrugged, scraping the remaining streaks of French eggless double chocolate mocha mousse from his bowl.

"That's how Mays changed my mind." He nodded to himself as he polished off the last spoonful. "That's how he saved my life."

T-Bone placed his spoon down next to the bowl on the table. You could have heard a pin drop. I guess he really did have a silken tongue. Maybe he had been quite the ladies' man in his day after all.

"Audrey! Manny's here!"

A voice from somewhere on the other side of the serving counter broke the silence. Audrey was like the rest of us, watching T-Bone, not knowing what to make of this weird moment.

"AUDREY!"

She rose, still staring at T-Bone, then glanced at me and backed away toward the crowds behind the serving counter. A general murmuring resumed as T-Bone leaned over and whispered in my ear.

"You think I shoulda gone with the mangled puppy thing instead?"

Chapter 12. PRINCESS

I had trouble sleeping that night for reasons that had nothing to do with the chilly late March weather. A strange thing was happening, an almost imperceptible change I wouldn't fully understand or formally diagnose until much later.

My fantasies had started to return.

One might have thought an active fantasy life was a necessary escape mechanism from the daily hardships of an underground existence. I found the opposite to be true. Fantasy was a luxury I didn't dare indulge in. Fantasies meant a future, even if a hopelessly optimistic or unrealistic vision of one. Fantasies meant hope. Now I found that all of my childish, obscene, wish-fulfillment, ego-centric fantasies began to creep back into my consciousness, despite my best efforts to shoo them away. Audrey and I holding hands. Audrey bent over in a French maid's outfit. Audrey understanding everything. Me saving the soup kitchen. The return of my fantasies represented the first blips of life on my heretofore flatlined psychic and spiritual electrocardiogram.

Other tell-tale signs that I was no longer one of the living dead began to appear as well. Bathing, for example. The nearest running water to the Bat Cave was a treacherous hike to a decrepit work restroom further along the abandoned track. As in the wilderness, any public water source was a life-giving commodity and had some amount of risk associated with it, and the expedition I made the day before my next shift at St. Christopher's was my first trip without T-Bone. I followed the route I had travelled with him at least a dozen times before. About fifty feet away from my destination I slowed down, where the tunnel ended at a T junction. Straight ahead of me, on the far wall, should be where the closed door with the broken lock lay inset in the dirty cement. I slowed to a stop and listened in the darkness. Was that the sound of trickling water? I took a few more steps forward, clutching a dirty folded towel containing a disposable razor and a toothbrush. An empty plastic milk jug dangled from my other hand, to fill with drinking water and bring back to the Bat Cave. I felt like a deer creeping closer to the waterhole, in a kind of sensory overdrive looking for any sign of the alligator lying in wait just below the waterline.

There was a *CRACK* ahead of me that echoed through the tunnels like a gunshot, the sound of the door swinging open and slamming against the wall behind it. A flashlight beam appeared ahead of me, and a dark figure in the doorway let out a low-pitched bellow that echoed throughout the tunnels.

"Princess!"

I lunged to the side of the tunnel in the darkness, in doing so knocking some metal objects that then sent a rattle echoing up the track. There was silence, and then footsteps in my direction. The beam from the flashlight swirled on the walls around me as I stayed crouched along the side of the tunnel. As the footsteps got closer a heavy breathing, almost panting, became audible. The figure passed me no more than five feet away, and I heard a familiar voice.

"... 'til I find that bitch ... niggers are going to be held *accountable* for their actions ..."

It was Kendrick, who continued past muttering to himself semi-coherently and issuing occasional angry outbursts.

"It's his dog. Princess. Disappeared a few years back."

T-Bone was looking through a rack of pornographic magazines, tastefully concealed inside a closet within the otherwise impeccably decorated lobby of a fertility clinic in northern New Jersey.

"After that he stopped going to the VA clinic. Which was supposed to be the whole reason he moved up here in the first place. Where he used to live, there were only two in the whole state. Somewhere down south."

I already knew which magazine he was going to pick. Anything with a black woman on the cover. Sure enough he reached for a magazine with a naked African American woman lying on a zebra skin and making a wild expression, with a tabloid-style sensationalist headline that read "Jungle Fever!"

"You never know with him. Sometimes he talks, sometimes he doesn't talk. Sometimes you can go near him, sometimes you gotta stay away."

I quickly perused the selection, although at this point pretty much just the sight of a plastic screw top receptacle specimen cup was enough to set me off.

"I tried getting him a new dog, but he still thinks she's coming back. That's what he does when he disappears, goes looking for her."

I grabbed one of the newer periodicals depicting two well-endowed soccer moms pleasuring each other and flipped through it.

"I knew you were going to pick that one." T-Bone chuckled as I swung the closet shut and we made our way toward the collection rooms, armed with our pornography and spoo cups.

"He missed his shift again yesterday," I mused. "Yvette was pissed."

"It was better when he was on his meds. He even had a job at a French restaurant on the East Side. Won a prize during restaurant week. Still has the certificate."

Really?" I asked, my interest piqued.

"One of his recipes. Says it's his specialty. His signature dish."

"What is it?"

"Don't remember exactly. Something French. Something—"

We both entered adjacent collection rooms and slammed the doors shut, only to emerge moments later.

"—duck I think. Duck Lorraine. Duck Stroganoff. Something like that."

"You want to make duck à l'orange for 300 people?"

Yvette peered up skeptically through her wide-rimmed glasses at Kendrick, T-Bone and me from behind the desk in her office.

"That's correct," I responded.

"And how many ducks would we need to do this?"

"Sixty."

I was unclear why she looked so pained. I would have thought we were doing her a favor.

"I only have a budget of about $500 per meal—"

"T-Bone and I are prepared to make up the difference out of our own funds. We've reviewed the budget with Kendrick and he's confirmed we have more than enough to cover it."

T-Bone and I had close to $300 between us and figured we could pick up another hundred in the next week, which Kendrick assured us would be enough if we bought the ducks wholesale down in Chinatown. Kendrick nodded his head vigorously.

"Nothing to worry about Yvette," T-Bone chimed in. "I'll be the executive sponsor on this baby. Everything goes through me."

Clearly that didn't inspire confidence in Yvette, who looked at me almost pleadingly.

"Mr. Mays it's not that simple. I have health codes I have to abide by, if anything is served improperly we could get shut down—"

"We aren't trying to circumvent the normal process for getting something put on the menu," I added as reasonably as I could. "Perhaps you could tell us what the typical procedure is?"

"The menu gets submitted by the Food and Beverage Director to the Executive Director a week in advance."

"And who is the Food and Beverage Director?"

Yvette sighed.

"That would be me, Mr. Mays."

"Really?" I raised my eyebrows in surprise. "Well that means we have everyone we need right here in the room!"

Yvette lowered her voice, speaking directly to me.

"Mr. Mays, I understand you have good intentions. It's natural to want to help. It's not always that simple. Do you understand what I'm saying?"

Whatever it was she read in my face it was clear to her that I did not. She rolled her eyes and picked up a black magic marker from her desk and leaned over to the wall where a dry-erase calendar listed the meals for the next month.

"You mess this up, people go hungry. You understand me?"

I nodded solemnly. She shook her head and marked the calendar, a week from the following Friday.

"And I want to see the ducks first."

Chapter 13. DUCK LORRAINE

I beheld the rows of hanging ducks with a grim fascination as the sounds and smells from Chinatown bombarded me. The whole thing had the morbid appearance of a kind of duck execution chamber, with fully feathered ducks looking like they might have been swimming in the park only moments earlier now hanging from their necks by plastic twisties tacked to a wooden board.

"No, fellas, no, not these ..." I protested.

A young, largish Chinese man dressed like a longshoreman shouted out loudly in Chinese, presumably counting off, as he pulled the ducks from their gallows and dropped them into the shopping cart we had stolen from the Shop Rite a few blocks uptown.

"These are too ... too duck ..."

Crowds were swirling awkwardly around us, and my arms were full of shopping bags filled with a seemingly random array of ingredients and equipment we had picked up that morning, spending most of our savings before we even got to the ducks. Next to me T-Bone was inspecting each duck as it entered the cart as he negotiated the price with an older, smaller Chinese man, clearly the brains of the operation.

"What, these ducks die of starvation?"

I was trying to get the attention of Kendrick, who was being harassed by the purveyor of another duck death camp at an adjacent stand. He was waving a duck in his face, which Kendrick inspected dutifully.

"Three dollar, three dollar, how many you need—"

"Look, why can't we just get the frozen ducks from the supermarket?" I reasoned.

All of them, T-Bone, Kendrick, and our Chinese colleagues immediately stopped and waved their arms in disgust at the idea.

T-Bone insisted that he had negotiated a brutally effective deal with our Asian vendors despite the fact that we didn't have enough money left for the subway or a cab ride back up to the soup kitchen. We were completely cleaned out. Not that the sight of three homeless people with a shopping cart heaped with dead birds was likely to entice many cab drivers to stop anyway. We ended up walking the fifty blocks all the way back to St. Christopher's, New York being perhaps the only city where people will brush past a rolling monument of dead fowl without a second glance. Kendrick and T-Bone seemed to be magically energized and skipped ahead of me, chattering like a couple of schoolgirls. Now and then T-Bone would shout back instructions like "Make sure we use REAL cream" or "Serve left, clear right."

By the time dinner approached the kitchen had degenerated into a kind of cooking school gone horribly awry. All of the food prep stations were overflowing with half-prepared meals, and stacked dishes were overflowing in the wash area. What sounded like an extraordinarily loud blender was running from somewhere, which mingled with the clinking of broken glass being swept up over by the dishwashers. I was covered in grease and duck feathers, having been assigned the unpleasant task of defeathering the ducks. The process involved cutting off the head and wings with shearing scissors, leaving one of the legs as a handle, then "rough" plucking the duck, or manually pulling out fistfuls of greasy, dirty feathers by hand until the bird was bald and hairy with wisps of down. Holding the duck by its lone leg, it was then dipped into a large bucket of hot water and paraffin until it was covered with a waxy coat. After dipping it into a bucket of cold water to harden the wax the whole duck was then peeled like a tangerine, producing a down and feather free bird you would expect to find shrink-wrapped at the supermarket. Kendrick even showed me how to make a long incision and pull out the liver for pate. It had taken me all afternoon to prepare less than half of the ducks.

To make matters worse, Kendrick had disappeared.

I followed the sound of a steady metallic banging to find Rosa, near the pantry, trying to separate oysters with a small canned ham.

"Has anyone seen Kendrick?" I shouted to her.

She shook her head no and I continued looking, pushing past Kwami at the dessert station. He looked like a welder, the reflection from the flame of a crème brulee torch mirrored in his sunglasses as he moved it over the tops of bowls set out on the tray before him with a creepy intensity. Toward the middle of the kitchen I could make out Yvette speaking animatedly to T-Bone. I couldn't hear what she was saying, although one voice, a man's that I couldn't recognize, bellowed above the din.

"Yo, where the saucepan at?"

I made my way toward the main entrée station, a giant wooden table in front of the industrial ovens, which was the epicenter of most of the commotion.

"Where the motherfucking saucepan at!" the voice rang out.

"Watch it!"

I was blindsided by Mrs. Daugherty, who rammed into me at full steam carrying a tray, spilling the contents onto the kitchen floor. I would not have thought her capable of the withering glare she shot me before bending down and placing the tray on the floor to salvage the remains. I stammered through an apology and kneeled down to help her.

She was putting back together what looked to be deviled eggs, except they were smaller and the egg whites were a deep crimson. I held one up to examine.

"What are these?"

"Quail eggs. Tell Kendrick he can do the rest himself. I'm done." She was scooping the yolk filling off the floor.

"Why are they purple?"

"I had to soak them in beet juice, pain in the ass," she explained rolling her eyes, and was on her way again.

As I approached the entrée station I was able to make out the conversation between Yvette and T-Bone.

"Every menu has a concept. That's the thing you don't understand."

"I did not give permission for a concept, T-Bone, that isn't what we discussed." I heard Yvette reply. She was wearing one of those strips across her nose that are supposed to keep your sinuses open and was squeezing an orange ball and taking deep breaths between every statement. I had the sense that every stress management technique in her repertoire was simultaneously firing on all cylinders. Next to me the building manager, Mr. Chin, not usually involved in kitchen duties, was holding down the button on an enormous, antiquated food processor. He was tossing in a random collection of diced vegetables, eggs, mushrooms, and other foodstuffs without any discernable theme.

"Tell Kendrick where the duck liver!" he shouted at me over the blender. However I could not take my eyes off what appeared to be four large flesh colored, hoof-shaped pieces of meat on the cutting board in front of him. One by one he tossed them into the blender.

"Are those pigs' feet?" I asked Mr. Chin.

Before he could answer screams filled the kitchen as flames shot upward from the dessert station. Kwami stepped back from the tray, holding the flaming crème brulee torch in one hand and a bottle of cognac in the other.

"GET AWAY FROM THERE!" Yvette shrieked above the chaos.

I found a wet dishrag and sprinted over. As I approached, I could see bowls covering the tray filled with cherries apparently floating in brandy, some of which were overturned. The flaming liquid covered the tray.

"I GOT IT I GOT IT—" T-Bone screamed, arriving with a fire extinguisher. Kwami let out a curse as foamy spray extinguished the flames and knocked all the bowls off the dessert tray, coating him in the process.

Kendrick was gone, although with the help of Mrs. Daugherty and Rosa we were able to consolidate the ducks we had completed along with most of the ingredients into a kind of orange duck stew. Between that and the other smaller entrees in varying levels of completion there was enough food for everyone who came, even some leftovers. The quality probably wasn't up to Kendrick's standards, but it was edible.

I stayed late to clean up. I was glad to be alone. Needless to say, I felt miserable. I questioned how much of my leap-first exuberance had come from a genuine desire to help Kendrick, or was merely a vain attempt to get attention, particularly from Audrey. The whole thing seemed so misguided I started to question how Yvette could have ever allowed it, although to be fair she had done everything in her power to discourage it. My attempts to unfairly pass the blame only furthered my self-loathing. I did my best to salvage any unused groceries or uneaten food. There were pots of soup and servings that never made it to the counter in all the confusion, including a funny shaped pasta thing I was able to save and a soggy onion bruschetta tart that I was not. Most of the dishes had been cleaned but not racked, so I finished those, and was debating whether I felt guilty enough to complete the dishwasher station break-down when a voice startled me.

"Willie Mays."

It was Audrey. She was standing a good distance away from me, on the other side of the illuminated serving counter, which cast strange shadows across the now dark and cavernous dining hall. I could barely make her out.

"I have a question for you."

I stepped out from the canyons of dishes, holding a plate of some unidentified meat I had scraped off the floor, and stepped forward warily.

"That story that T-Bone told that day. About how you changed him. Was that true?"

She waited for an answer as I walked slowly toward her, my mind racing.

"Of course."

Audrey reached into her purse and pulled out a pack of cigarettes.

"You don't believe it?" I probed gently.

"No. I don't think so."

She pulled out a lighter and lit her cigarette.

If I didn't protest it would look suspicious.

"Why don't you believe it?"

"That's what I always tell T-Bone. I don't think you can change people like that. That's why I like T-Bone, we have good conversations."

Her response surprised me. It was an interesting thing for someone in her position to say, I thought.

"Isn't that exactly what you're trying to do in your job?"

"Me?" She rolled her eyes dismissively. "I'm not even a real psychiatrist or anything. I'm 'sposed to be the independent living facilitator. All's I can do is refer them. Food stamps, the methadone program, the Veteran's Center, the shelter."

I continued walking toward the serving counter where the overhead lights illuminated the puffs of smoke around her face.

"I don't know that I ever really made any difference with anyone here. I don't know that nobody has really."

She took another drag on her cigarette, considering it.

"Sometimes I think we just say that so we feel good."

"Maybe it's not the kind of thing you can see that easily. Maybe it's not the kind of thing that happens overnight. Or two Thursdays a month."

I immediately recognized my mistake of letting on I was following her work schedule, but fortunately it didn't seem to register with Audrey, who only shrugged.

"That's what Yvette says. Except now she doesn't even know if they can pay me after the summer. That's what I come by tonight to talk to her about, but she says after the day she had she's 'not in a mental place to discuss it.' Whatever that means."

As I got closer I could see that she was dressed differently than she normally was at St. Christopher's. She had on heels and a skirt and jewelry under a leather jacket. She smelled different too. She was dressed up, clearly going out.

"You look nice."

She smiled, pleased that I'd noticed. "I'm seeing my OB-GYN."

I wasn't sure how to respond. She must have read the confusion on my face.

"He's taking me to a club."

"He's going to examine you there?"

"No silly. We going dancing."

"Your gynecologist asked you out on a date?"

"It's weird, right?"

I was certainly not in a position to be judgmental, so I didn't tell her that it was so weird that I didn't even know how to put into context how weird it was. Although, as we learned in medical school, a surprisingly large percentage of doctors do choose their profession because they are, in effect, peeping toms. I decided the Socratic Method was the best approach.

"What do you think?"

She gave it some thought as she took a puff of her cigarette.

"I don't know. I was flattered. I mean, he be checking out pussy *all day long*."

Her natural reaction made me laugh, which made her crack up as well. We were both laughing. I was intoxicated. I couldn't remember the last time I had flirted with anyone, or been flirted with.

"Better to get them when they're young and in medical school. Like me."

Audrey laughed again.

"Oh really?"

"Absolutely. I'm like a ball of clay you can mold."

"Hmmm ... no, I don't think that's a good idea, but thank you, Willie Mays."

I was surprised at the immediate and unambiguous response.

"Nothing personal. Just not my type."

Wow.

Wow.

Well, fuck her.

"What type is that?" I asked. I wasn't trying to be combative, but was genuinely curious. I didn't even know I was a type.

"Just another white boy in love with himself," she shrugged with a smile.

I smiled as well, only because I didn't know what else to do.

"That's who you think I am?"

She laughed again. "*Puhleeeze.* You think you're hot shit. Let me guess. You worry about making a certain amount of money by a certain age. You probably talk about your career all the time. You worry about what kind of car you drive. Right? Am I close?"

I could feel my smile fading.

"Don't get mad Willie Mays."

"I'm not mad."

"Yes you are. Why you mad?"

She was right. I was mad. I was fed up. With everything. Fuck her. Fuck finishing the dishwashing station break-down. Fuck the whole soup kitchen. Fuck the ducks, and Kendrick, and T-Bone, and the Bat Cave.

"Because you don't know me. You don't know anything about me. For all you know I could need your help more than anyone else in this place. Who knows? Maybe I'm that one person you can change."

I could tell my response surprised her.

"Maybe I'm that one person you make a difference with."

I had made my point. I was pleased. I placed the plate with the mystery meat on the counter.

"I saved you some pate."

It seemed like the moment to make my exit, so I turned around and headed back toward the dishwashing station until I heard her voice behind me.

"You like roller coasters?"

I didn't miss a beat.

"Maybe" I replied coolly, turning around again. It was another unexpected question I instinctively responded to with a lie. With my gentle stomach, I hated everything about roller coasters. The waiting in line part. The being flung around at high-speed part. The screaming part.

"I promised Rosa I'd go with her family to Coney Island on Sunday. They always go opening weekend, it's like some big tradition with them. She told me I can bring a friend."

"That works," I managed to get out, feeling suddenly faint. She rummaged through her purse and produced a pen.

"Gimme your hand."

I approached and extended my arm, and she proceeded to scribble her number on the back of my hand.

"You need me to walk you—"

"No, Prince is outside in the car." She backed away.

"Your gynecologist? Is that really his name? Prince?"

"Yes."

"Is he a Doberman or a German Shepherd?"

"Bye, Willie Mays."

I watched her leave. I had a hard time holding it together until I heard the thump of the wooden doors closing. When they did, I felt as if there must have been some cosmic shift in the universe. It was as if the God of Love had suddenly decided to make amends for my thousands of unrequited crushes. I was trying to decide if what had just transpired had actually happened, or was it a product of my warped imagination. But it had to be real. I had her phone number on my fist to prove it. I was trying to control my breathing, and staying on my feet was of concern, although bouncing up and down in place seemed to keep my knees from buckling.

"Mr. Mays, why don't you head on home?"

I turned around, still jumping in place. Yvette was standing at the opening of the hallway to her office.

"We can get this tomorrow. You've had a long night."

I did a kind of gallop out the back exit, and continued loping down 8th Avenue. It had rained at some point during the evening and my feet splashed through shallow puddles on the wet sidewalk. I paused at a red light, leaping straight up and down as if riding an imaginary pogo stick. Out of my peripheral vision I could see a crowd of teenagers laughing and pointing in a packed SUV at the light next to me.

"Go get 'em, Slick!" a voice called out as I continued down the avenue, now at a full sprint.

I didn't care. I just wanted to run. I just felt like running.

Chapter 14. THE RAGE

For optimal yield most fertility clinics require waiting at least 48 hours between ejaculations.

I was trying to give my fifth specimen of the day.

In the thrill of the moment I hadn't realized I had spent all of my own and T-Bone's money to help fund the duck fiasco. I had twenty-four hours in which to come up with enough cash to pay for my date with Audrey. I was sitting in the reclining leather chair in the collection room at ReproChoice Laboratories with my jeans pulled down, furiously flipping through my mental rolodex of erotic images. In my plastic cup was a minute smear of semen that barely covered the bottom. Clearly, I had reached the point of diminishing returns. On the other side of the door I could hear T-Bone's voice negotiating with Sonja, the lab assistant.

"Just a couple more minutes ..."

"I have to close up, T-Bone," Sonja protested.

"Five more minutes. He's under a lot of stress ..."

"He's been in there almost an *hour*."

Pornographic magazines were spread out on the table and floor around me. I silently cursed the fact that the length of my toenails were just short of the magic inch threshold where I could sell them to the cosmetics company. My payout from this morning, minus the transportation expenses, would come to just under a $100, which was pretty much pocket change in New York. It would barely cover two 1-day passes at Coney Island, let alone dinner afterward. I could say that I wasn't hungry. I would probably throw up from the roller coaster anyway. I needed another injection of cash. Delicately clutching the throttle, I began one final push.

There was a low moan, steadily rising in pitch and intensity. I realized in horror that the voice was my own.

"That's it, Mays, milk and honey baby!" I heard T-Bone shout from the other side of the door, over Sonja's shriek.

"I'm leaving, T-Bone—"

"Wait—"

Four hours later I was on the floor of the kitchen at St. Christopher's. The curly wire from the antiquated wall phone which hung above me was stretched to its capacity to the receiver tucked under my head like a pillow. Audrey's voice on the other end of the phone sent a warm rush through my body and temporarily made me forget about the dull ache between my legs.

"I talk a lot sometimes. Rosa warned me not to talk too much to you but I told her guys usually like it, it means they don't got to worry about talking so they can just chill until I start talking about something they wanna talk about. If I talk too much you'll just tell me, and if it's time for you to say something I'll tell you, okay?"

I had figured that she talked a lot, having spent the better part of the last hour listening to her life story. It was amazing to me that anyone could maintain such an outwardly cheerful disposition, even if there was a kind of desperate, forced, hanging-on-by-a-thread undercurrent to it, when she'd had such a grim history. She and her step-brother had been raised by their paternal grandmother until she died, and then after a short stint in a group home spent most of their lives in and out of foster homes. She told me all kinds of horror stories about their unfortunate string of foster parents, many of whom were only interested in the monthly stipend they received from the state and exploited the system by racking up as many foster children as they could as their sole source of income. One pair fed them primarily ketchup and other condiments for days on end; another would tie her up to a radiator with her step-brother whenever they went out. It was enough to drive her now estranged step-brother to madness, who she assumed was either dead or surviving day to day on the streets. It was clearly one of the prime motivators for Audrey's mission to help others, which she continued to pursue despite the obstacles she had been forced to overcome since birth. She passed her high school general equivalency exam and had even completed coursework at City College toward an associates degree, working as a temp as her schedule allowed and taking occasional babysitting gigs through Rosa's family (who also provided occasional financial support) and friends around the neighborhood. For the most she lived off the meager $700 monthly stipend she received for her work at the soup kitchen, and even that was dependent on outside donations and tenuous at best.

"I just believe everything happens for a reason," she told me as explanation of her ferociously positive life outlook. "Like, if all that shit didn't happen I wouldn't be the person I am, I would never have met Rosa, or want to go to school to help people. I mean, it's like this one big salad, don't you think?"

"What's like a salad?"

"Everything. Life. Don't you think? Not one of those stringy ass salads you get at the bodega but the fresh kind with beans and peas and the little corn things and it's like all these flavors they all look all different and they feel different in your mouth but when you put them all together and it's all just so *fucking* good."

I couldn't be certain but it sounded like she was getting choked up on the other end of the line, almost to the point of tears, presumably over an imaginary salad.

"Sorry, I get all emotional when I think how blessed I am, how beautiful everything is, I mean every little thing, it's all like this miracle, don't you think?"

As I heard her blow her nose on the other end of the phone I tried my best to think of something life-affirming to say but, of course, being death's unofficial champion, came up with nothing.

"You don't think every day is like some miracle?" Audrey asked.

Even if our opposite life views weren't a good omen for our long-term prospects, I was heartened by the fact that I had met someone potentially even more damaged than myself.

"You don't think life is like a salad?" she repeated.

My mouth was open but no words were coming out.

"Hello? Time to say something, Willie Mays."

I arrived at Coney Island just after dawn on Saturday. I finally gave up trying to sleep and took what passed for a shower out of the sink at my normal underground watering hole and hopped on the subway before the sun came up. My immediate concern was funds, or the $92.57 I had stuffed in the pocket of my jeans. It was tied to the larger worry that some question about my source of income, living conditions, or history would unravel the web of lies I had been weaving. The more I thought about it, the more remote the possibility of pulling off this charade seemed.

It is a good ninety minutes by subway on the N train from Manhattan to the Stillwell Avenue Station at Coney Island out in the far reaches of Brooklyn. Once the largest amusement park in the United States from its opening in the late 1800s through its peak around World War II, the modern Coney Island is a gritty, working-class seaside boardwalk on a tiny island peninsula near Brighton Beach. A period of decline over the course of the last half century brought on by rising crime and a declining local economy had robbed much of its grandeur, although there were black and white photographs and iconic structures such as the Parachute Drop remaining from the 1939 World's Fair that served as reminders of its storied history.

The mid-April weather was unseasonably warm, sunny and beautiful. So was Audrey. She had a mouth full of rice when I found her that afternoon, and blushed when she saw me. Rosa and their neighbor Eloise were laughing hysterically at her as she sheepishly kissed me on the cheek. There were picnic tables and lawn chairs set up, with a dominoes game going on and a football being thrown around. Audrey introduced me to Rosa's extended family and their friends. They couldn't have been more different than the family I grew up in; they screamed at each other, hugged, laughed out loud, all kinds of outward display of emotion and affection that were completely alien to me. I had trouble remembering most of their names, except Manny. He was huge and covered in tattoos, sporting a goatee and a backward black baseball cap that said FRESH in silver and gold and just smirked when Audrey introduced me. Audrey offered me a beer out of one of the mammoth coolers they had brought, which I gratefully accepted, along with a cigarette.

"You just open me up, find my stomach and staple that shit up. Leave enough room for like one happy meal from McDonalds and that's all."

"It's more complicated than that," I protested. Audrey was trying to talk me into performing gastric bypass surgery on her, kindly steering the topic of conversation onto one that she thought I would be able to contribute.

"They didn't teach you that yet? How about when they slice you open and vacuum out all the fat?"

"You need special training. You have to learn how everything works first."

"What kind of doctor school you go to anyway?" Rosa's neighbor Eloise asked good-naturedly.

"Last one," Audrey squeezed my arm. "I promise. When I die I want to have my brain frozen. They freeze it then bring you back to life when it's the future and they smart enough to know how to wake you up. Manny told me about it."

"Manny wants to have his brain frozen?" Rosa asked incredulously.

"Just his dick."

"You'll just be a brain sitting in a pan somewhere," I countered. "You can't see. You can't listen to music. You can't talk. Just thinking all day. You really want that? You'll go crazy."

"No, they'll put in me some skinny bionic body like this," she responded, holding up her pinky finger to indicate just how svelte her robotic host would look. "You can just switch into a new body whenever you want, like getting new shoes. All's you got to do is wrap up my brain and stick it in the freezer behind the pork chops."

Before I could respond, a herd of children swarmed around us. A girl of about six looked at me pleadingly with big brown eyes.

"*¿Es tiempo de ir en el Ciclón?*"

Rosa's husband Lionel saw my blank response across the table and laughed, then asked me a question that sent shivers down my spine.

"You ready for the Cyclone?"

"I don't think Manny liked me too much," I told Audrey moments later as I forked over cash for two Half Day Classic Rides wristbands, shooing away her attempts to pay for her own. My heart sank as I silently counted the grand total of $32.57 remaining savings with which to win over my soulmate-to-be.

"Manny is a very beautiful person. He still has feelings for me even though we just friends now. See this?"

She pulled a necklace out of her tank-top with the word LOVE made out of twisted wire.

"He made that for me in hobby shop."

"Hobby shop?"

"When he was upstate. At Sing Sing."

"Do they really call it hobby shop in prison?"

My words were drowned out by the roar of the roller coaster whizzing above us as we approached the entrance to the Cyclone. Just the sound tied my stomach in knots, and I silently prayed I would be able to hold it all together for what would be an exceedingly unpleasant three minutes. As we approached Rosa's clan already waiting in line, Audrey whispered into my ear.

"Just be sure we don't sit behind Rosa's nephew Bruno. That little peckerhead always throws up every time we go on the Cyclone. Shit is disgusting."

The Cyclone remains the oldest commercial free-standing wooden roller coaster in use today, and as such has something of a cult following both with the locals and roller coaster connoisseurs worldwide. Unlike its more contemporary high-tech counterparts with elaborate corkscrew loop-de-loops, this was the old-fashioned rickety kind, where I could brace myself against the sides and lower my head while I gripped with white knuckles the filthy worn metal guard rail that pinned me to my seat. I tried to put on a brave front, which lasted until the first drop when I quickly decided I was better off looking like a coward than spraying the contents of my stomach like a blender with the top off. As I clenched my eyes shut I could hear Audrey's blood-curdling screams of excitement from the seat next to me. Rosa's extended family took up the entire train of cars, including her nephew Bruno of the projectile vomiting incident directly in front of us. Overall I was pleased with my performance; both Bruno and I were able to complete the ride without regurgitating. As I dazedly staggered onto the platform however I could tell I probably looked as bad as I felt. Rosa and the others kept asking me if I was okay. Manny just smirked. Audrey, on the other hand, could not stop laughing.

"It's because you have to scream, let it all out. That's the whole point." She was sympathetically patting down my frazzled hair.

"It was safer to keep my mouth closed."

"What you wanna do next? You wanna do something easy? You want to go on the Inferno?" She pointed to a twirl-a-whirl kind of contraption behind a fiery sign with the words Dante's Inferno emblazoned on the side.

My stomach churned at the sight, but I played it off coolly.

"Nah, the ride is never as good as the book."

I saw another ride that was a little more my speed and, throwing caution to the wind, took Audrey by the hand.

"Follow me."

"I bet you hold in your farts too. That shit ain't good for you. You gotta let it out." Audrey was riding side saddle, facing me on the carousel.

"These things are a lot faster than they look," I mused, watching the park spin past from my own horse as I gripped the bar on the front of the saddle.

"Like, sometimes late at night when I can't sleep I'll turn on those shows asking for money with kids from Africa or somewhere," Audrey continued, waving her arms and only occasionally touching the bar her horse rose and fell on. "All bony and starving, and the announcer lady is crying and everybody is crying, and I'll just bawl my ass off for an hour straight, and then afterward, I feel so good, after I let everything out, like taking this huge dump. All light and everything."

"I can't do that. I'm physically incapable of crying."

"For real? Even when you was little?"

I just shrugged, not wanting to pursue this line of conversation.

"How come? Come on, tell me."

So I reluctantly started to tell her about the wintery November day in Lexington. I was eight years old, and school had been cancelled because of the two feet of snow that had accumulated overnight and all that morning. I was rummaging through some boxes in a closet where my mother kept all the scarves and mittens and I found her stash of chocolate and junk food. When I could remember my parents talking to each other (which was only very early in my childhood), my mother's weight was a constant source of friction between them. It was one of the few variables my father was unable to manipulate in his meticulously controlled environment. He came home early to prepare for some social function they were planning to attend that evening and found me in the closet covered with chocolate frosting and a mouth full of Twinkie. He seemed to comprehend immediately what had happened. What followed was one of the worst cases of The Rage I had ever seen, his face turning beet red as he took the box without saying a word and marched upstairs to the bedroom where my mother was getting ready to go out.

"My dad, he was always the exploder," I explained to Audrey as we completed our third consecutive carousel ride. We had moved to the seats in the make-believe carriage where it was easier to talk. "We never knew what was going to set him off. It terrified me. My mother. I didn't ever want to be like that. That's probably why I hold everything in."

"So what he do? Your dad?"

"So then I hear all this crashing and screaming coming from my parents' bedroom. Finally I make my way up the stairs. The door was still open."

The scene in the bedroom is still indelibly etched in memory. My mother was in her underwear and bra, her face covered in chocolate but there was blood around her mouth. She was always so perfectly put together — my father always insisted on it — it was strange to see her so disheveled. Her coifed hair had come undone, and makeup and mascara streaked her face beneath tears as another picture went flying across the room and shattered amidst the splotches of food on the wall. A giant mirror on their bureau had been shattered, and there was a hole in the wall where my father had kicked it in.

In truth I didn't completely comprehend the meaning of what I saw, or the words that were exchanged at the time. It was only years later that I gradually came to understand what I had witnessed. My mother was wildly screaming out anything that might get some reaction from my father, how much she hated him, how she knew who he was fucking, how she sucked our neighbor's cock when he was away. Things no eight-year-old should hear. I remember watching the scene escalate as my father held her wrists, wrestling her down onto the bed until she was face down. Placing his knee on the small in her back, he then attempted to insert an individually wrapped cream-filled golden sponge cake dessert into her anus.

"That was when he finally heard me crying," I explained to Audrey as the carousel slowed to a stop, signaling the end of our fifth ride. She was listening to me with rapt attention, and the ride attendants didn't even bother us anymore.

"I was bawling my eyes out, pleading for him to stop. And he does. For a minute. He leaves my mother and carries me to his wine cellar."

I left out the part about my father taking a belt to me there, only because it was too embarrassing. It had to be the most awkward beating in history. My father was simultaneously struggling to take off his belt while pulling down my pants, all the while I was squirming to get away. He finally gave up and just spanked me with his bare hand, which still hurt so much I lost all bladder control and peed all over myself and him, which only further fueled The Rage. I had scars for days afterward.

"Finally he explains to me, if I'm going to cry, I can't be around people. I shouldn't ever let anyone see me like that. I should excuse myself and go where no one can see me."

The wine cellar was just an unfinished basement of rough-hewn concrete at the bottom of a rickety wooden staircase. A single light bulb that hung from a cord in the center dimly illuminated racks of musty wine bottles. Despite the many eye-witness accounts of rodents my father steadfastly denied it and one never even mentioned the possibility of their existence in his presence. It was a dark, dank, creepy place of unexplained sounds that terrified me and, no doubt sensing this, my father used it for solitary confinement for any punishment.

They never did make it out to their event that evening. My mother spent the night locked in the bedroom and my father was passed out drunk on the couch downstairs. I spent the night in pitch blackness, stinking of my own urine on the top step of the basement. It wasn't until the next morning that I heard my father unlock the door from the other side.

"It seemed like that was the moment I knew that everything was wrong," I explained to Audrey as I slid the plastic ring that dangled from a long piece of string tied to my fishing pole around the neck of the beer bottle that lay on a platform on the other side of the railing before me. "From the very beginning. My mother and father being together. Me even being here. It was all this horrible mistake that never should have happened."

I lifted the bottle slowly by the rim, waiting until it no longer swung from side to the side, careful to keep the line centered until the bottle was almost at a ninety-degree angle with the ground. I supposed I should have tried one of the more macho boardwalk games, like throwing footballs through tires or shooting a target with a toy machine gun, but those didn't play to my strengths: intense concentration and fine motor skills. It was why I was always the best in my class at stitches. From the first year practice board with shoelaces and rubber bands to chicken breasts and then finally surgery patients who weren't conscious to object to being the first human subject to a jittery third-year medical student, I had always been the Suture King.

"The thing is, what I'm saying, today … Rosa's family. You. This just seems like the first thing, in so, so long, that matters. That is good."

A final tug, and the bottle wobbled on the platform, then stopped, sitting proudly upright. I handed my fishing pole to the arcade attendant, who in return gave me some small ridiculous bean-bag animal probably worth less than the $5 it cost to play. It was a luxury I couldn't afford, being down to $13 and change, but after eight rides on the carousel this was the best alternative I could find. I handed the stuffed animal to Audrey.

"I guess I wanted to say thank you."

We walked down the boardwalk to nowhere in particular, and I tried to read her reaction. She was silent for a moment, and I suddenly felt like I had made a fool of myself rambling about my own personal weaknesses.

"You know, you should talk more, Willie Mays," she finally said. "I like it when the guy is just as fucked up as I am. It means I don't got to worry so much about how I act."

She had no idea. I wasn't even scratching the surface. It didn't take much math to figure out that my parents' marriage was a product of my mother's unplanned pregnancy with me. My father was a bachelor into his forties, and I doubted he ever intended to marry, let alone become a father. She was a pharmaceutical sales representative, quite beautiful (almost a job requirement) when she was younger, probably with idyllic visions of life as a doctor's wife. It must have degenerated very quickly thereafter into open warfare, as I have only the vaguest of memories of them even sleeping in the same room. The pervading atmosphere in our house in Lexington was a vitriolic cocktail of hate, resentment, and disgust that each of us coped with differently. My father was prone to binge drinking and tantrums, and would stay away from the house as much as possible, with me going days, sometimes weeks without seeing him. There was my mother's depression, spending most of her day in bed and medicating herself with junk food or pills or whatever was available to her. Then there were my own "adjustment issues" at a string of private schools and any social situation I was faced with.

Throughout it all my father would deny, rationalize, or obfuscate whatever was necessary in the name of maintaining outward appearances at all costs. No need to scare Audrey away on our first date, however. I decided it was best to save a little mystery for later; there was plenty Mays family dysfunction to last us.

"You never have to worry about how you act around me," I told her. It was the truth.

She was about to respond when something caught her eye.

"I know something that might help," Audrey said, and pointed behind me. I turned to see a man in a red and white striped uniform and a cap holding a bunch of helium balloons, each shaped like some cartoon animal I vaguely recognized.

"I need one of those balloons."

Panic of a financial variety shot from my brain to my stomach, as I looked back at her questioningly; she nodded encouragingly and I went up to the man.

"Six dollars," he said matter-of-factly. Every carefully formulated financial model for the afternoon went up in smoke. I was suddenly down to $7 and change, barely enough for the subway fare home. The vendor filled a new balloon from a large helium tank, only slightly larger than the one I had tried to kill myself with. I reluctantly handed over my cash, not wanting to negotiate in front of Audrey. I took the balloon by its ornate ribbon and returned to Audrey, who was sitting on a cement wall separating the boardwalk from the beach, and sat down next to her.

"No, you hold onto it," she said when I tried to give her the balloon. "I learned about this in one of my classes. Check this out."

She took my hand, the one holding the ribbon, and closed my fist.

"Now I want you to stare at it," she said, pulling the balloon down to my eye level. "Stare at it and think ... think of all that stuff ..."

I shifted uncomfortably.

"... the bad stuff, negative shit ... and look at the balloon ..."

I did my best to stare at the balloon as instructed, hoping to get past this exercise as quickly as possible.

"Now let go."

I took my eyes off the balloon and looked back at her.

"The balloon, I mean. Let it go."

"It's a six-dollar balloon."

"Let it go, Mays," Audrey repeated with growing irritation.

"Can't I just imagine I'm letting it go?"

"Give it to me," she finally said impatiently.

"You're going to let go of it."

"I won't."

"I don't believe you."

"MAYS! Give me the damn balloon!"

She grabbed the ribbon from my hand without waiting for an answer.

"Good. Now stare at it. Are you concentrating?"

I leaned over and rested my head in my hands, doing my best to focus on the shiny helium-filled bag before me.

"Yes."

The balloon began to ascend as she let it slip through her fingers.

"I knew you were going to let it go."

"Shhh! Watch it."

I did watch it. The wind had taken a hold of it as it rose past the roofs of the nearby boardwalk arcades and booths, but it was still visible as it made its journey out over the beach and toward the ocean. Audrey's face was right next to mine, and looked so perfect that I didn't even want to touch it, so I just lowered my head until our foreheads touched, then somehow our cheeks were touching, and then we began to kiss.

It may have been the overpriced placebo I had just purchased or the scent of Audrey's perfume that did it, but at that moment it did seem like the clouds had parted, and my troubles were as ephemeral and far away as the floating metallic helium bag, with the future as limitless as the ocean below it.

Chapter 15. ETERNAL HAPPINESS

A mere two hours later I am proud to say I had undone Audrey's button-fly jeans and was fingering her vajajay in complete darkness under the suffocating warmth of a heavy comforter. Neither of us had further interest puttering around at the boardwalk anymore, and we had been holding hands and generally touching each other all the way back to the one-bedroom apartment she shared with two roommates in Bushwick. It was about a half-hour via subway (including the change of trains at Atlantic Avenue) north of Coney Island. She lived only a few blocks away from the Aberdeen Street station on the L line, past the shops and bodegas of Knickerbocker square in a brownstone on a quiet, tree-lined block.

"Rosa's friend Theresa owns the apartment, that's why she gets the bedroom. She says she's been in a lot of TV commercials except I haven't seen any of them. She probably won't even be there, but if she is just tell her you recognize her otherwise she'll keep going on about did you see me in this and did you see me in that and name all these shows you never even heard of," Audrey explained as we rounded the stairwell of the fourth-floor walkup while she fumbled for her keys. "My other roommate, her name is Louisa, she's cool, we have good conversations, she's home all the time talking to her girlfriend on the phone. She's studying to be a philosopher or something."

We were immediately in a dimly-lit small living area separated clumsily with a large curtain that went diagonally across. Lying on a couch in the left corner covered in a blanket was a very large, pock-faced young woman with a unibrow that ran above her glasses. She was talking into her cell phone in the darkness.

"I didn't say I didn't like dinner. I said it was better than nothing."

Audrey gave her a wave, but her roommate, presumably Louisa (since she didn't have the only bedroom and I certainly didn't recognize her from any television commercials) barely responded.

The ten feet around the couch that she sat on was clearly her entire living space, with stacks of neatly folded clothing on the floor, a small bookshelf overfull with impressive-looking hardcover texts and a plastic bust of Plato or some other Greek philosopher with a bicycle cap placed on top.

"Do you agree that nothing is better than eternal happiness?"

Audrey took my hand and pulled me past a tiny bathroom and a bedroom door that presumably belonged to her other roommate, and through the curtain that divided the living area.

"So if dinner was better than nothing, and nothing is better than eternal happiness, does it not follow that dinner was better than eternal happiness?"

Audrey grabbed a remote control sitting on a small television on the floor and clicked it on, mercifully drowning out Louisa's voice with the sounds of an only slightly less abrasive music video. She leaned over to turn on a lamp next to a small futon mattress on the floor — everything in this neatly maintained corner of the world she called home was floor level — and we fell back on her onto her futon simultaneously kissing and tearing off clothing. My pants were unbuttoned and Audrey was groping inside.

"Aaaahhh!"

It was an involuntary reaction to her dry, rough handling of my extremely sensitive divining rod, like someone learning how to drive a stick shift for the first time.

"I'm sorry, it's just sore."

"Sore from what?"

I just gaped at her. Fortunately she found my panic amusing and gave a laugh, then started kissing me again, holding my head.

"Your hair is funny," she murmured.

"Mmmmm?"

"Like there's this tiny little piece that's all curly here," she giggled some more as she wrapped the lock of pubic hair that had been grafted to my head as part of an experiment around her index finger. Needless to say I was on high alert at this point, but Audrey only continued to kiss my neck, making her way down my chest as she slowly unbuttoned my shirt.

I tried to relax, leaning back and closing my eyes, wriggling off the rest of my pants when I suddenly became aware that she had stopped for some reason.

I opened my eyes.

Audrey was staring at my chest. Specifically, she was staring at the perfectly symmetrical squares of color that had been created from my hours laying under an ultraviolet sunlamp testing the effectiveness of a new line of high-end sunblock.

"What the fuck is that?"

I feigned confusion, as if a carefully shaved checkerboard of varying shades of red, tan and pink was the most normal thing in the world to have on your chest.

"What's what?"

"That," she repeated, gently touching my chest in bewilderment. "It looks like a flag or something."

"Oh ... I ... um ... joined a tanning salon ..." I was fumbling for the lamp on the floor next to the futon that was the primary source of light. I found the switch and turned it off, then grabbed the edge of the comforter on the other side of the mattress and pulled it over the both of us for good measure. One of my sneakers was removed and I was working to kick off the other when there was a scream from Audrey.

The comforter flew off and the light clicked back on.

Audrey was holding my foot, beholding the 9/10th of an inch-long toenails curling outward with a kind of morbid fascination.

I struggled for an excuse until she finally dropped my foot and walked quickly out of the room, closing the curtain that separated the living area between her and Louisa.

It was over. I knew it. What had I been thinking? I lived underground. I was a subterranean creature. It wasn't even that she was out of my league; she was a different species. It was a miracle I had gotten even this far.

The curtain slid open again and Audrey walked back in, then closed it behind her. She stepped toward me and thrust out her hand, opening her fist up to reveal a pair of silver nail clippers.

I took the clippers and crossed my legs, my relief quickly transforming into anxiety as I imagined the $100 bill I was ripping in half, at $10 per each nail I cut off. I supposed saving them in my pocket would have aroused suspicion.

"Mays!" Audrey screamed as I bent over to cut the nail off my little toe. "Not in the *bed!*"

To her credit, she ended up actually cutting them for me, a touching sacrifice although despite her screams of mock terror I think she had a gross obsession with them. She even made a little arts and crafts project out of the cuttings days later, a stegosaurus with toenails as plate fins adorning the top of its protective outer armor.

To be perfectly truthful, I would have to say my own sexual experiences up to that point had been pretty limited. Don't get me wrong. I wasn't completely inexperienced. At least if you counted college road trips and late-night frat party encounters in the dark with drunken half-dressed women who generally wouldn't have anything to do with me the next day. Still, it's fair to say that Audrey taught me more than a few tricks. We'd do it, talk, do it some more, and finally when I thought we were taking a breather she started giggling and told me she had something else that might loosen me up. I was expecting some other self-help exercise as Audrey rummaged in her closet, until she pulled out what looked to be a nine-inch dildo attached to a belt.

I was about to politely inquire as to when it had last been used and if it should be sterilized in boiling water or at least washed with anti-bacterial soap when she moved behind me and pulled back my head by my hair. I felt something hard touch the outside of my rectum. The coldness took my breath away, as did her next statement involving her ex-boyfriend who had been paroled after eighteen months in the New York State Penal System population.

"Manny used to *love* this."

Chapter 16. TOPSIDE

The thought of returning to the Bat Cave after I had just spent the most perfect hours of my life on the outer side of the Earth's crust was unbearable to me. I was a changed man, with a new love and outlook on life. If T-Bone had forced me to question long-held conceptions, Audrey completely turned my world upside-down, and I found myself re-evaluating my views on everything from life, death, religion, to the basic laws of physics and anal sex. I didn't want darkness anymore. I wanted light. I wanted to live.

I wanted to be topside again.

I called Audrey every day the next week on a new pay-as-you-go mobile phone I picked up after T-Bone and I completed a focus group for a new brand of adult diapers, and twice took the train all the way out to Bushwick to sleep over at her place. We watched television and drank beers out on her fire escape. Her bovine graduate philosophy student roommate Louisa joined us once wearing form-fitting, mildly obscene pajamas. I hadn't actually met the actress roommate who had the only bedroom, but could hear her doing her vocal warm-ups through the wall on occasion, a series of scales and tongue twisters that added to the eclectic orchestra of neighborhood sounds.

It didn't take long before my lack of acceptable living accommodations became an issue. I always offered to come to her place under the guise of chivalry, taking the long trek out to Brooklyn rather than forcing her to travel the opposite direction to upper Manhattan where I told her I shared an off-campus apartment. However, I was beginning to sense some hesitation on Audrey's part whenever I glossed over the my-place-or-yours discussion.

When T-Bone told me he had another place above ground I could use rent-free, I was of course skeptical. Still, I didn't have a lot of options. I was desperately hoping for a diamond in the rough, a loft in an abandoned warehouse or a one of those industrial-cool urban apartments that look more artsy and hip than dilapidated and unfinished. There were all kinds of commercial or deserted sections of the city that suddenly became hot real estate properties, such as the old Meat-packing District in Manhattan. Maybe there was some chance I was blazing a similar trail. That was the hope anyway, and why I had accompanied him on the subway up to the Bronx and through a deserted graveyard near Van Cortlandt Park. I had even packed up all of my worldly belongings, a few changes of clothing and some blankets that half-filled the garbage bag I had slung over my shoulder.

"You know, I knew this day would come. You got your own life. Met a nice girl. Makes sense to get your own place."

I had been putting up with the wistful, coming-of-age monologue from T-Bone since I had returned that morning from Audrey's apartment.

"This is a real find, spectacular seasonal views of the city. Plenty of privacy. Minutes from downtown. Great schools. Move-in condition."

T-Bone had stopped in the graveyard and was digging in a flowerbed.

"This should hold you 'til summer, then we hit the road to Longwood. Here it is!"

He pulled out a small object from beneath a rock, then wiped the dirt off under his armpit to reveal a metal key. I realized we were actually standing before some kind of structure, a mausoleum hidden beneath a large oak tree and so completely covered in ivy and leaves that I didn't recognize it. T-Bone pulled away a layer of tangled vines on one of the walls to reveal a weather-battered metal reinforced door.

"I figured this would be perfect for you, seeing as you're always talking about death and everything. Fits in nice with your interests."

He probed gently with his hand into the foliage until he found a rusted padlock the size of a fist, which he was able to unlock with the key. The door was stuck when he tried to open it, so he turned the knob and threw all his weight against it. It still moved only a quarter of an inch.

"Now it's a little tight in there, but last time I checked there were two empty. Plenty of room. Long as no one else in the family dies."

Again he threw all of his weight against the door, then again, and then yet again. Each time the door opened only a few degrees, making a hair-raising, nails-on-the-chalkboard sound as it scratched the concrete floor. I suppose I should have helped him, but I was too busy grappling with the most disappointing realization that the five-foot high mausoleum I was looking at was in fact the new living accommodations T-Bone had in mind for me. With a final thrust he was able to open up enough space to squeeze through, and disappeared inside.

"Oh yeah, we're good. You'll be all set in here," his voice echoed. A light appeared inside, and I peeked my head through the low doorway.

T-Bone was standing with a penlight in a tiny entry area about three feet wide by five feet (the width of the mausoleum) amidst broken glass and littered paper. In a concrete wall before him there were four crypts, two of which had been sealed with a marble plaque. The opening to the third on the top right was covered with a metal grate. The fourth, on the bottom right, was empty, a small but long opening in the wall that went back deep enough to fit a coffin inside. The metal grating protecting the outside had been removed, presumably by T-Bone, who pulled out bits of trash stuffed further back inside. By the flicker of his penlight I was able to read enough of the inscription on the sealed crypts to see that the mausoleum belonged to the Palmisano family.

I pulled my head back out and slunk down along the side of the building. T-Bone could obviously sense my displeasure when he emerged a few moments later.

"You know most chop shops up here in the Bronx will let you sleep on the floor for free," he suggested, trying to be helpful. "Like a cheap alarm system."

"That's not the point."

"What about a hotel? I can get you a room for fifty, maybe forty bucks a night."

"I wanted to look normal for Audrey. Topside."

"You need more money, we could move up to bone marrow. It pays better but you're on your side for a week, plus it lowers your immune system ..."

"T-Bone, no landlord is going to want to rent an apartment to a human guinea pig."

"I mean, you want to get more aggressive there's some underground stuff that pays real well. Real groundbreaking. Replacing human parts with animal parts, that kind of stuff. And you can always get a fair price for a kidney, even in a down-market—"

"T-Bone," I interrupted him. He stopped, and our eyes met. I spoke to him in a tone as gentle and contrite as I could muster. I knew full well it wouldn't matter, although I think on some level he knew what was coming.

"I need to get a real job."

T-Bone took the news about as well as I thought he would, which is to say he threw a tantrum of biblical proportions. Considering our next destination it was not inappropriate, although it was disappointing to waste one of the few experiments I was actually interested in getting yelled at by T-Bone.

"So what, you want to go back to med school? Become a whore to the insurance companies? Sell your soul to big pharma, is that it?" T-Bone demanded.

We were at the Fordham Theological Seminary in upper Manhattan, participating in an experiment for volunteers who believed they were Jesus Christ. After a quick screen we were invited to a kind of cocktail party in honor of the son of God.

"I'm not going back to medical school," I told him.

There were about fifty of us, and the sight of varying styles of Jesus (there was an Elvis Jesus, a country-western Jesus, an all leather-clad sado-masochistic Jesus) standing around drinking non-alcoholic punch out of paper cups made it feel like a veritable Jesus convention. As one might imagine it was a fairly contentious affair, with a number of ad-hoc theological debates breaking out. A handful of staff members (identifiable by their nametags) recorded everything on handheld video recorders and walked around the room asking questions of participants. Happily, all the commotion provided a fair amount of cover for T-Bone's continued rant.

"So what're ya going to do? Daddy got you a job? Is that it?"

I bristled, trying to ignore T-Bone and eavesdrop on the argument taking place behind me between a Jesus in a Hawaiian shirt and a more pimped-out Jesus wearing chains, rings, bracelets, and similar bling.

"You're wearing a cross," the Hawaiian-shirted Jesus asked. "Why would Jesus wear a cross?"

I wondered what the underlying experiment was. Challenging monotheistic beliefs? Holding on to long-held perceptions in the face of contradicting data? Or perhaps the limits to which people would degrade themselves for $40?

T-Bone, however, wouldn't leave me alone.

"Come on, I want to hear about your new career. What is it? Just put me in the ballpark. Bus driver? Librarian? Dental hygienist?"

"GET THEE TO A NUNNERY!" the pimped-out Jesus retorted.

"That's Shakespeare," the Hawaiian shirt Jesus replied calmly. "That's not the Bible. That doesn't even make sense."

"Bricklayer? Interior decorator? Air traffic controller?" T-Bone persisted. "Where'd you find this job anyway?"

"I found it on the employment board," I finally answered, hoping it would shut him up. The employment board was a bulletin board outside Audrey's office in the soup kitchen that listed a dozen or so jobs that changed so infrequently they could have been etched in stone, typically places that were so undesirable they were in a constant state of recruitment.

"What? You're going to work at McDonald's?"

For some reason among the unemployed and underemployed, a job working in a particular golden arched fast food chain represented the very bottom in terms of prestige. It was below such things custodial work and street cleaning, and certainly well below illegal trades such as prostitution and drugs, which at least had the possibility of the big score.

"No."

I didn't feel I owed him any further explanation than that, although after a long pause I volunteered:

"Telemarketing."

"Oh no. Nonononono. Please tell me you're not going to work for American Dickhead?"

It was actually called America Direct Marketing, and I was already signed up for their weekly orientation session. They seemed to be in a perpetual hiring mode since the 1970s, if the faded advertisement on the bulletin board at St. Christopher's was any indication. It depicted a melting pot of head-phoned, clean-cut professional looking young men and women all beaming, no doubt because of their lucrative and exciting careers as a telesales professional. The recruitment poster advertised flexible schedules, an air-conditioned work environment, and unlimited earning potential.

"T-Bone, I don't have a lot of options. It's temporary, okay?"

At least I hoped it was only temporary. Longer term I had a better chance of getting a real job, maybe graduate work somewhere or doing research in a laboratory or even finishing medical school, someday, once I had enough money saved up. I had been in enough of a free fall to understand that my long journey back up onto the shelf would be measured in small, hard-fought victories: a resume, a reasonable explanation as to why my studies were interrupted, an interview suit, verifiable references, college transcripts. All realistically weeks or months away. For now, I just needed a reasonable enough living space that Audrey would believe I wasn't homeless.

"Hey, if you see the sales director there, Jerry Manfredi, ask if he found the wristwatch I lost inside his wife when I was fisting her," T-Bone quipped. He reached into his pocket and pulled out a wad of crumpled paper, including currency.

"I'll tell you what. I'll pay you not to work. Here ya go."

He peeled off a $1 bill, then another, and tossed them on the floor at my feet, yelling at me as he continued to throw money in my direction.

"Go ahead. Take it. What, you know how long it'll take to make that kind of money at American Dickhead? That'll be three bullshit recipe card catalogs you have to sell. Here, you'll need to sell a dozen crap jewelry kits to make this. Whoa! There's six subscriptions to *Assault Rifle Monthly*."

"T-Bone, stop."

"Go ahead! Take it."

"I'll take it!"

A kind of science fiction Jesus in white robes with a minimalist crucifix and other intergalactic new-age symbols around his neck grabbed a bill. Another 1980s rock star Jesus grabbed a dollar bill near me, almost knocking me over.

"Hallelujah!" T-Bone shouted, obviously pleased. I wouldn't have thought it possible to cause a commotion big enough to attract attention in the midst of this freak show, but we had somehow found a way of doing exactly that. Wads of papers, some with currency crumpled inside, now rained down on me, making a rainbow arc from T-Bone's perch from atop a chair. I was surrounded by a crowd of Jesuses converging around me and fighting for the bills now littering the floor. I reached out for help to one of the staff members, but he only leaned in with his handheld video camera to get a closer shot.

"It's a miracle! Praise the Lord!" T-Bone shouted.

I just cowered finally, protecting my head and covering my ears in an unsuccessful attempt to block out T-Bone's shouting.

"Damn. You really don't believe in God at all? So you think everything is like, science? Like little cell thingies and germs and asteroids and shit?"

"That's what I used to think. Now I don't know what to think."

I closed my eyes in the darkness and held my cell phone against my head, imagining how beautiful Audrey must look in her apartment on the other end.

"That's what Louisa says too except she's all philosophical and logical about it. She says there can't be no God because if God created everything then who created God."

I let out a groan, which caused Audrey to giggle.

"Where you calling from anyway? It sounds like you're inside a tin can."

I cursed silently from my position inside one of the two remaining open crypts in my new accommodations, and carefully rolled over on my side in the torn sleeping bag that had been left by T-Bone.

"I'm at my place."

"How come you never tell me about your place? How many roommates you got?"

I thought about the sealed crypts and the mummified bodies that were presumably stored inside.

"Two."

"So what, they all trying to be doctors too? You guys sit around and talk about brain surgery and stuff?"

"Yes. No. I don't know. They don't say much."

"So you gonna let me see your place or what?"

Our theological discourse suddenly evaporated, and I found myself stammering to make up facts.

"Sure, there's just not that much to see."

"You're not hiding a girlfriend in there are you?"

"What? No!"

She had said it playfully, but my violent reaction only escalated her suspicion.

"That's what Rosa told me. I'm just saying."

I tried to sound as calm as possible, but my words came out as if I was speaking to her through clenched teeth, which of course I was.

"Audrey, you are welcome to visit my apartment whenever you want."

"How about tomorrow?"

A squadron of stress zits were burrowing their way to the surface of my forehead.

"Tomorrow is fine, would be fine, that's not a problem. Absolutely fine. If you want to. Like I said there's nothing to see—"

"I have to go in tomorrow to talk to Yvette about my work schedule for the summer. That bitch better get me some serious hours. I'm already two months behind in my rent."

I started at American Dickhead the next day, selling crap over the phone.

"I have work. A class. Until five. Why don't I come by St. Christopher's tomorrow after my class then? After five."

My stomach was already in knots and I was beginning to hyperventilate, harbingers of the full-blown panic attack that was brewing.

"That's when my class ends. It's a lab." I quickly corrected, although there was nothing to correct. This was all happening too quickly.

"A lab class. In organic chemistry." Another completely unnecessary clarification.

"We can go to your place after then," Audrey agreed cheerfully.

I struggled mightily to formulate an explanation why I could not show Audrey my living accommodations, only to hear the same words fall out of my mouth and onto the floor.

"That's right. After my class. Tomorrow."

Chapter 17. AMERICAN DICKHEAD

I didn't sleep that night. I couldn't fault my new accommodations, which in many ways were an improvement over the Bat Cave. To begin with, my relationship with T-Bone had deteriorated to the point where we were both relieved not to be sleeping in such close quarters in what was effectively a low-end bunk bed. Because of the isolation, it was also considerably safer, as there seemed to be little chance of anyone stumbling upon me. I had so far not encountered any vermin (there was no food or excrement), and the musty smell was preferable to the gamut of human, animal, and waste created fragrances I was likely to encounter underground. Despite the chilly early spring evenings, I was protected from the elements and fairly warm enclosed in my cocoon of fabric.

The irony was I didn't at present have a housing problem, despite the fact that my current abode lacked what might be considered basic requirements for a residence such as a bathroom, a legal address, a mailbox, or television. My problem was deeper than that. I was so far removed from the topside world that I no longer even possessed any of the trappings of a civilized life. I had only a handful of jeans and clothing along with some old blankets that I was currently using to insulate my crypt. I had no books, photos, appliances, furnishings or mementos of happier times. It was in fact a measure of the wasteland that was my emotional life up to that point, it occurred to me, that I didn't even have a single keepsake; something with no worldly value (like a driver's license or social security card), but a knickknack that brought about a sense of well-being. Even the most hardened street dwellers allowed themselves this luxury, whether it be a plastic doll, an old letter, or even a piece of jewelry with the word LOVE fashioned from twisted wire. For T-Bone it was a weathered photograph he kept in his Filofax. He'd take it out and stare at it at times when he didn't think anyone was looking. I never caught a glimpse of it, and he was so secretive I didn't have the nerve to ask him about it, but only wondered about the subject (a lover? an estranged child?), and what secret to his past it would unlock.

As I pondered my current dilemma, the least attractive course of action was telling Audrey the truth. It wasn't an option. Even if she didn't drop me like a bad habit, to confess the events that led up to this point would be so emasculating I wouldn't even be able to face her. My failure at medical school. My suicide attempt. My months living underground with T-Bone, and the lies I had been feeding her regarding my day-to-day existence. The best I could come up with at the end of my sleepless night working the problem from every conceivable angle, was that I would somehow try to escape from my web of lies by telling an even bigger lie. Hopefully one that would cast me in a flattering light.

I still didn't know what that lie would be as I took the subway downtown the next morning for my first day at America Direct. It would only be a temporary lie, I consoled myself as I wandered through the Chelsea neighborhood trying to find the correct address. Surely in the coming weeks I would be able to save enough money through some combination of legitimate employment and the continued sale of my body to secure new accommodations, and this transitory deception would be forgotten.

I was counting down office buildings on 23rd Street when a familiar voice called out to me.

"Seventh floor."

I turned to the voice instinctively to thank them. There in a tiny alcove in front of a chained fence blocking off the alleyway between buildings, in his oversized winter parka with a fur-lined hood pulled up to conceal his head, was an unmistakable diminutive figure.

"T-Bone?" I choked.

As he looked up at me I could see he was wearing dark sunglasses and had a scarf wrapped around his head, concealing his mouth and much of his face, giving him an almost comical undercover informant-type look.

"You are standing at the edge of a precipice."

I looked around, suddenly cognizant of all of the passers-by flocking through the revolving doors at the front of the building. I pulled him further into the alcove so we were no longer blocking traffic.

"T-Bone, Christ, how long have you been standing here?"

"The people up there," he motioned with his head to indicate the cold-hearted capitalists lying in wait up on the seventh floor, "they do not care about you. They don't care about human beings." His voice was raspy and had an eerie monotone quality to it. In all of the conditions I had seen him in before this was something completely new. Whether real or feigned for my benefit, he certainly had the exterior of someone who had been betrayed in devastating fashion. I softened.

"Look, T-Bone, this is just a way to pick up some extra money. That's all this is."

"They do not care about truth. They do not care about living a virtuous life."

I was getting impatient, and starting to feel self-conscious arguing with this vagrant Eskimo in front of what could be my new employers.

"T-Bone, no offense, but I don't care about that, okay? I want a real bed and running water. That's all I care about."

"That's all you care about?"

"Yes, right now that's all I care about. Look, I'm still going to do the experiments—"

"It doesn't work that way."

He reached into his coat, and at that exact moment I almost expected him to pull out a sawed off shotgun like the proverbial disgruntled postal worker. Instead he thrust a crumpled white business envelope in my hand. I looked at the return address: Longwood Clinical Research Facility and Medical Center in North Carolina.

"You got into the big JCN experiment at Longwood this summer. It was supposed to be a surprise." His voice faltered as became too choked up to speak. I grimaced and thrust the envelope into the pocket of my jeans.

"So what, we're breaking up then?"

"I don't know. Ask Audrey."

"What's that supposed to mean?"

"You still showing her your place tonight?"

I froze.

"What are you talking about? How did you know about that?"

There was an almost imperceptible shrug.

"She know where you live yet? You tell her everything?"

I felt my face flush. It was the first time I had ever felt real anger toward T-Bone.

"Is that what you came down here to do? To blackmail me?"

"No."

"No? Then why the hell are you here?"

"I came to give you some advice."

"You did?"

"For your first day at work."

"Fine. So give your advice."

He leaned forward.

"When things get fucked up. I mean completely fucked up, so fucked up you're starting to realize there are whole new levels of fucked up you didn't even know existed, here's what you do, see, you look them right in the eye, right in the eye like this ..." T-Bone removed his sunglasses. His eyes were beet red and beyond bloodshot, his left eyelid fluttering wildly. "... and you tell them: 'I understand *exactly* what you mean.'"

He put his sunglasses back on, repeating the line.

Before I could respond, or perhaps in the absence of any response, he was gone. I stood there a moment, my stomach in knots and my brain quashed under the burden of anger, guilt, lack of sleep and general confusion. With no beacon to follow other than the overriding truth that I needed money, I made my way into the building and up to the seventh floor to seek my fortune within the corporate sales offices of America Direct.

I was immediately put in a training room with a handful of other telesales representatives of varying ages and ethnicities. I would soon learn that I was in the presence of, in addition to three working mothers and two work-release prisoners from Rikers Island, a budding screenwriter, a voiceover artist, three models, and two rap performers. It was quite an honor to be part of this impressive artistic community. Our trainer was an affable bald middle-aged man with a radio voice and threadbare suit who insisted on being referred to as Mr. Z and liked to crack painfully corny jokes. We worked through a number of role-playing exercises, where we would pretend to call Mr. Z and read to him from our carefully prepared sales script that had been laminated and bound in loose leaf notebooks.

After a half-day training session they cut us loose on the phones. I got chatty with an elderly black woman named Collette sitting next to me who had taped pictures of her grandchildren to her temporary cubicle and clearly took pity on my cluelessness. She provided me with advice (I spoke way too fast on the phone, attempting to dispense with the painfully scripted sales pitch as quickly as possible) and gave me the skinny on the basic operations of the office. At any given time there were a dozen or so products being sold. They tried to keep salespeople of similar skill levels working on the same product since commissions were paid based on how much above the average you sold. Whenever somebody's average sales per shift got too far above the group average they'd move that person up into a higher sales group. Those hearty souls who were able to sell successfully above the average even in the top sales groups, a skill that required confidence, speed, and an utter disregard for any semblance of phone manners, were usually offered jobs as shift managers. Their base pay was barely higher than the minimum wage the telesales representatives were making, although they were officially full-time employees and had the opportunity to buy into the company's health benefits plan. It would also entitle them to collect unemployment if they got fired, a path some actively pursued as it would at least temporarily equal their actual pay and leave them free to pursue other career opportunities or sit outside on the stoop, depending upon their disposition. T-Bone was certainly correct about nobody caring about truth, or living a just life. It was a pretty grim environment, idealism being a luxury neither I nor any of the employees of America Direct could afford.

"Good morning, this is Mays Parker calling on behalf of *Christian Parenting* magazine. May I speak with Mrs. Estacia Hernandez, please?" I spoke into my worn and no doubt germ-infested headset in as bright and cheerful a voice as I could muster. "I'm calling because the publishers of *Christian Parenting* would like to send you some gifts to celebrate God's love, in the form of a nine-inch porcelain table cross. With its appealing, colorful design and inspiring message, this cross perfectly accents home or office décors. It's a wonderful reminder to live life letting your light shine for Jesus. Now, Mrs. Hernandez, keep in mind this is a $19.95 value that we'd like to send at absolutely no cost to you."

Our sales pitch was tailored to the product we were selling; for example, you could expect to recite pages of patriotic shtick selling additional insurance to veterans. I was staring at a flat computer screen that tracked statistics like the number of calls I had made, the number of no answers, the number of rejections, the average length of the call, and other metrics to track my efficiency.

"In addition, we'll send you three risk-free issues of *Christian Parenting* magazine."

It wasn't long before I found myself deviating from the script we were given. I was surprised at how starved I was for conversation, sharing a house with two corpses, and many of the retirees or housewives at home during the day didn't seem mind talking on the phone.

"If you really love this girl you must tell her the truth, my friend." Mr. Vijay Lakshminarayanan, an emergency services worker who drove an ambulance four nights a week in Alpharetta, Georgia admonished me in a Middle Eastern accent. "It is the only way."

"Trust me, I wish I could. I can't, I just can't. There has to be another way."

"Well," he sighed, "I suppose you could tell her that your apartment has been quarantined by the Department of Health."

I bolted upright in my chair. He said it so matter-of-factly, like he used the old Quarantined-By-The-Department-Of-Health excuse all the time.

"No. Really? You think that would work?"

"I certainly wouldn't want to go there."

"Quarantined for what? It would have to be believable."

"Legionnaires?"

"It'd be all over the news," I replied dismissively. "Although smallpox is making a comeback—"

Collette next to me cleared her throat to warn me, but it was too late. I looked up to see none other than Jerry Manfredi, the director of sales, turn into my aisle of cubicles and make his way toward me. The first thing you noticed about Jerry were his disturbingly large and unnaturally white dentures that suggested a great white shark zeroing in on its prey, accentuated by his permanently tanned face and complexion of worn leather. What hair he had left was feathered back, seemingly cemented in place, which coupled with the stench of his cologne gave him a chemically preserved, ageless quality. Under normal conditions he had the demeanor of an angry gym teacher, and at this moment was clearly in an even more elevated state of agitation. I was in deep trouble. I quite rudely tapped my keyboard to disconnect from Mr. Lakshminarayanan and pretended not to see Jerry, while reciting verbatim the script for a successful close in my most professional voice.

"Now remember you may cancel at any time during those first ninety days, and you will not be charged at all. Plus, we'd like you to keep the porcelain table cross, the Man of God money clip, the Jesus Lights The Way penlight *in addition* to the God's Direction Is Always Best tire tread gauge and ice scraper car tool just as our way of saying thank you. How does that sound to you?"

Jerry didn't even have to look at my screen to know I was talking to myself.

"Are you for real?" he asked me. His voice was like sandpaper and smelled like cigarettes.

"Um, I don't know how to answer that question," was my honest reply.

He held up his hand to indicate that I should stop talking.

"Warning."

He then held up one finger.

"Only one."

He then pointed to me with both index fingers, in case there was any doubt that I was the person he was addressing, and then touched his ears with the same fingers, presumably to indicate that I should listen.

"Stick to the script."

He then leaned down over my cubicle, moving his face close to my own.

"Or *say hello to Mary.*"

Once again I wasn't sure how to respond. He said it menacingly enough that it was clear that saying hello to Mary was something I wanted to avoid, although I had absolutely no idea what it meant. I assumed it was some kind of euphemism. Or maybe it wasn't. For all I knew saying hello to Mary was a legitimate alternative to sticking to the script, and if I only said hello to the named-but-unknown woman I could also forever rid myself of this painfully worded sales propaganda.

"Understood?"

It was noticeably quiet around me, as the other telesales representatives spoke in hushed tones or pretended to type on their keyboard. I deduced that they were in fact well aware of what "saying hello to Mary" entailed, and clearly didn't want it happening nearby.

"Yes," I responded firmly, looking directly into his eyes. "I understand *exactly* what you mean."

Chapter 18. NASOPHARYNGITIS

Needless to say any fantasy of America Direct as a long-term revenue stream was pretty much extinguished by the end of my shift, although I had no time to dwell on it. I ran the entire twenty blocks uptown to St. Christopher's, fueled by a combination of dread and anticipation. The door to Audrey's office was closed when I got there, although I could tell she was inside by the light seeping through the cracks behind the shade of her office window. I knocked loudly, then opened the door without waiting for an answer.

Audrey looked up at me from behind her desk. As soon as I saw her I could tell something was horribly wrong. Her face was streaked with tears. T-Bone sat next to her, having pulled the chair from the other side of her desk. His arm was around her shoulders in consolation. My first feeling was one of panic, which was quickly replaced by rage.

"What did he tell you?" I demanded. I pulled her chair away from T-Bone and swung her around so she was facing me.

"Listen to me, Audrey, whatever he said to you, it doesn't change anything. Do you understand? Listen to me." I took both her hands and dropped to my knees. "Just because, the things that he may have said about me, it doesn't change how I feel about you, it doesn't change everything that's happened, or that you're the very, very best thing that's ever happened to me, do you understand? Please tell me you understand."

"What are you talking about?" Audrey finally responded. Her face registered complete confusion.

"Why are you crying?" I asked, backtracking.

"Because I lost my job. Yvette said they don't got no more funding after next month."

Waves of relief flushed over me, to the point I had to grab hold of Audrey's desk to keep from falling over.

"What were you talking about?" she asked me, her despair now giving way to suspicion.

I looked up at T-Bone, who smiled back smugly, then to Audrey.

"Um, I was, confused."

"You said, 'What did he tell you?' What did you think he told me?"

"Yeah, that, I thought, I just thought, he told you ... something else."

"Told me about something else what?"

"Told you about ... the ... the acute nasopharyngitis."

Now both T-Bone and Audrey were looking at me in confusion. I was betting that neither of them knew the medical term for what is more popularly referred to as the common cold.

"There was an outbreak in my building. It's been quarantined by the Department of Health."

T-Bone scoffed, and Audrey shook her head in amazement.

"Are you for real?" she asked. It was the second time that day the question had been asked of me.

"Tell her, Mays," T-Bone admonished. He said it empathetically, like he was genuinely trying to help, almost like an intervention, but my response was pure venom.

"Stay out of this, T-Bone!"

"You're a different person now. It's okay. You're not the old Parkhill. The one that wanted to be dead."

"I'd rather be dead than be like you," I snapped.

Audrey gasped, then looked like she was about to say something but only covered her mouth with her hands.

"You have no life," I continued. "This isn't living. It's the same thing as being dead."

"How the fuck would you know what living is? I don't need to fuck people over to make money. Hey, how many sewing kits you sell today at American Dickhead?"

I could feel myself losing control as Audrey just stared at both of us in bewilderment.

"You couldn't hack it in the topside world." We were toe to toe, screaming at point-blank range as our words overlapped. "You want me to be like you. But I'm not. I'm not anything like you."

"Damn straight you're not. You got no balls. You don't have the sack for the street. Never did. Depressing fuck."

"You think anybody cares about what you think? You think anyone cares when you piss on a Fortune 500 company? They live in houses and have real jobs, T-Bone—"

"Why don't you try to off yourself again? See if you can do it right this time."

"—while we're masturbating into a cup for $50 a shot!"

"You get paid $50 to jerk off?"

Audrey's quiet voice silenced both T-Bone and myself. We stared at each other, out of breath. His face was beet red and his left eyelid predictably twitching uncontrollably.

"Fifty dollars? Just to play with yourself?" she asked again.

T-Bone and I both turned to her.

"'Play with yourself'?" T-Bone repeated incredulously.

"Well it's actually a lot more than just playing with yourself," I corrected her.

I wasn't sure I liked her choice of words. To perform as consistently as both T-Bone and I had over an extended period of time actually required a fair amount of discipline and attention to one's body, not unlike an elite professional athlete.

T-Bone answered on top of me.

"We are playing a huge role in the genetic history of the population—"

"Damn. I wish someone would pay me $50 just to jerk off," Audrey murmured wistfully.

It was her tone and T-Bone's reaction that set off alarms in my brain.

"Actually women in our industry have a whole world of opportunities open to them. It's supply and demand. You can pretty much write your own ticket."

"T-Bone, no. Audrey, no—"

"Ovaries, for example. Breast milk? I bet Mays here could have you lactating in no time."

It was meant to be a peace offering, but I was too aghast to respond. Audrey brightened immediately.

"For real?"

"Audrey, let's go. Please. Let's leave now."

"Sure! We could get at least a couple gallons a week from you easy. That's ALL profit."

"A couple *gallons*?"

T-Bone was literally jumping with excitement as the full horror of what was unfolding before me began to register.

"It's all about the nipple stimulation. Lemme show you—"

"NO!"

The shriek came from me. Audrey turned in surprise, but T-Bone only rolled his eyes and pointed in the general vicinity of his nipple.

"I was gonna show on me, I wasn't gonna touch her tits."

I didn't think he was going to touch Audrey's tits. In fact, I would have much preferred that he just cop a feel than recruit her as the newest soldier in his twisted army. I wanted to shout for him to stop again, I wanted to take Audrey away, I would have given anything for what was happening not to happen. However, it was as if the emotional whirl of the sleepless night and last twenty-four hours caught up with me. I was overwhelmed, and certainly no match for T-Bone.

"Not to mention the fact you smoke. That's three hundred bucks a month easy. Check-of-the-month club."

"Shut *up*!" Audrey shrieked.

"Audrey, I'm leaving. Do you understand? I'm leaving right now. This is me leaving."

"That's not even the best part! Wait 'til you hear about this, cause it's gonna blow you away! How does $3,000 an egg sound?"

"What egg?"

"Your egg!"

I was heading toward the door, hoping someone would stop me, but all I heard was Audrey sounding like she had just won the lottery.

"I can get $3,000 for an egg? How many can I sell?"

I walked out into the evening air to the subway that would take me uptown to my new accommodations in a northern Bronx cemetery. I was exhausted, confused, and more than anything else I needed time to think. About my first day back in the workplace, and whether I would return. About Audrey, and T-Bone, and the topside world in general, which after my months underground seemed as unyielding to me as the warped door of the mausoleum I shared with the Palmisano family, their final resting place in our physical world, and now also home to another one of its orphans.

Chapter 19. POWER BITCH

I was awakened by a series of thumps on the outside of the mausoleum. T-Bone's muffled voice was audible through the heavy door.

"Mays, open up!"

I groggily reached my arms out of the sleeping bag, clothes, and newspapers I insulated myself with and pulled my body out of the narrow confines of the crypt, worming my way onto the cold cement floor. I turned the knob to the door, which was then pulled open from the outside in short, screeching bursts. Blinding light poured in, followed by the silhouette of T-Bone's head, then Audrey's.

"Oh my god … how can anybody *live* here … oh my god," she said as she looked down at me, then at my general surroundings, then back at me inquisitively.

"Wait, you sure you're not hiding any bitches in there?"

T-Bone let out a guffaw and Audrey giggled uncontrollably. Not finding anything particularly amusing, I stumbled outside. The sun was up, but the late April morning was windy and chilly. I didn't say anything, and the three of us stood there a moment, looking at each other, wondering how we were supposed to react in the aftermath of the meltdown that had taken place the day before.

"We got that thing in New London. The phase three. Remember?" T-Bone said finally. I just stood there, wrestling with my bruised ego, trying to look indifferent.

"You coming?" T-Bone asked, taking a step backward.

I still didn't budge but looked to Audrey, who apparently would be accompanying us. I supposed we were some kind of dysfunctional threesome now. She just shrugged, and then T-Bone rolled his eyes, adding: "It's a hundred and seventy-five bucks."

An hour later we were on our way to a research facility in Connecticut near the Rhode Island border to receive $175 each for testing a liquid cannabinoid tincture, some kind of synthetic THC substitute. It was certainly one of the more benign trials, although I sulked and didn't say much all the way to the George Washington Bridge bus terminal. It wasn't until T-Bone dozed off in the seat behind us on the bus that I made any attempt at communication.

"What did T-Bone tell you?"

Audrey delicately related how T-Bone had told her how we had met, of our cohabitation and means of livelihood, and, to my horror, of the events that led me to volunteer at the soup kitchen. I was too ashamed to look at her, my head resting against the bus window as I stoically gazed out at Interstate 95.

"And what do you think?" I asked her.

"What do I think of what?"

"I don't know. Everything."

Audrey reached into her purse and pulled out a stringy tissue which she used to blow her nose.

"It's fucked up," she said, choking up to the point of fighting back tears. "Everything is bullshit. My job, life, everything. T-Bone is right."

I turned in her general direction, although I still couldn't look her in the eye.

"That's what I thought before I met you. Now I don't think that. Because if everything was bullshit it would mean that we're bullshit too."

Audrey touched my cheek, and I could tell she was searching for gentle words.

"You're just fucked up right now, that's all. You need something to grab onto. You want God or Marlon Brando or the meaning of life or some shit like that."

I assumed she was referring to Charlton Heston, but my reaction was quick and defensive.

"That's not true, don't say that."

"Someday you'll get your shit together again. End up with some quiet blonde bitch with big tits."

"So you just want to give up on everything and do this?" I pressed. "What about changing people? Helping others?"

"I can't even change myself. Look at me. I'm nowheres. Nothing I do makes no difference. How the fuck am I supposed to help other people when I can't even help myself?"

"That's not true! What about me? You changed me."

She eyed me suspiciously.

"You all better now? You not ever gonna try to hurt yourself again?"

I swallowed. "No. Never."

Audrey thought for a moment, then reached up to unhook her necklace with the word LOVE fashioned out of twisted wire.

"You know the day Manny made this for me in the joint he saw four guys knock the teeth out of this white boy and force him to go down on all of them. He told me he was so scared he didn't think there was no way he was going to make it through."

She let the necklace drop into the palm of my hand.

"If Manny could make it so can you."

Audrey closed my fist and held onto it with both of her hands. "I want you to swear on it that you won't never hurt yourself again no matter what."

"Audrey—"

"For real, Mays. Promise."

I felt the twisted metal in my fist and reluctantly looked her in the eye. "Fine. I promise."

She seemed satisfied, and took her necklace back and placed it around her neck.

"Now can we not do this? Just go back to the way things were?" I pleaded.

"Nah," she said dismissively as she hooked the clasp. "T-Bone say nobody cares about that helping people shit 'cause it don't create no revenue generation."

I cringed, and peeked back between the seats at T-Bone, who lay sleeping or at least pretended to be asleep.

"I'm gonna be a power bitch," she continued. "You watch."

"A power bitch?"

"That's right," she nodded defiantly. "In a kick-ass Armani business suit with a pearl necklace and Ferragamo pumps—"

"On your way to the lactation center?"

"What else I'm supposed to do, Mays? Go live with Rosa? Pretend like she's got room for me? She already got the baby staying in Celeste's room. *Everybody* makes money off of my body except me. Everybody."

I winced at another T-Boneism, and did my best to explain to her about realities of living hand to mouth without a permanent home, about the shelf, about how difficult it was to drop out of the topside world and then rejoin. It all fell on deaf ears. By the time the bus arrived, my stomach was churning, and my mind a scrambled mess with nightmarish visions of ways I might embarrass myself in front of Audrey during the day's proceedings.

We got into a cab and T-Bone read an address from his Filofax. I begged Audrey to stay close to me whatever happened, although T-Bone interjected that under no circumstances were we to let on that we knew each other, which might preclude us from participating in the same experiment. Like many rules with T-Bone it was one he broke whenever it was convenient. After checking in with a woman in a nurse uniform, who seemed more office assistant than nurse, we were each given a clipboard and a pen, which T-Bone handed over to me.

"It's easier if one person tells the whole story for all of us. Makes it more synchronius," he explained, and then checked to make sure Audrey was out of earshot. "The usual for me and you. Put her at 120, 125 pounds and give her an art degree. Occasional smoker, no allergies. No birth control or medications. Six days since her last period. Any questions, come direct to me."

I did my best to fill out the forms as accurately as possible, much to the chagrin of Audrey and T-Bone, who had little patience for my incessant questions. Finally, I relented and made up the remaining information, and we handed in the completed the forms in return for these black nylon badge things you wore around your neck that made it look like we were at some convention or trade show.

The packed waiting area held fifty or so mostly young people, college students with a few scraggly outliers like T-Bone. One by one our names were called, and people began to disappear behind a doorway, escorted by a mirthless elderly woman in a nurse uniform. Audrey leapt out of her chair and gave a fist pump when her name was announced.

"Go get 'em, Audrey! Focus, sweetheart." T-Bone turned to me, grinning ear-to-ear like a proud parent watching his daughter's college graduation.

As a reward for my thoroughness in completing our paperwork, I was the very last name called. I was led by the nurse to a small examination room and told to sit down behind a folding table. She tied a disposable plastic bib around my neck, like I was being served a lobster dinner, then placed a shot glass sized cup containing an opaque, green elixir in front of me.

"You'll need to hold the liquid under your tongue for two minutes," she informed me, placing a digital timer on the table.

The disgusting, alcohol based solvent had the piney taste one would expect from tree sap. I had trickles dribbling out of the corners of my mouth and down my chin, and the burning sensation made my eyes water so much I could barely see. I spit it back into the plastic cup after only thirty seconds.

"Water!" I gasped.

"Two minutes," she responded, handing me back the cup of green tincture I had just spat out. She reset the timer to zero, meaning I would now have a total two minutes and thirty seconds of sublingual medication.

I made it a minute this time before I had to spit it out again.

"I can't—"

"Would you like to be excused from the trial?"

I defiantly emptied the contents of the cup into my mouth once again, and she reset the timer. This time I made it the whole way, counting down the last seconds through tears, even though at this point my total exposure time was three minutes thirty seconds. I was rewarded with a new cupful of water to rinse with.

I wiped some of the gucky green mess off my mouth, and, as I did so, it felt like my chin was dripping off, like wax from a candle. For some strange reason this didn't cause panic within me, only a rising sense of concern, as I began to touch the side of my face to ensure it was still securely fastened. I also noted my cheeks and jowls had a fluidity to them, a molasses-like viscosity. I tapped them gently with my fingertips.

"How are you feeling?" the nurse asked as she filled out an index card with my name and other information. It occurred to me how unfair it was that she knew my name but I didn't know hers. I tried to make out the handwritten scribble on her identification badge, which seemed to swim before me.

"I'm feeling much better now, thank you, Doris."

"Dolly," she volunteered.

"Well. Hello, Dolly."

She didn't respond. I had to say it.

"Helloooooo, Dolly. It's so *nice* to have you back with us again."

I keeled over in hysterics, laughing until I saw that she made no reaction and was only continuing to scribble on my index card, glancing at her watch and checking boxes.

"I'm sorry ... so unlike me ..." I waved dismissively.

I continued to tap my face, alarmed at its transformation into a kind of elastic goop, and wondered why Dolly paid no notice. My tongue seemed particularly wobbly, like the wheel of a car that might come flying off at any moment.

"I can't feel my face," I finally prodded her, although it came out more like "Ah cahnt feel mah face," because I was now holding my tongue firmly between the thumb and forefinger of my right hand for fear of it falling off.

"It's the cannabinoids," she replied absently as she finished writing on my card.

An assistant appeared in the doorway, not a medical type looking assistant, but a computer nerd assistant, with glasses and a scraggly beard.

"The network is still down," he announced apologetically.

"He'll have to wait to get banded then. He can't stay here." Nurse Dolly was clearly annoyed as she slipped the index card into my nylon pouch that all participants wore. She removed the bib from my neck and replaced it with my new badge, my name, and other vital stats clearly displayed through the plastic window. The administrative geek wordlessly came into the room and gently took my arm.

"Wait!" Dolly shouted as we were about to leave, and I almost jumped out of my shoes.

She handed me a tissue.

"You have something on your face."

A fresh wave of panic rippled through my body as the administrative geek took me down the hallway while I madly dabbed at my chin with the tissue. It felt like my whole face was dripping. I wondered what Audrey would think to see the flesh melting off my face, or worse, if I would find her off in a corner with her own face dissolved into a puddle on the floor.

I could hear a cacophony of strange noises coming from behind a pair of swinging double doors at the end of the hall. My guide, clearly with more pressing matters on his mind, pushed one of the doors ajar.

"Just have a seat. Somebody will come by to band you."

I fumbled for the badge that hung around my neck. I had already been badged, I meant to answer. Was banding really necessary? Of course I had no idea what banding entailed, but didn't like the sound of it, not one bit.

It took a moment to process the sight on the other side of the doors. It was part kindergarten classroom, for there were a number of tables spread around with papers, pencils, magic markers, and part law library, with tomes of impressive-looking reference books on another part of the wall. The room was far too crowded, with trial participants, medical and technical staff all packed inside, making it hot and claustrophobic. T-Bone's voice was audible from somewhere. T-Bone's voice was always audible from somewhere during these things; he was almost always the most at ease and gregarious. I was also aware of the sound of a xylophone and someone banging on a bongo drum nearby, a ball being dribbled on the floor, along with other assorted noises I was unable to identify.

Before you dismiss my impression of the surroundings as tainted by a poor pharmaceutical transformation of one of the hundreds of cannabinoids found naturally in the hemp plant into liquid form, I would point out that, like weddings, each clinical trial has its own style and feel to it. A university study can include wine and cheese at a professor's house if they're feeling charitable. A product focus group was usually a slick corporate affair, with tons of attractive marketing people who would listen forever to what you had to say about marshmallow and chocolate on a piece of graham cracker. Pharmaceutical clinical trials varied depending upon a number of factors, although most tended to have a worn kind of hotel chain feel to them.

This particular trial had a very substitute teacher day feel to it, a much more amateurish affair. It seemed there were two warring armies. The first army was that of the nurses and the administrative staff who worked there, like my new drug dealer hookup, Dolly. The other group was the grungy, more technically inclined looking young men and women. I think even the women had facial hair. They were working on a row of laptops set up along a conference table, upon which a number of other assorted toys and instruments were strewn about. I couldn't spot Audrey amidst the chaos and pressed forward.

"Have you been banded?" a woman's voice asked me from nowhere in particular.

"We can't band him. The network is still down," another voice answered.

"Hey, Mays! Check this out! We can control the weather with our butt cheeks."

T-Bone was calling me from over by the window. He was bent over with his pants at his knees, his exposed bottom facing the window.

"C'mon, Mays, we're gonna make the sun come out!"

I finally spotted Audrey in the crowd watching him. A couple of other participants had joined in, and the staff seemed too preoccupied or too frightened to stop them. I forced my way through and stepped boldly up to Audrey, fully intending to declare my undying love and to serve her until my very last breath.

"Ah cahn't feel mah face," I heard myself say.

I realized I was still holding my tongue with the thumb and forefinger of my right hand.

Audrey looked at me with confusion. "What the fuck are you doing with your tongue?"

"Ah don wan ah blonde bitch," I tried to explain to her frantically, still gripping onto my tongue for dear life. "Ah ohly wahnt you."

"Mays, get your hand out your mouth."

I started to pull on my lower lip. It seemed like it would stretch forever.

"What's he doing with his lip?" T-Bone asked, suddenly standing next to me, his pants down around his knees. He was being trailed by none other than Dolly, who was reaching the end of her patience.

"Sir, you need to pull up your pants right now."

"What band are you at?" Audrey asked me excitedly. That stupid word again.

"The network is still down so they shut down the sims," T-Bone responded calmly, as though that explained everything. Why was it that nothing ever affected him?

"If I don't get banded then *say hello to Mary!*" I bellowed to no one in particular.

"Who's Mary?" T-Bone, Audrey, and Dolly asked simultaneously, all looking equally perplexed.

I felt like I was losing control of the situation, my ability to communicate deteriorating with every passing second. I grabbed Audrey by her shoulders and looked at her.

"Audrey, I didn't even want to, I mean, I couldn't even, until … you … not until you."

Audrey made shushing sounds for me to stop, but I had to finish.

"You changed me. You saved me."

"No, Mays, no—"

"Yes."

I put my finger to her lip and was surprised that she stopped talking. "Yes," I repeated, although at that point it seemed like there was only a distant relationship between my brain and my mouth. Much to my surprise, she nodded her head in the affirmative like she understood, which was remarkable considering I only had the faintest idea of what I was saying myself.

So I kissed her. A long, slow kiss, closing my eyes to block everything out, conscious only of the piney alcohol taste in her mouth, and snippets of conversation from the voices around us.

"You need to pull up your pants, sir."

"Did they just meet?"

"We need to create a new band level."

"No really, we're going to make the sun come out."

Our lips parted as we both seemed to become aware of something warm on our shoulders. We turned to the window to see the sun now peeking out from behind the clouds.

"It works," I murmured. The rays of sunlight filtered through the windows, illuminating a half-dozen naked butt cheeks from the stoned test participants and causing even the staff to pause.

"Oh my god!" Audrey gasped. "Oh my god ..."

"Oh mah gahd!" I repeated, grabbing my tongue again.

Hours later Audrey's jubilant voice penetrated the cool night air.

"Oh my god ... I mean oh my *fucking* god ..."

She was holding a wad of cash, our payment, counting it again while skipping down the sidewalk.

"That was *nothing!*" T-Bone bounded behind her. "That was small change."

I stumbled off the sidewalk, still feeling tingly, struggling to catch up with them.

"Mays!"

Audrey screamed as a delivery truck whooshed past me, an explosion of sound about two inches away from my ear. T-Bone yanked me back onto the sidewalk.

"He's good, he's good, we just need to keep an eye on him," T-Bone reassured Audrey as they each took an arm and walked with me in the middle. "And I want you to know that even though everyone else there thinks you're a band zero, you're still a band ten to Audrey and me."

"That's right, baby," Audrey concurred.

It was more of the same all the way on the bus ride back, with T-Bone extolling the life of wealth, leisure, and social consciousness that awaited Audrey as a human guinea pig. Not surprisingly, the T-Bone-fest didn't end when our bus pulled into the terminal at the George Washington Bridge.

"We staying at my place or yours?" Audrey asked me as we disembarked.

T-Bone let out another guffaw. His laughter died down, until the three of us were staring at each other awkwardly.

"Why don't you come stay at my place, with Mays?" Audrey finally asked T-Bone. I cringed.

"Oh no. Nononono. Definitely not. No way," T-Bone replied, in a false protest tone of voice that made it clear it was a foregone conclusion.

Had I known I would be forced to listen to the two of them bawling all night to public service charity infomercials on Audrey's TV about starving third-world children, I might have stayed back in the Palmisano mausoleum. T-Bone had a loud, overly dramatic wail he would let out for Audrey's benefit that even she had to ask him to tone down.

"It's so fucking sad!" he bellowed to Audrey, in tears next to him. "That kid, the one they keep showing, with the missing teeth ... I can't take it."

I wrapped a pillow around my head in a vain attempt to escape the noise, closing my eyes to the images of emaciated children that flickered across the television screen.

Chapter 20. THE LAND OF MILK AND HONEY

It increasingly felt like it was myself, not T-Bone, who was the third wheel in the relationship as I accompanied them to the public library the next day. There was no way I could possibly match their excitement as they compared the requirements, details, dates and duration of trials in different cities on a map, then cross-referenced them with bus lines and available accommodations. As I watched Audrey and T-Bone high-five each other over a two-day trial for insect repellant in western Pennsylvania, I tried to be philosophical about my predicament. Audrey was in the honeymoon phase with the experience, just as I had been. Certainly I was in no position to cast any judgments as to the relative worth of a life spent as the royal taster of the latest innovations in academic research, pharmaceutical compounds, or consumer products. Whether this was a legitimate alternative lifestyle or just a naïve and self-delusional distraction by three desperate people, I still am unsure. Perhaps it was both.

Of much more interest to me, at least from a medical standpoint, was the whole mechanism of inducing lactation. I had always just assumed the process was set off by some biological trigger during the prenatal development period. As it turns out, it is entirely possible for women to produce breast milk even if they're not pregnant. As T-Bone correctly pointed out, regular nipple stimulation and breast massage can raise the levels in the pituitary gland to the point where the critical mass of prolactin (the hormone responsible for lactation) is produced. I also found out that estrogen, for example in the form of birth control pills I knew Audrey was taking, is a lactation suppressant, which, as it turns out, wouldn't be an issue since T-Bone had already signed Audrey up for some kind of contraceptive vaginal ring study, whatever that was. Most research I found recommended no less than eight sessions of twenty minutes of nipple stimulation per day, since this most closely approximated a newborn's feeding patterns.

Even more remarkable was the online marketplace T-Bone
showed us, a sort of national classifieds for people buying and
selling breast milk. The going rate was $2 to $4 per ounce, higher if
the donor adhered to caffeine-free, gluten-free, vegan, or other
special dietary restrictions. A newborn baby consumes roughly 30
ounces of milk per day, so it wasn't inconceivable to bring in close to
$100 a day, shipped out in coolers packed with dry ice, dropped off
at any number of non-profit "milk banks" across the country, or by
arrangement (drop off or pick up) with an individual buyer.

And there I thought the sperm thing was weird.

Getting the whole lactation process up and running before
we hit the road to Longwood for our three-month trial in North
Carolina in July was important. Along with the sperm donation it
was the one thing we could depend on multiple times a week and
paid cash. Audrey had just over a month of her job left, so we had a
little runway to try to open the biological sluice gates.

It didn't really get to be an emotional issue with her until T-
Bone told Audrey's roommate Louisa about it. Louisa had an
advantage in that she was already the size of a cow and, despite a
newly minted Ph.D. in classical philosophy (including a
groundbreaking thesis on Moral Absolutism in Gender Identity),
was unemployed and as desperate as we were for a steady stream of
income. She was so enthralled at the prospect of generating her own
milk money that she went with her girlfriend to purchase a top-of-
the-line Milk Maid Deluxe 9600, the "Cadillac of breast pumps,"
which took about twenty batteries and came with its own carrying
case. Audrey was competitive to begin with, and this set up a kind of
bizarre woman-versus-machine rivalry.

Bags of Louisa's breast milk began appearing in their freezer
after only a week. Under pressure from Audrey, I began doing
research on galactagogues, which is a real word used to describe
anything that may promote lactation. I had no idea there were so
many. In fact, if one believes the popular folklore, it's surprising that
all of our collective nipples aren't like leaky faucets. Over the course
of the next week we tried asparagus, fenugreek, brewer's yeast,
blessed thistle, alfalfa, anise, flax, astragalus root, pumpkin seeds,

Bermuda grass, red raspberry leaf, burdock, nettle, fennel, goat's rue, quinoa, soapwort, vervain, marshmallow, althaea root, and oatmeal (not instant but the old-fashioned kind). Usually I'd make her a big marshmallow fluff sandwich and sprinkle in as much of the dry herbs as she could stomach. Once during this exercise Louisa came into the kitchen to deposit another armload of breast milk into the fridge in ziploc baggies. When I asked her how she did it she explained how her girlfriend was able to stimulate lactation using a peacock feather. I thanked her for the suggestion and returned to Audrey with her galactagogues sandwich.

"Who's gonna buy my milk with that cow giving away twenty gallons every day?" Audrey sulked one evening, as she lay on her mattress gently tugging on her nipples.

"It's not a competition," I explained wearily as I rubbed an experimental anti-bacterial athlete's foot powder on the soles of her feet. Her jeans were rolled up below her knees, and I was sitting in my underwear, my own feet already covered with the chalky pale blue powder. Her toenails were half an inch long, having committed herself to T-Bone's philosophy that no body part with any market value be wasted.

She reached for an open quart of milk on the floor next to her and drank deeply. "Why does T-Bone need to run his mouth like that?"

I massaged her foot and didn't mention that it served her right for letting him stay with us. Through the curtain behind me and above the steady churn of the breast pump I could hear T-Bone fawn over Louisa like a baseball scout who had just discovered an 8th grader with a 105 MPH fastball.

"I mean you're really gifted. You know that right? Do you know how special this gift you have is?"

I was correct about the fact that it wasn't a competition, or at least competitive. Louisa's output was nothing short of remarkable. After three weeks she was doing about fifty ounces, or a liter and a half, a day. She had already exhausted the purchasing capacity of all the local purveyors of breast milk (the Breastfeeding Center at the

Park Slope Woman's Hospital, the Williamsburg Lactation Center) and was expanding her reach to Manhattan, in addition to the online services that would let her ship it in pre-packaged containers with dry ice. It was actually helpful having her blaze a trail for us to demonstrate the nuts and bolts of turning the fresh milk into cash, but Audrey didn't see it that way.

"It's all psychological," was T-Bone's diagnosis. We were sitting on a park bench at a playground in lower Manhattan on a weekday morning, killing time before we visited the lab a block uptown to receive an experimental treatment for our non-existent acid reflux symptoms.

    "It's already been three weeks. Louisa started after only six days."

    "Everyone's different. Maybe you're an egg person."

    Around us African American and Hispanic nannies and babysitters were taking care of upper-class Caucasian preschoolers who ran amok around us, the spawn of affluent Manhattan bankers, lawyers, and captains of industry.

    "What if it never happens? What about all our plans? Aren't we supposed to be in Wisconsin or something in two weeks?"

    "Pennsylvania. It's gonna happen. You know, there could be other factors at work here. May I ask a delicate question? Have you and Mays been having normal sexual relations?"

    Before I could respond, or in an attempt to deflect my response, Audrey nudged me and pointed across the playground.

    "There. Over there."

    She was pointing to a thirtyish professional looking woman in a dark blue dress suit with perfectly coifed hair and stylish glasses, replete in heels and a tasteful strand of pearls around her neck. She was waving an exaggerated goodbye as she backed away from a line of strollers while at the same time speaking into her cell phone.

    "That's gonna be me. A power bitch. See?"

It seemed like such a heart-breakingly implausible transformation that I felt compelled to say something, although I tried a different tack this time.

"Maybe it wasn't meant to be."

Both T-Bone and Audrey stared at me like I had just said something blasphemous.

"I mean, if, like you say, everything happens for a reason."

I was using her own words against her. Audrey was steadfast in her belief in predetermination and the fact that we were only actors following a script that God had already created for us. It might not have been fair, but I still clung to the faintest of hopes I might be able to dissuade her from continuing down what I saw as the self-destructive path of human guinea piggery.

"Mays, you cannot blame yourself—" T-Bone tried to interject.

"I'm not blaming myself," I responded calmly. "I'm not blaming anyone. It isn't anyone's fault."

A posse of nannies pushing strollers and baby carriages toward the exit of the playground paused in front of us as a small plastic bottle of milk landed on the concrete. A baby's cry ensued.

"Maybe it isn't, you know ... God's plan."

The sound of the baby crying set off a chorus of additional wails from the adjacent strollers and baby carriages, making our general area sound like a maternity ward. Most of the nannies continued gossiping amongst each other as if nothing had happened.

"Maybe you were meant to make a difference some other way."

I peeked over at Audrey for a reaction, but she was watching the baby in the stroller nearest to her where the nanny returned the plastic bottle without so much as a wipe. I couldn't tell if it was a boy or a girl, but it couldn't have been more than a few months old, covered in layers of blankets and a knit cap. It was still screaming, a full blown baby cry that could have been a sound effect for a movie.

"Do you want to go somewhere else?" I asked her. She clearly wasn't listening to me and only stared at the crying baby, until she slowly reached inside her leather jacket and beneath her hooded sweatshirt. Then I began to get an inkling of what was going on.

"What the fuck ..." she murmured.

She pulled out a finger and touched it to her tongue.

"Oh my god ... oh my god ..." she exclaimed more loudly.

She reached under her sweatshirt again.

"I'm milking, check it out—"

She held her moist finger out to myself and T-Bone, who both fell off the bench recoiling in horror.

Audrey was simultaneously laughing at us and celebrating, attracting attention from the passers-by.

"I'm *milking!*"

In truth she wasn't milking very much, at least not by Louisa's standards. Still Audrey insisted on labeling the ounce and a half she was able to produce, using the same black marker and shorthand Louisa did for date and weight, and placed it in the freezer next to hers. Personally this would have made me feel worse, as the sight of all of Louisa's frozen bags next to her single twice-folded baggy looked pretty pathetic. It took another week before we were able to make our first subway ride to the Lactation Center in Williamsburg, where she filled out some forms to set up an account and had her milk weighed and tested.

"Is it soup yet?" T-Bone asked. It was like watching me selling my sperm for the first time all over again, right down to Audrey's giddy, childlike joy when the lab attendant unlocked a drawer, pulled out $80 and forked it over to her. I felt a mixture of trepidation, and perhaps embarrassingly pride and wistfulness as she gripped both T-Bone and myself in a gleeful embrace.

"Let's go to Wisconsin!"

It was Pennsylvania, for an insect-repellant trial, and we left two days later. Audrey gave up her apartment, the last vestige of her normal topside life, and moved into the mausoleum with me for the last few weeks before heading to North Carolina for our extended phase three trial. We weren't home but a few days a week anymore, and it made more sense to save the money since there was enough space for the two of us. All of her worldly possessions save what she could fit in a backpack had been stored at Rosa's, who also let us use her shower a couple of times a week. Blessedly there was no room for T-Bone, who stayed at the Bat Cave.

"The terrific thing is the commute to the city is completely manageable," I explained to Audrey as I tried to maneuver her legs into the crypt above mine. "Forty-five minutes to midtown door to door, and the neighborhood's safe too," I quoted T-Bone almost verbatim.

"Watch my leg!" she screamed.

I was holding her in my arms with my knees bent so I wouldn't hit my head on the low ceiling, straining under her weight. Her legs were inside the crypt, as she wriggled her way further down.

"And as long as no more Palmisanos die we're fine—"

"Mays, careful!"

She became still and the only sound was of my panting in the darkness, trying to catch my breath.

"I need a cigarette," she said finally.

"We're out," I responded, and then added wearily, "Fine, I'll be right back."

I started throwing my weight against the door to open it again as I heard Audrey's voice behind me.

"They got Chinese food around here?"

With the sale of her hair to the North Shore Academy of Cosmetology and Hair Sciences on Long Island for $225, Audrey's transformation was complete. I actually thought they did a credible job of stylizing the hair that remained into a cute, pixie-like, functional tomboy coiffure, but that didn't prevent Audrey from bawling through the entire ordeal. Rosa was similarly aghast when Audrey showed up for her last day at St. Christopher's, which only re-affirmed her growing suspicion that T-Bone and I represented an increasingly bad influence. T-Bone, as he did with me, saw himself as Audrey's savior, rescuing her from a corrupt economic system and a lifetime of debt and student loans that a two-year associate degree from City College would never begin to pay back.

Yet while it was true that neither T-Bone nor I were responsible for cutting the funding for Audrey's job at the soup kitchen, I couldn't say that I faulted Rosa for blaming me. While I ostensibly did everything in my power to dissuade Audrey from this questionable path, truth be told I was far too in love to care. It had never occurred to me that there could be a light so bright that it could illuminate something as dark and twisted as my life had been, so powerful that we could remain locked in a kiss in a tent of mosquito netting in western Pennsylvania completely oblivious to the clouds of insects that swarmed us. I had always believed The Rage, and my accompanying emotional baggage, would forever prevent me from reaching these heights. Yet having swallowed, inhaled, injected or shoved up my ass any number of dangerous medications, I can honestly say I found no narcotic as addictive, potent, or dangerous as love. And if our life is one big question, a search for truth and meaning, then let it be said that Audrey was the closest I have ever come to arriving at a satisfactory answer.

Chapter 21. MAYS LANDING

As our relationship became more intense so too, it seemed, did the experiments T-Bone signed us up for, with Audrey's encouragement and my own diminishing protests. The months leading up to our departure to North Carolina that summer for the extended trial at Longwood felt like an all-out sprint across the Northeast and Mid-Atlantic from one gig to the next, interspersed with Audrey's regular appointments at the NYU fertility clinic in preparation for the harvesting of her eggs. On top of the other medications we were already taking and Audrey's hormonal therapy for her egg extraction, we also needed to taper down her milk output. As T-Bone explained, we would be in "lock-down" mode at Longwood for three months, with all medication carefully monitored and no possibility of any extracurricular experiments on the side. At our current pace that seemed like a blessing.

While for me the off-the-grid lifestyle had provided (at least initially) a needed respite from the "real world" after my suicide attempt, for Audrey it was just the opposite. She genuinely believed she was pursuing a legitimate career path, climbing a corporate ladder that would lead to an idealized urban professional "power bitch" lifestyle that until now was beyond her grasp. It was a fantasy fueled by T-Bone, who was more energized than I had ever seen him, having not one but two apostles now under his tutelage. He seemed at his happiest tracking all the moving pieces in his ubiquitous Filofax, scheming with Audrey to scale our operation to a multinational corporate superpower.

"There's hundreds, thousands of us, all living together, see, and everyone gives whatever they can, sperm, eggs, milk, bone marrow."

We were in our customary last row of a Greyhound bus taking us from western Pennsylvania to upstate New York. Audrey lay with her head in my lap, scooping peanut butter out of a tub with her finger, while I applied calamine lotion to the welt-sized insect bites on her arms and face from the trial we'd just participated in. The Milk Maid Deluxe 9600 whirred reassuringly beneath a sweatshirt covering her chest.

"So you would have this stable of bitches, and I'm like some kind of assistant pimp?" Audrey asked curiously. It wasn't accusatory, merely a factual question.

"I wouldn't call it that exactly," T-Bone hesitated, himself with nary an insect bite. I attributed it more to his freakish super-human resistance than the efficacy of the chemical agent that had been sprayed over us.

"Like a farm," I offered, gently dabbing the last of the calamine on some lumps on Audrey's face, a mountain ridge just below her hairline. "Where you have chores, like milking and egging the females? Jacking off the men?" I wiped my fingers on the back of her neck.

"Hey, I like your thinking!" T-Bone nodded approvingly, as if the whole thing had been my idea.

By far the highlight of all the experiments for Audrey was spending the better part of a day at the Aurora Cryonic Life Extension Facility just outside of Buffalo, NY. It was meant to be a quick stop to donate a tissue slice for cryopreservation until we happened upon a tour that was starting. We had already been paid our $200 each along with a gift certificate for 50% off one adult admission at a nearby Niagara Falls amusement park that Audrey and T-Bone intended to use, so I didn't protest when Audrey insisted we stay to listen to a sales pitch for eternal life. There were a half-dozen other people on the tour, including one guy in a wheelchair suffering from ALS or multiple sclerosis or some other debilitating disease who didn't seem to have any voluntary muscle control. All of them were older and, unlike us, gave the outward impression of having the means to fork over $100,000 to have their entire body preserved indefinitely in liquid nitrogen, or $30,000 for just their brain.

"The cryopreservative never actually freezes, even at extremely low temperatures, so no damaging ice crystals form," the executive director explained to us, a Dr. Bernard. He was a slim, bald, bearded man, fortyish, and somewhat effete, who led the tour with the air of a luxury hotel manager showing off the first class accommodations. While clearly in sales mode, he seemed at least to be very intelligent and passionate about the subject of cryopreservation, and proud of what they had built at the Aurora Cryonic Life Extension Facility.

"Otherwise your brain is like a re-heated burrito," T-Bone concurred.

Dr. Bernard took us through the entire process from start to finish, beginning when a patient was declared clinically dead. The actual timing of the declaration of death was critical, as you needed to start the process before oxygen deprivation caused permanent damage to the brain cells. The dirty secret was that many physicians wouldn't even declare death until it was too late, which is why the facility had their own doctors on call, as well as a list of recommended physicians who were sympathetic to their cause. Discretion and privacy, almost to the point of secrecy, was apparently a big part of the culture in cryopreservation. It helped to protect the companies from law enforcement and legal action in the nebulous gray area between death and near death, as well as their clients from the stigma of being seen as crazy for paying tens of thousands of dollars for an unproven experimental procedure on the fringes of modern science.

The dead (or almost dead, depending on your definition) were placed in a giant vat of ice and treated with a variety of medications and chemicals to lower their body temperature to just above the freezing point. Afterward, they would be moved to operating tables where holes were drilled into the skull to wash out all the blood and bodily fluids and replace them with the cryopreservative, a kind of medical-grade anti-freeze. After this process, known as vitrification, the bodies (or severed heads, if you were just saving the brain) would then be cooled, placed in a plastic sleeve and moved to a secured patient care bay. There they would be stored upside-down (to protect the brain) in upright giant aluminum pods called dewars in liquid nitrogen at -106 degrees

Celsius. We toured the forest of shiny metallic pods emblazoned with the Aurora logo.

"If you think about it, when you die really what we're saying is: there is nothing else we can do for you now given the limits of science today," Dr. Bernard explained to us enthusiastically. "That could change in a hundred, even a thousand years."

Audrey followed every detail in rapt attention, even making us stay after the tour ended to watch a video on the current state of cryopreserved organ replacement. Dr. Bernard treated us to a catered lunch as we watched a close-up on a giant display of some doctor making stitches into a devitrified replacement kidney inside a living, breathing, anesthetized rabbit. It would later show the rabbit's creatine levels (a measure of kidney function) return to normal to prove it was functioning properly.

We even filled out all the paperwork to have our brains cryogenically frozen, providing the Aurora Cryonic Life Extension Facility with everything except the $30,000 payment required for each head. We'd come back with the money later, T-Bone assured Dr. Bernard, who played along gamely.

"Shoot, it's just like a real long experiment," Audrey whispered to me. "What do you got to lose?"

"Thirty grand each?" I offered.

"Fine," she shrugged. "I just be chillin' in a fridge somewheres while you and T-Bone get old and fat."

While our alternative lifestyle may have cheated Audrey and me out of some of the more traditional rituals of courtship, the intimacy we developed while selling both body and mind to science brought us closer together faster and more deeply than miniature golf or dinner and a movie ever could have. Few things will battle test a relationship, for example, like a week-long sleep deprivation experiment.

Psycho-stimulants like Adderall and Ritalin are typically used to treat mental disorders like Alzheimer's and Attention Deficit Hyperactivity Disorder (ADHD), although they are also widely abused in bastions of higher education because of their ability to allow students to absorb an entire semester of Econ 101 in a span of forty consecutive hours. Known as study buddies or steroids for the brain, our experiment was conveniently located at a testing facility outside a large state university in South Jersey, and most of the participants were college students. They brought textbooks, personal computers, music devices, portable electronics of just about every variety, comfort food, changes of clothing, board games, sleeping bags and other accessories spread out across the floor in the large recreation room where we were to spend the better part of the next week. Windows and chairs lined the walls, and there was a giant boxy antiquated television in a corner of the room playing 24-hour cable news. There was a small pantry area with a well-stocked refrigerator and sink, as well as scattered tables with an eclectic array of reading material. We were each given portable handheld versions of a Psychomotor Vigilance Task (PVT) device, a little box with a red light that would blink on every couple of minutes, and you would have to push a response button to turn it off to prove you were awake.

It felt odd watching the packs of students spread out like at a giant campus picnic from my corner with T-Bone and Audrey. Most of us who are fortunate enough to have had the privilege of attending an institution of higher learning (particularly if it was on someone else's tab) consider those sepia-tinged memories as some of the very best of their lives. That was never the case with me. I had found the whole experience to be a stomach-wrenching, stress-inducing, ritualistic exercise, from the freshman fraternity rush through graduate school and the intense hazing model of our medical hierarchy. Anxiety about meeting expected behavior always outweighed any temporary relief I was supposed to find through road trips, football games, and fraternity parties.

Still, my academic experience and medical training had given me a very intimate experience with sleep deprivation, which I hoped would finally give me an advantage over T-Bone and Audrey. While this may have been true for the first sixty hours or so, I was completely unprepared for the kind of punishment we were about to be subjected to. To be fair, T-Bone was full of sleep deprivation war stories that could have given me some warning, although I chalked that up to his typical bravado. He was a big hit with the college kids, recounting tales such as the disc jockey who stayed awake for fourteen days in Times Square and subsequently went insane, and some experiment during the second world war in which the Nazis used Russian prisoners who, according to legend, ate themselves alive.

I, on the other hand, was engaged in a much more important ritual for our overnight experiments, finding a safe location for conjugal visits with Audrey.

"You supposed to be saving it up," she replied matter-of-factly, arranging her medication in a plastic tackle box we had gotten her at an open-air flea market.

"We could be here for *five days*," I pleaded. She was not greeting the news of my discovery of a lockable supply closet on the floor below us with as much excitement as I had hoped.

"So? You get all backed up and then boom-boom-boom you shoot out a six pack, like five hundred dollars."

"It doesn't work that way."

She closed her tackle box and picked up the same copy of the *Atlantic County Register* she had already read cover to cover.

"Talk to me after I pump."

Once the hormonal therapy for her fertilization kicked in, Audrey's moods would swing wildly, and I had to tread lightly. She was also producing almost a liter of milk a day. Pulling off an extended multi-night gig like this was a challenge as she needed to pump approximately every four hours or her breasts would become painfully engorged. After she ran out of ziploc baggies halfway through, she started storing the milk in any container she could find: Tupperware, coffee cups, a small flower vase. When one of the study participants complained that the milk in the refrigerator "tasted funny" I didn't make the connection until I saw Audrey let out a yelp and go running into the pantry, where we ended up pouring over $100 of breast milk down the drain.

I spent the better part of the first two days in front of a large whiteboard creating a five color large-scale depiction of the human heart, meticulously labeling every detail down to the posterior interventricular sulcus. I didn't even fully realize what I was doing until almost an hour into it, although I had unusual clarity, like it was all right there in front of me in my *Essential Clinical Anatomy* textbook. I became completely engrossed, eschewing the take-out meals they brought in for us. The only indication of the passing of time I had was the occasional blinking light on my PVT box I would extinguish with the click of a button, and the research assistant making her hourly rounds to check in with each of us.

"And how are we feeling this hour, Mr. Mays?"

They would rattle through the same questions, making notes on a clipboard, logging the time and date and our verbal responses to (I discovered after sneaking glances at the paperwork) what was apparently known as the Epworth Sleepiness Scale.

"And on a scale of zero to three, zero meaning no probability, three meaning highly likely, what is your chance of dozing right now while sitting and reading?"

"Zero."

"Watching TV?"

"Zip."

"Sitting inactive in a public place? Talking to someone?"

"Nope."

"Lying in bed after a large meal?"

"Not happening."

It was true. As admirers would stop by and compliment me on my artwork, I was beginning to wonder if I may have been missing out on something, and that perhaps I could have dispensed with the whole formal education thing with far less time and fuss by taking a few minor legal and medical risks.

That was until the headaches started.

I suppose it makes sense that any muscle that gets a workout like that, whether naturally or pharmaceutically induced, would become sore eventually. The main difference is that there are other limiting factors that would have prevented say, my legs from running the six marathons that my brain felt like it had endured after two full days. It came on suddenly, like a cramp in my head, to the point that I was completely immobilized and had to stagger back to the corner of the room where Audrey lay curled underneath a desk.

"The headaches started?" she asked simply.

I just nodded, collapsing on the floor next to her, rubbing my temples.

"Wait 'til the walls start moving."

I became aware that I was lying on top of a local newspaper, the same newspaper that Audrey had read front-to-back repeatedly while I was drawing my human heart. I was staring at a photo of a beauty pageant winner, a not particularly comely woman with an unfortunate nose that one would have thought would preclude her from any contests of physical beauty, apparently the winner of Miss Atlantic County, New Jersey. Audrey's interest was piqued by the fact that she hailed from "the small seaside town of Mays Landing," which she thought was hilarious, showing the picture of "my girlfriend" to T-Bone.

At around eighty hours, the hallucinations began, and things got really interesting. As Audrey promised, the walls started to "breathe," bending inward and then outward, a side effect I was familiar with through our other trials and of no immediate concern. Much more disconcerting was watching my fellow subjects one by one reach their breaking point, suddenly babbling or shouting hysterically for no reason. The emotional investment in staying awake for such an extended period of time was such that one would actually develop a manic fear of falling asleep, and few simply nodded off peacefully at their PVT device. Many would beg incoherently to remain, sometimes through tears, as they were ushered away by staff members.

It first happened with an older gentleman, a burly man with a wide mustache who I had become obsessed with because of his resemblance to my "guardian angel," the mysterious stranger with the handlebar mustache who had surprised me in my apartment after my suicide attempt, and who I was sure I had recognized watching me months later. It was actually only a passing resemblance (his mustache wasn't twisted at the ends, and he was generally fleshier and less fit), although after three days a full-blown conspiracy theory was brewing in my sleep-deprived brain. I kept casting furtive glances toward him, despite the fact that he clearly caught me a number of times staring at him.

"I didn't do anything!" he finally screamed at me, and began swatting at imaginary flies in front of his face. He was immediately surrounded staff members, as well as an imposing woman I recognized as the study director, the boss of the whole operation.

"I did everything I was supposed to," he pleaded with me. "You understand? I followed all of the rules."

I just blinked, hard, in the hopes of clearing my eyeballs of what I prayed was just another hallucination.

"It's okay, Bennett, we know you didn't do anything wrong," I heard one of the staff members tell my mustached friend, apparently named Bennett. As I watched them lead him away I heard T-Bone's voice out of nowhere.

"It's the subconscious. That's what kills you. Not the staying awake."

T-Bone was lying on the floor next to me and staring straight up at the ceiling as though nothing at all was happening.

"It's all the stuff you try not to think about during the day," he continued. "The stuff that comes out in your head at night when you're supposed to be asleep."

I watched them wrangle Bennett toward the doorway. To my relief he turned his attention to the crowd of staff around him, pleading with them to allow him to stay.

"See, I'm different. I have no subconscious. Everything with me is on the surface. What you see is what you get. Most people though, when they get shit they can't deal with, they just put it in their subconscious. Let their brain handle it when they're asleep."

"WHY WON'T ANYONE LET ME EXPLAIN?" Bennett's voice echoed from the hallway.

"You don't sleep, the subconscious overflows."

The mood thereafter changed markedly from the languid pace of a Depression-era dance marathon to a kind of "who's next?" tension as participants were gradually eliminated from the study.

We were sailors lost at sea, treading water, waiting to be attacked by sharks; at least that's what it looked like when one of us would suddenly cry, scream, or shake hysterically for no apparent reason and have to be led away to the waiting cots and blankets in the basement. Bennett was the first of these "shark attacks," and after him they occurred sometimes as many as a handful at a time.

At the one-hundred-hour mark without REM sleep, verbal communication breaks down, to the point that you lose track of what you were saying in the middle of a sentence, or forget names of common objects. I did my best to keep tabs on Audrey's well-being, but by this point it was pretty much every man (or woman) for themselves. I was having enough trouble managing my own subconscious, as T-Bone would describe it. There was no question I was under the influence of some chemical agent, for my throbbing brain was clearly clattering along on all cylinders completely unaware that it was time to rest. The generally accepted best practice at this stage in the experiment was taking a comfortable position and holding the PVC unit close to your face, the bodies around the room flinching instinctively whenever their light turned red in a newly developed evolutionary adaptation that allowed fleeting intervals of a very poor substitute for sleep.

I don't remember how long I stayed in that position, or the incoherent responses I murmured to the attendants as they made their hourly rounds. I do remember at some point I drifted away, transported to the Cape Cod beach where my parents would take me to visit my grandfather before he died, although for some reason it was very clear in my head that I was in the small seaside town of Mays Landing. I couldn't have been more than five years old. It must have been long ago as my mother looked young and beautiful sitting on a blanket on the beach, before she gained all of her weight, laughing at my father and me down at the water's edge. I was trying to pull him in deeper, where the ocean waves were breaking, to show him how tough I was and how I wasn't afraid. I'm clinging to my father's hand as I am thrown in the surf. I look up and my father is laughing, and his smile doesn't have that dangerous edge now, and I laugh too even though I'm sputtering, gasping for air as another wave knocks me over, and there's so much I want to tell him right now if I could only hold on longer.

Then I became aware that I was not gripping the hand of my father, but the arm of Audrey. I was digging my fingers into her arm and flailing beneath the desk with her, and she was shouting at me to stop. A posse of attendants were all talking to me, and I must have been creating a scene because none other than the study director was in front of me, gently getting me to my feet while my PVT device was taken from me. I tried to explain about my father and other things I couldn't possibly have articulated even if I had a full month of sleep, sounding just as lost as the other shark attack fatalities. I remember Audrey crying and clinging to me and telling anyone that would listen that I wasn't crazy, I was just abnormal. People were trying to separate us until they finally led us both out together, clutching each other, through the door and downstairs into a basement area. A number of cots were lined up with flimsy pillows like you get on airline flights and what looked to be worn army blankets folded underneath them. Audrey and I lay on a cot together, clutching each other, eyes tightly shut amidst what felt like a whirlwind of commotion around us. A perfect storm of subconscious thoughts thundered through my brain: Audrey, T-Bone, my father, The Rage, and for some reason a small seaside town in New Jersey bearing a name similar to my own that I had never visited.

Chapter 22. FOR THE BETTERMENT OF HUMANITY

Regardless of whether going without sleep for the better part of a week had any permanent psychological effects, it represented a turning point in our careers as human guinea pigs. In addition to taking almost a full week to recover, for the first time Audrey began to join me in vetoing potential gigs. Money, particularly cash flow, was always an issue; we were living hand-to-mouth with no safety net, so we couldn't exactly pick and choose. Still, it was a relief not to be the only naysayer in the group.

"It's an easy five hundred bucks a month. You put it on your forehead, bam, check-of-the-month club," T-Bone explained to Audrey on the way back to New York.

"A tattoo? On my face? What's it gonna say?" Audrey's skepticism relieved me, although I literally wasn't in a position to comment. We were in our usual space in the back corner of an almost deserted bus, and I had my head underneath a sweatshirt manually sucking breast milk from her nipple and spitting it into the plastic receptacle we had removed from our no longer functioning Milk Maid 9600 unit. It was easier than arguing with Audrey, who grew frustrated trying to squeeze it out with her fingertips.

"Just an advertisement. Like a little billboard."

"So they make a for real Coca-Cola tattoo on my forehead, and I walk around outside so people can see it?"

"Nah nah," T-Bone responded, as if the thought were absurd. "It's mostly porn sites. Like getting paid to wear makeup."

"Except it says 'pussy.com' and you can't ever take it off." I blurted out from under Audrey's sweatshirt, milk spilling from the corners of my mouth. Audrey gave me a light smack on the head as a gentle reminder to remain focused.

"Getting a tattoo removed these days is nothing. Takes five minutes. You can hardly tell anything was even there."

Some jobs sounded reasonable enough until we actually arrived at the address, which meant we already had to shell out transportation costs. We left a trial for a new kind of synthetic skin after having traveled six hours all the way down to Delaware by bus when Audrey caught a glimpse of one of the participants leaving the test facility. It appeared to be a woman, or at least someone slight in stature, although it was difficult to tell beneath the hooded windbreaker, sunglasses, and light fabric decorative gloves they wore despite the warm weather. The face around the dark lenses of her sunglasses, the only part of her body that was not covered, was blotches of purple and blue and covered in scab.

"Oh my god ..." Audrey started to hyperventilate as the door closed behind her. "Oh my god ..."

"It's okay, we don't have to stay," I said, putting down a pile of release forms and taking her by the arm.

"What?" T-Bone asked in genuine surprise. "Where we going?"

"Oh my god ..." Audrey repeated as I led her toward the exit. T-Bone was only reluctantly following, protesting with each step.

"I didn't even think she looked that bad. Maybe it was an improvement?"

She had a similar reaction when she found a human eyeball floating in a mayonnaise jar in a refrigerator she was storing her breast milk in on an overnight. It was for some secret mad scientist club run by students from the Massachusetts Institute of Technology testing an intestinal medical camera, whereby we would swallow whole a synthetic pill the size of a grape that was actually a tiny encapsulated video camera. The three of us had to spend the night at a fraternity house outside Boston waiting for it to pass, which turned out to be a protracted and very painful process, while video of each of our respective gastrointestinal systems was streamed live onto a set of laptops and recorded for posterity. We could hear cheers of drunken fraternity brothers for what we first assumed to be a Red Sox game on television on the floor below as each of us sat on the toilet trying to expel the device. I learned later they were in fact watching the inside of our colons, having turned the whole event into an elaborate drinking game, making bets on when the excretion would occur for each of us, swigging beer and high-fiving with each contraction.

Thus, by the time we made our trip up to Arthur Avenue in the Bronx for what T-Bone had promised was a one-day brain stimulation experiment, we had reached rock bottom, worn down both physically and emotionally in a sludge of calamine lotion, peanut butter, and stale breast milk. T-Bone was working overtime to keep our spirits up.

"Twenty bucks each for walking through the door, and that's just the start," T-Bone reassured us as he pushed the buzzer to the ornately carved doors of a brownstone. It was a once beautiful building that had fallen into disrepair in what had been an Italian neighborhood before the riots and de-gentrification of the sixties, a vestige from a lost civilization.

We were buzzed in without a word, pushing through the doors and into a dark foyer with checkered tile floors and walls completely covered with portraits, mirrors, and other decorations. Stacks of books, mail, newspapers, and other assorted clutter were piled about, and there were small pedestals on which rested an impressive display of taxidermy, primarily stuffed birds and small animals. It had the feel of a museum or antique shop that had been long neglected, and the room had a musty, stale smell, like dirty laundry. I was drawn to a particularly prominent black and white photograph of a mustached man in World War II-era uniform. As I drew closer, I recognized the iron cross and swastika he was wearing and read the small letters at the bottom: Josef Mengele.

"We have to leave," I announced, recognizing the portrait of the famed Nazi known as the Angel of Death for his experiments with concentration camp prisoners. "We have to leave now."

As if in answer, down a dark spiral staircase came the largest Doberman I had ever seen, a truly terrifying beast with a spiked collar. It was dragging a leash behind it, and I froze in terror as it trotted directly over to me and stuck its snout in my crotch.

"What a cute doggie!" Audrey exclaimed, coming over to rub the ears of this dog that could easily have ripped the three of us to shreds. I watched astounded as the dog licked her face.

"Ampere!" a voice called from the staircase.

It was a man's tone but high pitched, with an accent I couldn't identify, something Eastern European. Descending footsteps followed, slowly, one step and then a rest.

"Ah, he likes you, yes. This is good."

Down the stairs came a very old, slight man in a worn plaid bathrobe over pajamas, with gnarled gray hair that stuck straight out from his head and bulging eyes that were magnified by the thick glasses he wore, like he had stuck his tongue into an electrical outlet. The most accurate description I could give is a wiry Albert Einstein on crack cocaine. He stopped at the bottom of the stairs to catch his breath and look us over, patting his dog as it came back and licked his hand.

He saw me next to the portrait of Mengele and stepped toward me.

"Do not fear science. It has no country. No political party. It does not seek power," he admonished. "We learned more about the limits of the human physiology from the Nazis than anyone before or since. Yet it remains ignored by the scientific community."

He said "Nazis" with a soft z, like "naz-zees" and in general spoke in spurts, as if the thought might evaporate if he didn't get it out quickly enough.

"You do not look like the usual volunteers," he commented, pulling a wad of money out the pocket of his bathrobe and peeling a $20 bill for each of us. He introduced himself as Doctor Katz or Doctor Schatz, but Audrey would later call him Doctor Whack, which seemed more appropriate, and how we would forever refer to him.

"We are not usual volunteers. We work in the name of science, and knowledge," T-Bone announced, stepping forward ceremoniously. "Please tell us how we may be of service in this most noble experiment."

I rolled my eyes at T-Bone's pandering, meant to suck every last potential dollar out of each experiment. Both Dr. Whack and the dog were clearly enamored with Audrey, however.

"Excellent," beamed Dr. Whack. "You have completed the paperwork?"

"Actually no—" I tried to interject, but he had already taken Audrey by the arm and turned away.

"Please come with me, my darlings."

We followed him through the foyer and into a narrow, claustrophobic hallway similarly covered with seemingly unrelated photos and memorabilia, walking single file as Dr. Whack spoke. His dog, still dragging the leash on the tiled floor, trailed behind us.

"You see, my dear, I began my research many years ago when my Ingala was first diagnosed. Two very small alternating signals of slightly different frequency. This results in current having a recurring modulation of amplitude, based on the difference in frequency between the two signals. The results have been extraordinary."

Audrey nodded sympathetically as if everything Dr. Whack said made perfect sense. He paused by a doorway and took off his glasses, touching his eyes. Was he crying?

"For my wife Ingala and myself, it has been nothing less than a miracle," he continued in a voice indeed seemed to crack with emotion. He finally looked into the room to his right and called in a cheerful voice.

"How are we today, my flower?"

The three of us peered through the doorway next to him, into what appeared to be a library equal in creepiness to the rest of the house, illuminated primarily through a giant bay window on the other end of the room. A lone thin silhouette sat motionless in a wheelchair, her features masked in shadow in a very unsettling Bates Motel kind of way.

"There. There is the inspiration for my research."

He put his glasses back on and beamed again at Audrey, who cast a desperate glance in my direction telling me to say something, anything.

"Nice," I finally offered.

"Her flesh is supple to the touch," he said as if in reply, and continued down the hall. "Of course, at even a few milliamps of current, no microorganism can survive. The Soviets knew about this, their space program, all of the astronauts received multiple currents per day, pulsed currents, eighty milliamps."

Ahead of us Dr. Whack stopped before a large industrial metal door that looked like it belonged on a meat locker, crudely chained shut with a padlock. He turned around and looked behind us.

"Come, Ampere. Come."

The dog had stopped following for some reason and stood watching twenty feet behind us.

"Come here, Ampere."

Ampere finally turned around and trotted off in the opposite direction. Dr. Whack sighed wistfully.

"She does not go downstairs with me anymore."

It took him six tries to open the combination lock, all the while reading a string of numbers he had scribbled on the door, which seemed to defeat the purpose of locking it in the first place.

"You've completed your paperwork?" he asked again when he was finally able to swing the door open, revealing a narrow staircase leading downward.

"Yes," T-Bone answered immediately.

We followed him down into a well-lit basement with a cement floor and cinder block walls, with long fluorescent lights lining the ceiling. Like the first floor, the walls were almost completely covered, this time with scientific looking graphs with cryptic, mostly illegible notations. The one exception was a large oil painting, a portrait of Nikola Tesla, whose name was inscribed on the frame. A quote superimposed along the bottom read:

"Science is but a perversion of itself unless it has as its ultimate goal the betterment of humanity."

There was a sofa and chairs scattered about, and an antiquated desk covered with dusty texts and papers. The centerpiece of the room however was what looked like a homemade reclining dentist chair attached the floor with straps on the armrests. Next to it was a tray table covered with clutter, beneath which some kind of antiquated electrical contraption the size of a large suitcase with knobs and protruding wires rested on the floor.

"Please, sit," the doctor offered, motioning to the overstuffed couch. "Perhaps you would feel more comfortable if I demonstrated on myself?"

"Actually that's not necessary—" I started to protest, having seen more than enough, but Dr. Whack was already saddling up in his dentist's chair, searching through trash on the tray table next to him. T-Bone yanked me downward onto the sofa where he and Audrey were seated.

"I usually give myself, every morning, just a few milliamps to prepare for the day."

Dr. Whack was ripping open what looked like packets of sugar, from which he produced self-adhesive padded electrodes.

"Most people are unaware they can reset themselves. They have a button to change everything back to when they came out of the factory, yes?"

Dr. Whack was affixing small metal clips attached to the wires protruding from the contraption to each of the electrodes, and peeling off the back like a Band-Aid. There were four in total, which he placed along his forehead, just beneath the hair line. Then he took what looked like some kind of wooden joystick with a button on the end.

"I must continually apply pressure. If I pass out, the current is interrupted."

"Safety first," T-Bone agreed.

I was about to protest, stop this man before he set himself on fire, when he pressed his thumb on the button. There was a click, and then a buzz lasting a few seconds while the lights in the room browned out momentarily. Audrey let out a gasp. The lights came back on full power to reveal Dr. Whack leaning back in his makeshift dentist chair, eyes closed, motionless. The wooden joystick dropped from his hand and clattered to the floor.

"Yes. Yes."

He blinked, then took a deep breath, like a junkie who had just gotten his fix.

"Yes, that's it. That moment. That one sublime moment of clarity."

Returning home from spring break during my sophomore year of boarding school I discovered that my mother had undergone ECT treatment for her depression, which would keep her bedridden sometimes for days at a time. No one ever told me about it; that wasn't our way, although I discovered literature on the subject in my father's study. He only spoke in vague terms about a "new treatment" my mother was undergoing, taking her to sessions every other day over a period of weeks. I didn't notice anything different about her other than perhaps additional memory loss and forgetfulness, although that was always an issue due to the steady stream of tranquilizers and sedatives my father fed her (many of which were likely at least partially responsible for her significant weight gain that so infuriated him). Truth be told we both might have benefited if he were the one getting 200 milliamps of electric current passing through the frontal and medial temporal lobe of his brain.

"We start at 50 milliamps for six seconds, then increase the voltage by ten milliamps each round," explained Dr. Whack. "I pay $10 per milliamp."

Dr. Whack reached down to pick up the wooden joystick and held it out to us.

"So. Who will be first?"

I got up to leave and was about to thank him for his time when I heard T-Bone and Audrey's voice behind me in perfect unison.

"I'll go."

"Splendid!"

I looked back at Audrey, aghast.

"No. Just no."

"I can only accommodate one at a time—"

"We're leaving." I grabbed Audrey's arm, but she resisted.

"Let go!"

"I got this," T-Bone said confidently, rising to his feet. "Five hundred bucks for six seconds? You kidding? Dinner's on me tonight."

"I'll make it a thousand for the girl," the good doctor offered generously.

"Do you understand what this does?" I sputtered at Audrey. "It zaps your brain cells and erases your memory."

"Of course it does," Dr. Whack interjected. "That's how it works. What is it do you think that makes you so unhappy?"

He was looking directly at me, as if in that eerie moment he was peering into my soul. I stared at him a minute, and then at Audrey, then realized he was right. Fuck it. I'd reboot my brain back to the factory preset. Maybe it would succeed where medication had failed. Hopefully it would at least jolt enough sense in me to stop wasting my life traveling from one freak show like this to the next.

"Fine. I'll do it."

My sudden change in demeanor clearly unnerved all them, including the doctor.

"Eh ... you need to change clothes," he protested, rising to his feet.

"Mays, stop," Audrey said quietly.

"I don't need to change clothes," I responded as I hopped into his dentist chair. "What do I need to change clothes for?"

"You need to wear the diaper."

"I'm not wearing a diaper."

"Stop, Mays," Audrey repeated.

"Stop what? I can do whatever I want," I retorted. "It's my body," I added, throwing in a T-Boneism for good measure.

"I'll go," T-Bone offered up, trying to defuse the situation.

"Fine, no diaper," the doctor relented, obviously sensing our ambivalence and anxious to close the deal.

"Mays, let T-Bone do it," Audrey persisted. "He's good at this shit."

I was about to protest again when she added a final, quiet "Please."

I reluctantly got out of the chair, as Dr. Whack produced a towel that he spread with great flourish across the seat.

"Not necessary, Doc. I got an iron bladder," T-Bone explained, making himself comfortable in the dentist chair. "I've had six gallons of saline injected into it without spilling a drop. All about muscle control."

The good doctor was a whirl of energy now, fussing with controls on the homemade ECT machine on the floor. At T-Bone's insistence he paid us first, counting out twenty-five $20 bills.

"This for both of our protection," the doctor added excitedly as he strapped T-Bone's forearms to the arms of the dentist chair. "And this for your mouth, to protect the tongue."

He found a mouthpiece from beneath the clutter on the side table and shoved it into T-Bone's mouth.

"Is that sterile—"

Before I could finish there was a click, then the buzzing from the ECT unit. Through the browned-out lights I could see the silhouette of Dr. Whack holding his homemade button-plunger, a freakish grin on his face, which was no more than six inches away from T-Bone's. The six seconds seemed like an eternity as T-Bone's body pulsated, becoming rigid at first and then convulsing wildly. Dr. Whack was holding his other hand over T-Bone's mouth, from which foamy saliva started spurting forth between his fingers. I leapt from my seat to pull him away, and he finally released the button on the wooden box. The buzzing stopped. I pulled away the mouthpiece that had become dislodged in T-Bone's mouth in a pool of froth.

"Talk to us, T-Bone. Say something."

I was pulling the electrodes off of his forehead; the wires were hot to the touch. T-Bone was staring at the ceiling, his face expressionless, eyes almost completely dilated.

"Can you hear me, T-Bone? Let us know you're okay."

I unstrapped his arms and found a pulse. His breathing was forced but steady.

"Say something, T-Bone," Audrey pleaded through tears.

There was the faint smell of burning flesh, along with the stench of urine as T-Bone finally looked down to his crotch area, where he had wet himself.

"It's okay, we're going home now," I said hastily.

"I need to conduct the post-treatment interview. It is very important for my research," Dr. Whack protested. Audrey and I ignored him, helping T-Bone to his feet.

"Come on, T-Bone, we're going home."

Strangely enough I did have an epiphany of sorts, even though it was T-Bone who had received the voltage to the brain. The experience of watching him get electrocuted gave me a newfound clarity of thought and perspective.

"I can't do this anymore."

It was a simple statement, and I made it to Audrey and T-Bone in a Bee-Line Bus heading back to Manhattan an hour later. We were sitting in one of those four-tops, with two pairs of seats facing each other. Audrey was directly across from me, picking pills out of a giant prescription bottle in which she had consolidated all of her medication for that day. T-Bone lay next to her with his head in her lap. His eyes were open, but he still wasn't saying anything.

"I don't care how much money we make. I don't care if we're saving the world. Not if it means we have to hurt ourselves."

We needed to get back to the NYU fertility clinic for Audrey's final checkup, two days before her eggs were harvested. She continued to select pills in a variety of colors and shapes from the bottle, then swallowed the fistful of medication dry.

"Not if it means hurting people I care about."

I felt good after I'd said it, and it occurred to me how long it had been since I had felt that way. Audrey just gave a weary sigh, replaced the top on her pill bottle and put it in her backpack, careful to not disturb T-Bone as she started rummaging through it again.

"So after going through this shit for two months you want me to stop now right before we get paid?" she asked, pulling a direct-from-manufacturer prefilled 12 cc. disposable syringe out of her backpack. She lifted up her t-shirt, exposing a stomach covered in bruises and track marks.

"All that legal shit we signed?"

She wasn't exaggerating. There were in fact so many details and obstacles that had to be overcome in the whole egg donation process that I somehow never believed we would make it to this point. First she needed to be selected from a list of donors in a medical database based on physical appearance or whatever other criteria the potential recipient was looking for. Then there were the regular hormone injections, checkups and ultrasounds at the clinic. By far the most stressful part to Audrey, however, was the mandatory psychological consult, required to ensure she was mentally prepared to undertake and complete the donation process. Audrey viewed it as a kind of final examination and referendum on her life. T-Bone had prepped her about what to tell them, obviously skirting over how we had made our living over the past months. I felt terrible for secretly praying either the psych exam or some elevated level in her blood work would disqualify her from becoming a donor. However, not only did the psychological consult turn out to be perfunctory ("They asked me if I like to smash shit, stuff like that," was her summary), but it turned out that physically Audrey was as fertile as a tropical rainforest.

Audrey ran her hand across her stomach, then gripped an inch of flesh firmly between her thumb and forefinger. I watched her as she bit off the plastic tip and jabbed the exposed needle into her side without flinching.

"You wanna give up $3,000 just like that?" she added, watching as the human chorionic gonadotropin emptied out of the syringe.

"Fine. So we do the eggs and then stop."

She extracted the needle from her stomach and absently discarded it on the floor of the bus. I picked it up.

"What about Longwood? It's like T-Bone said. Getting $4,000 just to chill for three months?"

"After Longwood then—"

There was an electric buzz around us as one of the passengers in the rear pressed the signal for the bus to stop. It was not unlike the noise emitted from Dr. Whack's antiquated ECT machine and all of us, including T-Bone, jumped in our seats.

"Okay," she said simply.

"We'll have enough by then to—"

"I said okay," she said again, in a why-can't-you-take-yes-for-an-answer-and-shut-up kind of way, so I didn't say anything more.

Egg harvesting is a much more invasive and potentially dangerous proposition than producing breast milk. The actual process of removing the eggs is achieved through a small ultrasound-guided needle inserted into the vagina to aspirate the follicles in both ovaries, which extracts the eggs. The procedure lasted approximately 30 minutes with Audrey fully under anesthesia, with a couple of hours' recovery time. Audrey insisted that we cash the check immediately, and the thrill of walking around with $3,000 in her pocket was enough to outweigh the mild after-effects of her surgery. After a celebratory dinner, the three of us capped off the evening by splurging on a budget hotel in the East Village.

Our celebration turned out to be short-lived. Audrey woke up that night feeling violently ill, nauseous and bloated, tossing back up her penne vodka and all-you-can-eat breadsticks from dinner. She similarly wasn't able to keep any food down the following day, and her symptoms and abdominal bloating grew progressively worse to the point that she could barely stand by the time we took her back to the NYU fertility clinic that afternoon. She was diagnosed with OHSS, or ovarian hyperstimulation syndrome. They proceeded to drain almost two liters of fluid from her abdominal cavity with a needle which, as unpleasant as the experience was, provided immediate relief. By the time they were finished with her, however, it was clear that the money she had received for her eggs wasn't quite the bargain she thought it was eight weeks before when she first embarked on this journey. As I waited for an elevator on our way back to the hotel afterward, I noticed Audrey lingering at the other end of the hallway, outside the entrance to the clinic, gazing almost wistfully inside.

"It's her," she called to me.

I walked back and followed her gaze through glass doors to the main lobby, where I saw what had caught her attention. Pacing in front of a row of chairs and speaking into a cellular phone was a genuine power bitch, replete in a dark business suit and an ornate necklace. She was older than us, late thirties, and was with a similarly professionally-dressed spectacled gentleman in a suit who was talking to the nurse at the desk.

"The one getting my eggs."

"That could be anybody," I protested.

"No. It's her."

There were tears in her eyes. I didn't argue. I suppose it didn't matter, it might as well have been her. At the very least, this clearly was not a woman who was there to sell her eggs for three grand.

"You did a good thing," I told her. "You know that, don't you? Forget the money. You did something good for another person. Even if it's not her. You did a good thing for someone somewhere."

The woman on the phone inside froze as she caught sight of Audrey staring at her through the glass. Their eyes locked.

"You helped someone. You changed their life. That should make you feel good."

I couldn't tell if Audrey's tears were due to her lingering OHSS symptoms, the culmination of the past months of hard living, or perhaps the growing realization that the path to Power Bitchdom lay not through the soup kitchens, research laboratories and fertility clinics of this world.

"I feel like shit," was all she said, and finally turned away.

Chapter 23. LONGWOOD

It was a disturbingly trivial matter to tie up the loose ends of our existence and lock up the Palmisano family crypt for possibly the last time. We departed with all our worldly possessions to North Carolina, for what I had every intention of being our final experiment, the exclamation point punctuating the end of this strange chapter of my life. I had no idea what would come next, or even where. We'd have three months in lockdown to figure that out, not to mention a modest nest egg at the end that, for the first time, would give us some financial breathing room. Truthfully I didn't care, as long as it didn't involve needles, pills, or experiments of any kind. As long as there was Audrey.

We gathered at a hotel off Interstate 40 in Durham for a one-day orientation where we filled out paperwork and listened to what was in store for us over the next twelve weeks before a line of buses took us to the Longwood Clinical Research Facility and Medical Center the following morning. I suppose any lucrative large-scale trial was likely to draw from the same recurring national pool of pharmaceutical test jockeys. Still, this was, even by my hardened standards, a bizarre sight. There were hundreds of people, a sort of convention or summer camp for professional human guinea pigs. T-Bone worked his way through the crowds back-slapping and swapping war stories with old acquaintances and introducing Audrey and me to other luminaries in the industry, rattling off their histories like he was reading the back of a baseball card. This included the original testers of the first contact lens, and an aging hippy woman who, according to T-Bone, was single-handedly responsible for the advent of roll-on deodorant. We also met an elderly gentleman of few words, introduced as Scratch, who had worked with T-Bone years back on an erectile dysfunction trial. He was in a wheelchair with an oxygen tank between his legs, and if his Little Elvis was still functional it was apparently one of the few parts of his body that was. Finally, there was a young wunderkind with a ponytail named Sergey who had just spent the better part of three days floating upside-down in a sensory deprivation tank for some classified experiment for the Department of Defense. I admit feeling a tad jealous when T-Bone built him up to be such a rock star. Sergey didn't even look up from the copy of *Pharmacy Today* he was reading when T-Bone introduced us but gave a haughty nod, barely acknowledging our existence.

I spent most of my time beneath a canopy in the sweltering North Carolina summer heat, busying myself with the paperwork left for me in my role as secretary of our little enterprise. It was clear we had graduated to the big leagues, at least from the number of forms I had to fill out and the level of security present. Each of us had to sign no less than a dozen non-disclosure, limitation of liability, and other intimidating legal documents waiving any right we may have to anything, anywhere in the universe. Hoping it would be my last time selling my body to science, or perhaps to ensure that it was, I spared no detail going into my own and my family's sordid history of depression and medication, even asking for extra paper when space on the forms ran out. It was one of the few studies we participated in that I was qualified for, if not over-qualified. If they were looking for a yardstick with which to measure the anti-depressive properties of their new wonder drug they certainly would get their money's worth out of me.

Dozens of Longwood staff members, all in blue polo shirts with the Longwood logo and khakis, milled about directing traffic, as well as representatives from the client, JCN Pharmaceuticals, who were clearly supervising the operation. We were given a JCN goodie bag filled with corporate trinkets, and then they herded all of us into a giant ballroom elaborately set up for a kind of pep rally, with fluorescent lights, lots of balloons, lasers, refreshments, and loud music. There were giant television screens, upon which we were first treated to a slickly produced video on JCN's history and products. Afterward a thin, very stylishly dressed young black man with nerd glasses and a headset hopped up on stage to welcome us, clearly a master of ceremonies type.

"Are you all ready for the biggest clinical trial in history?"

We all applauded good-naturedly.

"I can't heeeeeeeaaaaar you!" he shouted back at us, cupping a hand to his ear as the audience cheered more loudly.

The master of ceremonies went over some of the logistics with us, such as what a phase three trial was for the greenhorns who hadn't been to one before. We were part of a double-blind randomized control trial, generally considered the gold standard for any clinical trial. It was a placebo-controlled trial, meaning participants would randomly receive either JCN-4830, the compound being tested, or a placebo. Double-blind meant that neither the participants nor the researchers running the trial would be aware of who had received what. I wished I was sitting in the back of the room with T-Bone and the rest of the cool kids, veteran guinea pigs like myself who were too sophisticated for this primer on drug development. Audrey, however, was taking the whole affair much more seriously and insisted on sitting in the first row and used the pad and paper provided by the hotel to take copious notes.

The lights dimmed again, and we were treated to another short video introducing JCN-4830. From what I could glean beneath the layers of marketing propaganda, the theory was that JCN-4830, a magical concoction of antigens that simulated the physical effects of depression, supposedly worked like a traditional vaccination. Once exposed, your immune system would develop depression-fighting antibodies to circulate in the blood and trigger an immune response whenever the symptoms reappeared.

"*Why are we here?*" a soft, reassuring female voice asked us over pastoral images of running streams, mountain tops, and sunsets on video screens around us. "*What is the purpose of it all?*" she asked again, over a backdrop of traffic jams, a woman being chastised by her boss in an office, and other images of the travails of modern life.

"*And why can't I be happy? If you find yourself wondering these things, you're not alone.*"

Suddenly, we're hurtling through an animation of the human blood stream, watching an invading army of evil-looking molecules labeled as antigens by a foreboding subtitle.

"Scientists at JCN Pharmaceuticals have long suspected that our immune system, with its T cells that protect our bodies against attackers like bacteria, cancer, and viruses like HIV, has more to do with protecting our mental health than previously believed ..."

Animated helper T cells were now racing through the blood stream sounding the alarm in an over-simplified cartoon depiction of the cell-mediated immune response that occurs in the vaccination process.

"... linking depression and mood with raised levels of proinflammatory cytokines and other markers of inflammation through years of research and clinical trials for disorders such as allergies, autoimmunity, and inflammatory bowel disease."

We were now watching cytotoxic T-lymphocytes, or killer T cells, caricatured like super-heroes, answer the call and rescue distressed cells already infected by the antigens by fighting them off with tiny swords. Nearby B-lymphocytes, looking like little firemen whose hoses sprayed animated bullets called antibodies, stop the marauding antigens dead in their tracks.

"Through a groundbreaking vaccination with immunoregulation-inducing organisms — which contribute to the anti-depressive interactions of some of today's most effective medications — JCN is once again blazing new trails ..."

The battle is won, the invading antigens gone, however, a few of the T-lymphocytes and B-lymphocytes, now classified as memory cells another subtitle tells us, continue to patrol the perimeter.

"Empowering our body's natural defenses and immune system to protect us from the debilitating effects of depression and mental illness ..."

Back in the "real" world, a stressed-out mother is rubbing her temples as in the living room behind her, two young children clobber each other playfully with couch pillows.

"... enhancing our ability to cope with the many "cold pricklies" that life throws at us ..."

Back inside her blood stream the same depression-bearing antigens once again rear their ugly heads. This time, however, the patrolling memory cells know exactly what to do. The T cells become saber-wielding kamikazes once again, and the B cells start spraying antibodies. They make short work of the overmatched antigens.

"... and allowing us to lead happier, more fulfilling and productive lives ..."

Back outside her bloodstream, our stressed-out mother decides to smile instead of sinking into depression. She grabs a cushion from the couch and joins in the pillow fight, to the delight of her children. Mental health crisis averted. When the video was over, the master of ceremonies emerged on stage again, even more energized than before.

"And now it is my pleasure to introduce to you, our fearless leader, the big boss, please make some noise for JCN's Regional Vice President of North American Clinical Development, Mr. Stuuuuuuuu Jansen!"

More cheers, as the JCN staff standing by the walls all let out a low "Stuuuuuuuu" chant, which I would learn is what you were supposed to do whenever Stu entered the room. As he played with the crowd, cheering with them and then feigning embarrassment at their continued ovation, I tried to quantify why I had such an immediate negative reaction to him. He looked to be mid-fortyish, and his suit jacket was removed, tie loosened and sleeves rolled up to reveal a huge physique with big, beefy cop forearms that he was obviously proud of. Both his body and his fist-pump mannerisms screamed ex-jock to me, probably a football player years ago with a body and gut that had softened with middle age. He was no doubt an active member of the proverbial old boy network, the kind of guy who would fit in perfectly out on the links at some corporate golfing event. Someone who had spent his life sitting at the cool kids' table, a grown-up, overweight version of everyone who had ever bullied me in elementary school.

Stu leaned forward to speak into the microphone and it became immediately apparent that it wasn't functioning. After a tap he pointed to it and shouted out in a booming voice loud enough to make any amplification unnecessary.

"Uh-oh ... a cold prickly!"

Laughter and applause, as Stu called out to a woman named Penny, a waifish blond assistant who appeared with a working wireless microphone.

"Six years. Close to four billion, that's billion with a B, dollars in research and development. More North Carolina barbecue than we care to admit. And here we are," Stu announced. More cheers.

"That's bullshit, them talking about how much money it costs to invent a new drug," I whispered to Audrey. "Most of the money goes to marketing." I figured I would use the opportunity to show off my insider knowledge, but she only shushed me, clearly afraid I was going to get her in trouble with Stu, the Regional Director of Whatever at JCN. I slouched in my chair.

"It's been a team effort getting to this point. There's too many people thank everyone, but I do want to give a shout out to my staff, who have been busting their tail to make this moment possible. Schmatzie? Boom Boom? Roo? Tonto?"

There was more applause and hoots of enthusiasm as Stu called out each of his lieutenants by their nickname, which apparently was a requirement working for Stu, all with their ties loosened and sleeves rolled up exactly like him.

"Close to a $100,000," Stu continued. "That's what each one of you is costing us over the next three months. Almost a $1,000 per day. But it's not about the money. That's not what this is about."

He shook his head and paused for dramatic effect.

"JCN-4830 is about people. About you, and me. About our children. And their future. About making each of us the very best we can be. Think about that. Think about what a world like that would look like."

And for an instant I tried to do just that, imagining everyone back at St. Christopher's, the mole people, Jerry Manfredi at America Direct, my mother, my father, how different the world would be if we were all under the influence of this cold-prickly killing vaccination.

"How would that change how we treat each other? If we all could lead happy, fulfilling lives. All of us. Everywhere. What happens to things like crime? War?"

So JCN-4830 was the drug to end all wars. I supposed if Prozac was around in 1930s Berlin, Hitler might have just admired the sunset instead of invading Poland. Stu cleared his throat and, whether feigned or real, choked up, his voice quavering with emotion.

"I'd like to take this opportunity to thank you. Each one of you. And let me be very clear about what you are doing. By making each of us the very best we can be, healthier, happier, we can change ourselves. We can change each other. And together, we can change the *world*."

Music blared, and with that, Stu Jansen, JCN's Regional Vice President of North American Clinical Development, left the stage to thunderous applause, as if he had just accepted the Republican presidential nomination.

The first step to changing the world involved surrendering most of our personal belongings, including any portable electronics, cameras, phones, or anything that might be used to transport or copy information. We were then loaded onto buses and given a boxed lunch. The bus ride was almost two hours long through forests and North Carolina countryside, during which T-Bone and his cronies talked shop in the back.

"They have not had hit since Suprin," Sergey explained from his seat in the back corner. He was the only one sitting alone, a symbol of his exalted status, and didn't look up from his copy of *BioSupply Trends Quarterly*. "If this does not cut mustard, they clean the house."

"What about Provax?" someone asked.

Sergey snorted as if this barely warranted a response.

"Please. Another anti-viral. Is Rimadol in different shape." He turned the page of his magazine, continuing to read without looking up. "We are taking medicine for irritable bowel. Not anti-depressant. If worked they would test overseas like is standard procedure. Instead we come to Longwood."

Developing an anti-depression medication is a particularly risky and expensive ordeal in the high-stakes world of pharmaceutical development, particularly for a company like JCN that made most of its revenue from a family of anti-viral medications. Their last true mega-hit was over a generation ago, an anti-platelet medication called Suprin, a blood thinner that helps prevent and dissolve clots in arteries and stents. That was about the time that my father joined the board of directors. There was much skepticism surrounding JCN-4830, especially for a compound that began its life years ago as an immune suppressing medication to treat irritable bowel syndrome, as Sergey informed us. Moreover, most large-scale trials like this were typically carried out overseas, where it was much easier to attract participants at a fraction of the cost of a U.S.-based trial. Longwood, the testing facility of choice for Big Tobacco back in its golden years, was notorious for providing clients with the positive outcomes they were looking for. That JCN would pay this premium indicated either the importance of the drug in their pipeline, their lack of confidence in its efficacy, or both.

We finally got to a gate at the foot of a densely wooded hill. Our bus caravan was waved through, winding its way upward and through yet another gate and into a football field-sized parking lot. The first thing to notice as we pulled to a stop was a monolithic building of dark reflective glass only a few stories high but perfectly smooth and cylindrical. I would learn that this modern structure was in fact the administrative building, and strictly off-limits to test participants. What was striking about it, in addition to its futuristic design, was how completely incongruous it was with the rest of the buildings it overlooked, which were all nestled down a small hill from the parking lot and formed a rough square around a large grassy field, known as the Quad. It was as if a flying saucer had landed on a hill overlooking a bucolic college campus of stately buildings of stone and exposed brick, with large dormitory buildings anchoring each corner of the quadrangle.

We disembarked from the buses and were led down a series of marble steps to the main campus. A kind of college freshman orientation atmosphere of excited chatter surrounded me as we took in our new home for the next three months. During our tour, however, it was clear from the ubiquitous cameras and advanced security that we were not at an institution of higher learning. Most of the hallways had a spaceship-airlock feel to them, with a sensor on each big double security door requiring a Longwood staff member to press his or her thumb on before it would buzz open. We were guided through a state-of-the-art gym, and a commissary where we could buy candy, cigarettes, magazines, and various sundries. Our tour guide explained that throughout the study we would also be given the opportunity to earn "achievement beads," which could be cashed in at the commissary, or used for other privileges.

Finally, they took us into an expansive cafeteria that easily accommodated all four hundred or so of us. After serving us snacks and coffee they read off names to divide us into four dormitory units of approximately equal size and issue identification badges we were supposed to wear around our necks for the remainder of our stay. Much to my disappointment, Audrey wasn't in my unit, nor was T-Bone. Dour and irritated, I had little interest in exchanging pleasantries with my other Unit Four designees. Our team leader (there were a half-dozen teams per unit) marched us off to a barracks-type dormitory on the north end of the campus where we were divided by sex and put into rooms of eight each, four bunk beds per room.

Each day we were each given printouts of our schedule, although after the first week it was all routine. The first order of business was always the morning checkup, where they recorded our vitals and had us sit before rows of computers where the same depression assessment tests were administered. These included the Rafaelsen Melancholia Scale, the Beck Hopelessness Scale, Clinician-Administered Rating Scale for Mania (CARS-5), the Harvard National Depression Screening Scale, the Diagnostic Inventory for Depression, the Yale-Brown Obsessive Compulsive Scale, the Zung Self-Rating Anxiety Scale and a host of others. Every. Single. Day. Usually by the end of the exercise I was so fed up with answering the same questions about my feelings of guilt, hopelessness, and other nuances of my psyche I'd stop reading the questions and blindly race through checking boxes at random.

This poorly organized activity would usually drag on past nine, meaning I would barely have time for breakfast before Group Share. This was an insufferable exercise that entailed sitting in a circle with other team members and talking about your mood that morning, and things that affected your mood, and what you can do when things affected your mood. People would cry and you'd feel like a cad for quietly stifling a yawn. Three times a week we had physical therapy, where they'd measure our performance on treadmills and a number of weightlifting drills. We had no fewer than twelve EEGs (which measures brain electrical activity) a week, including an elaborate 300 channel setup where it took them a full hour to place the hundreds of tiny sensor sticky pads over the surgical-style electro caps that covered our skulls. EEGs were administered so often many of the participants just started wearing the caps full-time. I would watch three-dimensional color images of my brain appear on a monitor next to me as a Longwood lab assistant saved them into some clinical trial software program that tracked each participant by the number on our badge.

Once a week we'd have our individual session with one of the staff psychologists. I have to admit the one who was assigned to me, a Dr. Richards, or "Marci With An I" as she introduced herself, deserved much better. If I were to describe her in the most politically incorrect of terms it would be as a really smart lesbian. She was tiny and seemed intelligent and wore men's suits and thick glasses. To her credit, she was quickly able to detect the disdain for mental health professionals that had been passed down to me from my father and my experience in medical school. Either she took it all it all in stride or was simply too busy with her workload to care.

"I need a cigarette," I mused in her office, staring at the fluorescent lights on the ceiling.

"How long have you smoked for?" she asked, flipping through my extensive paperwork.

"About a year. I wish I had started earlier though. It's terrific. Like good food, good wine."

"Chlorpromazine, diazepam, secobarbital ... it looks like you were on medication for ..." she was counting off years in her head.

"Up until about a year ago. Bipolar II depressed affective disorder. I think the ICD code is 296.5. Twenty-eight on the Asperger's scale, if that helps," I offered, trying to save us both some time.

"And you stopped the medication cold turkey?"

I just shrugged.

"Was this under the supervision of a doctor or on your own?"

"On my own."

"You didn't find medication effective any longer?"

"It wasn't that none of them worked. They all worked. They all worked in different ways. That's the thing."

"And now you're here to try another?"

"I have an open mind." It was true. My foremost desire was for JCN-4830 to be the wonder drug it was cracked up to be.

"Do you really?" Marci seemed skeptical.

"My mother has been depressed her entire adult life," I sighed. "She has a horrible marriage. She and my father hate each other. It's not rocket science. That's why she's depressed. Do you have a pill for that?"

"Medication isn't always the answer. It can help people. It worked for me."

This got my attention, as was clearly her intent.

"I've been on Ruminex for almost six years now. It probably saved my life."

"Interesting." I was trying to sound as non-committal as possible.

"After my divorce I didn't get out of bed for a month. I didn't see any reason to."

"That's what I felt like," I offered before I could catch myself.

"You felt like this before or after you discontinued your meds?"

"Mostly after."

"Was there a specific event that made you stop?"

"Yes," I answered simply, in a way that I hoped would indicate that I didn't wish to pursue this line of questioning.

"And how did it feel when you went off your medication?"

"At first it felt great. Then it all just came apart. I couldn't get out of bed. Go to classes. I didn't know if I wanted to be a doctor. Then I didn't know if I wanted to live if I wasn't going to be a doctor."

"So what did you do?"

In truth I tied a 2-ply garbage bag filled with helium around my neck, although I wasn't about to go into the details of my suicide attempt. Instead I gave the summary version.

"I just decided life wasn't worth living."

It was a logical decision, an objective conclusion I arrived at with a head clear of any medication for the first time in many years.

"Do you think that now?"

"No."

"So what changed your mind?"

I remembered I was meeting Audrey next, as my team leader had cancelled our daily Group Share session and Audrey was free until her afternoon ECT. It was a quarter before the hour, another fifteen minutes to go.

Fuck it. I couldn't wait. I rose to my feet.

"Can't be late for Group Share," I smiled apologetically, rushing toward the door to her office before she could protest. I needed to find Audrey.

During the first few weeks I was fighting a recurring panic brought about by the fact that my time with Audrey was much more limited. I was only able to see her at meal time and during our infrequent breaks during the day. As was typical for any overnight stay, I immediately set out to find an isolated place where we could fornicate. The big obstacle at Longwood was the security. In addition to the omnipresent video cameras and staff that patrolled the residency units at all hours, most entrances and exits had that sensor where you had to physically press down your right thumb to gain admittance. Stealing someone else's badge to gain access wasn't going to work, which was probably the reason the precaution was put in place to begin with. Study participants were given access only to certain spaces like our residence unit, the gym, and other common areas. We had also repeatedly been told that any inappropriate relationship with other test participants would be grounds for immediate dismissal.

It was only with the greatest of stealth and duplicity that I was able to find an unlocked gardening shack behind the Unit Three residence building that would do nicely. I even arranged the fertilizer bags to form a makeshift bed. Audrey, however, wasn't impressed when I told her about it at breakfast as she polished off a western omelet.

"They'll kick us the fuck out if they catch us. No way we can sneak out after lights out."

She was right on both counts. I was prepared with a response, however.

"We can do it before dinner time, during Personal Reflection. Just say you're taking a walk. No one will know."

"I got to be with my unit. I got serious responsibilities. What about I just give you a hand job in the bathroom?"

I was crestfallen, my fragile ego shattered. Audrey must have read my reaction. "Fine," she relented, spearing the fruit salad in my bowl with her fork.

"The food is so fucking good here, everything is so fresh," she gushed with her mouth full, her mood brightening again. She noticed the string of beads hanging around her neck atop her ID badge and held them out for me proudly.

"You see my achievement beads?"

Chapter 24. JCN-4830

It was after the first week that they started injecting us with either the JCN-4830 compound or a saline placebo. From what I was able to glean from the staff during my attempts at small talk it was 20 milligrams to start for men and 10 for the women, which would increase or decrease each week depending on symptoms and whatever the magic formula the software program they were entering the data into told them. The rumor amongst the study participants was that some of us might feel an effect after two to three days. Our bodies needed that time to create antibodies to destroy this bacterial depression in a bottle, and store the configuration in memory T cells so that, should depression rear its ugly head, our immune systems would have the chemical information needed to obliterate it. In theory it worked just like any other vaccination, except that for reasons not fully understood the antibodies and proteins generated in humans injected with the JCN-4830 compound also seemed to cause a statistically significant increase in self-reported emotional health and heightened cognitive functioning.

I immediately experienced flu-like symptoms.

I woke with a splitting headache, sore throat, head and nasal congestion and a low-grade fever, and was sent to the infirmary. Having an adverse reaction to a vaccination (which acts like a mild case of whatever you're trying to protect against so your antibodies can build up a resistance) isn't unusual, although I appeared to be one of the few participants affected in this way. The campus infirmary was a surprisingly minimal, long room with a couple of dozen beds separated by hanging curtains. The nurse would come by and check on me every few hours and bring meals. It was a measure of the nurturing environment that was being fostered, or perhaps the effects of JCN-4830, that I had a stack of get well cards already waiting for me there when I first arrived, many from other test participants I had never heard of. I flipped through them in amazement as I settled under the covers of my bed, apparently alone in the infirmary. The only other sign of life was the low whir of a machine coming from the bathroom. Sergey finally emerged, in a bathrobe, holding an electric blow dryer. His ponytail was undone, and damp hair flowed down below his shoulders.

I sneezed uncontrollably, then wiped my nose with a tissue through watering eyes. I held out the tissue box to Sergey, hoping we could bond over our shared illness.

"You too?" I smiled weakly.

"No," he said, taking a seat on a bed a few down from me. He took a hair band off the table next to it and began fixing his ponytail.

"Is better to pretend symptoms when medication starts. Then you see first what happens to others."

I nodded, impressed, then looked around the empty infirmary. "Well, so far so good it looks like."

This elicited one of Sergey's trademark scoffs.

"The sick people they take to main clinic in administrative building," he said, motioning out the window behind his bed and up the hill where the dark circular administrative building sat overlooking the Longwood campus like an alien spaceship. Sergey finished adjusting his ponytail and picked up a copy of *Drug Discovery and Development* magazine, adding almost as an afterthought, "Where no one can see."

I was about to respond when there was a loud THUMP on the window behind my own bed, and I turned to see a group of study participants I recognized from T-Bone's unit, all waving and shouting at me through the window.

"Feel better, Mays!"

"We miss you!"

"God bless you, Mays!"

I could only see the tops of their heads as they all filed past in the quadrangle outside, each shouting words of encouragement as if I was one of their dearest friends, these people who I had merely passed in hallways and shared tables with in the cafeteria. Finally T-Bone's head appeared. He had to jump to get his eye level up to the window, giving him the appearance of being on a trampoline as he attempted to converse with me.

"How you feeling?" Jump. "We gotta talk!" Jump. "Remember the farm?" Jump. "Lots of interest!"

I reached back to the strings of the Venetian blind hanging from the window and pulled to release it.

T-Bone jumped again, wisps of wild gray hair flapping in the wind, waving his Filofax this time. "Meetings all next week—"

The blinds collapsed down onto the sill, blocking the outside completely.

I turned back to Sergey, wanting to question him further, but the curtain around his bed had been closed.

On my way back from the bathroom that night I saw another one of the beds was occupied, or at least the curtain was drawn almost completely shut. Coming from behind it was a woman's voice, older it sounded like, with a Southern accent.

"... so I said to myself, goodness gracious, Margaret, what have you done with yourself now, I better check with the team leader and sure enough they brought me here."

"Lamar is on his way," a voice I recognized as belonging to one of the nurses replied. "He'll take you to the clinic, and they're just going to run some tests to be extra careful it's nothing serious."

I tip-toed further down the row of beds, beyond where Sergey lay sleeping, toward the drawn curtain from where the voices emanated.

"Oh I met Lamar before, he is an absolute dear, just as precious as can be. I must say everyone here has been so helpful, they've been like one big family ..."

"Can I get you some more tea?" the nurse asked. As I got closer I could see shadows through the curtain, and their voices indicated the nurse was sitting at the end of the bed, with the other occupant propped up on pillows near the top.

"Oh goodness no, that's fine, I've caused you enough trouble already, I'm so sorry, I'm sure this is nothing at all ..."

I peeked around the curtain surrounding the bed, just far enough to catch a glimpse of the occupant sitting upright at the top. There in a Longwood bathrobe was an unrecognizable woman of late middle age holding a paper cup. Her face was grotesquely swollen, one of her eyes shut completely, and covered in black and blue eczematous crusting skin rashes and lesions that trailed down her neck. Her visually distressing appearance was eerily at odds with her cheerful, conversational tone of voice.

"... I do hope I'm not keeping you awake."

"It's no problem at all. Are you sure I can't get you another cup? It will be a few minutes before Lamar gets here."

"Well, only if you're absolutely sure it's no trouble ..."

The bed creaked as through the curtain I saw the shadow of the nurse rising, and I stumbled backward.

"... y'all have been just so helpful, I swear I don't know what I'll do when this all comes to an end ..."

I barely made it back to my bed in time, shutting my eyes just before the nurse walked past toward her office holding the empty paper cup.

I left the infirmary the next morning to find Audrey and tell her what I had seen. The people in her unit directed me to a classroom where she was participating in a voluntary focus group with the JCN marketing team. The door was open, and I waited out in the hallway, peeking in to see an impeccably dressed professional woman from JCN holding up colorful shapes and logo designs and gauging reactions while her assistant, seated at a desk behind her, jotted down notes.

"No, that looks like grape soda," Audrey chirped up from the front row. What looked like ten pounds of achievement beads hung around her neck.

"That's it!" she exclaimed at the next logo. "It's the whole inside going outside thing. Like before I used to always think that, everything I wanted, it was something, out there, you know? Something I had to go find or chase."

"A pursuit?" beamed the JCN marketing executive.

"Yeah, like every day I used to go out there and try to find something that's gonna make me happy. Like a job, or a guy, or just something ..."

Like the rest of the room I found myself transfixed by her. Her words sounded so sincere, and she almost seemed to be glowing with this aura of positive energy. Audrey was clearly becoming the star of her unit, the first poster girl for JCN-4830.

"But it's so simple. It's just me. Just ... being me. That's what it does to you. Every day, it reminds me, like it tells me all over again, a ..."

"Renewal?" the JCN executive prodded.

"An affirmation?" her assistant said in a whisper, clearly awestruck.

"That's it!" Audrey almost jumped out of her chair. "It's like my daily affirmation."

There was a moment of silence, and then a smattering of applause that grew into a full-blown ovation. The JCN marketing professional leaned over to her assistant, and I was able to make out only parts of what she said.

"Get Stu ... call him on his cell if you have to ..."

I decided not to wait for her and instead sought refuge in our secret spot at the gardening shack we used for conjugal visits. I must have dozed off on the bed of fertilizer bags because I woke up with Audrey perched on my chest, holding my face in her hands.

"You are not going to *believe* this shit!"

I was only half awake, and did my best to listen dutifully to her explanation of how she and another member of her unit enjoyed a private audience with Stu and a couple of other JCN executives to discuss the results of their focus group.

"And you know what they said? This is what they said, they said: You have a real talent for brand actualization. I don't know what it means but that's *exactly* what they said, and then they both gave me their cards, and guess what, you're never gonna believe this, guess what else?"

I just grunted in what I hoped was an engaged manner.

"They say they gonna get me the name of someone who maybe can get me a job as a *pharmaceutical sales representative.* Can you believe that?"

I groaned inwardly, or maybe it was outwardly as well. My mother had been a pharmaceutical sales representative. I was turning out to be quite the chip off the old block.

"You have to dress really hot and go door to door flirting with doctors to sell drugs," I observed.

"He say I communicate well and I have a very pleasant conversational tone of voice and not everybody has that."

I rolled my eyes. I didn't know why I couldn't be more supportive. Maybe because I was so fed up with Stu, JCN, and happiness in general.

"So that's great, right? I can be like a power bitch at meetings and you can be at home vacuuming and running errands and shit ..."

"Don't joke."

"Like I'll call you and tell you I'm gonna be late from work and you'll be wearing one of those aprons and taking cupcakes out of the oven with those big mittens ..."

"It's not funny."

"Yeah it is!" she protested. "A little? No?" She slid her hand into my shorts.

"Ouch! Gentle ..."

"Was it a little funny?" she pressed, lifting up my shirt and kissing my navel, then continuing southward. I chivalrously decided to take the high road.

"Maybe a little ..."

It became abundantly clear after the first month that many of the participants were under the influence of some kind of pharmacological pixie dust. The tangible euphoria also extended to the staff, who were either very pleased with the anecdotal evidence they were witnessing, or someone had spiked the coffee machine with JCN-4830. Stu in particular seemed positively intoxicated, dancing through the recreation room in our unit each day, high-fiving the participants and doing his jokes-that-are-so-bad-people-laugh-anyway shtick. He even held weekly putting tournaments, breaking out a ridiculously huge black golf putter that said Black Betty on the handle but Stu insisted people refer to as Mjölnir (pronounced MOLE-near, he even spelled it out phonetically on a whiteboard). It was the name for the hammer of the Norse god Thor, an indication of how Stu perceived himself out on the golf range. He would make jokes about whether people would have the strength to wield it, and the most irritating part was that everyone loved it. It was as if enough people were stoned on JCN-4830 that even the placebo recipients, which no doubt numbered among us, were caught up in the mood.

Needless to say this preternatural happiness had the opposite effect on me, making me even more sullen and annoyed at the increasingly saccharine surroundings. I kept the infirmary pass the nurse wrote me as a kind of get-out-of-jail-free card from all the overbearing good will, team-building and mental health exercises that filled our days, and used it to roam freely around the non-restricted parts of the Longwood campus.

"You know I don't usually make house calls like this."

Marci With An I was typing on her laptop in a lawn chair next to the bench I was laying on. She had tracked me down to my smoking spot outside where I had escaped for a cigarette. My trusty box of tissues was by my side, my flu symptoms seemingly determined to stay with me for the duration at Longwood. I was watching Unit Two file out onto the grassy quadrangle. I had the least interaction with Unit Two since neither T-Bone nor Audrey were housed there, but they seemed to be the most mystical, free-spirited of the four dormitory units. A large sub-contingent had started doing daily nature-worshipping yoga type exercises on their own, whenever the weather permitted. Many wore their cotton EEG caps on a full-time basis, which resembled tight men's underwear pulled over the ears to matte down hair and affix electrodes to. A few were almost completely naked; others wore a mix of Longwood shorts, t-shirts and bathrobes that had been tailored in some way. It was an odd sight to be sure, made even stranger when they arranged themselves in a circle, holding hands, then took turns as each person would shout out some life-affirming word toward the heavens, and then they'd all close in together in a kind of group hug and repeat it.

"Maybe people aren't supposed to be this happy," I mused, watching them frolic on the grass. "Maybe life isn't supposed to be served up like processed cheese or bite-sized nuggets. Maybe it's supposed to have ups and downs."

"Happiness," I heard someone in Unit Two cry out, and they all shouted it again in unison as they closed in a giant group hug.

"Is that why you stopped taking your medication?" Marci asked me. "You wanted to experience the ups and downs again?"

I took another drag from my cigarette. I had to admit Marci With An I had some skill. I found it impressive and annoying at the same time. I decided to reward her with a story.

"So I was almost at the end of my surgical rotation, and I'm assisting in exploratory surgery on an eight-year-old with acute lymphoblastic leukemia," I began. "Raymond William Rose Jr. That was his name. And so the surgeon, he explains to us, he's just going to look around, see if there's anything he could do, and if it was too far advanced he's going to close up and we're done."

Instead of continuing to type, Marci put her computer on the ground next to her chair, making a show that I had her full attention.

"And I'm so tired. You know, fantasizing about sleep. And I can't help it, the first thought that comes into my head is, please, God, I want to go home. It was just my body's response, to hear there's a possibility that this torture might be over. And as I look around the operating room, I can tell, I can just tell all of the people there, the nurses, the anesthesiologist, the intern, they're feeling the same way."

"Love!" echoed out across the quadrangle, with Unit Two closing in together once more for another group hug as they repeated the word.

"Anyway the cancer was everywhere, all through his chest. I visited Raymond a couple of times over the next month and a half. Met his family. Until one day he was gone. But the thing that really bothered me," I continued, "the thing I couldn't get over, wasn't that I had wished for this to happen. What bothered me was that the *next* time it happened the only difference would be that I wouldn't even give it a second thought. I'd be just like everyone else in the OR. That's what it does to you. Like my father. Like with my drugs. You stop feeling anything."

"Yeast!" I thought I heard someone in Unit Two shout out. I took the last draw from my cigarette, wondering why they'd wish for a single-cell fungi capable of fermenting carbohydrates into alcohol or carbon dioxide.

"Peace!" they all repeated, which I supposed made more sense.

"That's why I stopped. I wanted to feel more."

"And do you feel more when you're medication free?"

"Yes. That's kind of my problem. Knowing how much to feel."

"But don't you think medication might be able to help with that? Deal with some of those ups and downs?"

I tried for a moment to pinpoint my aversion to medication. It certainly wasn't any cultural stigma. I was fully aware that my brain was different, even broken at some basic level. I wasn't, for lack of a better word, "normal". Why didn't I want to fix that?

"Less highs maybe, but fewer crash landings?" Marci pressed.

"No," I finally decided. "Actually I think we'd all be better off if everybody felt more."

I was thinking about St. Christopher's, and the mole people, and the homeless person who had been set on fire, and my father for some reason. I didn't want to be normal. In fact if I had learned anything, it was that normal was the very last thing I wanted to be.

"Everything would be so different if we just felt more."

Chapter 25. COGNITIVE DISTORTIONS

By the end of the second month I was spending most of my time isolated in the gardening shack, staring into the darkness like I was back in the Bat Cave or my apartment at 125th street. The tell-tale signs began to reappear that I was, as Marci described, heading for another crash landing, ironically enough in this sea of chemically generated optimism and goodwill. It was extraordinary to me that no one seemed to particularly care that I was missing, as long as I showed up for my daily JCN-4830 shots. Or maybe that was part of the experiment. Maybe they were supposed to watch me go crazy. Of course that seemed ridiculous. I was just being paranoid. Or maybe I was being paranoid that I was paranoid. After what seemed like days of my mind spinning in a circular, downward fashion I finally ventured outside.

I found Audrey with the rest of her unit in the dormitory recreation room. Saxophone and soft synthesized electronic sounds wafted out of the darkness as soon as I opened the doors.

"I take your hand ... each of your fingers ..."

A voice, vaguely familiar, was speak-singing the words to a karaoke soundtrack. As I made my way into the dim room I could see members of her unit sitting together, many holding hands, swaying to the music.

"Then take your arms, just for a while."

The words to the song appeared superimposed over a constantly morphing psychedelic cloud on a television with a game console attached. The brightness silhouetted the wiry toned body and long flowing hair of the person singing, who was facing away from the screen and played to the crowd.

"I take your lips ... so I can kiss you ..."

I was trying to locate Audrey when I suddenly recognized the performer. I came to a complete stop.

"Then take your teeth and steal your smile."

It was Sergey. I couldn't believe it. He was playing rock star, now clad in a fashionably torn Longwood t-shirt. His ponytail was undone, the light filtering through his shoulder-length hair.

"I just want one thing ..."

It was only by following his gaze that I located Audrey with two other women, lying on their stomachs with their heads propped up on their hands near his feet. They gazed up dreamily, swaying back and forth in unison.

"... is all I am asking ..."

I rushed over to her, stepping on the hand of someone sprawled out on the carpet along the way.

"Your hair and eyes, so pale and blue."

"I need to talk to you," I hissed at Audrey, getting down on my knees next to her.

"I take them all now, and hold them near me ..."

Even through the darkness I could tell she was disappointed to see me, which made me even crazier.

"Shh! We're up next," she whispered back. "You wanna sing?"

"I just want every part of you ..."

"I don't want to sing. Can we go somewhere where we can talk please?"

"Where? Not the shack—"

"I don't care, anywhere but here."

"But this is where I wanna be. Why can't you *stop*?"

"Stop what?"

"Stop being such a cold prickly."

"Who are you calling a cold prickly?" I snapped back at her.

"That's what you are, all you want to do is be depressed."

I tried to ignore the paralyzing sickness gripping me as I struggled for a comeback, something factually substantive while at the same time packing enough of an emotional wallop to let her know I had the last word.

"So?" I glowered.

"Are you okay, Turtle Dove?" someone called out to Audrey.

"So maybe I don't want to be with a depressive cold prickly all the time!"

"What did he call you?"

"You're taking away my positive energy. You don't feed my soul."

"Did he call you Turtle Dove?"

"I sense disturbance," I heard Sergey murmur, moving behind Audrey. The song had ended and the lights in the room were on now. We were both standing. I was making a scene, my cold prickliness like an infection that was about to be snuffed out by lynch mob of human T cells.

"We're learning share each other's positive energy. You could too if you weren't such a cold prickly."

"I'm NOT a cold prickly!" I screamed, far too loud. I was aware that the whole room was looking at me in silence now, all seemingly crowding behind Audrey in her defense. I could feel myself shuddering but was powerless to stop. "Please stop calling me that."

Audrey took a step toward me, reaching out in a terrified kind of way. I could see she was in tears.

"Don't you see how you're acting? Maybe there's a side effect or something. Maybe the drug is making you crazy—"

"I'm not the one who's crazy! I'm sick, and we have no place to go and no future. We're supposed to be depressed, don't you get it? You're all on drugs! That is why you're behaving this way! I'm the only normal one here!"

I looked around at the eyes staring back at me.

"Why doesn't anybody understand that?"

The only thing to break the silence was another of my horrific sneezes. I stumbled around toward the exit.

"Mays, come back ..." I heard Audrey protest, but I stormed out, ignoring the cheerful salutations as I made my way across the quadrangle to T-Bone's unit. I needed reality, some escape from the unbearable diet of cotton candy I was being force-fed.

T-Bone was on his knees next to his bunk when I approached him, his Filofax off to the side. He was coloring giant intersecting pastel clouds on a sheet of poster board that resembled an Easter-themed Venn diagram.

"It's my mood chart," he explained matter-of-factly. Into each cloud he had written sometimes incorrectly spelled emotions: "Fear," "Greed," "Dezire."

"So much of my spiritual core has been stuck in Fear. Don't you think?"

"T-Bone, remember what you always said, about the people at the top controlling everything — the Grecian Formula — do you remember that?" I was almost pleading with him. T-Bone looked at me quizzically. "About how it's all just about manipulating us, selling us stuff, that's all they want to do? It's all bullshit, remember? Everything is bullshit?"

Finally T-Bone broke into a wide grin.

"I get it. This is a cognitive distortion."

I had no idea what that meant, except that it sounded bizarre coming out of T-Bone's mouth.

"We talked about it in group today. Catastrophizing. They have a disease named catastrophizing. It's when you always think everything's going to shit. And we were all laughing at lunch, saying, that's Mays, boy ..."

"You were all laughing about me at lunch?"

This wasn't even my unit. How did they even know me?

"I mean, not laughing, just, trying to, you know, apply what we learned in group. That's just what most people think about you. Not everybody though. Nelson thinks it's something physical, like you're a retard or something."

I immediately turned around to go back to my unit.

"Hey, I don't think that, Mays. I already know what your problem is."

I broke into a slight jog, hoping to reach the hallway and elevators before I heard T-Bone's diagnosis. It was a futile attempt.

"I already told you, it's your defense mechanisms. You got no mental filter, see. That's what's supposed to block all the bad shit from going into your head and driving you crazy. Except yours don't work."

I pressed the elevator button, hoping one would be there waiting.

"Your mental filter is like a used tampon. It don't absorb nothing. In fact, it sits there and *reminds* you of shit it's supposed to be filtering out."

I gave up waiting for the elevator and sprinted for the staircase, throwing my weight against the door to open it.

"Look, will you do me a favor, tell that to your doctor? The problem is your mental filter."

I was already down a flight of stairs while his voice echoed above me.

"Trust me, he'll know what I'm talking about!"

Back at my unit I dove into my long-ignored mental health exercises with a rabid intensity. I was going to win every achievement bead there was. They would have to create a new rank especially for me, a Band 11 or however the rating system worked here. I was going to be the superstar of my unit, just like Audrey. I was going to be the happiest prick at Longwood.

I'm not quite sure how many days passed while I sat there on the tiled floor next to my bunk, surrounded by piles of crumpled tissues, magic markers, pens, and assorted arts and crafts materials. I was having one of my manic episodes. I had long dropped any pretense of participating in the scheduled activities. People came and went, mostly ignoring me until finally I heard a familiar voice above me.

"I didn't know there were so many shades of black."

It was Marci With An I. She was staring at my mood chart. I sprang to my feet in excitement and gave what must have been a completely unintelligible description of the Bat Cave and the subtle changes in darkness in my own feverish, sleep-deprived manner.

"Mays, it's okay ..." she tried to stop me, but I had to explain everything to her.

"I'll be totally caught up, just need a few more hours, it's my 'should' phrases, I got stuck with them, the instructions were confusing—"

"You don't have to worry about the exercises anymore."

I froze, and a horrible realization swept over me. They were dropping me from the trial. I wouldn't get paid. I wouldn't see Audrey. Marci saw my reaction and immediately put on her don't-worry-relax face and spoke in soothing tones.

"It's okay. I just need you to come with me."

As we headed across the quadrangle from my unit toward the marble staircase leading up the hill to the administrative building, that dark circular death star from which no study participant ever returned, I became overcome with panic. The fact that I had just thrown away four grand and possibly irrevocably damaged any future with Audrey because of my anti-social behavior was beginning to sink in, and I was desperate.

"You know, it's funny, I actually think I'm starting to feel better. The last couple days I mean, maybe it's the drugs ..."

I pulled another tissue from the ubiquitous box I carried tucked under my arm like a football, interrupted by another bone-jarring sneeze.

"... or just all the, you know, the therapy, all the good work you've been doing. I feel like things are moving forward now and everything is positive, really looking up ..."

Marci was marching up the steps with a purpose, and I struggled to keep pace.

"I mean, life, it's great, right? It's ... precious ... a miracle ... it's ... like ... this, this—"

She was clearly preoccupied with other thoughts, and my lack of articulation wasn't helping things.

"Salad!" I shouted triumphantly. "That's what it is. This amazing salad," I continued. "With lettuce, tomatoes, plump cherry tomatoes, and those big croutons, and the tiny miniature corns—"

"Mays what are you talking about?" Marci asked, half confused, half annoyed, as we pushed through the dark glass doors to the administrative building. We were a world removed from the dormitory units and common dining and recreational areas now, entering a strictly off-limits facility I had never been inside. Marci led me to a circular security desk, where a guard had to call someone before giving me a temporary pass in the form of a sticker to affix to my soiled t-shirt. Marci led me through a turnstile and into a small elevator that was already crowded with four other people. Two were wearing scrubs, one a bit older, who reminded me of the attending during my surgical rotation. There was a tiny, rail-thin gray man in a lab coat, and someone I recognized from the dining hall who was pushing a dolly stacked high with trays. The conversation stopped completely the moment I entered, leaving only the aroma of savory chicken and the sound of a muzak version of a Beatles song. There were buttons for three floors and a basement, and Marci pushed the top button for the third floor.

When the doors opened on the first floor it was as if we had somehow been transported into another building. Stretched out before me was a sea of reflective glass and shiny metal of an expansive, state-of-the-art high-tech laboratory. The familiar fingerprint-activated double security doors blocked the entrance but the exterior (and subsequent interior) walls were of glass, allowing me a fleeting glimpse of what appeared to be translucent sub-cubicles of varying sizes occupied by figures in protective lab coats, gloves, aprons, head and face covering. An array of equipment including refrigerators, mixers and plate mills for grinding, refractometers, photometers, digital bench scales and a series of nitrogen desiccator cabinets cast an incandescent glow of light that refracted through the concentric layers of glass.

The small gray man in a lab coat exited and the doors closed again, the tableau of glass and metal before me disappearing as quickly as it had appeared, leaving us once again immersed in the muzak that wafted gently from above us.

When the doors opened to the second floor a completely different scene presented itself. It was the smell that hit me first, that familiar hospital smell resulting from iodoform, the disinfectant used in most medical facilities, and quickly overpowered the chicken aroma from the tower of trays next to me. Across a brightly-lit hallway before double security doors was an oval-shaped reception counter that blocked off an administrative area, where a minor commotion was taking place.

It was a clown, like a circus clown themed in JCN corporate blue and green colors offset against the white walls and fluorescent lights of the bright hallway. He was leaning against the desk arguing heatedly with a flustered young woman in a nurse's uniform behind the desk, who in turn seemed to be relaying his arguments into a telephone. Another nurse, an older woman behind the desk next to her, was talking to the clown in soothing tones, clearly trying to lower his level of agitation.

The two men wearing scrubs exited the elevator, followed by the food service worker pushing the column of chicken dinners. He was almost run over by two passing technicians pushing a portable plasmapheresis, or plasma exchange machine, which ironically I had become familiar with not through my abbreviated medical training but after multiple donation sessions at a blood bank in Staten Island in exchange for $100 gift cards. It was still covered in plastic and had Styrofoam blocks protecting its corners, like it had just been unpacked, and was on a collision course with the tower of chicken dinners until the food service worker let out a warning expletive.

It was a reception area that would not have looked out of place at a medium-sized hospital. It seemed remarkable that such a facility existed solely for the purpose of servicing the study participants, yet I could come up with no other explanation. An elderly male patient wearing a Longwood bathrobe over his hospital gown strolled past the traffic jam in the corridor before us pulling a mobile IV stand, as inside the elevator Marci impatiently pushed the button to the third floor again even though it was already illuminated. As the elevator doors finally closed the patient paused to peer into the elevator, revealing a face that was severely swollen on the right side, inflamed and covered in lesions like the woman I had seen in the infirmary.

It was only Marci and me in the elevator then, and it seemed she was being careful not to make eye contact to discourage me from asking any of my thousands of questions. So distinct were the first two floors I felt like I was channel surfing in front of the television, and when the elevator stopped again on the top floor I braced myself for what diorama would present itself next.

The doors opened into what was neither a high-tech pharmaceutical lab nor bustling hospital, but what looked like the largest office furniture and supplies showroom on the planet. It was only after Marci started leading me through pathways of cubicles and offices that I realized there were actual human beings occupying them. JCN staffers and Longwood team members in blue shirts swarmed about what appeared to be the operational and administrative nerve center. There was a definite upstream/downstream flow, with piles of receipts and papers being scanned, scribbled on and stapled together by mostly young women. They took piles from outbound trays on one desk and placed them into inbound trays on desks a few rows further back, closer to the other end of the colossal office space where we seemed to be heading. We walked past conference rooms named after JCN brand drugs, continuing through additional security doors and past colored index cards taped to the walls and whiteboards displaying squares and circles with arrows connecting them in scribbled magic marker. As we walked I overheard at least one mini-crisis having to do with the fact that the clown I had seen on the second floor was hired on a whim by Stu without approval, and they were unable to pay him because he wasn't on the approved vendor's list.

It got less crowded and the population older the further back we walked. It seemed that all the work was taken in at the front of the floor, funneled, approved, and consolidated into slick spreadsheets and graphs by the time it was delivered through a final set of security doors to the executive suite in the far back, which consisted of a single hallway lined with offices. At the far end of that hallway, at the end of our journey and this corporate assembly line, was Stu's office.

As we approached I could see people standing about, including the petite blond I recognized as his assistant Penny. She was guarding the doorway and motioned for Marci and me to wait outside the threshold when she saw us, putting a finger to her lips indicating not to speak. I peeked around the corner to see Stu inside his office holding his Mjölnir, carefully lining up a fifteen-foot putt into a juice cup that lay across a thin column of artificial turf atop the industrial carpet floor. A half-dozen other middle-aged executive types in suits with the jacket off, sleeves rolled and tie loosened just like Stu watched in silence from comfortable positions around the room. Stu shifted his weight back and forth a few times then gave the dimpled ball a short tap. There was a rising "ahhhhhHHHH!" as the ball approached its target, then an "OOOOHHHhhhh!" as it bounced off the rim of the glass.

"I'd like to introduce Mr. Parkhill Mays," Marci finally announced with forced cheerfulness, an unscripted comment that clearly upset Penny. Stu turned around and acted surprised by our presence, then gave a good-natured shrug and motioned for us to enter. I looked around what was clearly the crown jewel of the temporary workspaces in the building that Stu had commandeered. He must have transported some of his more important office trinkets for his stay at Longwood, including a Vince Lombardi portrait that hung above his desk, as well as some other sports memorabilia and family photos. As we filed in, Stu looked me over, then thrust out his hand.

"How's it going, Pops?" he announced confidently, and it took me a moment to realize he was referring to me. He took my hand in a death-grip handshake while he turned to Marci and mouthed in her direction, "This is him?"

"Yes," Marci replied, taking a deep breath and giving me a reassuring pat on the back.

"This is the father."

Chapter 26. UNIVERSAL DESTRUCTION

Somebody pushed a chair behind me and I collapsed onto it, as the reason for my presence hit me with the force of a freight train.

Audrey was pregnant.

I felt as if some seismic shift had suddenly taken place inside of me. Images of my childhood, my parents, my father flickered rapid-fire through my head. It seemed unfathomable to me: fatherhood. All eyes in the room turned expectantly to Stu. He took a moment, seemingly for dramatic effect, and then spoke gravely.

"So. I guess we know JCN-4830 is not an effective form of birth control."

Laughter erupted, too hard, except for Marci who noticeably winced. The laughter would quiet down until you thought it was going to stop, then someone would start laughing again and start it back up. I wasn't paying any attention, nor was I really listening when an exasperated Marci finally mentioned Audrey by name.

"... her blood test indicated a spike in her hCG levels. It's a glycoprotein that is secreted by the placenta shortly after fertilization, usually at least six days after conception so we'd estimate she's about two weeks along. We've already tested for STDs and Rubella and have been doing CBCs daily along with the other treatment ..."

All of my life I had been sure I would never reproduce. Having always wished I had never been born, the thought of bringing someone else into this world seemed sadistic. The Rage, I thought, precluded me from ever having children. What if Audrey wanted to keep the baby? The idea of the two of us raising a child together, especially in our current situation, was unimaginable.

"... as a precaution we've already tested her glucose tolerance, and we'll probably want to get an Rh factor for you as well. We'll have an OB/GYN perform a quad screen and an amnio because of the additional risks, that is, of course, should the two of you decide to take the child to term ..."

Yet as unimaginable as it was, imagine I did. What if we had a baby together? The concept ignited a tingly sensation that began to spread through my body. I became vaguely aware of one of the suits sitting across from me, with thin glasses and really thick black hair that was heavily gelled to a fashionable peak, who was chiming in now as well.

"At this time, though we are under no legal obligation to do so and despite the inaccuracies you provided during the screening process, clear violations of our behavioral code of conduct, wasted investment and significant expense we've already incurred for each of you, JCN is prepared to cover all relevant medical expenses ..."

Maybe our child would be different. Maybe Audrey and I would show our baby that everything wasn't bullshit. Audrey and I could teach them that. Or maybe they would teach us that. Maybe our baby would be the only thing in the world that made sense.

"... contingent upon your voluntary withdrawal from the trial, along with a complete personal statement and accounting of all willful violations of study protocol ..."

What if I was in fact the one who wanted to have a baby? Maybe it wasn't that I didn't want to be a father. I just didn't want to be *my* father. But I wasn't my father. It didn't matter that we both suffered from The Rage. I was someone completely different. That's what I understood now. It just took the prospect of fatherhood to make me realize it.

"... and provided you are completely candid and forthcoming in your statement ..."

I wasn't listening to the hair-gel man telling me we had been dropped from the study. I suddenly didn't care about the study, or money, or the fact that I was about to become jobless and homeless once again. There was only one thing that mattered now, and thinking about it flooded my very being with a lightness and exuberance that I hadn't felt in months. It was like a giant JCN-4830 suppository had been inserted into my rectum and undiluted euphoria surged through my veins, to the point that I had to leap out of my seat.

"We're going to have a *baby*!" I shouted.

It became silent. The faces in the room all looked back at me in surprise. Like I was missing the point or something. I didn't understand. Audrey was pregnant. How could that not be the point?

All eyes turned to Stu again.

"Family. It changes everything," Stu finally said. He walked over to his desk, still holding his Mjölnir, and took a small framed picture with his other hand.

"Time to get serious about your life, Pops. Time to start taking responsibility."

Stu stepped over and handed me the snapshot of himself posing sternly in an Eagle Scout uniform, with five pudgy younger boys of varying ages in slightly different scout uniforms, with equally serious looks on their faces. Opposite him was a heavy-set blond woman, like an older version of Penny, presumably his wife.

"No more wasting your life jacking off for beer money," Stu chuckled. "Quite a story. We're talking to your other friend now, getting his statement."

I froze as Stu took the picture back, pleased that this information had the unnerving effect he had intended. What had T-Bone told them?

"We all make mistakes. Bad choices. We've all been there. But now's the time to step up. It starts right now."

He placed the photo back on his desk.

"It's time to get serious about your life. Do what's right for the company," Stu said solemnly. "Do what's right for Audrey, and your family."

With great ceremony he then held out the handle of his Mjölnir toward me. It was as if he was performing a sacred ritual, at least in his mind, some rite of passage to manhood.

"A little luck, maybe someday you'll be the one running a billion-dollar clinical trial," Stu finished, still holding out the golf club expectantly.

I looked at Marci, who at this point was covering her face. Finally I just took the golf putter. I didn't know what else to do.

Stu turned back to hair-gel and gave a slight nod. "Schmatzie?"

The man with the hair-gel, and apparently an unfortunate nickname, addressed me once again.

"The first order of business is to get a complete accounting of your activities over the past six months, including all medication, prescribed or unprescribed. The more accurate you can be the greater our likelihood of tracking down the underlying cause."

"Audrey is pregnant," I asked, looking around the room in confusion. "Don't we know the underlying cause?"

There was another pause that seemed to make people uncomfortable before Schmatzie answered.

"I was referring to the cause of her other symptoms."

"Audrey seems to have had an exaggerated immune response," Marci finally jumped in. "We assumed her symptoms were due to the introduction of the foreign fetus, so naturally that was the first place we looked—"

"Until we asked her what medications she's been on in the last six months," Schmatzie interjected.

They all looked at me expectantly. My elation at the thought of fatherhood now gave way to the sickening realization that they had been right. I didn't get it. The point wasn't that Audrey was going to have a baby. The point was that Audrey was sick.

"What's wrong with Audrey?" I asked simply.

"There's been a dramatic drop in her white blood cell count," Marci explained quietly. "She's been running a high fever for the past two days and her edema has become widespread, more so than the other cases we've seen. The corticosteroids haven't helped reduce the inflammation, so they're setting up a plasmapheresis machine to try to remove all of the 4830 from her bloodstream—"

"The truth is it could have been any number of factors that caused this reaction," Schmatzie jumped in. "That's what we need you to make clear in your statement."

"I want to see Audrey," was all I could utter. Schmatzie responded immediately.

"Mr. Mays, if you want to help Audrey and yourself, if you want her and your child to get the medical treatment they need, you'll need to do exactly as we say."

"You take care of the company," Stu explained, "the company takes care of you."

"I'd like to remind you of the legally binding agreements executed by you and Audrey during the screening process," Schmatzie continued, opening a folder on his lap. "This includes the general waiver of liability and indemnification ..."

I held the putter with both hands and slowly lifted up the head, wielding it like a two-handed sword.

"... the patient informed consent waiver and blanket release statement—"

"Someone please take me to Audrey," I said quietly.

Now Schmatzie stopped speaking, and Marci slowly rose to her feet.

"Mays, I think we'd be more comfortable if you put that down."

"Give me that—" Stu took a step toward me, but I took a half swing into the air to keep him at bay. His eyes widened in surprise and his face flushed.

"Mays, you need to sit down now, this isn't helping yourself or Audrey," Marci continued. "I give you my word we're doing everything we can—"

"Someone call security," Stu snapped.

I was backing toward the door, still brandishing the Mjölnir. There were people in the room dialing on cell phones, and it occurred to me I couldn't stay there.

"Call security," Stu said again, staring at me. "Tell them to send Lamar."

"Where is she? Tell me where she is," I asked Marci desperately.

"She's in the clinic, she's safe—"

I was out the door before she could finish her sentence, and was halfway down the long corridor of executive offices before I could hear their voices behind me.

"Get Lamar!" Stu's voice boomed as I ran full speed, waving the Mjölnir. The security door to the executive suites was unlocked from the inside and I burst through it, back into the acres of office space outside. I ignored the passing glances as I veered hard to the right, wondering how to get to the clinic on the floor below and make myself as immediately invisible as possible.

There was a hallway in a far corner that branched off from the main office space that seemed less populated and I ran toward it. I sped past cables and monitors and what appeared to be other assorted audio-visual equipment stacked on chairs, stands and piled along the side of the dimly-lit hallway. Rounding a corner, I skidded past two glass doors that had been propped open, and was about to continue down the hallway when something I saw inside made me slide to a complete stop.

The room inside was dark, with work light filtering upward through thick braids of cable visible beneath a grated floor. The only other illumination came from flat-screen monitors that lined the walls. Flashing on each of them were different angles of the dormitory units, recreational area, the cafeteria, and seemingly the entire Longwood campus. Sitting before them were the silhouettes of Longwood staff, typing notes into computers and whispering to each other. A larger group of them was crowded around a series of video images of Stu, Marci, Schmatzie and the others running across the floor, presumably looking for me.

I was fixated entirely on something else though, a seemingly insignificant detail in the sea of live video feeds that swirled around this control room. It was so shocking to me that just a subliminal flash out of the corner of my eye had stopped me at a full sprint, and seemed to suck the air out of me as it drew me toward it.

One of the monitors in a far corner displayed the *inside* of the gardening supply shack Audrey and I had used as our little love nest. The fertilizer bags were left exactly as I had arranged them, a kind of lumpy twin bed with two sacks across at the end as pillows. I stared at the unchanging image, thinking about everything that Audrey and I had done in there, of how they had been watching, of how they *must* have been watching, and how it seemed like none of this could really be happening until a voice loud enough to penetrate my trance-like state yanked me back into the moment.

"Holy *shit!*"

The Longwood staff, most of them wearing headphones, had all turned around in their seats and were staring across the room at me in astonishment, looking every bit as bewildered as I was. I hesitated only a moment before continuing down the hallway. As I rounded another corner, my heart dropped as I saw ahead of me that the corridor went back into the main office space, until in the next instant a door on the side came into view with red lettering: EMERGENCY EXIT Alarm Will Sound. Lights flashed and a harrowing high-pitched electronic beeping siren rang out the moment I pushed it open, which unfortunately didn't stop when I shut the door behind me. I leapt down flights of stairs and burst through another heavy metal door to the floor below.

The beeping still echoed around me as I emerged into the brightness and antiseptic smell of the second-floor clinic that pulsed with flashing lights from the alarm I had set off. I was clearly further back from the crowded reception area I had witnessed in the elevator. Open doorways to what looked to be the patient ward rooms lined one side of the hall.

"Audrey ..." I called out above the racket, peeking inside one of the sparsely furnished single rooms which looked to be unoccupied, its lone railed bariatric electric hospital bed unmade. I checked another, which was similarly empty.

"Audrey!" I shouted louder, checking a third empty room, then realized I wasn't going to be able to physically look in every single room before being discovered. I backed out into the hallway again, then let out a desperate cry so loud it probably could have been heard back in the Bat Cave.

"AUDREY!"

I held my breath, the sound of my voice reverberating through the hallways and above the electronic ringing. I started running again, calling out her name repeatedly as I passed additional empty rooms until the hallway came to an end before a double security door that blocked me from proceeding any further. I spun around and ran back up the way I came, fighting panic at the growing realization that I was trapped in an air-locked subsection of hallway between security doors, like a lab rat inside a maze.

I slid to a stop where the hallway intersected with another. In the distance to my right a small figure in a nurse's uniform was frantically jiggling her hand on the thumb sensor by a pair of double doors at the far end. She cast a panicked glance back in my direction as the doors finally swung open with a buzz. I ran toward her at a full sprint, and she let out a shriek as she ran through the doors, continuing further down the hall as they slowly began to shut behind her. I was able to get within a few yards, lunging forward with the Mjölnir before the edges of the doors touched just beyond my reach, a nanosecond too late.

I proceeded to beat the outside of the closed doors with the Mjölnir, which only served to bend the putter in half. I threw my weight against them, damaging my shoulder, then started kicking with full force and probably would have broken my foot as well were it not for the voice I heard.

"Mays!"

I turned around to see Marci standing behind me, gasping for air, as Stu, along with Schmatzie and the rest of his lieutenants came to a stop behind her, equally out of breath. Then came a trail of additional Longwood staff, security in blue blazers bumping into them from behind, along with other curious onlookers including the techies from the audio-visual room. I was even able to spot the blue wig of the JCN clown peeking around the corner behind them.

"Stay away from me!" I shouted, swinging the damaged golf putter, my back to the closed double doors.

"Mays, you're not yourself now," Marci told me breathlessly. "You're on a very powerful medication that has serious side effects."

"Stay away from me!"

"Listen to me, Mays. You're paranoid right now. This is not you. It's the drugs that are making you act like this. That's all it is. It's just the drugs."

"There is nothing wrong with me!" I screamed back, still brandishing the putter.

The doors behind me suddenly slid open. I whirled around and beheld the person standing in the doorway. It was the final shock in what had been an escalating series of impossibilities, to the point that I knew Marci must be correct. I was hallucinating.

It was my guardian angel, the man with the handlebar mustache. The one I had seen in my apartment after my suicide attempt, and who I had caught watching me months afterward. He was flanked by two Longwood security guards in blue blazers. I just stared, trying to connect the dots to how he could be in front of me right now, how that world could possibly intersect with this one.

"It's okay, Parkhill," he said calmly, repeating the same phrase he had uttered to me back in my apartment. "Everything's going to be okay."

I could feel the Mjölnir lowering, my head suddenly aching. "Close the door!" I heard Stu bellow from behind me, as one of the Longwood security guards started fumbling with the thumb sensor on the other side of the open doorway.

"Audrey!" I called out desperately one last time to no one in particular.

And then I heard it.

"Mays!"

It was Audrey, coming from somewhere down the hallway beyond the man with the handlebar mustache. I immediately lunged through the doorway, pushing my guardian angel backward with the bent putter. The doors closed on both of us, then opened again.

"Close the fucking door!" I heard Stu shout again.

"Audrey!" I shouted once more as I let go of the golf club and twisted past him. I stumbled further down the hallway, where at the far end I could see a crowd of people spilling out from one of the rooms. Most were wearing suits, some talking on cell phones, stepping outside the room to see what the commotion was, eyes widening as they saw me clattering down the hallway toward them. Somebody caught me from behind, and then there were people wrestling me down to the white tiled floors. I was writhing furiously as through my own screaming I could hear Stu's voice saying "Hold him down, hold him down." I struggled to twist free, my eyes fixated on the doorway to the room further down the hallway until I saw, between the arms and hands and faces pressed near me, a last unmistakable figure step out into the hallway.

It was T-Bone. And in the instant I saw him, the very last time I would ever see him, I could tell he was different. It was his expression, one that betrayed all the feelings of remorse, despair, confusion, doubt, all the attributes that I would usually have associated with myself. It was as if I had somehow transferred them all to this person who called himself T-Bone, and he understood now that I had been right all along, that life really wasn't worth living. It was an expression that told me T-Bone had a subconscious just like the rest of us after all. It was right there on his face. It just took Audrey's condition to bring it out.

"T-Bone ..." I shouted, as something sharp pricked me in the back of my neck. I clawed somebody in the eye, and there was a scream, and I suddenly had some room to wriggle forward on my forearms, making it out from under the pile until I stopped to remove the syringe I realized was dangling from my neck.

I looked up again for T-Bone, but he had vanished. Of course he had, I thought to myself, as I was again set upon by a wave of Longwood blue, and I felt another pinch somewhere else on my neck, and I thought I called Audrey's name again but couldn't be sure as a wave of darkness overcame me.

And then there were more voices, and the darkness seemed to fold in on itself until a familiar, hideous creature emerged from its vortex. It was Universal Destruction, the graffiti skull monster Little Andre had created months ago. I tried to call out to Audrey one last time, to warn her, to warn T-Bone. A familiar sound now rose somewhere in the distance; the more I struggle the louder it gets. Then I recognize it as my own screaming and I'm fighting, throwing punches as the familiar sound of my own screaming gets closer still.

Then I'm falling through space, and I hit the ground and lift up my head and there's red, actually white tile with red on it, blood. Is it my blood? I stare at it until I feel someone grabbing my shoulders and I shoot forward, slamming into something else, a body, and as I continue to plow forward the other body is falling backward and I can taste the blood in my mouth. I'm in another hallway somewhere else and the other person and I are both on the floor. I struggle to my feet and everything is spinning, the floor, the walls, a gurney and blue shirts, but now I see a figure headed toward me who is different from the others. He is larger, with a shaved head, and muscular, like a body-builder, so much that his blazer almost doesn't fit him. As he gets closer my heart soars as I read the name emblazoned on his nametag: LAMAR. The name sounds familiar, and I'm thinking this Lamar may be able to help me, I just need to explain everything, surely Lamar will understand. He's steadying me, holding my chest now with his left hand until his face is close to mine. Then I see in his expression that Lamar is not going to help me. Lamar is angry.

Lamar is going to hit me.

He pulls his fist back and before I can do anything I am aware of a dull THUMP on the side of my head, and then I'm not aware of anything at all.

Darkness.

I have no idea how much time has passed. Maybe I'm dead. Maybe I always was dead. Maybe my initial suicide attempt had succeeded. Maybe everything that had happened since then — T-Bone, Audrey, the clinical trials, my whole life underground — had been another creation of an oxygen-deprived brain.

As the glint of metal reflecting the dim light filtering in through grated windows slowly came into focus I became aware that I was on a bed in some hospital room again. Was I back at Bellevue?

Footsteps.

Everything was happening all over again, just as it had started. The nurse was approaching. I wondered if T-Bone was going to be in the bed next to me. My door creaked open. A figure stood there a moment, silhouetted against the light from the hallway.

From the outline I could tell instantly it was not a nurse.

It was my father.

Chapter 27. THE CYTOKINE STORM

My father's appearance triggered a series of immediate Pavlovian emotional and physical responses, including almost emptying the contents of my bladder into the sheets.

"Hello, Parkhill."

I watched him enter the room, his sharp features and thinning but coifed gray hair moving through the darkness toward me until another light on a table next to my bed switched on. The brightness was overwhelming, and I covered my face from the glare.

"Does that bother—"

"No, it's fine."

He was peering closely at me through his bifocals, taking a moment to examine my face, including what I surmised to be the bruise around my throbbing right eye. Seeing him up close he looked much frailer than I remembered, his face gaunt and eyes sunken, like it was only the starch of his pressed shirt that was holding him upright. I didn't particularly care at that moment that I was probably the reason for the dip in his constitution. He was wearing a tailored suit — my father always wore a suit — and finally took a seat next to my bed.

"How are you feeling?"

"Where's Audrey?" I blurted out.

It occurred to me that I didn't even know if he was aware who Audrey was, or anything about my last few months. That was until I saw him hesitate before he answered. He made an expression that I didn't recognize, choosing his words carefully, making it abundantly clear that he knew exactly who Audrey was.

"Audrey is in a hepatic coma."

Then I realized why I didn't recognize his expression, and why his tone of voice sounded so different to me. He wasn't talking to me the way he usually spoke to me or my mother. He was speaking to me like a patient, or a member of their family. Someone that he needed to relay bad news to. He had switched to professional mode. It was a courtesy he never extended to his family, who were usually the recipients of one-word commands or angry tirades. The polite and respectful tone was something afforded only to paying customers.

"She seems to have had an extreme reaction to the JCN-4830 resulting in an overproduction of antibodies, specifically cytokines. She is suffering from hypercytokinemia. Her immune system has attacked her body to the point of catastrophic systemic organ failure."

I was focused on my father's delivery and demeanor not only because I wasn't mentally ready to process the content of his message, but also because it was so contrary to my experience with him. He seemed uncomfortable, avoiding eye contact with me, looking at his hands, beautiful surgeon's hands with long elegant fingers, then up past me as if he was explaining everything to the wall behind my bed.

"It is a condition known as a cytokine storm," he added. "She was initially placed on immune suppression medications, which was the correct course, first cyclosporine, then prednisone, then cyclophosphamide, then a combination of all three."

Like many doctors, my father used medical terminology, lab results and a smokescreen of factual information as a shield, protection from the hysterical spouse whose husband of 40 years had just died of a heart attack.

"In retrospect, the emergency plasmapheresis after the onset of sepsis was probably a mistake, as it caused the drop in blood pressure that sent her into shock. At that point I had Dick Winters flown in, a colleague of mine. You might remember him, the house in New Hampshire with the tire swing ..."

He was referring to Richard Winters, as in Palmer, Winters and Stevenson, authors of *The Handbook of Vertebrate Immunology*, the definitive text on the subject. Like my father, he was well known in medical circles.

"It was his idea to start her on the TNF blockers, although once she went into septic shock there didn't seem to be anything we could do to suppress her response. She had already suffered class C cirrhosis of her liver and was placed on the transplant list late last night, until her blood pressure dropped this morning and her kidneys reached stage five failure. It was clear she was in the final phases of multiple organ dysfunction."

Audrey was dying, actually closer to dead than alive at this point. She was in the last stages of septic shock and her liver was irreparably damaged and her kidneys were failing. For some reason, either due to the developing fetus or whatever god-forsaken chemical that was still in her system from our lab rat tour, her immune system had gone into overdrive. Or perhaps her body just liked the warm fuzzies it was generating and couldn't stop, the medical equivalent of friendly fire.

"Probably within the next 24 hours," he added, looking up from his hands. "We'll know more after the autopsy."

The image of Audrey's brain, kidneys, lungs and heart being dissected and laid out on a cadaver table left me momentarily unable to breathe and I thought I might pass out again.

"I am sorry, Parkhill," my father said finally.

It was his unmistakable concern that was the worst for me. I wanted to hate him completely and without reservation. Any indication or even hint that he may be anything other than completely abusive and uncaring, a brilliant surgeon and flawed human being who did in fact love his family, were the moments when I despised him the most.

"What happens now?"

I said it in a whisper. It was all I could think of to say, and I felt like I had to say something because I didn't want there to be silence. My father looked confused, then chose his words carefully.

"Well, obviously JCN is sensitive to any publicity, but it's gone to the ethics review board. Their lawyers will perform a risk analysis. Based on the efficacy of the medication, weighing revenue against potential litigation and settlement costs. All completely beyond my control ... there are forces at work here much greater than you or I."

He looked at me again, apparently reading from my expression that wasn't what I was asking about, which actually wasn't true since I didn't know what I had meant myself.

"What happens now with regard to Audrey ... that depends somewhat on the wishes of her next of kin."

I couldn't even fathom who Audrey's next of kin were, or how they would find them if they even existed.

"After some investigation all they can find is what she had provided in her pre-trial questionnaire."

As he said it I realized I did know, I knew exactly who Audrey had listed as her next of kin in her paperwork. I had been the one who had filled it all out.

"She listed you."

My father looked at me like he was expecting a reaction, but in truth I had none. I couldn't have one, not then, not there in front of him. There could only be one thought occupying my brain at that moment if I were to keep functioning at all, the one thing holding me together, the single truth I clung to in an increasingly bleak world that had turned out to be more hopeless than even I had suspected. I needed to be with Audrey.

"Please take me to her."

My father was about to answer when there was a knock on the door. An Asian woman, very young and professionally dressed wearing a wireless headphone poked her head through the doorway.

"Tell him we're ready," my father said to her before she had a chance to speak. She nodded and then disappeared, and my father turned back to me.

"I promise I will take you to her after Bob speaks to you. He's been waiting almost a day now."

I didn't know who Bob was, but was more confused about how someone could have been waiting for me for a day.

"A day? How long have I been out?"

My father glanced at the clock on the wall. It was approaching midnight.

"About eighteen hours."

The door re-opened and the Asian woman appeared again, this time holding the door open for a distinguished-looking gray-haired man. He was about my father's age, although with kinder eyes and an almost courtly manner, wearing a bow-tie and fancy suspenders. He politely asked his assistant, the Asian woman with the headset, to have an extra chair brought in, which she placed by the side of my bed. He then asked her to wait outside while he spoke privately with the Mays family. He had a faint Southern accent and spoke to me in a folksy, reassuring tone.

"Hello, Parkhill. My name is Bob McCormack. I'm the Senior Executive Vice President of Worldwide Research and Development here at JCN. I report directly to our chairman and CEO. I also hope you won't hold it against me that I've been friends with your father for longer than either of us care to remember."

He cast a glance over at my father, who nodded.

"I know there is nothing I could possibly say that could make any of this more bearable for you, so I'm not going to insult you by trying to do that. I also understand that I'm probably the last person in the world that you want to hear from right now, but I'm going to ask you to listen and consider what I'm going to tell you."

I certainly wasn't going to give him any help, so if he expected me to nod affirmatively he was wasting his time. McCormack didn't miss a beat, however, not to be thrown off balance by a featherweight like myself. He pulled his chair closer to my bed.

"I can see you distrust me. That's understandable of course. I'm prepared to earn your trust. Sometimes the best way to earn someone's trust is to offer them something valuable of your own. That's what I'm going to do now, Parkhill. I'm going to share something valuable with you. You aren't likely to ever hear a formal admission of wrongdoing from anyone, but as my presence here might indicate the buck more or less stops with me. I also am a father and a grandfather, and to the extent that it means anything to you, which I imagine isn't very much right now, I would like to swear to you, on everything that is meaningful or sacred to me, how sickened all of us are about how things transpired here. I've ordered a complete internal review to find out what protocol, if any, was violated, and promise you that the failures that occurred here will be corrected."

He leaned back, staring me in the eye.

"We hope, with your help."

He was scanning my face for a reaction. Truth be told I didn't have any idea what he was talking about. McCormack cast a quick glance to my father, then leaned forward again.

"We think JCN could use a man like you, Parkhill, and would like you to join our family. We need someone who has seen things from both sides and who isn't afraid to question the status quo. You would report directly to me. Should you choose at any time to continue your medical training, JCN will pay all tuition and expenses. I will see to it personally that any resources you need are made available."

I suddenly felt dizzy and nauseated, to the point that I considered asking for something to be sick in.

"If what you truly desire is to improve the system, to be an agent of change, there will never be a greater opportunity than the one I am offering you now. I give you my word."

He paused again waiting for me to say something, but I just stared back at him blankly.

"I have been with this company for thirty-four years," McCormack continued. "Longer than you've been alive. This company is family to me. Every family has its secrets, Parkhill. Dark chapters we wish we could change. We overcome them. Together. That's what makes us a family."

I looked at my father, momentarily unsure exactly which family he was referring to.

"Does what I'm saying make sense to you Parkhill?"

Yes, actually it did. I was being offered a golden ticket back to the topside world. A red carpet into civilized society. A real apartment. Hot showers. Restaurants. Vacations. It was amazing at how much sense everything made to me now, and at last I did have something to say.

"Yes. I understand *exactly* what you mean."

McCormack's gaze was transfixed on mine, searching for clues.

"Stu tells me the two of you have become good buddies," he continued. That Stu would characterize our relationship that way didn't surprise me at all. "I'll send him by tomorrow with some materials. He'll be able to answer any questions you may have. Plus, if you golf, he'll help your short game." He smiled, rising from his chair, then held out his hand.

"Thank you, Parkhill."

I shook his hand, and McCormack turned around and patted my father on the shoulder and whispered something to him. He exited the room, leaving the door open behind him. Despite the late hour I could see there were people congregating outside my door, all in suits, talking on cell phones and with each other. My father excused himself, again extending another formality he usually wouldn't bother with, and stepped into the hallway.

A minute later he came back holding a pile of folders, envelopes, and documents bundled together, including T-Bone's weathered Filofax. He was followed by none other than my guardian angel, the handlebar-mustached man, who was pushing an empty wheelchair.

"I believe you've met Mr. Borishansky?" my father introduced the mustached man. "I hired him at your mother's behest after you disappeared. He was actually watching from a window when you tried to end your life. In case you'd care to thank him."

I wasn't in the mood to thank anyone and Borishansky just shuffled his feet, embarrassed. I unsteadily transferred myself into the wheelchair, putting on a JCN bathrobe my father handed me.

Mr. Borishansky pushed my wheelchair out into the hallway. A group of JCN executives drinking coffee and milling about before a bank of elevators became suddenly quiet. My father motioned to one of the blue-shirted Longwood staff members, who escorted us down the hallway toward a double security door.

"These may be of interest," my father mused as he dropped the pile of documents in my lap. "You certainly made Mr. Borishansky earn his fee, didn't you?"

I opened one of the folders and flipped through photos of myself, T-Bone, and Audrey in various locations since my suicide attempt, including experiments I had forgotten.

"Did you really make $400 in one week selling your sperm? I can't even fathom how many grandchildren I'm up to."

I was marveling that Borishansky got close enough to take the photos without being noticed as I flipped through what might have been a scrapbook of my human guinea pig experience with T-Bone and Audrey.

"I'm assuming you've been off your medication. I thought we had been doing so well with the lithium and olanzapine."

Inside another manila envelope, apparently devoted to Audrey, I spilled out additional paperwork including a baptism certificate from St. Edwards Church, foster care out-of-home placement forms from the New York State Department of Family Services, a diploma of high school equivalency, along with certificates of completion for different self-help seminars on subjects ranging from "Letting Go Of Fear" to "Visualizing Your Way to a Better Life" issued by some Brooklyn-based organization called The Success Academy.

"Just JCN-4830 ..." I murmured.

"You were taking a placebo. At least we have that to be grateful for."

In another folder I found records related to T-Bone, or at least the man I knew as T-Bone. It was impossible to tell who he really was as I tried haplessly to string together the fragments of documents and pictures. There were family photos, different families, with different children, and different hairstyles from different stages of his life. There were photocopies of driver's licenses in multiple states, each with variations of the same name, a Florida and Pennsylvania real estate license, and then a revocation notice from the New York State Department of Licensing Services saying that his real estate license had been revoked for mortgage fraud. There were photocopies of legal documents, most of which weren't immediately clear to me, including a Writ of Execution, and Verified Motion and Affidavit for Citation for Contempt of Court.

"Yes, he spent six months in jail for felony non-payment of child support." My father seemed pleased as we waited for our Longwood escort to thumb us through the double security doors. "I suppose eight children by three women is some kind of achievement. One his daughters is severely autistic. I don't suppose he mentioned her."

Seeing my dad defensive about a competing father figure was another first for me, but I was completely occupied with the final item at the bottom of the pile, flipping through the pages of T-Bone's Filofax. Scribbled dates and addresses and doodles of geometric shapes flashed past until I found what I was looking for tucked inside the back cover. It was the worn photograph I had seen T-Bone staring at so many times before. I took it out and held it up to examine closely.

The photo had to be at least thirty years old. I immediately spotted the much younger T-Bone sitting behind a banquet table holding up a champagne glass in a toast with three other men, with another gray and older man, clearly the patriarch, standing behind them all with his arms outstretched across their shoulders. They were beaming in celebration beneath a banner on the wall behind them which read "RON BOSCO REALTY TOP PRODUCERS," with the year and the words "Tiger Team" below that.

"We had an excellent conversation. I listened mostly," my father went on as I stared dumbfounded at this photograph that had given T-Bone so much comfort.

"I doubt you'll be seeing him again," my father added as we stopped in front of another high-security examination room like the one I had been held in down the hallway.

"Why not?" I asked, looking up from the photograph as the Longwood staffer buzzed the door open with his thumb.

"Because I paid him," my father replied impatiently. "That's all he was after."

Borishansky smiled, shook my hand and wished me good luck as my father thanked him and the Longwood staff member in a tone that made it clear his presence was no longer necessary. Taking the handles of my wheelchair, he then backed in through the door and pulled me inside.

It was a cluttered, dim room illuminated mostly by the blinking lights that reflected off the glass, plastic and monitors of what appeared to be a hastily constructed intensive care unit surrounding the electronic bed on the far wall. As my father pushed my wheelchair closer to it, I could make out Audrey. Her skin was yellowish due to the jaundice, her blood filling with creatine and other toxic waste as her liver and kidneys failed. Her face was swollen, particularly on the right side where it was grotesquely inflamed, and her blackened eyes were swollen shut. Her mouth was full of the endotracheal tube connected to a compact portable respiratory ventilator on a stand next to her bed, upon which rested a pulse oximeter connected from a clothespin-like clip on her index finger. A pulmonary artery catheter that had been threaded into her heart was inserted into her upper chest, amidst the electrodes affixed there with sticky pads. Multiple arterial lines from her chest, neck, and groin all fed data to the no less than four cardiac monitors that each displayed different waveforms. A collection of tubes from multiple drip bags converged at a central venous catheter that was secured by sutures into the jugular vein in her neck. I recognized the plasmapheresis machine I had seen being wheeled through the hallway now discarded to the side, along with still unopened boxes of other equipment that were piled on chairs. A countertop with a sink ran along the near wall, and there was a small bathroom in the corner.

It didn't seem real to me, just as my father's presence, Mr. Borishansky, or anything else did right now. My father noticed that the pile of materials he had given me had slid off my lap and lay scattered on the floor around me. He knelt down to pick them up as I continued to stare at Audrey.

"He said you seemed lost," he said, pausing over the photo of T-Bone's celebratory dinner as a top producer for a realty firm over thirty years ago. "He said that you were having a hard time 'figuring it all out.' Those were his words. Is that true?"

My father shuffled the documents into a neat pile, then stepped in front of me to ensure he had my full attention.

"Well. If I may, perhaps, offer you some fatherly advice." His face was close to mine, the lights from the monitors and equipment reflected in his bifocal lenses, and he had that same solemn expression he had whenever he was going to say something he thought was important to me.

"Our presence here is the result of a meaningless confluence of science, circumstance, and in your case, some above average Cabernet. It does not come with any meaning attached to it. Our lives are meaningful only to the extent that we ourselves endow them with meaning."

I tried to look away, around him and back at Audrey, to will him, or myself, somewhere far away.

"If you'd like to help your friends, if you'd like to live a meaningful life, *however* you care to define it, would you not be better suited, would you not be better able to do that if you weren't living underground in your own filth ..."

I could tell he was trying to control his temper, wrestling with The Rage.

"... wallowing with the others on the tail end of the bell-curve?"

And then it hit me. The reason for it all — my suicide attempt, T-Bone, my whole underground existence — all of it. How I had spent my entire life trying to please my father, winning his approval and mirroring his success. And the end result? I was looking at him. Or rather, I was looking at me, or at least what might become of me, a prospect I had for so long both coveted and feared. That I would be just as arrogant, as insulated, trapped in a loveless marriage with unwanted and unhappy children. It was so simple, so painfully obvious that I almost burst out laughing. What I couldn't fathom until this very moment was that perhaps my greatest fear was not failing to live up to his exacting standards, but the even scarier prospect that I might actually succeed.

"We'll have to think of some plausible way to spin all this at Columbia, although I have some ideas." I became aware that my father was still speaking. "There are a number of complicating factors. I'm sure you're aware of the mess you left there."

It occurred to me that he might be referring to the ongoing investigation at the Columbia University Medical Center into assorted incidents of patient medication that had gone missing. I had been questioned twice about it.

"The dean there is an ex-colleague of mine, and was kind enough to notify me as a courtesy," my father added, in response to my look of surprise. "He put me in touch with the attending from your surgical rotation."

Third-year students are never allowed to order, administer, or handle controlled narcotics, making the pilfering of anything worthwhile a painstaking ordeal fraught with risk. It began a few weeks after I discontinued my regular meds and my symptoms returned. I began to self-medicate with anything I could get my hands on. By the time I threw myself a personal going away party the night of my suicide attempt I had accumulated an eclectic stash.

"I don't suppose you know anything about that."

"No," I answered unconvincingly.

My father was staring at me again with a combination of disappointment and frustration, no doubt wishing there could be something between us other than the same awkward silence we were both accustomed to.

"Well. It's late," he said finally. "I'll be back tomorrow. I had Margaret clear my schedule. I'll take you back—"

"I'm staying."

I was expecting an outburst but instead he hesitated a moment, then pulled something out of his inside jacket pocket and tossed it on my lap. It was my wallet, in case there was any doubt that I was back to being the old Parkhill Mays again. I examined it as my father turned to leave, then paused in the doorway.

"Do you have any questions?" he asked. It seemed like a strange thing for him to say, almost a plea for me to say anything.

In fact, I had nothing but questions. I wanted to ask him if getting old meant having your dreams replaced by anger. I wanted to ask him what my mother and I could have done to have made him so mad at us. Most of all, as Audrey lay dying before me, I wanted to ask him, as the individual responsible for bringing me into this world, what, really, was the fucking point of anything? I wanted to ask him all of those things but said nothing. I knew I wasn't about to get any answers from him, just as I understood now that even though my father could explain all the intricacies of how the human heart gives life by pumping blood through our body, he was as clueless as the rest of us as to why.

And so I continued to say nothing, as I usually did, which only served to frustrate him further, as it usually did. I could see The Rage pass through him like a wave, which in years past would have undoubtedly set off one of his outbursts. Except that it wasn't even The Rage anymore. That was what I realized as I watched the door close behind him. It had been replaced by The Sadness.

Chapter 28. HELIUM

The biggest lie about mental illness is that it can be separated or distinguished from our "normal" personality and behavior. As comforting as it may be to be told that it's not you, it's the disease, in fact you *are* the disease. Consider our current limitations in the surgical removal of even a purely physical disorder, an infestation of cancerous cells that grow into a malignant tumor. As anyone who has undergone chemotherapy can attest, the treatment is at best a bludgeon, a coarse high-level carpet bombing of both diseased and healthy cells, fraught with debilitating side effects and limited prospects for success. Attempting to remove the negative, even self-destructive aspects of our personality without fundamentally altering the underlying identity is as misguided and crude to me as Dr. Whack's efforts to erase only bad memories with his homemade ECT machine while leaving our necessary stores of accumulated knowledge intact.

At least, that's how it occurred to me as I prepared for my next compulsion-driven act of self-destruction.

I had my Exit Plan, just as I had a year ago when I filled a trash bag with helium. I had worked through as many of the details as I could in the morning hours between my father's departure and Stu's arrival, gathering whatever supplies were available to assist me and going through contingencies in my head. I was interrupted only by a nurse who popped in intermittently to record Audrey's body temperature, blood pressure, heart, and respiratory rate. Just as with my suicide attempt, I had an almost preternatural focus and resolve.

This time was different, though. I was different. The Rage was different, or at least how I perceived it was. It was still there; it would always be there. But I didn't fear it anymore, because I no longer feared becoming my father, or hurting my children, or falling in love. The Rage had kept me alive on the streets. It made me strong, more powerful than I imagined I could be. I had a different relationship with The Rage now. It was no longer the one-dimensional self-implosion kind which my suicide was the ultimate expression of. This time it would be more of an explosion. Just for today, I did want to be exactly like my father in at least that respect. I wanted to explode.

By the time there was a knock on the other side of the door early that morning I was settling back into my wheelchair in front of Audrey. There was a buzzing sound from the door unlocking, and then Stu stuck his head through without waiting for an answer. He was wearing a protective metal and foam patch over his left eye, taped with adhesive around the socket.

"You owe me a putter."

He smiled at his own attempt to break the ice. His arms were full with a small paper bag, a box of donuts, and what appeared to be folders and pamphlets of JCN marketing material. He placed them on the counter behind me, then took two cups of coffee sealed with plastic lids out of the bag and offered me one, holding it out like a peace offering.

"I'm very sorry about Audrey."

I took the coffee and placed it on the floor next to me.

"I'm sorry about your eye."

He shrugged, knocking a pile of boxes off one of the chairs nearby and wheeling it next to me.

"My eye will be fine. It's my putter I'm going to miss."

He disappeared behind me again to the counter, then reappeared with the open box of donuts.

"I got it for our leadership retreat in the Bahamas last year. I actually met McCormack in person the first time there. The guy you spoke with last night? First time after seventeen years with the company."

He sat down on the chair next to me, both of us facing Audrey.

"He's your boss?"

Stu scoffed, opening his own cup of coffee and taking a tentative sip.

"Nah, he's way up there, like three levels above. That's what you need to do, though. Get noticed somehow. At least that's one good thing to come out of all this."

He placed his coffee on the floor and wearily reached into the box of donuts.

"Don't get me wrong. You take care of JCN, JCN takes care of you. Never forget that. That's the gospel here."

I couldn't tell if he was trying to convince himself or me as he held out the box. I shook my head, no.

"But you do need to eat shit. A *lot* of shit," Stu confided as he bit into a jelly donut. "You sell yourself, you know. Every day. A little piece of yourself. Piece of your soul. All about making your PBCs. Personal Business Commitments. That's what they call them here. And forget about what you did last quarter."

I was watching a different side of Stu, a human dimension I didn't particularly care to see right now, preferring to hate him without reservation like my father.

"And ego," Stu continued. "Christ you wouldn't believe the egos I have to deal with every day. And politics. How they divvy up the pipeline, who gets the hot trials."

I attempted a sympathetic nod, but it was an unnecessary exercise. Stu wasn't paying attention to me, reaching into the box for another donut as he stared reflectively in Audrey's direction.

"You need allies. Someone with your back, who knows the way things really work around here."

I rose quietly.

"A coach. A mentor."

I went to the sink at the counter and turned the faucet on, letting the water run. Technically speaking there was limited benefit to scrubbing in, as very little about the procedure I was going to perform would be sterile. It was more about the comfort I found in my pre-surgical scrub routine.

"You even want to be on the development side? That's the first thing you need to ask yourself. Maybe yes, maybe no. It doesn't have the sex appeal it used to, you know."

I was washing my hands and arms, all the way up to the elbow. In between the fingers. Under the nails.

"They outsource everything now. Too expensive to do in-house. There's only so long you can work in a loss leader. That's how they look at us. A cost center. Don't kid yourself."

I reached over and put on a pair of surgical gloves from a cardboard dispenser, careful not to snap them too loudly. At this point, however, Stu seemed unaware of my presence.

"The revenue side of the house. That's where I should be. Give me a line of business. Something I can grow, not some bullshit vaccination. That's how you get noticed."

I quietly reached under the sink and removed the handheld fire extinguisher from the cupboard. It didn't weigh more than a few pounds but was metal and solid and blunt.

"When you think about it. I mean, really think about it, and trust me I have, that's all comes down to. Who brings in the revenue ..."

Turning back around I held the fire extinguisher with both hands and raised it high above the back of Stu's head just as he swiveled his chair around to face me.

"That's all that matters—"

I slammed the fire extinguisher into the top of his head. The chair tipped over backward as the extinguisher came loose from the impact and went crashing to the floor with a horrendous clatter. Stu was flat on his back, moaning something with his one visible eye half shut. I knew it would be unlikely that I would knock him unconscious cleanly on the first try, being far too afraid of breaking his head open, and was already straddled atop his chest pummeling his forehead with my fists. I thought about the house back in Lexington, and the wine cellar, and my father, hitting Stu until my surgical gloves were torn like rubber bands and my fists bloody. It was a huge release to channel The Rage toward hurting someone other than myself; perhaps my father had been on to something after all. I stopped finally, expecting to hear an approaching army of law enforcement. The only sound was my heavy breathing.

Knocking someone unconscious before performing surgery actually has a long precedent before the advent of anesthesia, most notably in the Napoleonic Wars and early days of dentistry. It takes a considerable amount of skill and effort by the performing surgeon (or "anesthesiologist"), and inducing a concussion can lead to significant and potentially long-term side effects. A much less traumatic means of effecting an unconscious state would have been to apply pressure to the carotid artery, although Stu wasn't likely to sit quietly while I wrapped my fingers around his neck. The irony of the situation dawned on me as I quickly examined him. He was out cold, a bloody knot already appearing on the back of his head. As I maneuvered him onto his stomach I realized that the tables had turned. Stu was in fact the human guinea pig now, and I was the one doing the experiment. At least it felt like an experiment. It was my first amputation, after all.

Kneeling on the palm of Stu's right hand, I wrapped my fingers around his thumb and gave it a sharp yank all the way backward until the tip almost touched his wrist. The bone cracked with a snap, breaking through the fleshy surface where his thumb met his hand. I twisted his thumb in an attempt to break the bone away cleanly. When that didn't work, I lifted his hand by the wrist and placed his thumb in my mouth, sucking it like a straw all the way to its broken hilt, tasting blood, salt and sweat and cutting the inside of my mouth on the sharp exposed bone. I attempted to align my incisors with the break in the bone at the bottom of Stu's thumb when it touched the back of my throat making me gag, and I had to stop while I dry-heaved. I gave it another try, finally biting down hard right below the proximal phalanx, the knuckle on the thumb, far enough down so I could be reasonably confident the fingerprint wouldn't be deformed. Flesh is more elastic that people realize however, and I was having a hard time completely separating Stu's thumb from his hand until I began moving my back teeth in a grinding motion and pulled his hand away from my face simultaneously.

Finally his thumb came loose in my mouth, and I spit it out onto the floor after almost choking on it. This time I did vomit, all over the floor and on Stu, a bright yellowish substance I assumed to be bile.

I applied some gauze with scotch tape I had found beforehand in one the drawers. I did my best to maximize the possibility for re-attachment through microsurgery, although the conditions were far from optimal. The thumb would have to be refrigerated fairly quickly, but I didn't plan on needing it for long.

I rinsed out Stu's cardboard coffee cup and placed his thumb inside, resealing it with the plastic lid, then did a mental inventory of all of the things I needed to bring with me. I reached into the pockets of Stu's trousers and removed a huge keychain and stuffed it into the pocket of my JCN bathrobe, where I checked to feel my wallet. I saw the pile of documents my father brought sitting on the counter and grabbed T-Bone's Filofax, removing the picture he had spent so much time gazing at for inspiration. For reasons I didn't fully understand I folded it carefully and placed it in the pocket of my bathrobe as well.

Disconnecting Audrey's arterial lines set off a symphony of beeps and alerts, as I struggled to move her and the drip bags into the wheelchair. There was a strap for a seatbelt but that actually made her more prone to fall forward. I had better luck leaning her against the side and sliding her down in her seat as far as possible, then tilting the wheelchair back on its rear wheels slightly while pushing it. I hesitated before exiting, rethinking my odds of actually making it out of the building in this manner, until sound of Stu moaning reminded me I was well past the point of no return.

The hallway immediately outside was empty, and I headed back in the direction my father and Borishanksy had taken me from, and where I had seen the bank of elevators. I didn't travel far down the hall before I reached my first test, a pair of double security doors with the thumbpad on the right, beneath which a tiny display glowed red. I had no idea if the amputation, if it could be called such, would somehow distort the fingerprint, or if it was sensitive to body heat, nor was I even 100% sure whether it was the right or left thumb they used.

I gingerly took the severed thumb out of Stu's coffee cup and placed it on the thumb sensor.

Nothing.

I moved it around, jiggling it on the sensor.

Still nothing.

Finally, I pressed down on the thumb with my forefinger, applying more pressure.

This time the light on the sensor turned green and the door buzzed. I peeked out into the adjoining hallway, almost identical to the one I was in, with doors to additional examination rooms and small offices lining one side. At the far end I recognized the bank of elevators, across from the same room I had woken up in. The hallway was empty, although I could hear the murmur of unidentifiable conversations echoing from inside some of the offices. I backed through the doors pulling Audrey in the wheelchair, and moved as quickly and silently as I could down the hallway keeping the wheelchair tilted backward at a constant angle.

Slowing to a stop before the elevators, I pressed the down button. Using the elevators was a huge risk, although both the alarms and the wheelchair made the stairwells not an option. The voices from the offices just a few doors away made each second I waited feel like an eternity. Finally there was a bell as an elevator opened in front of me. Much to my relief, it was empty. Pulling Audrey inside I pressed the button for the lobby, then held my breath as the elevator whirred downward and shuddered to a stop. The doors opened.

It was immediately obvious I had made a gross miscalculation thinking I'd be able to just wheel Audrey out the front door. The main lobby looked cavernous and much more populated than I had remembered when Marci had whisked me through, the morning sun creating shadows that crisscrossed the marble floor. The security desk that wrapped around the center of the room seemed to be teeming with guards in blue blazers. The dark glass doorways to freedom were a mere twenty yards away, past the turnstiles, but there was no way I would be able to make it across without being stopped. As I stared out in panic, one of the guards behind the desk looked up from his newspaper and glanced over in my direction. I immediately pushed the door close button, choosing the basement level this time as it seemed to be the only alternative available. The image of the security guard picking up a phone as he now most certainly looked in my direction was the last thing I saw before the doors finally closed. The elevator lurched down one level.

When the doors opened again the climate was noticeably different, warmer and humid. Washing machines vibrated from somewhere nearby, almost in rhythm it seemed with my churning stomach as I pushed Audrey into a dim hallway of white-painted cinderblock. We moved forward through the heavy air, the sound of the laundry machines getting closer as I made my way through the narrow passageway. I turned the corner and could hear the bell from another elevator arriving behind me, but didn't look back. I was focusing down the hallway ahead of me, just before it twisted out of sight, where there was a familiar metal door that read EMERGENCY EXIT – Alarm Will Sound.

I slowed as I got halfway down the hall, only twenty or so yards away from the door. There was an opening in the wall to my right, through which I could hear talking. Light filtered out from the inside. As I inched closer I could hear what sounded like some infomercial playing on a television.

"What I like about it, I don't have any of that hat head I get when I use other hair products like this ..."

Edging closer to the opening I peered around the corner and spied what was clearly some kind of employee break room. There was a coffee maker, vending machines, and a solitary figure reclined on a worn couch facing the general direction of the infomercial playing on a television affixed to the wall.

"None of the tackiness either, it doesn't weigh the hair down ..."

It was Lamar. He wore his uniform pants and a sleeveless undershirt. It wasn't until after my heart dropped to my scrotum that I realized he was sleeping, his chest rhythmically rising and falling. His head was tilted back ever so slightly, eyes shut, and he emitted an occasional snort. The glow of the television reflected oddly off of his shiny pate.

"... all the tangles are completely gone. It's been a complete transformation for my hair ..."

Approaching footsteps from the hallway behind me made me realize I had no option but to continue forward. I turned around, shielding the contents of the wheelchair as best I could and made my way past the open doorway to the break room where Lamar slept. The footsteps were louder now, causing him to murmur and shift fitfully. No matter. As I approached the rusty emergency exit door I realized the alarm would probably alert half the building anyway. I let go of the wheelchair and touched the dirty metal push bar that opened it, bracing myself for the terror-inducing racket that was sure to follow.

Before I got a chance, there was a hideous SCREECH as the door swung open on its own, pulled from the outside. There was no alarm, only blinding sunlight pouring in that forced me to cover my eyes. Through the cracks in my fingers I was able to discern a small figure in a white kitchen uniform and sanitary hat. Mexican, male, older, and overweight, he looked at me curiously as he took a last draw from a cigarette and tossed it to the side. For some reason I was immediately transported back to my escape from Bellevue with T-Bone, so many months ago, remembering his prime directive to exude confidence at all costs.

"Have you seen Stu Jansen?" I blurted out.

The man's look of utter confusion led me to realize he didn't speak a word of English.

"Stu?" I repeated. "I'm looking for Stu."

He finally broke into a wide grin, letting out the familiar cheer. *"Stuuuuuuuuuuuuuuuuuuuu!"*

He stepped backward to pull the door open wider, beaming as he waited for me to exit past him. I murmured some kind of thank you as I maneuvered the wheelchair down a three-inch step, then pulled the sealed coffee cup containing Stu's severed thumb from the pocket of my bathrobe and placed it in his hands.

"This belongs to Stu."

I was already halfway across the parking lot by the time he disappeared back inside. I hid Audrey's wheelchair behind a concrete pillar while I ran through rows of cars pushing the button on Stu's keys. It wasn't hard to find once I found the row of reserved parking spaces closest to the main entrance. I then drove back to retrieve Audrey. It seemed best to lay her down in the back, hanging her IV lines on the handle grip above her. Screeching out of the parking lot I felt little relief, but was instead preoccupied with the next set of to-dos for my Exit Plan. I had a long drive and a busy day still ahead of me, but found comfort thinking of the stiff shot of my beloved helium that awaited me at the end of it.

Flatlining, or the representation of an electrocardiogram displaying a perfectly flat line while emitting a high-pitched continuous tone is for the most part, except in cases of severe trauma, a Hollywood fabrication. Even asystole heart rhythms, which indicate a state of no electrical cardiac activity, usually display lines that are at least a little wavy. Audrey, laying before me on a gurney attached to a 12-lead EKG machine connected to her arms, calves, and across her chest, was actually now in a state known as pulseless electrical activity. Very low-level activity still registered on the EKG but, as I could tell from her limp hand that I was holding in my own, was no longer strong enough to generate a pulse.

"Audrey … I don't know if you can hear me," I began.

Showing up unannounced with a body in stage four organ failure isn't the way business was usually done at the Aurora Cryonic Life Extension Facility. However, Dr. Bernard, the bearded executive director who remembered us from our visit months ago, sprang into action like a wedding planner on the big day, giving rapid-fire commands to the attending staff. A new IV cocktail was prepared for her that included magnesium oxide, vitamin E and other antioxidants typically administered in the "pre-deanimation" stage of the process. An ice bath was being prepared, while immediately through the windows of the narrow confines of the sterile intake room I sat in with Audrey, I could see the assembled standby team of technicians in scrubs at the ready. They would perform a procedure to artificially circulate her blood after full cardiac arrest in an effort to keep the tissues alive, most importantly the brain.

"But I wanted to tell you what's going to happen to you now."

It was late afternoon by the time I pulled into the parking lot of the Aurora facility in Buffalo NY, making the nearly 600-mile trip in just over nine hours. I had made only two stops, one to get gas and another at a giant department store in western Massachusetts I saw a sign for along the highway. I figured there was fair chance they'd carry one of those portable helium tanks in the party goods section, and was rewarded for my effort. I also grabbed the trash bags and rubber bands necessary for my suicide contraption. After inarticulately attempting to explain my situation at the front desk at Aurora (still wearing my JCN bathrobe, shorts, and slippers) the receptionist wisely escalated my situation to Dr. Bernard. He politely but firmly stopped me every time I tried provide any explanation. The less he knew, he insisted, the better it would be for all of us.

"It's going to feel like you're swimming in ginger-ale," I heard myself say to Audrey, or whatever spirit was left of her.

After retrieving the consent forms and other paperwork we had completed on our last visit, I had planned to make a trip to the bank to cash out my trust fund to pay for both my own and Audrey's Neurocryonic Life Extension Package, but it turned out to be unnecessary. I was able to cover the entire tab, thirty grand each, splitting the bill between the parentally issued credit cards still active in my wallet. In return I received a card and wristband containing contact information and emergency instructions for the care and transport of my cadaver in the event of my (what I had every intention of being imminent) death.

"At first. Lots of bubbles," I continued to the unresponsive Audrey, "like you're floating in champagne."

Most physicians would wait for at least five of the EKG leads to display an asystole rhythm before declaring death. The one summoned by Aurora to make the formal declaration of death (and corresponding certificate of disposal from Erie County, NY) seemed unburdened by such constraints. A gaunt, gray man with a leather bag who looked every bit the part of the Grim Reaper himself, he was clearly sympathetic to the Aurora (and right-to-die) cause. I had been forced to wait outside the examination room, watching through a window as he took a small flashlight from his bag and checked her pupils. He donned a pair of surgical gloves and then went through some short tests, dabbing her eyeball lightly with a cotton swab then moving it from side to side to ensure there was no oculocephalic or corneal reflex. Using a plastic syringe he shot water into Audrey's ear canal while holding her eyes open to check for the presence of any oculovestibular reflex, then stuck a tongue depressor down her esophagus to see if she would gag. After pressing down sharply and rubbing her sternum to gauge her reaction to painful stimuli, he finally pulled a stethoscope from his bag. Ignoring the output from the state-of-the-art EKG apparatus in front of him, he held it to her chest for what seemed like an eternity.

"And it's going to lift you up, and then, and then the most amazing thing is going to happen ..."

At last Dr. Bernard told me they were ready, and that if I wanted to say goodbye to Audrey I needed to do it now. Then he placed the simple necklace Manny had made for her with the word LOVE fashioned out of twisted wire in my hand. I was immediately transported back to that day on the bus with Audrey, to the promise I made to her, on this piece of metal, never to hurt myself again. In an instant the only thing that remained for me to cling to disappeared into thin air: my carefully laid plan to join Audrey, my Exit Plan, to construct another suicide bag, to be together forever by doing exactly what I swore to her I wouldn't do. It was as brutally obvious to me as it was unfair, cruel even, to have come this far and not be able to take the last, most important step, to have to choose between keeping my promise to Audrey or having this Exit Plan fail just as my last one had. For first time since I could remember my eyes became dangerously close to welling with tears.

Instead of answering Dr. Bernard directly, I politely excused myself.

My father would have been proud.

"Everything will become so clear to you. In your head. All of the questions, all the things you've never understood. Why you were born, everything that's happened ..."

I was still squeezing that stupid necklace, the flattened metal making an indentation in my one hand as I touched Audrey's fingers with the other.

"This exact moment."

There were people filing into the room now, quietly, respectfully, and I realized that I was running out of time. I had to tell Audrey that I wouldn't be able to keep my promise, to stay alive, that there wasn't any point now, that there couldn't be any life without her, because she was the only thing in this world that made life worth living.

"This is just another experiment," was all that came out.

The gurney was being moved, and I clumsily tried to follow it, not letting go of Audrey's hand, tripping over feet and bouncing between the forest of technicians that surrounded it. I made it through the doorway and another room until we came to a large pair of double doors, each with small round windows of about four inches in diameter.

"... just another experiment," I kept repeating. I could feel arms gently restraining me as Audrey's hand slipped out of mine while the gurney continued ahead and disappeared through the doors, which swung shut behind it. I was able to pull free and lunged toward the double doors, only to find them locked. A salty wetness covered my face while I pressed against the tiny window and watched the team around the gurney recede down the hallway on the other side of the glass.

I was crying. Even more surprising to me was the fact that I didn't care that I was bawling like an eight-year-old on the top step of the wine cellar again. I watched through the fogged window while the crowded gurney got smaller down the hallway, finally disappearing through another door at the far end. As I crumpled to the floor, for some reason I remembered all of the rapture letters my Sunday School teacher made us write, and I wondered if I would be getting one from Audrey, and if they had late-night humanitarian commercials she could cry to where she was going, or whether or not people would even cry anymore, or whether there would even be such a thing as tears.

EPILOGUE

Darkness.

I point the beam of my flashlight around the littered ground of dirt and rock. There are some newish looking gum wrappers, not grown-up gum but loud, obnoxious fruit flavored bubble gum with some cartoon character on the foil. On further inspection I find a number of broken rubber bands nearby in different colors, each retaining the rough shape of an animal, a horse or dog or some other creature. They are the current fad now with the under-twelve set all over the city; I've seen children with what must be hundreds of them around their wrists and up their arms.

"Let's go back," my partner Ajay whispers pleadingly behind me.

"Take this," I hiss back, handing him the flashlight and taking the small wooden crate of oranges from him. The beam of light follows me as I carry it to a clearing in the darkness beneath the four-lane overpass under the Bronx River Parkway where trickles of light filter through.

"Turn off the light," I instruct Ajay.

"Are you serious?"

"Turn it off."

He reluctantly turns off the flashlight, and I look around, giving my eyes a moment to adjust. It's dim but not completely black, broad daylight compared to the Bat Cave. It's unseasonably warm for April, just over eighteen months since I fled the Aurora facility in Buffalo and abandoned Stu's car in a Brooklyn lot. The humidity is so thick the walls themselves seem to be sweating. I sense movement nearby, and clear my throat.

"Good afternoon, if anyone can hear me my name is Mays Parker. I'm with Operation HOPE, the New York City Homeless Outreach Project."

Covering the oranges with a layer of $1 cheeseburgers from certain golden arched fast food chain had been own my innovation, a much more effective bait than fruit or an already served loaf of bread donated by a local restaurant. The distinctive fried smell seems to travel much farther than the sound of my voice. I reach underneath my ill-fitting HOPE t-shirt into the pouch of the hooded sweatshirt I mistakenly chose to wear underneath and take one of the half-dozen small plastic single-dosed tetanus vaccination lancets from my pocket. They are branded with some pharmaceutical logo, happily not belonging to JCN.

"If anyone is in need of medical attention or would like to sleep in a shelter tonight, please make yourself heard and I can help."

The tetanus shots are also my idea. We had been administering them at the firehouse on 28th street during the New York City Marathon and I stole a handful of leftovers. It is highly unlikely anyone at HOPE would sign off on illegally vaccinating children without consent, so it remains a secret campaign of mine.

"If anyone is hungry I have oranges," I add, playing my trump card, "and a limited supply of cheeseburgers."

Now there is more movement in the darkness near me, faint, beneath the steady din of traffic above us. I bite off the end of the lancet, holding the rubber cap between my teeth.

He's fast, but I'm ready.

In the blink of an eye the crate disappears. I wildly grab a handful of t-shirt, finding a skinny arm, then thrust the lancet into exposed flesh. He or she is much smaller than me, although I have no idea as to the sex or age until I hear a frantic boy's voice.

"Get *offa* me bitch—"

I pull out the lancet and he is gone, almost certainly unaware that he had been vaccinated, disappearing into the darkness with the crate of food. I sit on the ground, shaken but hopeful that the number of life-threatening risks he faces on a daily basis has just been decreased by one.

On the long subway ride back to Brooklyn I can't help avoid another advertisement for JCN's new wonder drug. We pass a giant billboard upon which the now familiar Assure appears in soft letters, above the JCN logo, superimposed over a suburban mom standing on a beach at sunset hugging herself in ecstasy. Perusing an old newspaper a few months back during a "dumpster dive" to forage for food with my new freegan roommates I came across a full-page advertisement from a New York law firm directly appealing to anyone who had suffered adverse immune responses or debilitating side effects from the drug abrixumab, brand name Assure. They may be entitled to a significant financial settlement as part of a federal class action suit. Clearly JCN made the business decision that it was more profitable to fight the lawsuits and continue marketing the drug. I'll need to pee on a pharmaceutical company the next time I'm in Manhattan, I think to myself. I've been getting into a rut marking my territory on Fortune 500 finance and media buildings because they're easier to find. That's just plain lazy.

I get out at my stop in Bedford-Stuyvesant and swing by Prospect Park to kill some time before heading back to the warehouse I'm sharing with the freegans, where over my worn mattress hang not one but two keepsakes: T-Bone's old photo and Audrey's necklace. It's cooler outside in the park, and I'll want to eat before I go back. Spending money on food or clothing is in violation of the house rules, as is my part-time job as a nursing assistant at Lenox Hill Hospital; they say it creates further waste and perpetuates an inherently corrupt economic system. Whatever. More wilted arugula and moldy Portobello mushroom salad for someone else. I wouldn't be back until well past the communal dinner hour anyway and all that would remain would be the leftovers from their urban foraging (or the leftovers of other people's thrown-away leftovers, as it were).

Outside the park entrance a group of business-clad professionals are breaking down a booth that has been set up on the sidewalk for a local bank. There are dozens of balloons with an apple logo on them adorning the booth, behind which rests a helium tank, one of the old-fashioned refrigerator-sized models. I take a balloon. One of the women cheerfully asks if I would like to open an account and I pretend not to hear her.

I sit down on the grass in a clearing near the Cherry Esplanade and consider the balloon I hold in my hand. It reminds me of the day at Coney Island with Audrey and the $6 balloon I bought for her, transferring my negative energy upon it before she set it free. I still have no shortage of dark thoughts to channel onto this balloon before casting it away into space. There are the ever-present battles to control The Rage, and the nightmares about Longwood. For months afterward I expected a battalion of police officers to come crashing through my door, although certainly the folks at JCN would be motivated to keep the whole affair quiet. Perhaps in the end it was just another mess of mine that my father had to clean up. I feel genuine remorse for Stu Jansen, who deserved a less traumatic farewell then the one I gave him. He might, however, be a candidate for a procedure I remember reading about in school that was done to a West Coast fisherman who lost his thumb and had it replaced by his second toe.

I still think about finishing medical school, to the point that I've researched some programs that offer deferred tuition and loan forgiveness for practicing in high-need areas. Strangely enough, however, I've been getting a surprising amount of satisfaction from my part-time gig as a nursing assistant. The work is menial: changing beds, taking vitals, dressing and bathing patients, as well as catheter and toilet care. And here I thought third-year medical students were at the bottom of the health care food chain. I do, however, get tremendous energy from being able to do something, however trivial, to bring comfort to someone who is suffering, as I get to do every shift I work. It's a desire I share with most of my fellow nurses, along with our disdain for doctors. Plus, there's always the hope that I'll someday get to watch my father's expression when he finds out his son is a nurse's aide.

I think about T-Bone. Just as my father predicted I have not and do not expect ever to see him again. I have purposely stayed away from the Bat Cave, which I'm sure is now home to some other family of mole people. I've remained almost exclusively topside outside of my volunteer work, although I've done my imperfect best to maintain an off-the-grid, freegan lifestyle. I'm not sure if T-Bone would approve. I miss him daily. He had always been truthful about everything and I begrudge him nothing, least of all the same defense mechanisms he tried to instill in me. Perhaps our relationship had run its course. Natural conclusions happen so rarely in life I am dread to disrupt something resting peacefully in memory, and instead am content to end each day with the wish he is safe, warm, and fed.

I think about how little I know, and how humbling it is, and whether everything I feel now is temporary, or this is just what living feels like. I don't find myself thinking much about The Big Meaning of Life anymore, preferring to break things down into more manageable chunks, living moment to moment, and filling my days with simpler pursuits.

Finally, my thoughts return to Audrey, as they usually do. Before I am overcome with emotion, I let the balloon string slide through my fingers, setting it free into the night air. Stretching out my arms and lying back on the grass I watch through moistening eyes as the balloon rises steadily, clearing the tree line where the wind catches it, knocking it fitfully, upward through the dark wisps of cloud toward its proper landing beyond the stars.

Made in the USA
Monee, IL
13 May 2021

68500628R00157